Med

Book Four

The Royal Court

By Lina J. Potter

Translated by Kristina Tatarian

Copyright © 2018 LitHunters Ltd. (http://lithunters.com)

All rights reserved.

ISBN: **9781720279556**

LitHunters, 2018

Contents:

For the child, in love with globe and stamps,
the universe equals his vast appetite.

Ah! How great the world is in the light of the lamps!

In the eyes of memory, how small and slight!

One morning we set out, minds filled with fire,

travel, following the rhythm of the seas,

hearts swollen with resentment, and bitter desire,

soothing, in the finite waves, our infinities:

Some happy to leave a land of infamies,

some the horrors of childhood, others whose doom

is to drown in a woman's eyes, their astrologies

the tyrannous Circe's dangerous perfume.

Charles Baudelaire, Le Voyage

Chapter 1

Ativernian Cobweb

Karl Treloney swiftly downed a shot of cherry brandy, topped it off with a succulent bite of meat, and exhaled in delight. *Outstanding! I would even say wonderful!*

The day went incredibly well. Karl even managed to sell something that had been lying in stock for ages, and for a good price, too. Moreover, some gentlemen were going to visit him tomorrow.

What else does a man need for happiness? My affairs are more or less in order; spring is coming; it's bright and warm!

Karl had received a large sum of money in mid-winter, which had proven quite handy to him. He had already managed to multiply his profit and, given that nobody came for him, he intended to do it again.

Karl had no intention of cheating the people he dealt with; they were dangerous. He could not resist, however, making a little extra on the side. Even death itself could not stop him. Karl was the kind of person who would wake from the dead to make a profit. *Profit...hoo boy!*

A single thought spoiled the wonderful spring morning—the thought of Baron Avermal.

It is no feat for the noble-blooded to be trading, but they still don't care for minding their own business. I pray that one day the rage of Maldonaya falls on them!

In the past, Avermal would never go as big as he went last winter. He dug out some extravagant goods and began to trade. *The goods seemed to appear from out of nowhere! Take the lace for instance!* Karl knew its price perfectly well. He knew that one of the Khangans had laid out two piles of ducats for it and even thought that to be a good deal.

What about the amber? Let alone the ordinary marine honeysuckle, Avermal traded white and blue as well. *And the mirrors that reflect so clearly that one's blood runs cold? By Aldonai! All the profit goes to Avermal alone!*

The merchants did not like to trade in the winter, but Avermal had a ton of clients who realized his precious items could make them a fortune.

Karl wanted to join in the business. *But no.*

After carefully considering Karl's proposal, Avermal politely sent him away. He said it was his partner who was against having any outsiders involved. *A bloody Virman!*

If only Karl knew the person who provided Avermal with all his treasure, he would make use of the opportunity. On top of that, his master would pay him for such news. In the capital, for instance, the mirrors and lace were already on the go... but only the King, the princesses, and a handful of nobles owned them.

They got them from the Countess Earton, Karl knew this for sure. But again, he could not ask the Countess herself. Earton was far away. *Besides, how did they come by such miraculous objects there? Considering the place is a dark hole.*

∗∗∗

The sound of a slamming door interrupted Karl's thoughts.

"Uh!" The merchant flinched and froze as a whole procession of people entered his store. First came Virmans. They quickly inspected the place and peered into the back room. Karl heard the clanking of the latch being shut. *Bad luck he had let his assistant go!* Although, if he had three assistants, it wouldn't make a difference. *What chance could those youngsters stand against such sharks?*

Karl had a feeling that even a royal guard squadron would not save him. The Virmans who broke into the store seemed to be way too resolute. Two of them approached the merchant from both sides and grabbed him by his shoulders.

"Don't move."

"G-gentlemen..." Karl's voice shook. The merchant wanted to demand what was going on, but his feeble attempts were cut off.

"Is there anybody else?" The inquiring voice was certainly female.

"No one, My Lady." The Virmans sprang to full attention and straightened their backs as a lady walked into the store. *A Lady with a capital L.*

Is she a Virmaness? It was difficult to tell. Such golden tresses most often belonged to Virmans. One could take a Virmaness from an island, but to make a noble lady out of her was impossible. The lie would reveal itself as soon as you heard her speak.

What distinguished the woman was her noble posture; her luxurious dress made of black silk; the emerald bracelet on her wrist; the signet ring with a Earl's crest; and her manners.

The woman was used to subjugating others. She was fearless and...angry.

The lady stopped right in front of Karl Treloney. She looked him straight in the eye. Her eyes were stunningly green, like two shining emeralds.

She wore the Earl's bracelet. Karl was no fool; he figured out who he was dealing with.

"My Lady?"

"That's right, my dear." The Countess' voice was seriously alarming. It made one think of gallows and torture chambers.

"I am Countess Lilian Earton, and you have got yourself involved with the Darcy family."

Karl gulped in astonishment.

"Well yes, the Darcys. That's right. They get their money sent from the capital," Karl said.

"By Whom?"

Karl did not hesitate to give away the truth. *Why lie?* "The money is brought by the captain of the ship named the 'Scarlet Seagull.'"

"Whose ship is that?"

Merciful heavens, how would I know? I'm not a city dweller, my region is Altver—a little trade in Ivernea but that's about it. What is this interrogation about anyway? Why me?

"Well, My Lady. It's pretty straightforward. He is a respectable man."

***

Lily could tell the man was telling the truth. He had been given the money, and he passed the money on; he got handed the letter, and he sent the letter off. He did not question "'who, where, or what for.'" *One lives longer knowing less.*

"Letters? I delivered them and therefore sinned. As to reading them, I never did; I realized that sometimes it is better not to know. But I delivered…"

"The Earton Estate? Yes, I've heard about it…"

"My Lady, would you mind explaining one thing…"

"I am the one who is asking questions here," Lily retorted sharply. In the end, Karl did not know much. In fact, he knew too little…

"The 'Scarlet Seagull'…were there any other ships?"

"There was one, the 'Golden Lady.'"

As the interrogation continued, Lily made a record of everything that was said in order to show it to Hans Tremain, including the captain's name, the names of the steersman, the boatswain, the assistant, and the sailors…

What was the ship like? Did it have any features? A figurehead, patches?

How often did he show up? When was the last time? How did he go about sending letters? Ah, attached to a pigeon leg, without monitoring where they went? And you never read them?

Not convincing.

Ah, you did. But did not copy them? No…and what do you remember from what you read? Tell me everything if you wish to keep your fingers and ears intact. Otherwise, I might unleash the Virmans; they have been dying to put their hands to action.

Aha! And what did you suspect? No idea? Leif! Oh, so you had some suspicions after all. And now in greater detail, what were they about?

I see.

Now take this sheet—this is paper—and write a confession. Then, copy it out on the parchment.

Have your hands gone numb? The Virmans can fix that with an axe; they will carve your hands anew, Pinocchio.

Lily interrogated the merchant in this fashion for about three hours.

Karl protested, screamed, and resisted the questioning, but since he was alone against the two dozen Virmans, all attempts were in vain; Lily found out what she wanted.

When the Countess finally left, Karl made a circle of Aldonai, took out a cherished bottle from the counter, and downed it as swiftly as if the liquid inside had been water.

What a nightmare! Not a woman but a Maldonaian spawn, a real monster. But what's left to do? Report it to the client who passed on the money? Hmm. Karl had a feeling he shouldn't do that. *What then? Live in peace. I haven't seen, haven't heard, haven't said anything, and I know nothing. Period. Perchance, the storm will pass me by. It uproots large trees, but maybe it will leave me, a meek flower, untouched…*

Karl desperately wanted to live.

***

As the sun went down, the day seemed less successful than before.

"My Lady, maybe we should return and stab that rodent?" said Olaf in a low voice.

Lily shook her head. "No, don't. If he is foolish enough, he will get into trouble anyway. But if he is smart, he will stay still and quiet. He might prove us useful. He is not a governor, but if we throw a respected merchant into prison…"

It was clear from the expression on the Virmans' faces that they would send Karl to prison regardless, no bother. The prison would teach him; the Virmans had no respect for landlubbers.

"We do not need any fuss, lest the key enemies slip through our grip…"

The Virmans nodded in approval., *So far, everything is going smoothly, Lily thought.*

***

They arrived in the city that evening, and Lily decided to pay a friendly visit to the most significant man in the whole ugly plot—the one who handled the payment for her murder.

Later she would go to the ship, dine, and sleep. From tomorrow on, she would get on with her affairs. *Let them prepare the ships and stock provisions! A couple of days should be fine, and then to Laveri, by sea. Eww...*

***

The morning sunshine peered through the window. Sea waves rocked the cabin. Lily was used to it by now, but she still had a need to distract herself from the nasty feeling of nausea. So she sat with a frown on her face, re-reading the merchant's testimony.

Oh my. The main enemy is in the city capital.

What does he want from me? She had no clue. It seemed like there was nothing personal. That hatred was directed at Jess. They wanted to get rid of her because she got in their way; get rid of her and Miranda.

No way! I will not let that happen. To protect my child, I would tear their throats out with my teeth! The bastards would repent! Even for the crimes they haven't committed...repent posthumously.

Like a shadow, Mirrie crept into the cabin.

"Mother?"

"Yes, my baby?"

"Can I go to a fair?"

"Which one?"

It turned out there was another fair in Altver. It was not big, but it was open every day, something akin to the daily market.

Lily nodded in agreement.

"Who will go with you?"

"Mark and a couple of Virmans…"

"Who will be in charge?"

Somebody shuffled behind the closed door, and Ivar popped into the room.

"May I take her along, My Lady? We will take our women, they will look after the children…"

"I warn you, you will be accountable for Mirrie, even if she breaks one nail on her finger," Lily threatened him.

"Is Ingrid going? I hold her responsible as well," Lily added.

"Everything will go well," Ingrid ensured her. "Leif and I will personally look after Mirrie."

The Virmaness was a couple of months pregnant and looked incredibly beautiful. She did not suffer from toxicosis, so she was in good health. In fact, she belonged to that rare category of women who blossom in their pregnancy. Her eyes shone, and her mouth was curved into a permanent smile. She seemed to inwardly glow with her future motherhood.

"Ingrid, I am putting you in charge."

"Of course, My Lady..."

"My Lady?" Pastor Vopler crept through the entrance like a ghost. "I would like to…"

"Yes, Pastor?"

"Pastor Leider invited me to pay him a visit. I suppose…"

"I agree. If we go together, it will be more useful. When?"

"Maybe today?"

After some thought, Lily shook her head.

"We cannot. Today I intend to see Torius Avermal. You will go, too, by the way, as my religious teacher. Tomorrow morning, however, we can go to the service and after that…"

The pastor mused a while and agreed with a nod. "I suppose that would be better."

Lily smiled.

"Pastor, could you speak to Lons and figure out what gift is best to offer Pastor Leider?"

"A book perhaps?"

Lily shook her head.

"No. We will be in Laveri. Over there, we will meet the birds who fly higher than Leider. You should get used to it, Pastor. Now, you are not a vagabond from the middle of nowhere anymore; you are the religious teacher of the Countess Earton, herself. Carry yourself with dignity. You should also go around and speak with your fellows."

"With whom, My Lady?"

"With other pastors. I will not invite a random person to Earton, so take a close look at them. Later, we will hold interviews before heading to the capital."

Pastor Vopler only nodded. Lily knew he thought she was simply trying to advance herself, which was true to an extent. She adapted to the new world, took a small break, and was now driven to conquer new heights.

Is it dangerous? And what about Earton, will I ever be safe there? As if!

The end of winter, however, was peaceful. She might as well feel at home in a port tavern. At least there, it was clear which sides people took. *But here, anything and everything is possible.*

Lily sighed. She looked at the Virmans and Mirrie.

"During the time you are here, they will sell out everything at the fair."

Everybody got the message and vanished. Lily looked back at the pastor.

"Pastor, I cannot give orders to you. But I plead with you instead."

" I will try to fulfill your every wish, My Lady."

" I beg you, think about the people. You know better than me that there are people who serve God and those who serve only their own selves."

The pastor winced but refrained from responding. He agreed with Lily.

"I would never ask you to lie. But if you decide there are things that should remain solely between you and God..."

The pastor nodded.

"I will think about it, My Lady."

Lily nodded. The pastor left her alone, and she approached the mirror to look at her reflection.

I should do some exercise and later send a little note to Avermal. It needs to be done.

***

Baron Avermal received her letter during breakfast. The whole family was seated at the table—the Baron, his wife, their two sons and three daughters—when someone knocked on the front door so loudly that it echoed in the dining room.

A minute later, the frightened servant announced the visitor. "Sir, the Virmans wish to speak to you."

The Baron sighed, smiled at his wife, and left the room. *The stew will definitely get cold...*

However, as soon as he saw who his visitor was, his mind went blank.

"Ivar? Good morning... I am glad to see you."

"Baron Avermal, I am equally glad", the Virman produced a convincing bow. "My Lady, the Countess Lilian Earton, has arrived in Altver."

"What!"

"It would be her pleasure to see you."

"The feeling is mutual."

Torius didn't exaggerate. He was ready to greet, love, and worship the lady who had doubled his income for the winter. The Baron didn't think too hard about what to do next.

"Ivar, I invite you to join the meal. Tell the Countess she is invited to a dinner in her name."

"The Countess passed this on to you..."

Torius took a small envelope from the Virman's hands.

"This?"

"My Lady asked me to pass it on to you," the Virman repeated and smiled.

Torius unsealed the envelope and rubbed the green-tinted paper, which looked nothing like parchment.

He looked at the note:

Dear Baron,

I am in Altver for a couple of days. I will be glad to meet you.

Lilian Elizabeth Mariella, the Countess of Earton.

Nothing excessive, short and to the point.

***

"Has My Lady found a place to stay?"

"No, she decided to stay on her ship."

"Would the Countess be happy to accept my invitation to spend a couple of nights in my humble household?"

The Virman shrugged. "I suppose she might…"

"Yes, I will ask her personally. Hold on, I will get ready and call for a horse. I wish to come with you and invite My Lady in person."

Ivar nodded.

"I will wait for your return."

Torius briefly let his wife know he was departing for an urgent meeting, pecked his daughters on the cheeks, and called his son over for a word.

Darius obediently followed his father out of the room.

"Darius. I am inviting the Countess Earton to dine with us tonight."

"The shrew!"

Smack!

"Unless you can behave in a decent way during dinner, get out of my sight and everybody else's, too. Say you are sick. Understood?"

Darius frowned in agreement. He felt sick from his only memory of the Countess. Although the wound had healed long ago, the memory of it still hurt.

"Father…"

"Darius, I know you don't like her, but we need her. Do you understand? Do you like throwing away money in taverns? And what about the horse I bought you? The hound at Lorels'? That's right. If the Countess refuses my partnership, we will lose many of the privileges we have now. As for the Countess, she can easily replace us."

Darius pursed his lips but didn't reply.

The Baron's attitude had been appropriate—carrots and sticks. His son got the sticks all the time, but the carrots…they had their place, too.

The word 'gain' had special powers. It tamed the wildest and extinguished the fiercest spirits.

"I…it's better if I disappear for a night," exhaled Darius.

"Please do. Understood?"

"Yes, father."

Torius patted his son on the shoulder and left the room. *It's okay. Soon the fool will transform into his father's right hand.*

Whipping sometimes proved to be enlightening. Lily would say whipping activated the cerebrum through the stimulation of the spinal cord. But Torius had no intention of revealing any specifics about his family to her.

***

The Countess had already had breakfast and was sitting at the table in her tiny ship cabin. She was busy writing when someone knocked on the door.

"Baron Avermal, My Lady."

"Let him in!" replied the woman immediately.

The door opened and Torius literally flew into the cabin with a trail of compliments on his tongue. "My Lady, you are unusually charming today!"

Lily smiled. "You flatter me, dear Baron."

"My Lady, I speak the truth—your beauty deserves to be serenaded."

Lily almost snorted. *How much benefit, I wonder, does the Baron get from this agreement?*

Her reflection in the mirror revealed quite a lovely face. *I'm certain, though, that there are better looking women, too. It would be nice to have slimmer cheeks; there is still a remanence of a second chin; and the hips are too wide. It's okay. Compared to what it was before, these are only life's small concerns. It is so frustrating that the last layers of fat disappear the hardest—that dense sedimentary fat that is impossible to break up. Only exercise, nothing else will help.*

"Let's talk about our affairs, sir."

"Of course, My Lady."

"I suppose you're satisfied with our treaty?"

"Y-yes ..."

"I am, as well, and I propose to extend it. The only thing is that the goods will have to go to the capital."

To be fair, Lily did not particularly need Torius. *But why spoil the relationship?* She saw him relieved and realized her assumptions were correct.

"My Lady, will you allow me to invite you to dinner tonight? We can discuss everything then."

"Baron, I'd be glad to accept your invitation. But I have my daughter with me, her name is Miranda Catherine Earton."

"I'll be glad to see her."

"And the eldest son of the Great Khangan, Amir Gulim, as well."

"Has he recovered?"

Lily shrugged. "It is no surprise; Tahir Djiaman din Dashar is a great healer."

"My Lady, I hope you will pass my invitation on to His Highness?"

Lily shrugged. "I believe you know, dear Baron, that the Prince needs at least a dozen men to accompany him."

Torius looked inspired. "My Lady, just tell me how many people you want. I assure you I will not fail the reputation of Altver, nor that of Ativerna."

***

Following his father's instructions, Darius chose to stay with a friend, far away from the house. Tommy suggested they take a walk to the fair—go to a tavern, in other words—to unwind.

The result proved to be immediate.

Alas, the fair in Altver was not as big as a modern shopping mall. It was quite a humble place. The Virmans who accompanied Mirrie stood out as if the Hound of the Baskervilles appeared in a group of pugs.

For a moment, Leif got distracted as he paid for leather gloves. Mirrie saw a beautiful green cloth and made a dart for it to buy it for Lily. Ingrid rushed after the girl, only to run into Darius and his friend, Tommy.

Mirrie managed to get away, due to her being little and restless, and neither Darius nor Tommy was acquainted with her. But Ingrid... She was difficult to forget.

"You!" Darius yelled, and Tommy went speechless.

Indeed, Ingrid was incredibly good-looking. She had golden tresses, a slim silhouette, and was no longer wearing the Virman dress, but the clothes Lily designed. The dress was executed in empire-style, blue, with a ribbon encircling the waist, matching the ribbons in her hair. The sight of her made Darius impulsively reach out to her with his hand. His fingers grabbed the end of the ribbon on Ingrid's blue dress. Leif arrived just in time to push Darius away, and with so much force that he fell over and landed in a puddle.

In his turn, Tommy shouted at the top of his lungs, "Guards! Over here!"

Bad luck! The guards came running almost immediately.

Almost fainting, Ingrid hid behind Leif's back; the young Baron struggled to get out of the deep and muddy puddle, and Tommy screamed as hard as he could, "Get them! Don't let them get away!"

In all fairness, Tommy would be scared to confront the Virmans alone, but one sight of Ingrid produced such an effect that—being used to getting away with everything—the young lads forgot everything but their attraction to her.

***

Darius might have recovered, but no one let him. Before he could get out of the puddle, which turned out to be deep and viscous, a spear was already aimed at Leif, and the Virmans were prepared to start a fight.

"Stand still!" The scream was childish but quite overbearing. And the little person wedged between the two opposing groups looked like… Lily took care not only of her own appearance but also of Mirrie's, so the girl looked like a little princess, in some ways even better.

To go to the fair, Mirrie had chosen skirt-style trousers, a green vest, and a yellow silk shirt. The outfit was decorated with embroidery; the lace collar beautifully encircled her thin neck; an amber brooch on her shoulder was made in the shape of an owl. The object unobtrusively emphasized that the wearer was not a mere noblewoman. Not many could afford such a rarity as white amber, let alone have it executed in such an elegant manner—an owl with a nut-brown body, white head, and gold eyes. Mirrie helped Helke make it and valued it beyond any other. The girl's black hair was fastened with a comb made of the same kind of amber.

The guards hesitated. They weren't stupid. They knew detaining such a party could cost them their heads.

God only knows who they are…

Mirrie chose not to keep everyone in the dark.

"I am Viscountess Miranda Catherine Earton, daughter of the Earl of Earton. How dare you attack my people?"

Her demand sounded adult-like. Even the broken voice at the end of the phrase did not mar the impression. *It is scary indeed. I am tiny, and the spears are big…and there is not even a watchdog guarding me by my side. He stayed with Amir.*

Mirrie shuddered but did not show her fear. These were her people. More than once, Lily had explained to Mirrie that Lily herself was responsible for her people, and, in their turn, they were accountable before her…and before Mirrie as well.

I am Viscountess Earton!

"A Viscountess!" mocked Tommy. "You're lying!"

Leif produced a blow that immediately sent Tommy into the same puddle, knocking over Darius who had just managed to get out of it. The lads huddled in the mud like two wrestlers.

"Leif! Stand still!" Mirrie shouted. *Ugh, why is it that Lily can roar, whereas I can only yelp!*

The guards would never willingly confront the Virmans—they weren't suicidal after all—but everyone was on edge, and Leif's actions were taken for aggression.

"Noo!"

Mirrie rushed forward and, with her whole body, hung onto the handle of the spear one of the guards brought out.

In any case, she would not let him throw it. If fighting began, she would definitely be the first one to get crushed.

The guard wanted to shake off the impudent girl with a blow, but a man arrived just in time to grab Mirrie and drag her aside.

"Drop the weapon! Don't you dare! You will be hung!"

Mirrie took a breath.

It was Tahir.

Well, at least something...

"Sir Din Dashar, we were walking around the fair when these two attacked us." The girl's finger jabbed in the direction of Tommy and Darius.

Who cares if the gesture is improper!

"And when my people tried to protect us," continued Mirrie, "they set the guards on us!"

The spears slowly sank.

Tahir Djiaman din Dashar only shook his head.

"Dear order keepers, praise the holy Mare of Heavens I happened to be here. You could have inadvertently harmed the Viscountess Earton..."

The spears were meekly put out of sight.

"We had not touched anyone!" Darius yelled from the puddle; he finally came to himself and realized what his father would do to him for quarreling with the Eartons.

"Guards, I demand we all be brought to the magistrate and for news to be sent to my mother, the Countess Earton," Mirrie repeated after Tahir, who was quick to prompt her.

The guards were happy with this. All instigators, so to speak, would be delivered to the governor; let him deal with them. The main thing was that the guards would not be held accountable.

***

Two hours later, the incident was over.

The guards indeed sent news to the Countess. Lily moaned and rushed to the magistrate, turning a blind eye to road safety and the traffic. It was only by a miracle that Lidarh did not run anyone over. The guards in their turn caught up with her midway, which made the people quite unhappy.

The magistrate, on the other hand, looked splendorous.

They did not even attempt to detain Lily. Judging by the woman's face, she could have trampled an elephant, stepped over it, and rushed on. The officials did not consider themselves elephants and did not want to meet with Lily's wrath. They let her hurry to the second floor.

***

Torius yelled at his offspring; Miranda sat in a large armchair and drank something pink from a cup; Tahir stood beside her, holding her wrist to count her pulse; Tommy hid in the corner waiting for his father to come; and Leif consoled a crying Ingrid. The rest of the Virmans gave Darius and Tommy such fiery looks that it was a miracle their clothes did not catch fire.

"Is everyone alive?"

Miranda flew off the chair and rushed to Lily.

"Mother, I was so scared!"

Lily picked up the girl in her arms and incinerated the Baron with her angry look. He answered with a guilty grimace.

"Tell me, baby girl..."

Mirrie obediently retold all that had happened. Lily listened calmly. Then she kissed the girl on the nose.

"Miranda Catherine Earton. I am proud of you. Your behavior was totally just."

Not quite, but how can a little child understand everything? Incredible! The girl is not yet eight but is already so resolute! What a clever child!

Lily turned to Leif.

"So. Leif Ericson Erquig. Maldonaya take you! Why on earth would you get into a fight? You had a pregnant wife and a little girl on your hands...and what did you do?"

Leif looked down.

"Yes, I kind of only pushed them..."

"Lord Baron! Have you inspected your son? Does he have any bruises? Abrasions? Scratches?"

Torius shook his head.

He did not have any bruises; not counting those he got from tossing about and falling into a puddle. Besides, Leif did not hit him properly; it was just that the balance of strength was completely uneven. On one side was the Virman, who was accustomed to steering his ships in stormy weather. On the other, was a jerk who could be knocked down by a slight kick.

"Leif, if this happens again in the capital—"

"If someone dares to grope my wife with his dirty paws, I will not hesitate to let it happen again!" bellowed Leif.

"Ingrid?"

The Virmaness nodded.

"They wanted to—"

Lily had already found the half-torn ribbon on the blue dress, and her wrath fell on Torius Avermal.

"Lord Baron, we're setting our ship to sail. We are leaving."

Torius howled, realizing this was the end of their professional alliance—a total end. He could not manage to say anything.

Darius was not a complete idiot. He rushed forward and fell to his knees in front of the Countess.

"My Lady, my father is not to blame for the failures of his child..."

Lily swiftly stepped aside. She suppressed a great desire to kick the cretin in the jaw. *So that you would spend your whole life eating dried soup.*

"You are guilty because you did not raise your son a man. My daughter, who is seven years old, behaves better than a nobleman who is already twenty!"

Darius bit his lip.

"My Lady, if you want to behead us, do it. Only do not get angry with my father."

Torius clenched his fists tightly. He had no idea what to expect from the Countess.

Lily's anger softened.

"Had a single strand of hair fallen from my daughter's head, I would have beaten you myself. Presently, I do not demand punishment. We are leaving."

"My Lady, are you not on good terms with your own father?" Darius gasped.

"My Lady," repeated the Baron, "I do not dare ask you for mercy..."

"He's not a bad person, mother," said Mirrie.

Lily shook her head.

"Stand up, gentlemen. I do not want to see you again. Baron, we sail tomorrow. Your wife does not need to prepare a formal dinner. There is no need or occasion for such formality."

Torius had difficulty keeping his breath steady.

She is angry, fair enough, but she will not break the partnership. It would be unreasonable. And maybe it is best not to lash Darius so hard this time. In the end, it would not make any difference.

***

Lily could barely endure the time it took to get to the ship, where she kicked off at Leif. However, she did not yell; the times of yelling were long gone.

She did make sure to remind him about his pregnant wife, about the people, and about his duty before them. She spoke so forcefully that the Virman flew out of the cabin with red ears. The rest of the party got their share, too.

Fools! Leif will teach you an even better lesson.

Lily thanked Tahir, then attended to her little girl with all speed. The experience affected Mirrie. The girl was shaking; her teeth were chattering even though the cabin was hot and stuffy; she was clinging to Lily and muttering about how scary it was to see those spears, how Lily's education proved useful, and how Leif and Ingrid could have died there.

Mirrie clung to her puppy so hard that her fingers turned white. They had to take the dog away before she strangled him to death.

Lily somehow got the child to take an herbal sedative, put her on the bed, and sat by her side. The prince was there as well.

Amir Gulim had arrived almost immediately. He was angry and indignant; he promised Avermal he would tear off all the protruding parts of his body and feed them to the desert jackals.

Torius Avermal had arrived with Tommy's father, Clemens Triol, a prosperous merchant.

The Prince began telling Mirrie a fairy tale, and Lily went out to the men. Both men bowed and began to vigorously apologize for their offspring, saying they had not intended for the incident to happen, and that their children grew up foolish.

"And the beauty of your friend, My Lady..."

Lily made a spitting sound, dismissing all their excuses.

"Baron, tomorrow we will attend the church service, and after that, we sail with the evening tide. I do not accept your invitation. You can understand why. I'd rather stay with my daughter."

"You have a wonderful daughter, My Lady," Torius said.

Clemens, too, began to praise Miranda and lament that his son grew up a fool.

Angered, Lily advised the men to turn to beating, but she knew that if it were not for Tommy, everything would have turned out fine. *That idiot felt the need to yell!*

The men began to bargain. On the one hand, the mess was the fault of their sons because they were uneducated and unbeaten children. On the other hand, Leif acted heatedly. Lily immediately dismissed this argument, announcing a warrior would never have to run first to the judge to protect his wife from any rubbish.

The men were impressed. They all agreed on a decent compensation for Leif and Ingrid, for inflicting moral damage, in Lily's words.

Lily did not demand an execution or flogging.

They are your children, and it is your responsibility to teach them.

The parties separated more or less reassured—Torius by the fact that the Countess would keep doing business with him and Clemens because the Countess would not demand a showdown.

Lily herself was satisfied with the situation in general. *I really didn't want to make enemies, but maintaining my image is also important. And besides, today, I should go to bed early. Why not? I will babysit Mirrie and lie down to sleep right there.*

***

Lons Avels was waiting for her in the cabin. "My Lady, can I ..."

"What else?" said Lily with a groan.

"Can I have a word with you?"

"I'm listening."

"My Lady, will you continue working with Avermal?"

Over the winter, Lily had acquired good manners from the Chevalier. And he, unknowingly, had adopted some of the jargon of the 21st century.

'Working' with Avermal! Before, he would not have used 'working' when speaking of a lady.

"I don't know. Why?"

"What is going to happen at court is a mystery, but you are Countess Earton. If worse comes to worst, we will return here..."

Lily nodded; she understood. *If anything happens, Lons and his wife will definitely look for refuge here; the last thing he needs, therefore, is to cut all relations with Avermal.*

"What do you suggest?"

"Send the goods to him. Leif will receive the money from him."

"And Mirrie? Imagine if something had happened to her!" Lily started shaking.

The Chevalier sighed.

"My Lady, nothing happened."

"But it might have."

"Darius is not much to blame. It was the one who yelled…"

That's also true.

"Okay. I will send the goods, but without the gifts."

"Offering gifts is excessive as it is. We can make use of them in the capital," Lons agreed immediately. "My Lady, should I make the order?"

"I will do it myself. Call someone from the Virmans, Olaf for example, or Ivar…"

Lons left, and Lily rubbed her temples. It was at such moments that she wanted to shave her head bald. The crown of braids pressed unbearably against her skull.

Okay. Now, I wait for the Virmans, and afterwards, sleep, sleep, sleep… Only one more thing needs sorting out.

***

Torius was not pleased upon his return home.

Darius got a clout on the ear, his wife, a swearing, and the Baron locked himself in his office, where he downed alcohol until someone knocked on his door.

"Baron, a note from Countess Earton…"

The Baron jumped to his feet and rushed downstairs.

The chest was small, but handled very carefully. Two Virmans glanced at him without affection, but they did not take out their weapons.

"My Lady, the Countess, asked me to pass this on to you."

The letter was brief.

Baron,

With regard to the current circumstances, the dinner will not take place. However, I will not break our contract because of the stupidity of your offspring and his friend. Therefore, I am passing on to you all the goods due for sale.

Lilian Elizabeth Mariella, Countess of Earton

While the Baron wrote a letter of reply, the Virmans were treated in the kindest manner, given food and drink, embraced and kissed.

My Lady,

I can only fall at your feet once again, begging for forgiveness. I wish to emphasize that your generosity is not inferior to your beauty.

I am grateful to you, and I hope to see you again tomorrow during the service.

You can always count on me.

Yours sincerely,

Torius, Baron of Avermal

A few mirrors, a bit of lace, glass-colored beads, glass cups of different colors...a mad profit.

Darius's father did not whip him this time. Instead, he ordered him to be fed only bread and water for thirty days and to say prayers for further discipline.

For his part, Darius was happy that he got away so easily. He even felt grateful to the Countess. He could imagine what would happen if she broke off the partnership.

Tommy had it much worse. He could not sit on his bottom for over thirty days—it hurt from whipping—and he was locked inside the house with only bread and water for food.

**

Who is the bastard that decided to start the service at sunrise? What an idiot!

Lily did not want to go to the service. But there was no way out of it; she had to make an appearance.

The Virmans and Khangans stayed on the ships. Lily was accompanied by Pastor Vopler, Lons Avels, Miranda, Leis' people and a few artisans and lace-makers.

Lily walked to the church to make a sign of reverence.

**

She met Torius Avermal next to the church. He arrived with his whole family, except Darius. He bowed to Lily in greeting, full of kind words and compliments, but she took them coldly.

You don't deserve my full forgiveness yet, thought Lily. *A business agreement is not friendship.*

The service began.

Pastor Leider sang beautifully. Still, it was dawn, so Lily preferred to close her eyes, napping for as long as possible. When the ceremony finally ended, Lily decided to wait until everyone finished conversing with the pastor. That took a long time, but soon Simon Leider approached Lily, bowed and invited her to pay him a visit.

Lily sighed. She left Miranda with Marcia and, together with Pastor Vopler, followed Leider.

***

It was nice and warm in the living room. Flames danced in the fireplace, encircled by broad armchairs. The pastor personally walked the Countess to one of the chairs, kissed her hand, and smiled in a way that made Lily want to slap him.

Don't look at my cleavage with your slimy eyes!

"My Lady, you are even prettier than when I last saw you!"

"A righteous life in the wilderness benefited me," retorted Lily impudently.

She was leaving Earton. In the capital, though, she would try to improve her relationship with the aldon. It was best to not destroy the relationship while she was still in Earton, but she was a countess, and he, a provincial pastor.

"Oh yes, the Eveers, the Virmans, the Khangans…the sight of your retinue leaves one convinced of your righteousness," the pastor accepted the challenge.

Lily smiled at him in return. "Holy Liara lived among the Virmans, trying to convert them to the real faith."

"Do you pair yourself with a saint?"

"Not at all. That's why I do not live among the Virmans, and they don't live in my house, but the pastor can confirm that we tried to convert them to the true faith."

Volper only blinked.

"Oh yes, Pastor, I cannot say how many of them wished to be christened, but the Virmans' children know the holy word, and attend the service."

Very rarely, and only after tedious talks by Leif and myself.

Lily did not intend to encroach on someone else's faith. At the same time, she needed to maintain peace in Earton. That was why, approximately once a month, Leif and his crew got bored at a service. They treated it as an additional duty, made a schedule, and honestly came to listen—if not, to sleep to the sounds of singing. Being real warriors, they successfully managed to sleep both standing and with their eyes open. So, there was peace in Earton. The pastor was happy to have the pagans listen to him, and the Virmans were happy, too, since the people stopped laughing at them. Even though they were pagans, they went to the service, and the rest thought that, in this way, perhaps, they might become more civilized.

"Is that true? Many of them wished to be christened?"

"We are working on it, Pastor."

We are working on it. How could anyone prove the opposite?

"What about the Khangans?"

"I guess if you don't like the Prince of Khanganat Amir Gulim being in Earton or Altver, I can write to his father. He will certainly take pity and show understanding."

Lily's smile was so wide that it made the pastor almost swear.

"And what about the Eveers, are you also trying to…"

"Convert them to the true faith, yes."

"Are there any righteous people in your environment?"

"Were those who came today not righteous enough? Pastor, what is wrong? I built two churches in Earton, not counting the one in the castle. I listen to the words of my religious teacher with the utmost care." Lily was overtly pushing her case. "You say they are infidels? So are those in His Majesty's court! Do you suggest we throw the ambassadors out or make them convert?"

The pastor's eyes shone wildly.

"Is your husband aware of this, My Lady?"

"Why don't you ask him yourself?" Lily evidently got him there. Jerrison would not even think of replying to the pastor.

The pastor made grimaced as if he had gotten pepper up his nose.

"I do not understand, Pastor, on what grounds you interrogate me?" Lily switched her tactic and began attacking him. "What have I done to you to be treated like that? It is as if you looking for a flaw in me to point out."

"How could you even think that, My Lady! I only care for the people's souls…"

"It is your duty, I understand, but the priest can confirm that I almost never miss a religious service and that I always listen to him with utmost care."

The conversation lasted for about fifteen more minutes. The pastor twisted and turned, he tried to catch Lily out at least somehow, but he could not keep up with a girl from the garrison town.

Only imagine! Everyone is on the spot; you sneeze in one place and hear "bless you" on the other side of town; any piece of news remains current for a month. One involuntarily learns to spread gossip. Besides, the two things go together.

Lily was very good at making up excuses.

The most important thing was not to confess—in no circumstance and at no cost. The confession could diminish guilt but would increase the punishment; that was certain.

Therefore, the pastor attempted to fight with Lily but gave up in the end. His focus switched to Pastor Vopler.

"My son, would you like to confess to me?"

The priest nodded. "Yes, Pastor. I would like to pour out my heart to you and, if possible, get advice. I struggle…"

"Pastor, we will be waiting for you."

"Don't bother, My Lady."

"Pastor, yesterday my daughter nearly got hurt. If anything happened to you, I would not forgive myself. This is out of the discussion; we expect you with us."

With these words, Lily made her way back to the church.

She did not give Pastor Leider the honor of a farewell or forgiveness. On the contrary, Lily made a note to herself to find out the reason why he was exiled, and if possible, to send him even further away—to a place like a gulag, to the far depths of hell.

He imagined himself capable of tripping me up, and in such a manner! What a sheep!

***

It had been difficult for Pastor Vopler. He was not at all foolish. He saw a lot, understood a lot, and pondered many things. There was one little thing, however; he was painfully honest in his faith.

In his youth, he knew that Aldonai existed, and he was ready to convince every one of them, and to live only according to his covenants.

Later on in life, fate crushed his dreams.

Volper discovered that when one starts leading the life of a pastor, one sees that religion and the act of believing are two different things—nearly the same as a parasite feeding on a helpless animal. Volper could not call out his church-fellows for using the people's belief and naivety for their own profit. *Alas!*

It turned out that the church had many fraudulent tricksters, who did not care for saving souls but only for their own profit. Those people who came to them were at the mercy of being slandered, abused, or sent away to such dead ends where there was not even a single doctor to be found. Volper understood that he would forever be trapped in Earton. Even worse, when his wife died, he lost all hope for happiness. All that was left for him to do was to protect and give education to his son, Mark. But everything changed from the moment Lilian Earton appeared.

He remembered the church in flames, remembered the sense of sharp despair. He could recollect how he was afraid for his son, because all of his savings were gone. He worried that he would not be able to feed the boy during the cold season.

But no.

Lilian Earton took them to the castle, dressed, and fed them, and brought Mark to study. On top of that, being near the young Countess was akin to being near a miracle of nature; a mercy from the skies; a gift from Aldonai.

Volper tried to thank the Countess, but she brushed away the topic as if her help was a mere trifle.

"Pastor, do you really think that I could leave someone to die of starvation? What does this have to do with gratitude? This should be the order of things. This is my duty as a Countess."

Yes, but it was also true that a sense of duty did not include everything that Lilian Earton gave to him. Volper regained the meaning in life.

He perfectly understood that the Virmans did not take his preaching seriously, but let them stay pagan. There was something out there that was more important. If he succeeded to put at least one seed of true faith in their own souls or in the souls of their children, his efforts would not be in vain.

It may happen gradually, but the seed would grow. As for Mark, Volper was prepared to kiss the Countess' hands. He could not imagine the price he would have to pay for her kindness, but agreed to anything.

Alas! Only after some months, did he come to understand that Lilian Earton did everything completely out of a good heart. She did not expect anything in return. Perhaps only moral support that he should have given her anyway; that was all. She did not demand gratitude, she did not trade her kindness, she merely did what she felt she had to do. The pastor's heart was filled with gratitude.

He saw the strange sides of the Countess' personality. He also saw that they did not bring bad to the world. In fact, the opposite was true. If used in a correct way, they would give fruit to many. She cured, educated, and cared for her people; she worked as much as anyone else and never sought recognition.

Pastor Leider, on the contrary, did not invoke good feelings in Volper, for he belonged to the caste of social climbers and church chiselers.

Volper went down on his knees in his usual way in order to confess.

"Oh, brother in faith! My soul is pure and calm right now."

"Is it not disturbed by the pagans?"

"The Countess does everything to make them see the light of true faith. Being unworthy, I am still trying to aid her in this task."

"And the behavior of the Countess herself, does it trouble you?"

"Dear brother, I am close to the Countess. She is kind, smart and noble. If she had at least one dark place in her soul, I would have spotted it. However, she guards herself against the tricks of Maldonaya."

"Is it truly so?"

Pastor Leider listened, but Volper did not mention many other things. Neither did he mention the smugglers, nor the assassination attempts. *Why would I?*

These were the matters of the body, not the soul and useless for blackmail.

Thus, an hour later, Volper left Leider quite unsatisfied, and went to meet up with Lily and her people.

He knew that the next day, he would talk to his fellow believers; he would talk to the real believers, unlike this greasy rat. They would leave for Earton, while he would join the Countess in departing for the capital.

I am afraid, no doubt, but perhaps this is a challenge of my faith sent by Aldonai. Faith be in Aldonai.

***

The ships departed from Altver with the evening tide.

Lily stood on the stern and struggled against sea-sickness, immersed in her grim fantasies about the invention of trains, or better, airplanes.

In general, the first visits were not bad, not counting the incident with Avermal, of course. In all fairness, he should be left to teach his son better. *What rueful behavior! He saw a girl on the street and lost control! His spermotoxicosis needs to be cured, lest someone else decides to fix it by cutting off his head.*

Leif had more or less composed himself as soon as he received a big sum from Avermal. Torius also offered his apologies. He would pay thrice as much to prevent invoking Lily's anger; that was certain.

To break all ties with Torius was not an option yet. If they decided to return to Earton, the Baron would be a priceless contact, and in all fairness, Lily would not mind this.

Over the winter, she got to appreciate the perks of living in faraway places. They had peace and calm in them and good neighbors, too. *If only Jamie would get approved!*

Do I want to live in a capital? Let it go to hell. Dirt, boredom, and stinking, and all other incidents.

On the other hand, she was a doctor. In Earton, all her skills would be lost. *Maybe it is worth staying somewhere by my father's side?*

She didn't know, and one thing she could not take into account was Jerrison Earton. *What would he do after he got a hard wallop? It is hard to tell.*

Masculine pride is something else. It is not worth trampling on it, for fear I would get into serious trouble. On the other hand, what else is left for me to do, let myself die?

Lily's stomach rumbled louder than ever, and bending over the side of the ship (she had already learned that it was better to vomit toward the leeward) she thought grimly that to die would be faster.

They would reach the capital in two weeks.

Bleeuurrggh!

***

"Are you all set to go, Richard?"

Richard looked at his cousin.

"Yes. And you?"

"The servants are slow, but we are almost ready. So, on the road?"

"Yes, it's time. And then Bernard will be offended that he has almost no time."

"He will be offended. Judging by the gossip, he is a terrible brat. He keeps his own daughter in rags."

Richard made a dismissing gesture with his hand.

"Once she is a queen, we will dress her up. Otherwise, it is of no importance."

Someone knocked on the door.

Richard opened it and almost gave out a whistle. The doorway revealed Anna Wellster. Jess jumped behind the curtain before he could be seen. He would not tell anyone, and in case Richard needed a witness, he was ready to give testimony.

"Your Highness, would you let me…"

"Of course, My Lady. Come in. But how do I deserve your—"

Anna raised her hand.

"Your Highness, I don't have much time. I need to return immediately. I only wish to…here."

The princess' hand revealed a locket that looked too big for her tiny palm.

"What is this, My Lady?"

"This I wish to give you in memory of our adventure in the woods…and about me, lest you shall never come back."

Richard sighed.

"My dear Lady…"

Anna put her hand over his mouth.

"Do not promise anything. Say nothing. I only want you to know that…I will be waiting for you. I will pray for you, even if you never come back."

The girl came closer to Richard and touched his cheek with her lips. The touch was very timid.

She moved away immediately. A transparent tear ran down her cheek. The girl let out a sob and rushed out of the room.

It was only in her own bedroom that Anna managed to compose herself.

The idea of giving Richard a medallion was suggested to her by Altres Lort, and he also found her the gift. Anna herself could not think of a better way to part.

It seemed to her now that Richard would come back, at all costs.

***

Jess revealed himself from behind the curtain and shook off the dust from his garments. Richard showed him the gift from Anna. "Look!"

It was a simple golden locket, the outside of which was engraved with the face of a lynx.

Inside there was a portrait of Anna completed in the most skillful manner. Enclosed in it was a lock of dark hair. It looked like she had given it to him as a memory of herself.

"Richard, do you think we will come back?"

"It depends on what Bernard offers. But I strongly suspect that we will."

Richard stared at the door. His cheek retained a feminine touch of lips, and pity stirred in his soul.

She is still a child, she is more fit to play with dolls…a child.

For men, however, pity and love are far from being the same.

***

Adelaide Wells was also preparing to depart.

Duke Falion strongly regretted that he could not send off the scoundrel to Ativerna, but the chances for it were slim. For some reason, Her Majesty Milia of Shelt began to favor the wretch. With her in the picture, in the embassy, it was impossible to come close to Adele.

It would be different if she were at home, in Ativerna. There, it would be easy to get rid of her without making noise, then to shrug shoulders at her disappearance.

The night was dark, the robbers broke in, we are deeply sorry, what a tragedy, ah-ah-ah…

But until they were back, their hands were tied.

The Duke was satisfied because, once in the embassy, Adelaide turned wild. The others even tried to avoid communicating with her unless it was a matter of urgency.

***

This did not affect Adelaide too much. She already made a bet on Alters Lort and was now in the process of figuring out the best way to act when in Ivernea.

It was clear how to behave on the way there. *I am a woman suffering from the blows of fate. My cousin tortured me, Earl Earton deceived and left me, I lost a child. I have to be suffering.* Adelaide knew how to suffer. She could pull it off in Ivernea, too. Maybe that could help her make friends with Lidia. All women like to hear about the sufferings of others.

*Besides…*Adelaide's fingers touched an expensive casket made of fragrant wood. Under its velvet bottom lay a handful of little flat bottles—a sleeping drug, an aphrodisiac, a slow poison, a quick venom.

As Altres had explained, and even demonstrated on rats, each flacon was enough to put down five or six people. Therefore, it was necessary to use each with care.

Which one will I give to Lidia depending on the princess' luck?

Adelaide saw her goal clearly. Richard had to leave Ivernea, quietly, but definitely without holding any ties to Lidia…she had to disappear from the embassy in the time he was traveling away.

Altres made her learn a couple of destination names and promised her that if something happened, he would move her to Wellster.

And once she was there… *My apologies, but I don't guarantee giving you a noble status in court. You must understand why…But a rich husband in the middle of nowhere—easy! It is better than nothing. In five years, when the noise has settled, we will see.*

Adelaide considered this a generous offer. Nothing held her in Ativerna. It was true that she had been entitled to a house there and to some money, too, but she still had to claim it. She would be detained when crossing the Ativernian border. All she would be left with was a slap in the face.

Damn it! The house and the money—if I remain alive I can earn it. I can find someone to get under—only ahead. The ships of the embassy will go through Limaiere and be escorted across the border with Ivernea. Ugh, going by ship again.

Although Adelaide did not suffer from seasickness, either way, she did not like ships. They were stuffy and disgusting… *Eww!*

***

Altres Lort was getting ready, as well.

He could not leave for Ivernea, himself, but he made sure that his agents got the most detailed instructions. *To count on Adelaide Wells alone? What a joke!*

He had enough of his own agents. A couple of coins here, a few letters there, and people would begin to work for him. This, Altres knew how to do.

Ah, if only Edward would not let his offspring choose… It is not right to judge him for this though. When a man is forced to do things, he rebels, but when he is given a free choice, you are left with tied hands.

"Why are you so pensive?" Gardwig used a secret passage to enter his brother's chambers, and now he stood by the curtains and looked at Altres.

Altres jumped to his feet and helped his brother to a seat, hissing about the steep dark stairs, his aching leg, and his stupid folly.

Gardwig paid no attention to this. His brother was the only one who was allowed to give instructions to the King, as well as to reproach and criticize him (to a certain extent), and even to issue orders on his behalf. Altres had the King's full trust. The King trusted him like he trusted himself.

"Stop croaking..."

Altres snorted, but fell silent and began to look at the suzerain.

"I hope your people will not fail?"

"I myself hope for the same."

"Anna did everything right?"

"Even better. If we push it and slander Lidia even more, Richard will come back here."

"More precisely, we will have to go to Ativerna."

"Both of us?"

"Either you or me. I guess I'll go. You will stay here. I will grant you the regency in my absence, you might need the troops... You will manage."

"And Her Majesty?"

"With the children on her hands? I'll take the eldest, they are girls anyway…"

"Hum! Brother, should we leave them with Milia? It is not good to bring up the princesses in such a dark wilderness. We somehow failed to think of that."

"We should arrange for them to marry, better abroad. Think about it. Maybe it makes sense to have a talk with the Khangan..."

"It makes sense to take the young ones and present them to the heir of the Khanganat."

"To the heir?"

"Before, I didn't know the whole story. But now I can report it to you. One of the most famous doctors of our time was visiting Earton. Tahir Djiaman din Dashar."

"Khangan."

"Well yes. And now imagine, the Great Khangan sent his heir in the middle of winter, with three ships, through the damned channel, to Tahir, so that he could heal the prince."

"How now?"

"The treatment was more or less successful. It turned out that the youth was being poisoned."

"With what?"

"My agent did not understand... he wrote something about the blood of the Mare..."

Lily had not particularly talked about the illness of the heir. Gossip, rumors...and the Virmans, who went to Altver in winter and early spring and allowed themselves to unwind in taverns. That's where they caught up with Royce. He gave out drinks, kept asking questions, and then sent reports.

"All right, this is not important. Was the youth cured after all?"

"Not entirely. And now they are departing with the whole crew to Laveri."

"Why?"

"As far as I understood, Lilian Earton is a favorite student of Tahir; he cannot part with her."

"Is that so!"

"Edward, in his turn, is asking her to join the court."

"Hum! So the girl to the court, followed by the doctor, followed by the prince… Is Edward not afraid of undoing the boy?"

"He wanted the Countess to come in early spring. That did not work out. The prince was not yet strong enough, but now…"

Gardwig nodded. "You say a good doctor…"

"And here I've got…" Altres took out the scroll with Lilian's questions copied out. "I can send them the answers, but you understand. It's better if…"

"Can you not call them in?"

"No."

"Then we'll see what happens next. If everything goes well, I'll see you at the wedding. As for now, have a think. What can be of interest to this doctor? Who knows?"

Gardwig unconsciously rubbed his leg, and his brother's heart began to ache. *The death of a loved one is a terrible thing. Even more terrible is the death of the only dear person; the one who shares your every breath. But the worst thing is when the loved one*

*is slowly dying before your very eyes; when you see and understand
everything but cannot help him; when you are prepared to give up
your life for his, but they won't take it.*

Gardwig caught his brother's gaze. " Enough sorrow. If you
snivel, I will make you marry."

"Screw you," muttered the fool. "I see that His Majesty dares
to threaten me!"

Gardwig was not offended in the slightest.

"And then...will make you marry this student. In this way, I
will provide my children with a doctor, with a posh Khangan
student."

"Is it of no importance to you that the Countess is a 'little'
married?" Altres inquired.

"It is not accidental that you are the head of the secret
service. One day, she has a husband, another day, he is nowhere to
be found."

"Ugh. You are mocking me, Your Majesty."

"Why not? Shall we have a drink?"

"You don't drink wine."

"So what? Have you run out of ale?"

Altres snorted and took out a jug from under the table.

"No ale. Something else…"

"Cherry brandy?" Gardwig smiled. Altres had a sweet tooth,
that was one of his few weaknesses. He, of course, carefully
concealed it, but not from his relatives. The buffoon preferred cherry
to the best ale.

"Pour me some."

***

Anna inspected her jewelry casket. Over the winter, she had received a lot of precious objects. *After all, I am a princess! Not a beggar in a wretched castle, but a real princess. If only I had known that earlier, I would never have gotten involved with Lons!* Nevertheless, the damage was done. She was still afraid of Altres, but she was safe until she completed her mission. She was still useful for them.

It was evident that Richard did not love her. Yet, she could discern some strange uncertainty in his eyes. It showed in his patronizing behavior. She was younger, he protected her, she owed him for it. Such a state of affairs feeds a man's pride. It flatters men, even more, when they see love and admiration in the eyes of a young woman.

If Lidia does not prove herself to be even better, Richard will come back. I have done everything in my power for it to happen. Until then, I have to live my life. As long as Richard doesn't make his choice, they will need me; they will protect me. And yet, just in case…

Anna's eyes stopped on a well-hidden flask of poison.

Is it for me, for Count Lort, for somebody else? She did not know. *A rat is dangerous when it's cornered.*

Fate had not forced Anna into a corner just yet. Nevertheless, the girl was prepared to show her teeth.

***

"My lord and master, I fall at your feet—"

His Greatness interrupted the speech of glory. "What about Amir?"

He knew the captain perfectly well. Nazar Halim din Harnari from the clan that was sent to find water. He had selected and sent him with Amir.

"My Lord, Prince Amir instructed me to return home, bring you this letter and gifts, and send him your reply."

The Khangan took a quiet breath. "How does the prince feel?"

"Much better. The Countess says it will take about a year until full recovery, if not more, but right now his life is not in danger."

"Who? Tahir?"

"The Countess Lilian Earton."

"What is that supposed to mean?"

"The prince explained everything in the letter. I do not mean to disrespect you, but…"

The Khangan dismissed the captain with a gesture and turned to the letter.

My son is safe and sound; what else does a man need for happiness? Be you thrice a Khanghan, the children remain the most important. And this says it all.

    My beloved Father and Master,

    Let your way be forever paved with rose petals and lit by the rays of the Sun. Let the Heavenly Mare favor Your Majesty and mark your doorstep with Her footprints.

The Khangan let his eyes skim through the greetings and read on.

    Upon sending me for treatment to Earton, my father, you have shown truly great wisdom. I did not write to you before because I have not had a chance to send the letter; I did not want to keep it where anyone might easily come across it.

    The first thing that I wanted to tell you is that I am on the road to swift recovery, even though the Countess does not recommend me to touch the poison for at least three years. After that, I will easily be able to attend church. The Countess herself, I must say, is a marvelous woman. On top of being clever, she is also not afraid to show her wit. The public trusts her blindly. Although, I must say, there is a certain strangeness about her.

    The Heavenly Mare puts some people above others, and this is the natural order of things. But the Countess does not know and does not want to acknowledge it. For Lilian Earton, I am a human being above all; she sees my titles of the prince and your heir as secondary. It is the strangest feeling!

She treats everybody with respect, but at the same time, she is equally friendly to a goldsmith, to an artisan, to Virmans, and to my people. I must say that Rashad was genuinely surprised when the Countess asked him to teach the Virman children our language. Furthermore, together with those children, the Countess teaches her own child, the Viscountess Miranda Catherine Earton. I am aware of her being extremely mad at the teachers when they allowed themselves to praise the girl only because of her blue blood.

Rashad did not refuse; it was the first time I saw him so bewildered. It seems he intends to teach his own children in the same manner and the children of his kinship as well.

The Countess is a very odd person. It seems like she is good at everything. She speaks to the goldsmith about jewels, and I found out that it was the Countess who revealed a way of making red and white amber. She talks about ships with the Virmans and listens to their tales with great interest. She even gave them advice once. Her invention called the "telescope" is at a premium. Let alone gold, the Virmans are prepared to pay for it in precious stones worth the peculiar object's weight. I had looked into it myself and, although the device slightly distorts reality, with its help, one can see thrice as far as with one's own eyes. And considering the visual distortion, the Countess mentioned her working on improving the device.

In addition to this letter, I am sending you several gifts from Earton. The Countess noted that should you take interest in any of the objects, she will be happy to cooperate. Here in Earton, they make wonderful lace and produce colored glass.

Speaking of medicine, my doctors do not leave the Countess' side and look at her in awe. During the third week, I realized that I, too, had begun to regard her with the same awe. I do not know for a fact what she will do or say from moment to moment, but I am assured that it will be something unexpected and interesting.

Her daughter, alone, is worth a fortune. On the second day of my visit, she told me they did not need a prince in their household because he is useful for nothing, after which I decided to join the children in learning the goldsmith's trade from Helke. I

am still amazed at how the Countess managed to invent all of this!
The Countess Earton might be a woman, but she is one of a kind...

Upon finishing the letter, the Great Khangan unwrapped the gifts and gave off a whistling sound of surprise. He had seen such lace before. Not quite the same, but it cost him a fortune to get some of a similar kind for his wife. The Earton lace was even more exquisite, a wide cloth made of lace, with amber beads woven into it.

Wait a minute, not amber. It is clearly glass, colored glass! But how?

The pen and the spill-proof inkpot left him slightly surprised, for they were bountifully encrusted with precious stones. No one ever thought of giving him such necessities.

It had not been viewed as a necessity by others, that is why.

A collection of glass goblets made a strong impression on him. Different colors, elegance, simplicity, beauty; they were all different, but at the same time they were of the same mold.

And the last object was a box with tokens—a beautiful, expensive box...without hesitation, Lily had sent the ruler a game of backgammon.

It was most exquisite, and came with instructions. Lily had taken a sheet of the best paper (still thick and greenish), set up text blocks on a board, and printed detailed rules for the game.

"What is it?"

Nazar helplessly shrugged. He knew nothing about the printing press.

Lily managed to leave another monarch bemused.

Chapter 2

About capital dwellers, who 'judge a book by its cover'.

After almost three weeks, the Countess Earton, who was now considerably thinner, pale, and sultry, watched Laveri from the deck of the ship.

The city was not impressive. It could not compare to the view of Sevastopol from the sea at night. *What a beautiful sight it was!* Lily had seen it, in that other life—a swimming sea of lights, something truly magical.

In contrast, even an avid romantic would not call Laveri a magical place. Lily was in the Middle Ages, after all. Light from candles, heating from a stove, knee-deep in mud, she was fed up with how nothing was done for social benefit.

Either way, Lily would have to live like that for a while. There was no getting out of it. She would manage. Although it was good to live on the outskirts of the capital instead of in the center, getting there made her blood boil.

Oh, why can I not remember how springs are made? There were some significant gaps in Lily's education. For example, she was oblivious to everything that concerned technology, as well as mathematics, economics, philosophy, literature or history...a kind of compensation for the amount of extra-curricular activities she had taken on. She had learned to make a lot of things by hand, but they did not teach the basics of political science at university.

Ugh, life is a pain.

"My Lady?"

Lily looked at Lons with a tinge of melancholy. "Me?"

"Perhaps I should send a messenger to your father..."

"And to my mother-in-law."

"You believe it necessary?"

"Do we have a choice? Unlike my father, Alicia Earton is the most avid palace resident. Who else do we question if not her?"

"Her turn will come, but first…"

Lily sighed. Realizing that Lons was right, she sent a letter to August. Thinking about it made her stomach squeeze, and she retired to use the bathroom.

He is not a servant. He is your father! Okay, the father of Lilian Broklend. What if I make a mistake!

The thought of it made her stomach turn again.

***

"My Lady, the officials have arrived for inspection!"

"What officials?" Lily was genuinely surprised.

"Well, we must make sure that we do not import anything illegal into the capital; we need to make a record of all the ships. The port agency is involved," explained Leif.

"Would it be better if I spoke to them?"

"No doubt, My Lady," smirked the Virman.

"Do we owe them anything?"

"The entry fee. One golden coin for each ship, and five copper coins per person."

"Anything else?"

"Are we going to trade?"

Lily contemplated.

I don't want to pay. Especially if it is a tax on my belongings! To hell with that.

"We have no goods, only the personal belongings of Countess Earton."

Leif crooked his lips into a smile.

"On all the ships?"

"Do you think, you ignorant Virman, that one ship is enough to fit the Countess' personal belongings? At least five! Not to mention Miranda! She, too, needs at least one ship to fit all of her clothes, but we are forced to make everything fit inside only two. How disgusting."

Leif snorted.

"My Lady, if Ingrid was not with me..."

"Go, meet the officials, you flatterer. And do not forget to take the biggest axe, and put your armor on... You know what to do."

"So even before meeting you they shi—"

"...Shine at the very thought," corrected the woman. "Quick! March!"

***

There were two port officials. The first one had a balding head, was short and rather large; Lily's proportions faded in comparison.

The second one was tall and bulky with thick curly hair.

I see. This place brings yield. Why did these parasites not go to Altver?

Well, Lily had gone there with the ships only once. Even so, she could not imagine any official daring to tax a governor's friend. That would be trying to jump over their heads. If Torius had found out, it would have cost them their heads; so they stayed away. But at present, there were a lot of ships and only one capital...

The capital-dwellers have a certain snobbishness about them; there is no escape from it. Not everyone has it, but there are some exemplars who are firmly convinced that life in the capital gives them priority over the rest. Judging by the look of these two officials, they were just like that.

Snobs. Goons. And I don't care that they don't know the meaning of such words. Surely they bow. Obviously, everything is very polite in appearance. But there is something in their eyes... something rotten.

"My Lady..." began the curly-haired one.

Judging by the tone, they received dozens of countesses at port every day.

Lily sat at a table, making no effort to get up. She gave the "customs officers" an unkind look and smirked. Somewhere nearby, Leif was tossing about with an axe.

"That's right, the ships are mine. How much tax?"

"My Lady, someone needs to make the calculations."

"That is why you have come here, dear fellow," Lily played with her fountain pen, twisting the goose feather between her fingers.

"Three ships...with a load of goods," pronounced the curly-haired one.

"Wrong, my dear," Lily was the epitome of kindness. "Three ships which belong to the Countess Earton!"

"And ..."

"And about the cargo, that's a lie. Countesses are not merchants; they do not trade goods."

"But—" the second one tried to object.

"If you have doubts, you may appeal to His Majesty."

"Forgive me, My Lady, but the hold is full of trunks!"

"These are my personal belongings and those of my stepdaughter and my people," retorted Lily. "Do you think that Countess Earton travels like a commoner?"

"My Lady—"

"Three ships, three golden coins, one per ship. As for the people... Leif!"

Leif banged on the floor of the cabin with such force that it scared Lily.

What if he breaks it?

"How many people do we have on the ships?"

"One hundred and eight people, My Lady."

"In total, five hundred and forty copper coins. To round up, five hundred and fifty. Eleven silver coins."

Lily counted the required amount and laid it on the table.

The customs officers gulped and began to put it on paper.

The Countess Earton.

Three ships.

The cargo is her personal belongings.

***

The Khangans did not even pay, for Rashad groaned and wept, "They humiliate, they insult, they try to scrub money from the heir to the throne! Good people, what is the world coming to?" The customs would have paid any price only to get rid of him.

But this was only the first act of the tragedy. The second act opened with the ships having to move away from the shore and anchor in the middle of the bay to avoid theft. Sentries were put to watch over the ships, eight persons per ship. Otherwise, thieves stole anything and everything that was not nailed down. They would approach by boat to get on the ship, take a little, and divide it among themselves.

The last thing Lily needed was to be robbed, so she wrote a note to her father and asked Leif to send it. Meanwhile, Lily tried to decide where to stay. On the one hand, the Countess must live with her husband.

No way am I going to a house that is as close to Earton as getting to the moon by foot! According to Mirrie's stories, the house was not great. It would fit twenty people, but was unlikely to accommodate more.

What about safety? Thought Lily. *I need guards. And the Virmans? And the Khangans? Well, they also have an embassy there… First of all, Amir is my patient. Secondly, the boy does not want to go to the embassy. And thirdly and most importantly, they simply won't fit there.*

Ativerna and the Khanganat are on opposite ends of the continent. *Why on earth would they need each other?* No borders, no trade, excluding some small stuff and curious objects so the embassy was beautiful and richly decorated with Oriental ornaments but was tiny. It held twenty people at most, including the servants. Lily wanted to find a compromise.

How do I manage to find a place where I can accommodate everyone?

* * *

August showed up the next morning. Lily was already awake. She had just finished her morning exercise and was talking with Tahir when someone banged at the cabin door.

"Madam, your father is about to come aboard!"

The words felt like a lashing whip. "Ask him in," broke Lily's voice, revealing her moment of weakness.

Here we are. This is your first exam in this new world. It scares you to death, but if your "father" accepts you, it will be easier later. And if not… Do I kill him?

Lily bit her lip.

To kill a person who has done nothing wrong to me, whose sole fault is that he loves me? Something inside Lily vigorously resisted the very thought of it. Still, Lily understood that if worse came to worst, if she were left no other option…

The door creaked, and Lily rose from the table. An elderly man stormed into the cabin. "My daughter!"

Lily attributed her own reaction to the remains of Lilian Earton's personality.

"Father!" The exclamation was full of such sincere love that even the best actor would fail to imitate. Lily hung on the man's neck.

* * *

For about five minutes, Lily wept aloud. Then the man somehow tore her away from him and began wiping her face with a damp handkerchief.

"Well, my little one, do not cry, it's all right."

Not a chance! The tears came streaming down her face. It was no less than ten minutes before Lily could blow her nose and say something. Even so, it did not stop her from inspecting August from under her shawl. *In his youth, my father was a hell of a heartbreaker!* Even now, he made a strong impression.

Slightly taller than Lily, broad-shouldered, with completely gray hair and unexpectedly black eyebrows, August had strong hands and the tanned face of a man, showing he spent a lot of time in the open air.

Like father like daughter.

His genes alone were enough to explain Lily's inherited beauty. A warm hand stroked Lily's hair. She did not even dare to imagine that she would find a family in this strange world. But now…whatever August was like, she clearly understood that she could not order for his removal. She could not do that to him, although had she chosen to kill him with her own hands, not a soul would be able to detect the foxglove extract here.

"Father," she said.

"Now, take away the cloth, let me have a look at you ..."

A strong hand lifted Lily's chin and the woman modestly lowered her eyes.

"You grew thin, your eyes are as big as plates."

"I lost my child," confessed Lily to her own surprise.

"I know." August flashed his bright young eyes. "If I get my hands on Earton, I'll tear his balls out!"

"Is it worth it?"

"Why do you ask? Do you love him?"

Lily shook her head.

"I used to love him…a long time ago. But then… Well, it doesn't matter. What use is it to complain now?"

"Lily…"

"Do not ask, Father. Do not… It's disgusting. When I lost my child, the flame of life died out in me."

"I could make Edward agree to arrange for a separate lodging for you and Earton."

"You could, but not just yet."

"Why not?"

Lily sighed.

Well, what I would like to say now will be as risky as jumping into the abyss… If that goes through, though, the rest will be easier.

"Because I am more profitable for our business if I bear the title. Therefore, we must first try to settle the issue in an amicable way. Only then, if everything works out well…"

August gave off a whistle; he glanced at his daughter with special intensity.

Lily raised her head and met his eyes with her cold look. She could picture herself the way she looked in his eyes right now.

A young blonde with a long braid, she had a slightly plump figure and was dressed in white and green, with a bracelet on her arm and a ring on her finger. She looked beautiful, even though she had been crying. She hoped her father could also see her wit and determination, which the former Lilian did not possess whatsoever.

"So that is how it is?"

Lily silently nodded.

She let him interpret the unsaid, but August remained silent. Lily did not say anything either; there was no need.

"I see that you have changed, daughter. I did not expect to hear such speeches from you…"

"When one is left without love, sympathy and protection, one learns fast." Lily looked ahead, straight and calm. "I have changed, Father.

I hope I have grown wiser. I am still your daughter, but I am not so small anymore."

August looked surprised. Lily helplessly shrugged in response.

"Last time you saw me was almost two years ago. During this time, I lost a child and they tried to kill me... I already lost count of how many attempts were made on my life. I learned that my husband had a mistress, and that he did not care a thing about me. It would have been unbelievable if I had stayed the same. Not even! If I remained the same, you would now be praying to Aldonai and asking him to save my soul."

"That is true."

"So, dear father, will you be able to accept me the way I have become? It is easy to love a child. It is easy to protect a helpless woman. What about protecting the woman I am now?"

There was silence in the cabin. Lily waited for an answer, biting her lips.

Come on...

"I am proud of having such a daughter. You know, you look so much like your mother now... only her eyes were blue, like the sea ..."

"I know!" Lily sobbed. "I've got something to show you..."

For the next two hours Lily kept August busy. He approved of her lace and her Mariella Glass; admired the telescope and demanded to have such a miracle. Immediately, he was given three pieces, each enclosed in a beautiful case. He was then impressed by a kaleidoscope, and met Miranda and Prince Amir. He also managed to have a couple of words with Leif; he asked something about Eric Erkwig. Leif's answer made August's lips stretch in a smile of exultation, rejoicing that his old friend was in good health.

Lily watched him from the side. She increasingly liked this serious man. Something in him reminded her of her father from the other world, Vladimir Vasilyevich. August resembled him in his thoroughness, humor, and firm attitude.

If only everything would work out, thought Lily.

***

When they found themselves in the cabin, Lily ordered a drink for her father and snacks, and asked for a familiar meal for herself, fruit and vegetables. Fortunately, they had them in the port so Lily could allow herself to eat as much as she wanted. August drank a couple of glasses of wine, paid tribute to the kitchen staff, and looked at his daughter with apprehension.

"You do not eat anything. You will soon blow away in the wind."

In Lily's opinion, she needed to lose at least thirty more pounds, but she refrained from arguing.

"I do not want anything yet. Shall we talk about our business?"

"What kind of business, My Lady?"

August was obviously teasing his daughter, his eyes glowing in soft mocking.

"About some important business!" smiled Lily. "I'm in the capital, and His Majesty wishes to see me."

"As soon as he finds out that you have arrived..."

"When?"

"Hmm... It would take three or four days. I guess a report will then be laid on his desk."

"It follows then that I have three days or so to drop my anchors a little, and after that, I must immediately go to the palace."

"Good girl."

"I know. I have a few questions. The first is my people."

"What are you thinking?"

"It is out of the question; they must stay with me."

"And where will you put them? Who do you plan to take with you?"

"Well, I will not take the crews. Someone should stay and look after the ships," Lily wondered aloud. "Furthermore, I have about thirty Virmans, a little more including women and children; then Miranda, the servants, the artisans... In short, one needs to expect around seventy people. There is no need for special facilities, the main thing is that we stay together."

"What about the Khangans ..."

"The prince has not recovered yet."

"So let them live in the embassy with...what's his name...Tahir."

"It's out of the question. Father, Tahir teaches me how to treat people."

"There is no way I can let this go on. You are the Countess!"

"The Countess who is absolutely useless at every trade!" Lily knocked her hand on the table, forgetting about a pear which was clutched in her hand. Its juice splashed in all directions. The pair simultaneously swore, exchanged glances and snorted.

"Here, take a napkin." Lily handed her father a thin cloth and August began to clean his waistcoat. "Father, I understand that you have acted in good faith, but that does not make it easier for me."

August pondered and shook his head. "You were raised as a noble lady."

"In other words, I was raised to be an utterly useless creature. I could not make my husband take an interest in me; I could not spot the murderers who tried to poison me; I could not even protect my child... You know, later on, after the miscarriage, I was lying in bed thinking to myself that if I had known earlier, everything might have been different."

"Do not blame yourself; it was Earton's fault."

"Do you think he found any pleasure in looking at me? Marriages of convenience are often successful, but only if both parties work on it. Has anybody taught me this?"

"If nobody taught you then, how do you know it now?"

"I've learned it by myself, that's the truth of it."

Lily curled her lips. August was obviously half-mocking her, but there was something else in his question. *Is it pride?*

It seemed like it was. He felt love for her and was proud of her, too.

"In short, I will continue my studies. Who knows, I might invent something useful. Therefore—"

"You need a house for seventy people. I understand." August was a picture of holy innocence.

"Here."

"I guess I can find what you need. But it has to be in the countryside."

"That's even better."

"Are you sure? A lot of people are willing to sacrifice everything to come to the capital."

"Let them give up their lives for it, even, if that's what they want."

"I have an idea... Did you know that Alicia Earton owns a small estate near the capital?"

"How small is it?"

"It is tiny, I would say. But you can house your entire suite in that estate. It has stables, outbuildings... she is hardly there because she spends all her time at court ..."

Lily immediately seized the idea.

"That means that she can lend it to me. That way, I'm not in the city, but in the estate of my mother-in-law, a good way to keep up appearances."

"You are a bellibone!"

"A chip off the old block," Lily returned the teasing.

"Write to Alicia. Tell her to come. We will discuss it together as soon as she arrives," her father said.

"Where is she?"

"In the palace, of course! She is a lady-in-waiting for other princesses, where else should she be?"

Lily sighed. She got out a pen and a sheet of paper. This immediately caught August's interest.

"What is it?"

Lily quickly wrote down the message, sent it away with one of the Virmans and began to explain to her father the use of those objects. It was necessary to demonstrate a piece of paper and printed text, and explain that it could be used with seals, with watermarks ...

The man could only shake his head.

✳✳✳

Alicia Earton received the note immediately. The royal guard was not made up of fools; they did not wish to incur the "old viperess's" wrath.

So, Alicia unfolded an unusually soft and rustling envelope, rubbed the paper with her fingers and raised her eyebrows.

She did not expect Lily, at least not so soon, and that was understandable. Lily wrote to August from both Altver and on her way there. But she did not even think of sending a word to Alicia. There was no need to fill her in.

> *My Lady,*
>
> *I arrived in the city and will be happy to meet with you to have a conversation—the sooner, the better. I am asking you to either follow my messenger or inform in writing when it pleases you best to grant me a visit.*
>
> *Yours dutifully,*
>
> *Lilian Elizabeth Mariella Earton*

The viperess did not get her nickname without knowing how to keep cool under any circumstances. She turned to the servant.

"Where is the person who delivered this letter?"

"It was a Virman, My Lady," the servant was full of respect. "We asked him to wait in the guardhouse, for he could not be taken to the palace."

Yes, the Virmans should not walk around the palace. If they denounced everything to Edward, everyone would suffer.

"We are going. Lead the way," decided Alicia. There was no need to pack. She was always on alert when in the palace. Only at home— outside the city—did she spare the time to relax, and it did not happen often.

***

The Virman waited in the guardhouse. He was a huge fellow— three feet wide in the shoulders and 6 and a half feet tall.

"Ivar Helvisson Reinholm, My Lady." He executed a clear and quick bow. It was not very courtly, but better than nothing.

"It's good to see you, Ivar. You brought me a letter from my daughter-in-law..."

"Indeed, My Lady, the Countess Lilian Earton, asked me to tell you that she is now with her father, so if you want to see them, she will be glad to host you."

"I will call a carriage now."

"I will wait here, My Lady."

There were several carriages at court. His Majesty allowed them to be taken only by those courtiers of whom he was fond. It was a great favor to use a royal carriage, but Alicia had the right to do so. Thus, an hour later, the carriage arrived at the port, and Alicia climbed aboard the ship.

***

It was not Alicia's first time being on a ship. Therefore, the first thing that struck her was that everything was surprisingly clean. It looked as if the ship got cleaned six times a day. Ivar caught her surprised look and chuckled.

"My Lady, the Countess said that she would tie a rope to any filthy deckhand who refused to take a bath and give them a ride overboard."

"Is she that rampant?"

"Not really. She just doesn't like dirt. Please, come on board, My Lady."

Alicia was led by the elbow, with all honor, to the cabin, and washed over by comments like "If you slip, or else get hurt, the Countess will skin me alive." Finally, she was met with the two equally gleeful smiles of August Broklend and his daughter.

Alicia refused to trust her vision.

This woman is… Lilian Earton? Surely not! What happened to that other lady, shy and chubby, covered in pink lace from head to toe, who could not even string two words together?

There was no doubt the woman beside August was Lilian Earton, despite being slimmer, but the look in her eyes… Jyce himself never looked that way. It was the look of a person who sees enemies in everyone, in all circumstances, before everything else.

Lily lowered her lashes immediately, smiled and looked up at Alicia again radiating amity.

"I'm glad to see you, My Lady! I hope my messenger was polite. If he wasn't, I deeply apologize, for the Virman people are not courtiers..."

It seemed to Alicia that she only imagined Lily's wariness. The woman decided to keep watch. She broke into a smile.

"My dear mother-in-law! I am so glad to see you! You have gotten prettier since our last meeting ..." Lily smiled, slowly rose from the table, and greeted Alicia with a light bow.

They both had the same title of Earton. Lily was younger in age but higher in position. Therefore, Alicia should have greeted Lily first, but the Countess gave her elder friend in the Eartons the opportunity to save face.

"My Lady, if there was some lack of tact in any way, I ask for your forgiveness. I wish to assure you that your visit is an honor for me."

Everything was polite and sincere. Lily bowed again.

Alicia nodded and sat at the table.

Fortunately, August had time to move the chair for her. "It is good to see you, dear Countess."

"You do not show up at court. Otherwise, we would see each other more often," Alicia sighed.

August shrugged helplessly. "Courtyards and palaces are not my home, but my daughter..."

"His Majesty is very interested in the Countess."

On hearing that the King was interested in them, others might get nervous or delighted. Lilian, on the contrary, gave a simple shrug.

"I want to get settled in the capital and appear at court. I suppose the invitation will follow as soon as the news of my arrival reaches His Majesty?"

"Today?"

"No. It must be at least another day."

Alicia nodded in understanding. Any normal woman would not have been able to immediately appear at court, she would need her servants, her dresses, her jewelry...

"I need to find my people somewhere to stay."

"Your people?" Alicia was genuinely surprised. She realized that Lily had servants, but not that they would need housing.

August chuckled.

"Including Lilian, there are around seventy people. I suppose she will want to keep them near."

"And they would not let me go far from them either," Lily grumbled to herself. She then started to explain to Alicia where she got such a crowd from.

One must pay tribute to Alicia. Without any hint, she made the correct proposition.

"I suppose I can invite everyone to my estate outside the city. It's not far, only an hour or two by horse, there's enough room for everyone, and hosting the Prince of the Khanganat is an honor for me."

Lily's lips curled into a smile of delight. "In his turn, I believe that Prince Amir will mention your kindness and generosity when speaking to the King ..."

"His Majesty the King will certainly want to see him at court."

"As for my part, I will make any repairs to the estate, and since it would be impudent to take your kindness for granted, I will pay for our stay."

"Payment is out of the question!"

Alicia was outraged in a genuine way. One could spot devils jumping in the eyes of Lilian Earton.

"I do not offer money!"

"What then?"

Lily got up, went to one of the chests and opened the lid. "What do you think, My Lady? How much will it cost when it appears on the market?"

Alicia only gasped.

Fans made of lace, gloves, handbags that were fit to hang on a wrist, and something else…

"What is this?"

"This is for couples," smiled Lily, seeing Alicia turn purple, beginning to understand how these lacy panties were made to be worn. For now, the only difference had been the addition of thin straps.

"I suppose that any husband would be happy to see his spouse wearing these modest little things...or at least his mistress. Do not fear; the wives themselves will catch up," Lily said.

"That is obscenity!"

"Why? I'm not suggesting they walk around the street wearing them."

Not yet. She would see to that later.

"Look at this..." Lily pulled something out of the chest and gave it a shake.

Alicia gasped in delight. It was a lace dress.

"Wait a minute," exclaimed Alicia, "it is not a whole dress. It's rather..."

"...an overdress, to put on the shoulders. It looks rather good. By the way, I have one for you. I could not guess your size, but it can be fitted in a day or two ..."

"It's too luxurious." Alicia shook her head.

"Too luxurious even for Countess Earton?"

"The Princesses—"

"Will be left with nothing but envy? I have predicted this," Lily continued, unperturbed, "and made the same ones for them. Please remember, it will be expensive only at first. Besides, it took about ten days to make this dress."

Lily carelessly shook the cloak and threw it on a chair.

"How?"

"Using a conveyor."

"Er..." The word was strange to Alicia. Lilian herself seemed strange. Everything was done at Lilian's request. *Unpleasant,* thought Alicia, *but it is a part of life.*

"The production is divided into ten parts. One artisan knits the sleeves; the second, the back; the third, the hem; and so on. The tenth joins the pieces, and we are all left to enjoy the outcome."

Alicia only shook her head. "Very beautiful. But is it worth cutting the price for these wonderful products?"

Lily shrugged.

"It is not a cat to hide in a sack. My idea is more profound. Let them imitate. I want my workshops to always remain in the lead. The others will follow us. The products of my workshops and my Mariella Lace will become a sign of quality."

Alicia contemplated the idea and found it worthy.

It's true. They can copy her, but it would take a lot of time and skill before they could outdo her. Lilian will not stop at what has been achieved either...

"What does Jerrison think about it?"

Lily raised her eyebrows.

"He should worry more about my reaction to his mistresses, as well as everyone else...We have a lot to talk about during our next meeting with him."

Judging by the woman's face, she had hit the nail on its head; Alicia chose not to go into more detail.

Instead, she asked about how Lily was going to accommodate everyone at the humble estate. Getting there would be difficult; it was unlikely that they had brought horses along when traveling across the sea.

"We will sort out this problem," retorted August. "I will order the ships to be taken to my shipyards, they are not too far from here. Once there, we will easily find working hands, carts, and carriages."

"Meanwhile, I will head to the estate," thought Lily aloud. "I want to see how it is."

"Do you still suffer from sea-sickness?"

August looked quite understanding. Lily sighed.

"When the ship is docked, I can bear it. But why should I torture myself? Besides, Miranda will go. She likes the sea. Amir adores her, indeed."

"The Prince?"

"Yes, he gets along with Mirrie."

Alicia could only shake her head.

Let it be. I will have enough time to figure out what is going on. It is unlikely that Lilian Earton is a better diplomat than me. As for now...

"I have two crews. I can also give orders to Jerrison's servants. He has a couple of carriages."

"Perfect."

* * *

Later that evening, Lily was sitting by the fireplace at the estate; it was real, warm, and cozy.

Restless streaks of flame danced wildly and made the wood crackle. Lilian could not quite call it happiness, but it was not misery either.

Lily found Alicia's estate to her liking. Moderately big, it was not as pompous as Earton. It was cozy and neat, although slightly neglected since the owner was always at the palace.

Lily was the first one to see the new home, but she was not alone. A dozen Virmans accompanied her. There was also Leif (who refused to let the Countess wander around alone); Lons (who made a scene); Martha (who had sworn not to let go of her "girl" and who wanted to prepare the room for Mirrie); and Alicia herself.

That's right, the widowed Countess excused herself from the court for a couple of days and came along with Lilian, who suspected that it was not just a simple act of kindness on Alicia's part.

This was what Lilian was thinking when she heard quiet steps behind her back.

"Do you mind me joining you, My Lady?"

"Feel welcome, dear Countess."

Alicia sank into a chair next to Lilian. The table contained a bottle of wine and two tall silver goblets. Lily took one of them in her hand and turned it to make the gleams of fire reflect in peculiar and uneven facets. For a while, there was silence. Lily decided to help Alicia ease off the pressure; either way, the questioning was inevitable, so Lily decided to make the conversation take a favorable course.

"Have I surprised you, My Lady?"

"Most highly."

"I am sure that His Majesty will ask you about me."

Alicia responded with a little laughter. "That too. But I do not inquire out of mere curiosity."

"I understand. One might cause way more harm by being ignorant."

"You understand my intentions correctly. I did not expect to see such changes in you."

"You mean my makeover? That's right. The wedding was…have you ever seen any woman being herself on her wedding day?"

Alicia refrained from snorting. Alicia herself had been different, her wedding with Jyce had been a mere transaction that had her shaking.

"I nearly lost my mind. Before the wedding I did not even know who my future husband was; no conversation, no time to think; I was left confused and upset, my legs and arms shaking. And after the wedding, my husband got utterly drunk," Lily said. "And then I was immediately sent to live in the wilderness. The only brief visits that he granted me happened once every three months."

***

Alicia nodded as if in sympathy, but in reality she could not feel sympathy for anyone. *Why would I?*

Take Lilian Broklend Earton. *Why would I sympathize with her?* Lily was beautiful and far from dumb, she came from a family without a title but still far from poor; she married an earl; and her father was devoted to her. *And she complains that her husband does not love her! She should be thankful that he is not fiendish. What did she do to make him love her? Embroidery in silk? Of course not.*

Alicia, on the other hand, was not a beauty, and could never be one. Thin, ugly, with hips too thin to even bear a child, without any dowry.

Her father, a player and an idle spendthrift. Her mother, a downtrodden broody who hid away from life in a dark corner. As for her brothers, it was best to forget their existence. It was Jyce who managed to ward them all off quickly and forcefully. They significantly spoiled Alicia's girlhood.

Her father did not even take her to court. *Why would he?* They should thank him for even bringing them to the city. But even when in the city, she was made to sit at home and not complain, unless shopping. Walking around was not fit for her reputation. Alicia had no servants; her father thought that coddling was excessive. He thought women could get dressed and clean by themselves. Alicia's father would not pay to keep a maid so Alicia was made to run to the shops, and her mother prepared the meals. Either way, when at home, her father only drank.

Her meeting with Jyce had been a stroke of luck. Alicia was just running from the shop when she suddenly stumbled, twisted her foot, and hit herself hard against the stony pavement. That is when Jyce found her, sitting in the mud, tears streaming down her face.

Unlike his son, Jyce always tried to treat people well. Not out of a good heart, no, but he thought that people worked better when their master was attentive and respectful toward them. Alicia had often heard him repeat this. When she asked why Jyce had stopped to help her back then, he only shrugged. He said he could not know who she might turn out to be. Any information bore fruit; any person was useful in their own way. Maybe not immediately, but he did not mind waiting. So, Jyce collected people in case they might prove useful in the future.

But Alicia had not known that back then. Sitting in the mud, she burst into tears and told her whole story. About poverty, about relatives, about herself.

Jyce listened attentively. He wiped away the girl's tears, handed her a delicious pastry and asked to accompany her home. Two days later, he paid a visit to her house and confessed his intentions.

Alicia was infertile, as was he. She needed peace, security and, of course, money. He would provide for Alicia. He needed someone to confide in; he also needed the approval of his sister's children. His relatives were already filled in. If Alicia could be so kind as to marry him…

Alicia was most kind. Jyce was beautiful. After all, even a pig can dream about meeting a prince. And back then, Alicia's dream seemed to come true. *However, in what perverted disguise!* Alicia was offered what she wanted, and even offered a man, that the naïve girl immediately fell in love with. There was only one thing…

She was not going to become his real wife, not even a mistress. She was there to keep up appearances. That truth hurt her terribly.

It had been an incredible effort for Alicia to humble her pride, gather herself and conform to Jyce. She answered that if dear Jyce wished it so, then under certain conditions she would agree.

Not for a year or two, but for many years she had to face the hard challenge of watching someone else's children grow up. *They could have been my children*, she thought. She had to witness Jyce's love for her sister, which she thought she could never get, she had to look at her dream of happiness being so close, but so out of reach. Jyce laid with her only once, as a formality after their wedding. That was an end of it. Such a life could turn the most miserable worm into a fiend. She was far from being a worm, so she turned into a viperess.

What is so special about Lilian Earton? Alicia could not even imagine the position Lily had found herself in.

***

Although Lily did not know the whole story, she could sense that Alicia was not a bad person and had not turned fiendish from living a good life. Still, Lily could spot the droplets of venom in Alicia's eyes. There was no escape from them.

"This is not the horrible reaction I expected." Lily's stare was calm. Inside, too, she felt calm. She cared the most about her father, and since he gave her much desired recognition, Alicia played an important, but not vital part in her scenario. Therefore, Lily had to try to make a positive impression; but it was not the end of the world if she failed to do so. Alicia would still take care of her and offer her protection only because Lily belonged to the Eartons. Any slander associated with Lilian's name would stain Alicia's reputation as well.

"I guess…" nodded Alicia as she drank from the cup, "I have never lost a baby, but everybody says that no other evil can surpass that grief."

"The loss of a child is the hardest, that is true." Lily rolled the wine inside her glass, and noted that the goblet shaped like a tulip was quite exquisite, but the twist at the end was certainly excessive. "You know, there are things in life which feel way worse, at least to me." Alicia did not even have to pretend that she was interested; the words struck her.

"The worst thing is mere existence. The worst is when no one gives a damn if you exist or not." Lily noted the confusion on the face of her mother-in-law and, after a long pause, began to explain herself.

"I meant nothing to my husband. He already had the shipyard and was to receive an heir. And what was I to him...a trophy? I did not even know how to give orders. Even if I did, I was being poisoned with datura nectar that left me incapable. The servants took advantage of that whenever they could."

Lily continued, "I was lucky. Yes, after I had a miscarriage they were scared to continue poisoning me. The only person left beside me was my faithful servant Martha. She was the only one who protected and defended me; she gave me water and changed my chamber pot. A lady of her age cannot be of much use. But she, on the other hand, gave me everything she could. I love Martha like my own mother. She is a mother to me, indeed. Mariella Broklend breathed life into me, and so did Martha by curing me from death. I have two mothers." Lily thought she heard a sound at the door. *Was Martha listening? No matter. I am not embarrassed by my feelings, and Martha should always know she is loved.*

"And then I woke up. I was unwell. For a couple of days, I did not even know whether I would survive. Imagine, I am ill to the bone, I come downstairs, I did not have a soul to ask for a drink. Martha was away, the servants pretended not to hear... Of course, they were all gathered in the kitchen. They drank wine, touched the female servants and laughed loudly. They did not care a thing about me. They did not care if I was alive or not. I might as well have disappeared, that would not change a thing. The only person to blame for this was me alone. They were having fun while I was dying. And I had no one beside me except the woman who loved me unconditionally."

Alicia sighed.

That's life. I do not even have someone like Martha. My life has passed; it is almost over…

"That was the first time I lost my temper. Before that, I did not even know how to be angry. A red cloud of fog dimmed my sight; my hands were shaking. I had a go at everyone that time; I roared and screamed to make everyone leave my sight. I put an end to their feast. A little while after that, I was lying in bed, thinking. The servants bustled about, I looked at them and thought to myself that never again would I let others treat me like I am nothing. I would not allow this to happen ever again. I was ready to go through hell and back, to eat a frog alive, to learn everything I didn't know before. I would do anything to prevent this from happening. Never again, will I let others treat me like that!"

"And did you get what you wanted?" Alicia asked the question before she realized how silly it was. "I mean, yes. You became the woman you wanted to be. What next?"

"Next? 'To come further up, to go further in,'" laughed Lily, quoting from *The Last Battle* of *The Chronicles of Narnia.* "Only further. First, I want to receive my own title for my achievements for the state. Second, I want to open my own production line and have it protected by the Crown. And obviously, I want to fix my relationship with my husband. We had many disagreements, but both of us were responsible for weaving this spider web."

"It is good that you realize this." Alicia sighed with relief.

She liked this new Lilian. But the woman realized that if Lily and Jess quarreled, Alicia would suffer, too. That war would allow for no neutral parties; it would not have any winners, either.

"I realize it well. Jess did not make an effort to meet me halfway. But I am no perfect wife myself—"

"Although you can become one."

"Only if I give birth to the heir, or better, deliver twins to then die quietly after."

"You don't have to be so bitter."

"I do. That would be a perfect outcome for everyone but me. How strange, is it not?"

"Very strange." Alicia paused looking at Lily. "Please call me Alicia."

"Okay. I suppose to call you 'mother' would not be appropriate. It doesn't suit such a young and pretty woman like you."

Alicia's eyes glimmered. Lily was absolutely genuine and calm. She was not lying. It was quite true; judging by the standards of the twenty-first century, Alicia was quite attractive. Not too tall, very slim, thin-boned and graceful. As for her face…although she was plain, she only needed to pluck her eyebrows a little and put some color on her eyes and lips to obtain a distinctive look.

Like that, she would resemble a vigilant bird of prey. It seemed like the widowing Countess realized this and nodded. "I will call you Lilian."

"Close friends call me Lily."

Both women exchanged meaningful glances. All limits were established and all priorities were made clear. One of them desired to preserve the status quo and strengthen her reputation at court. The other one needed a title and money, and a family. If both of them tried hard, those aims could become compatible with one another. Such a conclusion left them space to talk about the mundane.

"You know, Lily, I need to seriously take care of your look. It is unacceptable for a noble lady to have tanned skin; you need to pluck your eyebrows and slightly touch your cheeks with white powder."

Lily shook her head. Although she didn't utter a word it was a clear protest. "I respect you enough to not argue with you, but I will not follow your advice."

"Lilian?"

"I will not conform to the whims of fashion," shrugged Lilian. "I will set a trend myself."

"So that's what you choose." Alicia squinted. "You are aiming to become a royal favorite?"

Lily smiled. "No."

"In that case you do not stand a chance. Baroness Ormt is the one who dictates fashion now.

"A close friend of His Majesty?"

Alicia agreed with a smile.

"I guess I will need to be introduced to the Baroness, even make friends with her."

"The princesses despise her."

"Does His Majesty love his daughters?"

"Very much. The Baroness is a woman, a mere entertainment for him, likewise for any other man. A daughter, on the contrary, is quite another thing."

"A memory about a woman he once loved?"

"Yes, her name was Jessamine. I do not see why everyone was so charmed by her, to be honest."

"Was she beautiful?"

"Yes, but dumb and helpless at the same time."

Lily snorted. "Alicia. Speaking from my own experience, I would put it in this way. Men love those creatures that need to be taken care of. To be with a strong and wise woman is obliging. If you want to tame a lioness you need to become a lion, not a goat. A doe is easier to keep. You give her a little grass, a little milk, and she is tamed. Who do you think a man would choose?"

"You are smart."

"I am trying to be. Who else dictates fashion beside the Baroness? It cannot be that she does not have rivals."

"You are absolutely right. The Duchess of Tarness."

The conversation continued in recollecting titles, connections, in discussions of friends and enemies. The two women made a pact of peace. However, it was purely bilateral; the rest of the world was open to war.

***

Lily's next morning began with a pleasant visit.

"Inform My Lady about the arrival of Hans Tremain."

This piece of news put out her burning headache. Lily yelped from excitement and flew out of the dining room after trying to stuff herself with bonny-clabber to make herself feel better. She did not get drunk yesterday, but her head was bursting like a balloon. She could not remember the last time she had to put so much energy into something, at least not since she had ceased to be Aliya Skorolenok.

"Leir Hans! I am so happy to see you!"

Hans bowed in accordance with all rules of courtesy, kissed the Countess' hand, and made her a compliment.

Alicia Earton was still resting. Therefore, Lily did not think twice before inviting Hans to the table and inquiring about everything.

The man accepted her invitation without a shade of embarrassment and began munching his breakfast with great delight.

"I am terribly sorry, dear Countess. I did not even have time for breakfast before arriving to see you."

"Why rush so much?"

"I wanted to talk with you before you get introduced to the court."

"You have my full attention, Leir Hans."

"Do you remember this man called Alex, a cousin of Lady Wells?

"I do," Lily said, her face darkening. The scar had not ceased to burn yet. "Did he not get executed?"

"He did. I have something to show you…."

Hans laid a pile of letters before the woman.

"What is it?"

"Please, have a read."

Lily obeyed and when she got to the third letter could not refrain from swearing anymore.

Of course! This was proof that Alex was the one standing behind the attempt on her life, him and Adelaide together. Whatever the others were saying, it was clear that Adele was the one giving out the orders. Although these were the drafts of his letters, it was evident that he replied with detailed reports about how to execute the crime.

"Very sweet. Leir Hans, what do you want to do with them?"

"I have already used them for what I wanted. My Lady, you are a straight-forward person, therefore can I speak frankly?

Lily nodded.

"When you get to the palace, His Majesty will not let you leave so easily. That is for certain."

"I don't have any doubts about it."

"It is clear that you might want to spend your time in your own dwelling, get your own things done, *et cetera.*"

"So what?"

"Your father was looking for a man who is capable of completing similar tasks to my responsibilities at the Royal Service."

"He hasn't introduced me to anyone yet." Lily looked at the letters and then glanced at Hans. All of a sudden she realized what he wanted from her.

"And you wish to…"

"Yes, I would."

"It doesn't look like you are trying to bribe me, it looks like a gift in return for my good treatment." Lily smirked. "Who else knows about these letters?"

"No one. Royal hangmen who guard the prison have their ears stuffed with wax, lest they hear what they are not supposed to know. Otherwise, they get thrown into—"

Lily interrupted with a nod.

"And where is this coming from? Why so suddenly? Leir Hans, I understand everything, you are a clever person and a strong man—"

"Yes, and I want to live long and happily. I want to get a home, a family, a child… all of this is impossible if I work in the Royal Service. The only way to leave the service is feet first…"

"And my service is possible to ditch at any time, am I right?"

"My Lady," Hans was being serious. "I am not much older than your husband, but have seen much more and it turned half of my hair white. You are generous and wise. I am making you a proposition. I will be in your service for ten years. It is not because you are kind to me, but I know that you are always loyal to your people. During these years, I will find you good people for service and will teach them everything I know myself. When the term expires, I want to leave, to the Khanganat. There I will marry, raise my children, and die of old age in my own lodging, and not from a stab in the back in some dark alleyway."

Lily nodded and began thinking. *Hans is a professional. I will be pleased to have him on guard. But there is one thing.*

"How can I trust you? You could be loyal to the King before being loyal to me."

"First and foremost, all of us serve the Crown, and only after, do we serve the people, My Lady."

"Either way."

"The King does not know about these letters."

Lily sighed. Once again, a difficult choice fell on her shoulders. There was no one to advise or to help her. *What do I do, what do I do?*

"All right. I will meet the people my father found. That is important; he worked hard, and I do not want to offend his feelings. If none suit me, I will appeal to speak to His Majesty. Only with his permission, will I be able to hire you."

Hans nodded. It seemed that this was more than he expected.

"My Lady, I hope that the letters…"

"What letters?" Lily gave him an innocent look. "Leir Hans, I haven't seen or received any letters in my entire life!"

Their eyes met, and the room was filled with whole-hearted laughter.

"Leir Hans, I hope you will extend your visit? Miranda will be glad to see you. I, too, wanted to catch up on the news…"

"Of course, My Lady. How can I refuse the wish of such a charming woman?"

Lily wrinkled her nose. "I accept your compliment. There is no need to refuse my invitation. Help yourself to food, and we shall talk after breakfast."

"My Lady, I could—"

"There is no way I am talking about your courtiers on an empty stomach. Never! It is a sure way to get indigestion!"

"They will love you at court."

"Considering Alicia's stories, they have all lost their minds. Half of them were born without brains. It is the other half I would like to talk to you about."

"Alicia's stories?"

"Yes, the stories of my mother-in-law."

"The old viperess accepted you in her circle, after all? That is remarkable."

Lily shook her head. She refrained from mentioning her art of weaving intrigue.

"She has not exactly accepted me, no. She is not my friend, but not an enemy either. I can become useful to her, so she will support me. But if I let myself do something that might endanger my husband, or the Earton family in general, she will not tolerate it."

"You will not do such a thing, My Lady?"

Lily shrugged.

"I love my husband, but if he intends to continue treating me like a speechless doll… Would you have personally liked such treatment?"

Hans shook his head.

"I understand that there are women who cannot even get bread without help from the side. But I am not like that. I hope that the Earl will realize this."

"I harbor the same hope."

***

Hans nodded to himself, deep in his thoughts. *The Earl has to realize that it is not worth obstructing his wife's plans. Otherwise...* No, Hans did not intend to murder him. *Not just yet.* He put everything in Aldonai's hands, who was the most merciful and omniscient ruler. *And that's the end of it.*

After breakfast, Tremain thought it truly necessary to go through the list of courtiers with the Countess, or at least mention the main ones, and prepare her for what awaited her.

It was around midday when Alicia joined their animated conversation, and the discussion extended until nearly four o'clock. Lily soon wailed, demanding to leave her boiling brain in peace, whereas Hans and Alicia found some urgent business they had to attend to, and everyone left the hall.

***

The following evening, Alicia approached the King.

"Your Majesty."

"I am glad to see you, Countess Earton. What happened yesterday? You failed to attend the reception."

"Your Majesty, I have been hosting my daughter-in-law."

"Is that so? Is Lilian Earton in Laveri?"

"Ay, Your Majesty."

"Why is she still not here?"

"Your Majesty, I am here to implore for a three-day deferral for the Countess."

"A deferral?"

"Lilian has just arrived from far away, and she finds sea voyages terribly painful."

"The same as August, I understand."

"She needs a little rest from the journey, some time to sort herself out. Only then can she attend to Your Majesty."

"You are speaking the truth, My Lady. Perhaps I can send her an invitation to a small reception that will take place in three days. This should be enough time for her to get ready, should it not?"

"More than enough, Your Majesty. My gratitude is as bountiful as your generosity."

"Leave your gratitude, dear Countess. There is no need for you to flatter me!"

"I have not said a word of flattery, Your Majesty! I speak the plain truth."

Edward smiled. *It might be flattery, but it is sweet to the ear.*

"Dear Countess, tell me about your daughter-in-law. I suppose you have already had time to speak to her and create a first impression."

Alicia hesitated for a moment, but soon smiled and took an offered seat.

"Your Majesty, my daughter-in-law is a very unusual person. Upon questioning her, you might need to be extremely careful in order to make her interested and ward off her caution."

"And yet, what is her biggest fear?"

"I suppose she is afraid of becoming a powerless toy in someone else's evil hands."

"Why is that?"

"As I understand it from her words, her servants did not respect her. However, she does not blame anyone for it because she realizes that there are two sides to blame in any quarrel."

Edward nodded. *That is good. I do not need a scandal, or worse, a divorce. Lily expressed her hope to find mutual ground with her husband. At the same time, she harbors certain fears.*

"Lilian is clever, well-educated; she is beyond ordinary. All these qualities cannot appear in a day. How did my son not notice it? Why did he send his wife to Earton? Is it because of her looks?"

This made Edward think. *Jess did not want to get married in general. He did what he had to do. But how did he fail to see such a diamond right in his bed?*

The King only shook his head.

"I do not know the answer to that. Has Lilian explained it in any way?"

"She said that she was left in shock. The wedding, the wedding night, the swift departure."

"And have they not tried to speak to each other since?"

"August mentioned that Jess is sometimes prone to a certain kind of...despotism."

Alicia did not continue further. But Edward did not need elaborations. *It is true that even during the wedding itself Jess was already disappointed, for the bride looked way worse than her portrait. Therefore, it seemed possible that the wedding night might have been quite drastic.*

"I could understand the Countess. Could you explain to her, though, that the wife must follow her husband, but sometimes..." Edward's eyes radiated gleeful sparkles, "...sometimes there can be exceptions to the rule. Isn't that so?"

"Your Majesty, you are most wise, as ever, and just, too."

"I hope so. The King, after all, is made the head of the kingdom by Aldonai himself."

"There is no doubt about this, Your Majesty."

"Now, tell me what your daughter-in-law wants. What are her aspirations? Her dreams? Her thoughts?"

Edward could see that Alicia was trying to choose her words with care. But even so, what she told him left the King in much surprise.

"Production?"

"Lilian showed me some of her handicrafts. Your Majesty, her lace and her glass are things worth encouragement."

"Show me an example."

Alicia took out a little toy from her bag. It was made by Lily herself. It was a small glass figure of a kitten with a bow tied to its neck. It was completed from glass of an average quality. Lily had not managed to get the shade she wanted. In her opinion, the figure could have been better and more eloquently executed. Nevertheless, it genuinely struck Alicia. The cat was of a pink shade, it had a big bow and a gracefully curled tail.

Yes, it looks complicated. But with a certain effort, skill and material, especially if it was not done for the first time…

"Is that all?"

"Lilian wanted to show you the rest in person. She does not wish anyone else but you to lay eyes on her craft, Your Majesty."

Edward nodded. "I will have a look. Figures like that one do have a charm about them. "

"Wait until you see her glass china! She will show you her windows, her mirrors…everything."

"Your daughter-in-law makes windows?"

"Lilian did not explain much, but I have understood that, provided she has the required equipment, she can make a glass pane as tall as a human."

Alicia spread her arms in a helpless gesture. It seemed like she was speaking the truth and got Edward thinking.

"What does the Countess want, may I ask?"

"She realizes that the government needs to own such big scale production. She is ready to teach artisans; she will show and explain the secrets of her trade."

"Clearly not for free."

"Your Majesty, you are clearly the first ruler after Aldonai," grinned Alicia. "I believe a reward of thirty percent for the first fifty years to be quite generous."

Edward considered it a fair ratio, although the workshops would be built on his land and he would need to provide the materials and workers. Plainly speaking, raw materials would have to be his, but the knowledge and the ideas... *How much can they be worth? Sometimes, intangible things are priceless.*

"Is that everything?"

"No, your Majesty. My daughter-in-law also wants her own title."

"Is that so? What for?"

"Baron Broklend is without an heir, he is of second kin."

"And Lilian wants to get a Broklend title of third kinship and make it hereditary?"

"Yes. She will stay the Countess of Earton. In the future, if everything works out well, the title Broklend will be inherited by her second son."

"That is reasonable."

"Or to the son who will inherit the skills of his grandfather. Lilian said that she is fascinated by her father and wants the dynasty to be—"

"There is no need to continue. Overall, I like it. If your daughter-in-law is able to prove that she is useful for the Crown, she will get a title."

Alicia smiled.

In fact, Lilian Earton does not ask a lot, and kings care nothing for titles. Besides, August already has his own land. "Moreover, if she will confirm her advance payment, I will give her authority over Broklend."

"Are you sure, Your Majesty?"

"Her crafts are promising. We will have to see." The King smiled lightly. Edward thought himself lucky. He had love and happiness. *Is that not enough?* It was more than enough for the King.

"August is going to die one day, and after his death, his estate will have to be passed on to someone. So I will make the Broklend title hereditary and let Lilian Earton rule over the estate until her son is of age; the estate will then be passed on to its heir."

"Your Highness, you are most generous."

"The Crown is generous to its loyal servants." Edward curled his lips in a subtle smile.

"What else can you tell me about Lilian?"

***

"Amalia, my dear, how are you?"

Amalia, pretty waxed in the last months of pregnancy, looked at her husband.

"Like a cow!"

"You have become more beautiful, my dear. Trust me…"

Amalia grimaced, but did not argue. She realized that she had gotten significantly fatter, her skin was uneven, and the swelling had turned her once slender legs into stumps. *Alas, I will give birth soon.*

It had not been like this in her first pregnancies. *Maybe that was because I let a lot of time pass in between? Enough of that.*

The woman touched her stomach. The baby immediately responded with a kick of his tiny leg.

"I will soon give birth. The last term is approaching."

"Darling, I have found you the best doctors to attend to you any time of the day."

Amalia nodded.

She listened to her husband, looked at his face. *Dear Peter! He is so kind, so loving and so…different.*

***

The next three days turned Alicia's country estate into a madhouse, slowly but surely. The house was divided into several parts, and the residents split themselves into clans—the Virmans, the Khangans, as well as Lily and her people.

The mass of people made noise, kept shifting around and arguing, only to reconcile and hurry to clean the mess later on. If Lily had not kept repeating to herself that the arrangement was temporary, she would definitely have given up and fled to the other county. She was the one who suffered the most.

First of all, Marcia and her friends seriously began to attend to their Countess. The girls were firmly convinced that their lady had to look splendid, for it was *their* Countess. Therefore, they went through her dresses and fit them once again. *Poor Countess*, the women exclaimed, *she lost so much weight during her voyage on the ship! A terrible sight! It left us with so much work to do…*

Second, Madame Trimes madly scolded Marcia. She was a local fashionista of Laveri, but the times when the girls trembled from every growl from their mistress were long gone. All of Lily's artisans realized they were unique specialists, and they were ready to defend their taste. This made feathers and bows fly in all directions.

Leis and Leif were like two Siamese twins, chasing their warriors up and down the estate. They were the personal squad of Countess Earton. Everything must be blindingly polished, no exceptions.

The Khangans, too, were determined to save face. The entire treasury of the embassy had moved to the other part of the house. After the tributes of courtesy were paid to the Prince, his part of the estate soon turned into chaos. The only difference was that Amir Gulim, not Lily, was the key victim of it all.

Miranda, in her turn, was trying to run away from the turmoil by escaping to the stables. Lily personally caught her and declared that it was her duty to attend court with her, although it had been against all rules.

Alicia was about to object, but later did not argue. *Let it be. There are Angelina and Joliette, maybe Miranda will get along with them better than she did with Sessie and Jess Ivelen.*

In addition, Lily had to give her attention to the doctors and Lidarh, whom the journey left in relatively good health, although he also required her love, attention, understanding and…horse riding. Attending to August's artisans also took quite a bit of time.

* * *

Fortunately, everything has to end sooner or later. On the evening of the third day, Lily found herself seated on that same chair before the fireplace where she had sat talking with Alicia for the first time. Mirrie approached in her usual way, tucking her head under Lily's arm to slide through the hole and climb onto Lilian's knees. Lily gave the girl a tight hug. The dogs spread their paws on the carpet beside them. One of Tahir's mongooses appeared out of nowhere and curled up on the stone shelf, his tail hanging. Thus, for a while the woman and the girl sat speechless, enjoying the silence.

"I am scared, mother…"

"What are you scared of, my baby?"

"Tomorrow we have to attend court and see the King…"

"So what! You already know the Prince."

"Amir is good…"

"His Majesty Edward is good, too, take my word for it."

"Are you sure that they won't harm me there?"

Lily laughed and kissed the girl on the nose. "Mirrie, darling, listen. Me, your puppy Liliona, our people—we will all be by your side, at all times. You also have a knife, and you know how to use it. Who do you think will dare to hurt you?"

"Sessie and Jess used to always mock me."

"This is your chance to fight back."

"Will you defend me if I fail?"

"I promise. Not a soul will dare to hurt you. And if anyone would, I promise to murder them with my own hands."

"Promise?"

"Well, we have managed to defeat Baron Donter, haven't we?"

Mirrie held tighter onto Lily. "You are nice, Lily."

"As are you, my splendid little lady. I love you dearly. I will not let anyone hurt you, ever."

"Do you give me your word as a countess?"

"I swear by Broklend, I will keep you safe."

Chapter 3

On Life at The Capital

"We have arrived! We have arrived to see His Majesty! Salut! Bonjo-o-ur! Hello-o-o!"

Lily was trying to calm Miranda down, despite being nervous herself. If it hadn't been for her strong, surgeon-like skill of self-control, Lily would not have looked so cheerful to Alicia, who was surprised at her daughter-in-law's placid disposition.

Lily teased Miranda, petted the dogs, argued with Lons, and wagged her finger at Amir in response to the flattering compliments addressed to both herself and Mirrie, the latter being "tender like the first ray of sunshine in the morning." In short, Lily was trying to act normal. She was happy to be wearing her gloves made of thin lace; for it made it impossible for her to bite her nails.

They arrived at the palace of His Majesty, Edward the Eighth, which had been occupied by seven other Edwards in the past. Lily had never been to palaces before, but her imagination pictured castles with high towers, haunted by ghosts and guarded by dragons. The palace looked like Hampton Court, only built in white brick, and not so wide in size. There was no famous court of Henry and no fountains. Despite the palace being two times smaller, the resemblance was still there.

The huge park around the castle was to Lily's liking. It was Edward's country residence, where he preferred to spend time in the spring. It was abundant with Lilac, Jasmine and Honeysuckle; the incense of their blossom was even stronger than the perfumes of the courtiers.

At first, Lily was charmed. As they approached closer, she noticed the cracks in the road; she could see dung under some bushes; the grass was nothing like the classic English lawns. It was only from far away that the castle looked impressive. On approaching it, she noticed it was built in different time periods and discrepant styles. The result was an evident lack of harmony.

But it would be too harsh to pick on faults. It was the Middle Ages, after all, not the Renaissance.

Mirrie, on the other hand, had been extra excited that day. She could not sit still. Lily threatened to put the girl on a leash together with the dogs, if Mirrie did not calm down. The threat worked…for some three minutes, no more.

As they were entering the castle gate, they were met by the guards, who spotted Alicia and looked at the invitation with the stamp. After that brief process, the party was immediately let through. Going down the rocky street, the carriage began to shake; it forced Lily to clench her teeth.

Can someone be kind enough to invent the damn springs? I wish I had gone with Leif by horse, but it would have ruined my dress and hair.

Lily decided she did not like the carriage for one simple reason: she had been desperately prone to motion-sickness. Walking by foot was beyond acceptable for someone of her title. So she had to endure until they reached the palace.

"Boy!" exclaimed Lily. Her first thought was that the historical chronicles told lies, compulsively. They said nothing about palaces being so dreadfully dirty, neither had they said anything about their accompanying smell. There was no mention of narrow windows or dust, cobwebs or torches or lamps splashing fire.

There had been no mention of the weird stains on the butler's livery and about his stinking smell, which scared away even the dogs; and also about the idlers swamping at the front entrance where Lily found herself the center of attention. To enter the palace premises, one had to hold a special invitation or arrive with the royal carriage. Lilian borrowed her carriage from Alicia. She had to put it in order before arriving at court. Alicia almost never went by her carriage; therefore, it was covered with dirt. It took the stablemen three days to make it look presentable. With a great deal of swearing and fresh paint, the carriage was painted white and green. The Earton crest and white curtains decorated the doors on both sides; the spiked wheels were coated in silver paint.

Too pompous? So what? The same as in Russia in modern times. If you were a governor's wife you could not travel in a Soviet-made car, or else your husband's name would be rhymed with some very peculiar terms, right in the middle of parliamentary hearings.

Was the name of Lilian Earton famous in the higher circles of the kingdom? Not at all. For now, she was an "O without a figure", as Shakespeare's Fool would have put it. In this society, the figure was her husband, who had been absent from his rightful place. As a result, Lily had no strong shoulder to hide behind.

The silver paint on Lily's carriage was worth it, regardless of being too expensive. *You are going to see who is who*, thought Lily. There must be a lot of bauxites and nephelines in nature, the only task is to find them. Producing aluminum and aluminium powder, on the other hand, was a matter of time and patience. Lily would think about that later.

Leif, who accompanied Lily's carriage, wore polished armor; he made such a good impression that even the dogs ceased barking. The carriage stopped. Leif approached it and opened the door. One could spot a couple of courtiers walking along the footpaths of the park, gossiping, as they watched the first visitors jump out of the carriage. It was Nanook and Liliona, who froze in a classic pose, with their ears and tail alarmingly pointing upwards, their bodies strained, their noses cautiously sniffing the air, their eyes scanning the surroundings to spot any signs of potential danger to their mistresses.

Back at the estate, Lily had doubts about whether or not to leave the dogs behind, but Alicia had said it was fine to take them. The King did not mind; besides, the dogs' fangs might have been of help during the journey. It would not do the dogs any harm if they happened to bite a trickster. Furthermore, having dogs would help to put the palace curs into place, otherwise known as courtiers. A dog is not a human; it won't ask for a duel.

Following behind the dogs was…a little doll. One could not find other words to describe Mirrie, who looked charming wearing her white and green dress. After careful consideration, Lily had chosen green for both Miranda and herself. White dresses were impractical for walks in the park. So she chose green, the noblest color and added a bit of white, here and there. Mirrie had white gloves and a belt made of lace; white lace collars and lace sleeves; and a white silk bow on her head. Thus the girl looked like a real porcelain doll. Her look was unanimously approved by a minute of admiring silence.

Alicia followed Miranda out of the carriage. She was dressed in a relatively simple way. The viperess did not need diamonds. Again, she was in mourning. She, therefore, chose to wear a modest dress of dark green fabric, which she made look fancier by adding emeralds as a symbol of County Earton and a white collar made of lace. One of the only luxurious items of her dress was a cameo brooch made of white amber and gold. The design had been Lily's idea. The jeweler highly appreciated it and made a couple of exemplars. One of them was given to Alicia. The woman pinned it at her collar and was delighted. She had never seen such items, but she considered it beautiful.

The interest of the gossiping courtiers grew bigger on seeing the little girl put her two hands on the backs of the dogs; they watched her nod when Alicia whispered something serious in her ear.

Finally, the third guest descended the carriage. The sun rays created a halo around Lily's tresses like a golden crown. Lily chose to hide her titular bracelet with wide lace sleeves. It was her father August who made the effort to get pearls for his beloved daughter. She wore a long pearl chain on her neck, a pearl ring, pearl earrings made by Helke and a couple of pearl strands in her hair.

Styling her hair turned out to be most difficult. Miranda could tie a bow; Alicia's hair hardly reached her shoulder blades and was done in courtly fashion, twisted in the shape of a snail and fastened with dozens of pins. Lily had a thick long braid that came down to her waist; putting it up would be a sure way to a migraine. Lily had given up thinking and tied her hair in a French braid. With Marcia's help, she weaved strands of pearl and lace into it to create a simple but expensive look. An invitation for tea was not an occasion for fancy dress, but such a method of braiding hair was a novelty in this world. Alicia found it very extraordinary.

Lily looked around, smiled and nodded at Mirrie.

"Come here, my baby."

Miranda put her hand into Lily's. They did not pay attention to anybody else. If anyone wanted to introduce themselves, they would have to come up first. Curiosity was always stronger than pride.

Alicia looked at the women and nodded.

"Let's go."

Leif made a sign to his people. They lifted the box with presents and followed the ladies. As it went, the Virmans were not welcome on the royal grounds. Ativerna was a marine state and the Virmans were sea pirates. Lily did not break any formalities. *The Virmans are not my official guard. But a noble countess could not be expected to carry her own luggage!*

The palace unfolded its winding corridors before Lily.

* * *

Lily was happy that she chose to wear the green dress and that she did not follow the custom of wearing a heap of underskirts underneath it. She put on only two underskirts, both made of very light material. She could grab them with her hands instead of letting them sweep the unclean floors.

No one had taught the noble courtiers to wipe their feet, or else, to not step in animal and human excrements. As a result, the floor was marked with a certain stain of a nasty color; the castle itself smelt like a pile of compost. The only measure they took was to drizzle the floor with straw.

Lily was quite skeptical about this agricultural product after she and Alex had once tried to recreate a mediaeval scene in their bedroom. In short, they wanted to make love in a heap of straw. It took them a long time to get all the straw out of certain places.

Miranda followed her mother's example and also lifted her skirts.

"Do they not clean the floor here?"

"I suspect what they do is just take out the straw and burn it," murmured Lily, feverishly concluding that the straw might be a pasture for fleas. She thought to herself, *If I find even one flea on either Miranda or myself, I will wash the whole of this domicile with vinegar; from basement to roof! We will need to give the dogs a wash, straight away upon return.*

"Eww!" snorted Mirrie.

It has not been half a year but the little Miss has already wrinkled her nose at the sight of dirt. Maybe she will manage to open some Roman baths in the palace, with massage and swimming pool, and hide there from the local inquisition.

A noble courtier passed the ladies. He made a slight bow and continued on; a few moments later, the whole party heard a characteristic sound, which made it obvious that the named courtier had had beans for breakfast. "Eww!" repeated Miranda. This was the first time Lily thought that Mirrie's husband would have a hard time keeping up with her capriciousness.

✱✱✱

"Open the boxes. I need to make sure they do not contain poison."

Lily looked at Alicia who gave her approval. Lily then ordered the Virmans to let the inspector have a look. The bloke did not touch the presents. He looked, nodded, and allowed the Virmans to close the lids.

"Who is the girl?"

"My daughter, Viscountess Earton."

The man nodded once more and called the butler forward. The servant opened the door and yelped in a way that made Lily almost jerk.

"Her Highness the Countess of Earton, her highness the widowing Countess of Earton, the Viscountess of Earton!"

Mirrie held on tightly to her mother's solid hand.

Lily took a step forward. It was certainly unpleasant with a crowd of people watching. Lily suddenly remembered her seminars at the university, with the crowd of hundreds of people. She could burst into tears after, but she would have to deliver results. The university life was certainly worse than this tea party. *Away with fear! Embrace the sass!*

Lily felt a familiar feeling of her shoulders pulling back and the muscles on her face stretching into a grin. *Who wants to fight me? Is anyone here tired of life? I can fix that.*

The whole party made their way to the King's throne. They did not walk, they glided gracefully across the room.

Like an icebreaker, Alicia walked in front. Two dogs trotted along. Lily and Miranda followed the dogs along the narrow corridor, and two grumpy Virmans closed the procession. *They are not happy to be in the palace, but what can they do? Someone needs to carry the boxes.*

Alicia abruptly stopped, which surprised Lily, who was not looking ahead for fear of getting her dress dirty. The mother-in-law kneeled in a bow.

"Your Majesty!"

Lily let go of Miranda's hand and whispered quietly to her, "Repeat after me, my baby."

The mother half-lifted her skirts, bowed her head, stuck out her chest and bum and went for a low, confident bow. Lily's position resembled that of a horse stance in martial arts.

No one would be able to tell, for long skirts covered her legs and even the ends of her shoes. In her previous life Lily could stand in this position for hours. The longest she could stand like that now was around ten minutes, if she didn't want to collapse on her butt. That would make a sure impression, with her butt in a pile of straw. When Lons saw this martial art trick back at the estate he was in shock. Wearing tight fit trousers, it was difficult for him to hide his surprise. He decided to consider the trick once again; after two or three rehearsals, the bow looked superb.

"You may rise," said the King in a domineering voice.

Lily obeyed, but could not refrain from looking up from under her lashes.

The man on the throne was handsome and about sixty years of age. His appearance surprised Lily, for the man in the crown looked a lot like Sean Connery if the actor was blonde and grey-eyed. Two pretty girls stood on both sides of the throne. The first one was a little older than the other and had an arrogant look on her face. It seemed like the other one had a softer character. Even considering those differences, both girls resembled their father in the face and build, only more feminine, with soft oval faces, an exquisite shape of lips and the same smile. The two girls were the princesses. The older one was Angeline, the younger one, Joliette.

"We are glad to see you at court, Countess."

Lily cast a quick look at Alicia. The woman lowered her eyes in approval, as if telling Lilian to go ahead.

"Your Majesty, I am honored to be worthy of your attention."

"You, Countess, you are a remarkable person. Unusual people always attract my attention."

Lilian made another curtsey, thanking him for the compliment.

"I hope that the road did not tire you out too much?"

"Not at all, Your Majesty. I am prepared to travel thrice the distance if it is to fulfill your command."

Edward turned his eyes to Miranda. His face slightly softened.

"Young Viscountess Earton. How are you doing, Miss?"

"Your Majesty," the girl clearly imitated Lily. "I am happy to have received an invitation to court."

"You look most wonderful, dear Viscountess"

"Your Majesty," Mirrie was holding herself with royal dignity, "I tried hard."

Her response made Lily's lips stretch in a genuine smile. *Honey-boo*, Lily caressed her inwardly. Only a few moments later did she realize that Edward's eyes had been on her the whole time. He addressed Miranda, but kept Lily's reaction in check. And he seemed to be pleased with what he saw.

"I am pleased with you, Countess. Please stay after the reception, I want to converse with you and your daughter."

Lily dropped in a curtsey.

"Your Majesty, your will is law to me. Will you grant me permission to give you my modest gifts and dismiss my people?"

Edward took a few seconds to think and gave a slight nod.

Lily called the Virmans forward.

This time, she made emphasis on glass and prepared three caskets. She had already presented the gifts to Alicia; Amalia's turn was yet to come. Now was the time to present the gifts to the King.

"What is it?"

Leif, Olaf, and Ivar took a couple of steps forward; in a well-rehearsed manner, they went on one knee and held out three caskets; an image of a crown was carved out on each of their lids. The King's casket was the biggest. The caskets of Angelina and Joliette were a little smaller.

The girls glanced over to their father, who gave kind permission for them to proceed. *The sisters begged him like puppies, pity they could not wag their tails.*

The two girls swiftly ran forward and attacked the Virmans, who opened the caskets before them. There were two pairs of crocheted fingerless mittens, encrusted in amber, pretty little things. They looked stunning and were not hard to make. The size was easy to guess, it was enough to take a girl of the same age and measure her hand. Lily had had such mittens herself, a long time ago, when she learned oriental dancing. It took her around four days to knit them with crochet hooks.

The girls looked at each other in confusion. Lily pushed Miranda with her elbow asking her to demonstrate. The girl carefully opened the fan tied to her wrist; she played with it, hid behind it, fluttered her eyelashes and winked from behind the lace. The girl was wearing the same mittens. For the sake of convenience, Lily made sure they weren't too loosely knitted. Mirrie was a little girl; after all, she might catch onto something and get hurt.

The princesses liked the mittens and immediately put them on. Lily thought that she had made a good gift. The good thing about those mittens was that one could wear rings with them.

The girls started inspecting the second gift. Upon choosing the presents, Lily had born in mind that the two princesses were little girls. She knew that every girl liked little trinkets.

So Lily decided to make little glass statues. It was not a difficult job. A cat, a dog, a snake…her main worry was for them not to break in transportation, as Lily had realized glass was of very bad quality here. Colored glass was even worse; it was highly overpriced and never used to make such miniature objects. Medieval technology was not yet that advanced.

Presenting the glass toys filled the room with shrieks of excitement. It took the girls five minutes to move onto the third plaything.

It was an ordinary kaleidoscope. Lily used to own one as little Aliya, only in plastic. This one was made of metal and glass. It looked incredibly impressive. When Lily saw the childish faces, she realized that by letting them play with toys, she had managed to win their hearts.

Edward could only shake his head. It seemed like the King was also curious why the girls were oohing and aahing when looking into a metal tube, but he could not let his interest become obvious to the public. He would ask them about it later.

"Countess, it is the second time already that you have managed to please my daughters."

"I, too, have a daughter, Your Majesty."

Edward understood what she meant. If Miranda liked something, the other girls were also going to like it. The way Lily had put it when she said 'I have a daughter', surprised the King. He wondered why she did not say "*we* have a daughter" or "my *husband's* daughter". *I am the Countess of Earton and this is my daughter*, that was what Lily implied. Edward liked this. In the end, Mirrie was his granddaughter. The King loved his son, too, but he realized that it was the mother who raised the child. In his knowledge of the latest events, the King could appreciate the Countess' endurance. Had he been in her place, he would have demanded at least a separation. She, on the other hand, endured. *Is it for Miranda's sake? Most likely,* thought the King. He only had to notice the way Lily looked at Mirrie, so lovingly and tenderly. It was the same way Jessamine had looked at her daughters.

"I will look at my present later." Edward smiled. "Countess, I suppose your daughter can spend some time with her cousins. Girls, you have won, I let you go out and play, but only today and only because your cousin is here." The princesses made a curtsey and flew across the room; and Lily thought that their effortless curtsey had looked way better.

"Mirrie, will you talk to the girls?"

"Yes, mother. Will you get me after?"

"I promise. I will do it myself."

It was said in such a low voice that even Edward could not hear anything. Only Alicia, who stood nearby, intervened. "Your Majesty, let me take the girls to the playroom."

"Yes, I suppose…"

Leif put the present by the King's feet, and the butler immediately seized it and took it to the office.

"Dear Countess, I want you to stay till the end of the reception. We will talk then. Let my people show you the way." Once again, Lily did a horse stance, so to speak, dropping into a low curtsey.

* * *

Miranda followed Alicia. The princesses marched ahead, not letting go of their toys. Lily's guess was perfect. They finally approached the door. Two guards saluted them, and the butlers opened the doors. There were a couple of women in the princess' living room. Upon seeing them Alicia hissed, and Angelina, as the elder child, gestured in the direction of the door.

"I suggest we speak with the girl in the small living room. Do not follow us."

The Virmans put the boxes on the floor and left the room. Miranda knew that they would be waiting for her. Alicia sent the girl a smile and left as well. Mirrie followed her cousins to the small living room and looked around. It was quite nice, but a tiny bit dirty. Her own home was cozier. On the other hand, the ceiling was covered in cobwebs, and the floor needed cleaning. Mirrie was used to the tidy floors in Earton, where even a needle would be noticeable. The palace was way dirtier.

Lou-Lou sniffed the air around her and sat next to her owner. Mirrie sighed. It was her responsibility to wash Lou-Lou. It was her dog, so she obviously had to do it. Lily would certainly ask her to wash the puppy.

Angelina and Joliette cast their eyes at Miranda. The girl looked back at her cousins. It had been a long time since they last saw each other, at least two years. She did not remember the visit very clearly. She was always hiding behind her father, and the girls had been chattering between each other privately. Then, she accidentally spilled soup on herself, and her father took her home. That was basically it.

Edward would be happy if Miranda was closer to her cousins, but he did not know how to arrange that. Alicia almost never saw her granddaughter. Jerrison was always busy. *Who would be taking care of the baby girl? The Yerbys?* Edward did not like the Yerbys very much. Yes, Magdalena had been a perfect match for Jerrison. She had a big dowry and was not bad looking, not that it was of much importance. Magdalena was a daughter of Baron Yerby from the first marriage. The second marriage brought him four more daughters and a son. All of them were ginger-haired, freckled and loud; they were clothed in multi-colored attire and reminded Edward of a flock of seagulls painted by a mad artist. The sight irritated Edward. Yerby also had another son from the first marriage, but after an unpleasant incident, the Baron banished him, and no one had ever heard of him again.

Yerby raised his daughters almost alone, took them to balls and tried to find them husbands, which had been quite a difficult task. Yerby's first wife, Miressa, came from a good family and in addition had a big dowry, which, according to the agreement, was to be split between their son and daughter. The second wife, Valiana, was born into a family of landless nobles. Her only virtues were her red hair and ample bosom.

She sold those virtues for good price, but could not bring her husband anything else— not even managing his household. It was driving Yerby mad. Even the banishment of his first son did not help. According to the agreement between Yerby and Merissa's father, if her children died or disappeared without a trace, his grandchildren or his children's' offspring were the ones to inherit everything. That meant that Miranda Catherine Earton was an heir to that dowry, and it was unthinkable to ask those who lost a lot of money because of Miranda's birth to look after her at court.

***

"What is the name of this thing?" Angelina was first to break the silence.

Miranda smiled at her cousin and suddenly realized that Lily had spoken the truth when she said that one can be lower in age or status but higher in wit and experience.

"You mean the kaleidoscope or the fan?"

"Ka…do…"

"This," Mirrie pointed with a tip of her fan to the kaleidoscope Angelina clenched in her hand, "is a Ka-lei-do-scope. It was created for entertainment. Well, you can also remember the patterns and copy them when embroidering. It is best to hold it against the light; it will make the patterns brighter."

"And where did your stepmother get it from?"

"My mother!" Miranda sharply corrected. She did not have any recollection of Magdalene Yerby, and Lily had quickly become her mother.

"Our father told us that your mother died, like ours," intruded the younger Joliette.

"I don't remember her. Lily, on the other hand, loves me. She teaches me, takes care of me, she even gave me a dog…"

Lou-Lou made a strong impression. You bet! Puppies grow fast and the endearing lump of fur had turned into a little elk-looking creature whose head was on the same level with Miranda's tiny shoulder. His rows of teeth were impressive, too.

"A dog is nothing great!" moaned Angelina. "Our father promised us—" But Miranda could hear uncertainty in Angelina's voice.

"And my mother will get me an Avarian stallion."

Mirrie shrugged. "Amir confirmed it, too."

"Amir?"

"The prince of Khanganat. Amir Gulim. He is great. He gets treatment from my mother and he knew that she promised me a horse. He also promised; he already wrote to my father."

In an automatic gesture, Mirrie ran her fingers though the dog's fur and patted him on the back.

The princesses exchanged glances…the cousin from the province turned out to be not so simple, contrary to what the two girls had previously thought. Mirrie had a gorgeous dress, beautifully styled dark hair, a huge dog beside her who would grow even more; her mother promised her a horse and introduced her to a real prince…

"Why did they send the Prince to your mother?"

"Because she had cured a Khangan once. He turned out to be from the royal guards of the caravan trail. He is very nice. They have very strict rules out there: if you have an injury you cannot lead a caravan. But my mother cured him. He does not even have a limp any more. Sometimes his leg hurts from bad weather. He was the one who gave us a horse. The stallion's name is Lidarh. At first mother wanted to give me his son or daughter, but then she decided that it would be faster to order me a horse from the Khanganat."

The princesses did not have any words left. Only emotions.

Mirrie told them about these things so casually, like it was in the order of things to befriend a prince and to have been given a horse.

"How did the prince get his injury?" squeaked Joliette.

"Mother told me they gave him poison—cinnabar, the blood of the Heavenly Mare. Lily teaches me little by little so I am now able to tell between herbs and things."

"How does she know it herself?"

"Well, grandpa Tahir is her teacher." Mirrie did not think about the order in which she told them things. But Angelina and Joliette did not care either. They were curious to hear more...

"Grandpa Tahir?"

"Well, he's not exactly *my* grandpa. But he teaches us all. His name is Tahir Djiaman din Dashar and he is the most famous physician of the Khanganat. He poorly understands poisons, though...and is useless at catching criminals...but so are the professional detectives."

"And who are detectives?"

Mirrie smiled. *How do they not know this? What kind of princesses do they raise nowadays?*

"Let me explain. They are a special kind of people who...no. Once upon a time in London there lived Sherlock Holmes on the road named Baker Street ..."

***

After the King gave Lily permission to retire, she went to the guestroom. *God, how good would it be to lean on something*, thought Lily. The dirt on the walls reached up to her ears, and if she did lean, she would need to get her dress washed.

It turned out that Lily could pop royal tea parties like chewing gum; she chewed, she popped, and she spat it out. This had been only the first round. There would also be a second, a fifth, and a twenty-ninth, but this one was won by her. Lily had demonstrated her power, her strength, showed that she could be of use. She also destroyed her image of being a cow.

On the one hand, Lily could not blame her husband for not being interested in her. It was true, she used to be a cow who only ate, embroidered and prayed. *Who would love her like that? Did she think that there was no competition?* That seemed very strange to Lily now.

On the other hand, what had my husband done to make his woman feel like a queen? It is easy to act by the principle out of sight, out of mind. He could have tried harder... However, it was unlikely that Lilian Broklend wanted to learn.

Off with these thoughts. Lily shook her head.

She took a thin lace handkerchief from her pocket and wiped her temples. Then she suddenly felt a cold wet nose touch her palm. *Nanook, darling!* The most important thing for Lily was Mirrie's safety.

She sent the Virmans to look after the little one. It was dangerous for anyone to even think of hurting Lily herself, but Mirrie was deeply affected by the kidnapping. It left her suffering from nightmares.

The dog began wagging his tail energetically. Lily let her arm get lost in the animal's thick fur. *Nanook, my sweetie.*

"What did His Majesty find in this country girl?"

Lily listened closer. It was the two ladies next to her. One was wearing sapphires, the other one did not have any jewelry. The rule was strict here. You could wear any jewelry or choose to wear none, but you must always wear a signet ring to establish your title for everyone else. In case one did not have a title and was a landless nobleman, one had to wear a ring with a golden topaz, a kind of a stamp on an identity card. If a baroness had enough money, she could wear a necklace with rubies; but she would still have to wear a square sapphire ring, similar to the emerald shining on Lily's hand.

"I do not even know. Perhaps her aim is to become the King's 'favorite'."

"Do you think? The Baroness will eat her with bones!"

"I would not be so sure. She is a countess, after all."

"So what? Melissa is already unhappy."

"The whole court is tired of Melissa's requests and whims, why does His Majesty let her get away with so much?!"

Lily looked closer at the ladies.

They were fine looking women of about forty; one wore blue that matched the sapphire on her finger, the other was dressed in a yellow gown. If both of them had a wash and did their hair and makeup correctly, they would look decent.

The two of them were looking straight at her. All they discussed was clear as day. She could not just come up to them and introduce herself. She needed to have someone to introduce her.

If the King was really fond of Lily, she needed to flatter him more, and tell him, for instance, that the royal favorite did not like her. *Where is that lady in favor?* Lily scanned the room with her eyes and quickly met the eyes of a woman in a dark blue dress. Well, His Majesty could have used better taste. Baroness Ormt was a short, plump lady with big breasts and tiny blonde curls. She had a prolonged face with features that reminded Lily of a ferret—a ferret with two viciously glittering blue eyes. Her waist was tied up in a corset that seemed too tight for her, judging from the lacing, and her legs were short. Lily did not care. It was up to the King who he slept with. She turned away indifferently.

A parody of Picasso! If need be, I will put her through the wringer. This is not the time to argue now.

"My Lady?"

Lily turned around.

"His Majesty instructed me to accompany you after the reception."

Lily nodded gratefully to the servant and once again regretted not having a watch. There was no other option but to endure the slow passing of time. *What are the other ladies discussing out there?*

"Have you seen that lace on her dress?"

"I am wondering where I can find it for myself."

"It will probably be worth its weight in gold!"

"If not more. And her hair? Do you think it is possible to do something of the like…"

"I need to talk to my maid, she has golden hands..."

"Where did she get all of this?"

Lily smiled widely. She knew exactly what the women liked. Fashion, beauty, luxury...

What is a woman willing to do to become more beautiful? Lily knew the answer to that question. *Whatever it takes, end of story.*

✳✳✳

Amalia clenched her stomach and let out a moan.

"Darling?" asked Peter worriedly.

A wet puddle emerged on the floor.

"The waters broke. I'm in pain…"

Peter picked up his wife in his arms and carried her to the bedroom.

His father nodded and began writing to Alicia Earton. It was not that he loved the old viperess, but it was about her daughter and her grandson.

He should let the granny know about such an event.

✳✳✳

"Your Highness…"

The heavy door of the royal office opened before Lily. She remembered her etiquette classes and, before dropping into a low curtsey, she took three steps forward to prevent the doors from smacking her butt. She remained in her bow until His Majesty told her to stop.

"You may rise, Countess. Please, feel welcome."

Lily obeyed. She could not resist throwing a glance around the room. It was quite nice. Someone else might have found the room dark, but

Lily liked it. It was furnished with heavy furniture made of dark wood, heavy curtains in brown and gold, a fireplace in the corner, and two chairs opposite to it. The owner of the office sat at the table. On it, there was a non-spill inkpot and a feather pen. The chest with the gifts stood beside the table. Lily felt like a schoolgirl in the principal's office. Edward looked for the key to open the casket and realized that the keyhole was made purely for decoration.

"You don't even seal it?"

"I do not have thieves, Your Majesty."

"Is that so?"

Lily fluttered her eyelashes and fanned herself a couple of times. *What did you expect, Dear King?*, thought Lily. *It is so, unless my husband hired someone again. And if that is the case, I will deal with him in private.*

"That's a nice toy."

"Your majesty, I hope that you will accept my humble present."

The first thing inside was a fan, a male version of it. It was made of thick dark material and lightly embroidered with amber and gold; these details gave it a moderate, stylish touch that was not at all feminine.

Edward took out the fan, folded and unfolded it, fanned himself a couple of times, imitating Lilian. "Not bad at all. My receptions are often stuffed with a lot of people so it would prove highly useful to have one."

"I am happy to have pleased Your Majesty."

"What else have you brought to please me? What is the use of these objects?"

"Let me show you, Your Majesty."

"Please."

Lily approached the table and took out a kaleidoscope. She understood the mechanism perfectly well because in her childhood she had constructed and deconstructed them with her own hands. Lily's first kaleidoscope was made out of curiosity; she made the second one when her mother said she would have to fix the one she broke instead of buying her a new one.

"It is a kaleidoscope. And you have to look through it, Your Majesty. It helps to relax."

Edward paid tribute to the ornaments; they were beautiful. And it was true that one could twist and turn the kaleidoscope for a long time.

What else is in the box?, thought the King.

"Another kaleidoscope?"

"No, Your Majesty. If you turn to the window you will see."

His Majesty could not have expected to see what he saw; he peered through the telescope into the distance.

"Good Aldonai!"

Lily left the King to figure it out. It was one of her best telescopes. Making it took a lot of time and energy.

"Where did you get this, dear Countess?"

"My people made it."

"And how does this thing—"

"It is a telescope, Your Majesty."

"Wonderful. Tell me, are such telescopes difficult to make?"

"It is not very difficult, Your Majesty. But I have only two craftsmen who are able to make them."

The King understood what Lily was trying to say.

"Good. We can correct this. And what else do you have in stock for me?"

"A magnifying glass, Your Majesty."

"A magnifying glass?"

The magnifying glass was a success, without exaggeration. Although to grind it was long and boring, her people had managed to do it. Lily carefully extracted the glass from its case and took out a sheet of paper with printed text.

Edward raised his eyebrows.

"What is this document, dear Countess?"

"A children's tale, Your Majesty."

"And how could you make the letters so identical to one another?"

"I did not write, Your Majesty; I printed them."

It took Lily about ten minutes to explain book printing. By the end of the story, Lily was already feeling quite comfortable alone with the King. Edward, too, had forgotten that he wanted to annoy the obstinate girl. He no longer saw the reason for it. She was a real treasure for the court; the printing press opened up incredible horizons, as did the paper.

Ativerna had enough reeds and nettles, the King could order the peasants to collect such weeds and they would bring full carts of them immediately. Speaking of the magnifying glass...

As the years went by, Edward's vision deteriorated. He had to hold out a document at a distance of almost a yard, or even make his secretary read it aloud. The magnifying glass would help him to keep matters under control.

Lily refrained from mentioning the existence of spectacles just yet, realizing that it required another level of knowledge and skills to produce them. She could make a lens, but to make two identical and adjust them for each eye would have been hardly possible.

Let them use the magnifying glass for now, thought Lily.

In the future, she would also invent calipers. Her father had them in the other world, and it was a delightful mechanism. But for now that was all.

"Paper can be sold. Paper with stamps, with prints, and sell it to issue petitions, complaints and pleas."

***

The idea was so pleasing to Edward that he even squinted in delight. For any king, his treasury was the most important thing to him. *The Countess is truly magnificent. If affairs continue in the same way, screw the title, in Maldonaya's name. I will give her the title, if only for inventing the telescope! This was not the end, surely.*

This got Edward thinking. *Why on earth was Jess so negative about his wife? Did he not have time to sort things out with her?* The King realized that Lily was a wise woman and had a calm disposition, too. She was not at all capricious or hysterical, other than she was constantly looking back at the door. To top it off, she was also good looking, a real beauty he would say. He remembered her being nervous during her wedding. *Or maybe the past made an impact on her?* He could try to find out.

"It looks like you are eager to end our audience, Countess, is that so?"

"No, Your Majesty. It is just that I left my dog behind."

It was true that Lily had left Nanook with the King's secretary and she was worried about the dog. He was a great dog but still a puppy, and everything around was strange to him.

"Invite your dog," the King gave an order. The sight of Nanook made him whistle. Edward liked dogs, he was a big connoisseur of them. He could see that the Virman shepherd dog had a promising chance of growing twice as big as the Hound of the Baskervilles. Nanook was clever and evidently trained; he kept a constant watch on his owner.

"Good boy," said the King and added, "Has anyone informed you, dear Countess, that I do not tolerate Virmans?"

"Yes, Your Majesty."

"I hope that you did not…"

"Your gracious Majesty, I beg you to not forbid me to hire the Virmans as my guards. If it weren't for them, Miranda and I would not be alive now."

"Hans told me a lot of things, Countess. But I also wanted to listen to your side of the story. Sit down," the King pointed at the chairs in front of the fireplace. "I will order you some wine and fruit. Your daughter is with the princesses now. No one can distract us from the conversation. Tell me, what happened to you?"

* * *

Fanning herself with her silk fan, Lily sent the kindest smile to the monarch.

You want a story? I will tell you a story. Besides, it would be a great chance to complain about Yerby and stick up for Hans.

Three hours later, Lily walked out of the royal office. The only thing she had energy for was keeping her back straight and looking arrogant, but that was it. Her only wish was to find a place that was a little bit clean, lie down and do nothing. She did not want to sleep, only to get her thoughts and feelings in order.

The clock struck three. She was happy to realize that it was not easy for the King either. She was craving cold, spring water, half a liter inside and three or so on the head.

Edward had asked her about many things, and Lily had given him her 'honest' answers. It would have been unthinkable to reveal the whole truth; however, it would have been a great story.

Your Majesty, your nephew drove his wife to such a state that she could not endure any longer and died. No, the body is the same; it is the soul. Shall we talk about an honest barter?

It seemed to Lily that after such a story they would either send her to a madhouse or burn her alive, but they did not burn people at the stake here, they interrogated the victims and killed them by hanging. *How very kind! Oh well.* Their conversation went well. Edward tried to question Lily about family. Lily honestly confirmed that her husband had gotten rid of her by sending her away. He visited quite rarely, and their communication was limited to the missionary pose. She immediately blamed it on the incognito poisoners. She said that if it were not for them, she would have made all the effort in the world. Her spouse, too, would have changed something. *But what could I do at the times when I did not even recognize myself in the mirror?*

Edward shook his head expressing regret. He said he would make sure they found the criminals and punished them so that the others were deterred.

Lily also nodded, as if saying, *Find them, Your Majesty; I will pray a hundred years to Aldonai for your soul.* As if saying, *My husband is useless, he himself gave birth to and spread bastards, take only Adelaide Wells!*

His Majesty frowned and asked if Lily was going to demand for a divorce or separation on the grounds of adultery. After all, the law was on her side.

Lily remembered the fable about an elephant and three pounds of chocolate and noted light-heartedly that she was obviously distressed and sorrowful because her husband had cheated. But on the other hand, the poor soul did not have a choice.

After her painful miscarriage and subsequent treatment, she was banned from all intimate contact; being pregnant again would put her life in danger. Lily also inquired if they had found the medicus Craybey. The answer was 'no' and it left Lily in dismay. In a few years, when she recovered her health, she would be just fine, she kept explaining.

That was why she was so fond of Miranda, "the poor child with her father never there."

The King objected to this, saying that Mirrie was never denied anything. In her turn, Lily noted that giving an education is very different from spoiling and that being a father, himself, His Majesty should understand this. This made the King angry, but he agreed. *What else is left for him to do?* Lily was behaving like a royal lady, beyond all expectations and praise. She loved Mirrie, she was going to fix things between herself and her husband, if he himself was ready for it. The issue of bringing up children and love was important, in any family and in all times, no matter if you were a King or a swineherd.

So, His Majesty got the answers he wanted and was left satisfied. The Countess was not going to ruin the family; it was all up to her husband now. If his attitude remained the same, then Lily could not change anything. Lily said that his behavior could make even plankton angry; she might be a woman, but she was far more evolved compared to plankton. After all, he had tried to get rid of her by sending kidnappers, slave dealers, seducers…

"Seducers? Tell me more," interrupted the King.

"Your order is law to me, Your Majesty."

Lily explained that the seducer was now imprisoned in one of her ships. His name was Damis Reis. He claimed that a certain man by the name of Yerby sent him.

"Yes, Your Majesty, the man might be lying." added Lily. "You understand that it happened after the departure of Hans Tremain, and for a fragile and weak woman like me, it was hard… How would I know how to question this villain?"

His Majesty suggested moving the scoundrel into the royal prison.

"Thank you, dear Majesty! You have taken a heavy load from my shoulders. After all, they are Miranda's relatives; I do not want her to be affected by it."

Edward nodded in agreement and suggested giving the job to Hans, since Lily seemed to get along well with him.

Lily could not resist asking. "Your Majesty," she said, "forgive me for my terrible impudence, but would it be possible for Hans Tremain to look after me while I am in the capital? He is a real professional, and we work well together… You were planning on finding someone for me anyway."

His Majesty agreed and was contented. It was true that he was planning to appoint someone anyway. The fact that the Countess was asking for it herself made the affair even easier. He would speak to Hans. It was settled for now. The conversation proceeded.

"What are you going to do in the capital, dear Countess?"

Lily decided to take her chance. "First, I wish to manufacture glass in all its shapes and kinds, colored glass, mirrors, china and other nice objects. I want to sell it to ordinary people. As for more serious things, I wish to produce lenses—magnifying glass, telescopes and microscopes, and also spectacles for reading."

Why not? Lily could imagine the scale of it. The job would keep busy not just her, but also her children for many years. The main task was to make it so Ativerna got all the fame, just like Venice from Murano.

Making lace, sewing, knitting and fashion was also possible to organize. Lily refrained from mentioning Mariella Fashion House just yet. Everyone should get used to the idea that Ativerna was to become a fashion center first.

The third thing she wanted to implement was medicine. Lily was not going to miss out on any bit of knowledge. *Chemistry? Definitely.* She could also include pharmacology, anatomy, pediatric therapy, gynecology, and of course her favorite dental surgery. Lily did not elaborate the third part of her plan. She just painted her vision in broad strokes, justifying it by saying that she wished to make sure no one ever found himself tricked by doctors like Craybey, a doctor regarded as one of the best in Ativerna.

The King was more or less pleased. The state would give Lily land, machinery and students who could learn and continue the trade. It would take them a long time to become artisans. The whole profit would go to the treasury; Lily would receive thirty percent, for her ideas and assistance.

***

At first sight, it seemed absurd to pay for an idea. Exhaled by one person, a sea of ideas was floating around freely, in the open air, until inhaled by somebody else. But Edward was smart; he realized that Lily did not offer him empty ideas.

It took this woman a few months to invent something that other states did not have. Perhaps she could do even more? August, for example, makes incredible ships when he is inspired. He has an inborn instinct for ship craft, and he knows how to place the crew. I gave him the freedom to do whatever he wanted. As a result, the ships of Broklend are famous around the whole kingdom. August even gets orders from the Khanganat. Lilian Earton resembled her father. How could Jess not appreciate her?

He was being quite objective. Putting the romantic component to the side, if the King had Lilian for his wife, she would easily become his ally, his companion and friend. That is why, when talking to Lilian, Edward subtly implied that preserving the status quo opened up many doors. *She wants a title? Why not!*

"You would be the third Baroness of Broklend, and one of the few women who was honored thus. But you would have to deliver results first. For example, produce glass on the Royal land. If you do it, you will get the title. You will have money anyway. And later, your second-born son, or whichever you want, can inherit the title. You can decide yourself what to do with your title. About book-printing… Why not? But for that we need the blessing of the church."

Lily had a pastor with her, she said, and he gave his blessing. The only thing left was to agree with the aldons. The King asked her about the possibility of printing sacred texts and prayer books; he also inquired about whether it was possible to print stories with illustrations. Her answer was yes. She said they did not have enough required material, only amber. He asked who got the amber. Taris Brok, August's trusted person. He did not steal, she said.

It made sense. Lily confirmed that Taris did not steal, but even with him stealing, the business would be a lot more profitable than before, thought the King; he had to think who else he could send from his own people. The King assumed that the Earl of Earton would not mind, to which Lily replied with a compliment, saying that His Majesty was the wisest of all. The King then asked where Lily had gotten the game she sent him. The Countess told him that it was called backgammon and that she found the rules in an old scroll which was now lost. Perhaps, it was stolen, she said, during the time when she was ill. Things like that happened, agreed the King. The conversation painfully proceeded.

"Tell me, Lilian, what was the disagreement between you and your neighbor? Baron Donter?"

"He tried to steal Miranda to get a ransom."

"What a bastard!"

"He might have wanted to marry her."

"Countess, you were in the right to get rid of him."

"I had nothing to do with his death. He died in an accident during the chase."

"And how many times did he fall on the sword as a result of an accident?"

Lily met the sarcasm with her impassionate look. The King gave in.

"I jest. You did everything right, Countess. The King has no objections. It would be necessary to find the land a new owner."

The conversation went on. Lilian told the King that there was a real baron. At first, the King only laughed, but Lily remained calm. She explained that Baron Donter was born as a result of incest and that his father had something to do with it. The King emphasized that it was a serious charge against the Baron, but Lily had the documents with her to back it up. To be precise, she had the copies of the documents, and the King wanted to have a look at them. Apparently, the real Baron had hidden in Altver and then fled to Earton; the King wished to talk to him and then decide whether to confirm the claims to be legitimate. Lily informed him that Taris Brock was looking after the neighboring estate. The King sighed.

"Dear Lady, do you not think that you take a lot on yourself?"

"There was no one else to help me, My King. My husband was not around, I did not want to die, so I had to take care of things.

"Including taking and distributing land, I see," said the King. "Tell me, how long had they been poisoning you by thorn apple? Do you have proof?"

"I have also brought it with me," said Lily. "The Darcy family is involved."

"Excellent. Pass the proof on to my people."

"I will order the Virmans to do it."

"Countess, are you aware that I disapprove of the Virmans?"

"Ay, Your Majesty."

"Are you not afraid of my anger?"

"There was no one else."

"What do you mean, there was no one else?"

Lily realized that it was best to let the King talk, so, she paused.

"Hans said that a whole squad of Virmans arrived with Miranda! Do not tell me you didn't know about it, that your husband did not let you know or that Aldonai did not take mercy on you!"

"Aldonai only helps those who help themselves," was Lily's only answer.

"Good words, everyone should remember them. But then, why did you not dismiss them after? Did you think that they could bring benefit? These are sea robbers! And their oath of allegiance means nothing!"

"I was afraid to dismiss them after the man from Leis' squad attempted to kill me, Your Majesty."

"Ah yes," the King went softer. "Hans reported the unfortunate news to me. Very well, Countess. You can leave your sea-rascals for your service. But I want it to be the last time that they accompany you to the palace. This is my last word."

"You are most gracious and merciful."

"Would you like to play a game of backgammon?"

"No, Your Majesty, I would not. I am afraid I can beat you, and kings do not forgive such things."

"They do not forgive rejection. Why are you so confident in your victory? You have to prove your words in action. If you do, I will let you have Virmans in the palace."

They played, and Lily won, five times out of six. It was not easy to give in, for although the King was a beginner, he was not a bad player, either. He would notice if she cheated in his favor. As a result, the King had to agree to have the Virmans in the palace.

He waved his finger at Lily.

"Do not think that you can get away with things like that again," he said. "There will be time for a rematch."

Lily ensured the King that the game was designed for men, and that her weak brains could not compete against his wit, to which the King reminded her how she treated the heir of Khanganat. Lily said it was Tahir who did, and the reason why he did not treat him in Khanganat was that he traveled, learned new things… She said she was happy to know about Tahir's arrival. After the former doctor's death, explained Lily, the place was left without any medical assistance, and it made Lily worry about Miranda. She told the King about Prince Amir Gulim, who lived with her and whose health was getting better. His Majesty did not send the Prince an invitation to the palace, so the Prince decided to wait for it.

The King said that he would send the Prince an invitation for a special reception as soon as possible.

"We throw ourselves entirely at your mercy, Your Majesty."

The King then expressed how happy he was to know that the prince was getting better.

"I am also very glad," said Lilian, "Amir is still a child. It is a lot worse when such things happen to children. He is almost Miranda's age, a little older. You said something about establishing diplomatic relations? Nay, your Majesty, I am just a woman, I do not occupy myself with things like that. Everything is at Your Majesty's mercy."

* * *

Finally, The King let Lilian go.

In general, everything went well. It was true that His Majesty had been quite domineering. He exerted influence, retreated, tried to approach the conversation from different angles, pretended to be angry, swiftly changed his wrath to mercy. Lily was aware of these methods. They were similar to the methods of interrogation. One sought to provoke the victim, to make him nervous. The strategy consisted of a forcing move, a calming gesture, and a retreat to neutral ground and ended in another attack.

Everything else was transient apart from knowledge. The house could burn down, the loved one could leave, the boss could fire his employee, the country could be consumed by war; everything was possible. But what one had in their head, the skills one had in their hands, would always give one a chance for survival, an opportunity for oneself and one's loved ones. Aliya Skorolenok always remembered this, and just now, in the King's office, Lilian Earton had a chance to experience it firsthand.

She recognized what the King was doing, and she replied with dignity. When he exerted pressure on her, she played the fool. Her responses were something along the following lines, *I am a weak woman, defenseless, anyone can offend me…but do not come near.* If the King praised her, Lily flattered him shamelessly, "You, dear Majesty, are the wittiest, the most experienced and the wisest." Although she realized that the King had no break from flattering speeches, she cared nothing for subtlety. One never got used to flattery. There was not one king in the whole world who would get tired of praise, especially if one praised him well.

When the King softened his tone, it was Lily's time to ask for favors. She batted her eye lashes, making her eyes big and begging; she asked bit by bit, never with impudence. The process of interrogation was like dancing in pairs. If the victim followed the rhythm, he had a chance to corner his interrogator. The King made his conclusions about Lily, but so did she about him. She recognized in him an ordinary man who was old, good-looking and sad. Her upbringing proved useful as she talked to the King as equals. She saw that Edward was tired, quite lonely, and rather soft with his family. He seemed to love his daughters and even his son. He surely used to love his wife, otherwise he would not have put a portrait of her in the most visible spot where he could admire her image at all times.

Jessamine was a beautiful woman—dark haired, blue-eyed, with a warm smile. Lily recognized the type. Such women were alike cats that were fluffy, domesticated and docile. They had no claws, no teeth, no strong character, but they knew how to love and purr. The children would take such a cat and drag her to and fro, and she would not even make a sound in objection. Such a woman would not make a strong queen, but at least she would make the King happy. That had been the case.

Although Lily realized all of this, it was not enough to understand, she had to put her knowledge into practice. *To hell with these thoughts! I need to take Miranda and leave. I want a long sleep.*

✳✳✳

Deep in his thoughts, Edward twisted a backgammon peace in his fingers.

Well, he was defeated, and not only in backgammon. He wondered where the Countess got such talents from.

Although Lily realized what the King was trying to achieve, Edward was not stupid either. He quickly understood that he would not get the desired result from the conversation. That did not make him end it either because even if his victim understood what was done to him, he would usually give something away. Something, somehow; the King was looking for some scraps of information, but Lilian Earton held herself with dignity.

His Majesty was able to realize a few things. The woman was certainly clever, strong and very tough. It was hard to tell whether she had been like this from the start, or whether the loss of a child had produced such a change in her. But there she was. Edward understood that he had never met anyone like that. Her behavior, her manner of speaking, her personality, her mind...everything was unusual to the King, unusual and exciting.

The King was curious to study her. What interested him, even more, was that she was also studying him, although the woman did it very carefully. No questions, no insolence...it was his reaction she was watching, and with great care. But again, she had been very polite, very obedient.

Edward had no doubt that she would obey any of his orders, although, to a certain limit—like in a children's fairy tale, where the King ordered his servant to bring the moon from the sky. The boy led him to the lake and said, "Here is the moon, and not in the sky." The King then asked the boy to his palace, but not by foot, by horse or by carriage. The boy tied a hare to his leg and showed up. The King's order was obeyed, but the boy was the one to gain the victory.

Yes, this woman could bring a lot of use. She would make a wonderful friend and a decent enemy. Even so, Lily was friendly, and she demonstrated it as hard as she could. She offered presents, made promises, took care of her husband's affairs. She was even ready to make peace with him. *She was not faking it, it was not a lie, no.*

Edward realized that Lily was the kind of woman who would turn any affair to her benefit. She would obey his orders, but only to fulfill the order's formality, not its essence. At the very least, she would find a way to get out of it.

August was more simple-minded. His daughter was far more complicated than her father. The King decided to not let her get away so easily. *Let Jess come, take his wife from the King's hands, and he would make sure that they made peace.*

He also thought about a place for glass and lace factories.

***

It was not the first time that Lily realized having a secretary was most useful. Even when the secretary was not a nice girl in a mini-skirt, but a bony man in luxurious dress with the face of someone who swallowed his axe. Lily approached his desk and said that she had no idea where her daughter was, for she was taken away to the princesses' room. The secretary leaned out of a tiny window that led to a waiting room and called a butler. He ordered him to take the Countess where she pleased.

Lily wanted to reward the secretary with a chocolate bar, but there were no cocoa beans in this world. Therefore, she took with her about five little mirrors; each was the size of a chocolate bar of a quarter of an ounce. She was right in her approach, some methods never failed. The mirror magically disappeared and the secretary told the butler to keep the lady happy, unless he wanted to lose his head. Lilian strolled along the palace corridors with confidence. The hygiene in the Gestapo was a lot better than here, she thought.

Yet again, a cold, wet nose touched her palm. *Nanook, darling...*

***

"Look who I found, Falion. What a charming woman," said a male voice.

The butler immediately disappeared, as if dissolved inside the walls of the palace. For some reason, Lily did not doubt that the servant would reappear if she needed his help. But he had not been foolish enough to interfere in quarrels between the noble people.

One of them was younger and considerably taller. He was not bad looking; his dark-blond hair had a dusty tint to it; he had thin lips and a long nose that was slightly crooked at the end. The man's grey eyes looked calm and even curious. He wore a simple dark dress; the dagger fastened to his waist seemed to be simple as well. However, Erik had explained to Lily about knives, and the handle of this one, made of shark skin, was rare and pricey. If the dagger was as good as its handle, then the man before Lily was dangerously armed.

The second man was plump and lively. He was dark-haired, brown-eyed, and had a broad smile. That kind of man was welcome in any company and was considered a good laugh; he was also prone to causing trouble.

"What do you want, gentlemen?" Lily's voice was arctic-cold.

Lily's cold response left the men unsatisfied. The second man would only back off if hit by a heavy object.

"Madam, forgive me for being too straight-forward, but I hope that your beauty is tantamount to your generosity. By Aldonai, it is impossible to let such a woman walk past!"

"Give it a try." Lily smiled.

Her head ached. She was not capable of being polite right now. She wanted to take the child and leave. Lily was not at all scared. The corridors were dark, she was alone, and if something happened, there would be no witnesses. And Lily was not so kind as to assume that these two medieval men were pure in their thoughts. But she was as dangerous to them as they were to her.

Besides, Nanook was capable of biting off even the most important of manly parts. In addition, Lily had a small dagger hidden in her sleeve, which was covered by a special sheath. Aliya Skorelenok was able to work with knives. After all, she was a surgeon and used knives to cut people open. So it was not for fear that she wanted to stay alone.

"Let's go, Tarney," said the tall one. The other lad seemed to be affected by Lily's response.

"No, Falion, we have to at least find out the name of the beautiful lady. Mistress, would you be so cruel as to deprive us of the smallest mercy? I need to find out your name, or else I will die and my miserable death will stay on your conscience."

"Die then," Lily spat. "I suppose your companion could lend you a dagger."

"What did you say?"

Lily grinned. *Medical students are far more advanced than you, guys. If you were a part of the medical faculty you would quickly learn how to bite!* "Are you going to die if I do not tell you my name? Well, so be it! Die, My Lord. My conscience will have to bear this terrible load."

The lad was clearly taken aback. He could not imagine how to get out of the situation without losing face, but then he caught the sight of Nanook.

"Is this your only male companion then? She brought a dog to the palace! What next? You might as well bring goats and sheep!"

"As far as I can see, the palace is already full of goats and sheep," retorted Lily. "What an exquisite royal society, don't you think?"

The man's politeness ended at that. "You, you little...!"

But he did not finish the line. The tall youth managed to pinch his companion on the shoulder so hard that the plump one grimaced in pain.

"Madam, please forgive us our impunity. Your wish is the law. We are retiring."

Lily dropped in a curtsey.

"I would be very grateful if you left me alone."

She did not have to repeat twice. The fat lad would not have gone so easily, if it weren't for his companion dragging him along. Lily curled her lips into a crooked smile and stroked the dog.

So that's how it was. Palaces, Kings…and thugs like that, who, like locusts, move from one century to another. Lily suspected she would have had a hard time getting rid of the fat guy if it wasn't for his buddy. *Anyway*, thought Lily, *it was good that I managed to get away from them.*

The butler reappeared from nowhere and was immediately questioned. "Who were those two?"

"The heir of Duke Falion and Baron Reynolds, My Lady."

"Well, well."

I remember you, Duke Falion, old bastard and intriguer. Quite rich, you have the land on the border with Wellster. You take part in the affairs of the embassy in the same place where my husband is. Your heir is known for his hobby; he breeds racehorses and sells them for a lot of money. He dreams of making the horses no worse than the Avars, but he miserably fails. Baron Reynolds. He lives for his own good, drinks, he is a womanizer and a player. In short, he is nothing. He lives from the money from his estate.

Lily caught her breath. She should have stayed out of trouble, but there were no witnesses, so her reputation and her ego remained intact. She seemed not to insult them openly, everything was within the boundaries. Lily was a countess; Reynolds was a baron. Everything was clear-cut. He asked for it. On top of that, it was not Falion who started it, he did not care for the Countess personally.

"This conversation did not happen," whispered Lily.

"If someone finds out about it, I would come to the palace again. Nanook bites well. Understood?"

The butler nervously nodded. Lily nodded, content.

"Very well. Take me to the princesses' bedroom and wait until I let you go."

***

Alexander Falion dragged his companion to the end of the hall. He let go of him only when the doors behind them closed shut.

"Have you gone mad?" exclaimed Tarney.

"I haven't. Better explain to me what came over you! To be playing with a woman like that! Besides, she was a noble lady, not a maid. A little longer, and there would have been a scandal. The King disapproves of you as it is."

Tarney made a face.

"Hey, who was that bird? I have not seen her before at court."

"I also have not."

"We ought to find out—"

"You can if you want. I have no time for that."

Indeed, Marquess Falion was late. That was what always happened when he spent his nights with ardent ladies. This time he overslept, too; it was only by accident that he ran into Tarney that day.

"Have you not seen how gorgeous she was?" Tarney elaborated his narrative with very expressive gestures which were meant to show what advantages the woman had.

"I did see."

One could not say that Falion was indifferent to female beauty but he was not eighteen any more to jump on every woman. However, the strange woman did make an impression on him. It was not her looks. She was beautiful, that was out of the question. But he liked the way she had turned away Tarney, quickly and without fuss. The woman did not care for empty compliments; to get such a woman, one needed to put forth effort. It was easier to find a girl who, upon being given one sapphire ring, would be ready to show them every acrobatic pose.

Unlike Tarney, Falion had noticed both the emerald ring and the wedding bracelet glistening from out of Lily's luxuriant cuff. It made him conclude that she was a countess.

I also wonder what her name is.

✳✳✳

Mirrie was narrating the tale of Sherlock Holmes.

When Lily began telling her this story, she was faced with a cruel truth of life. She had to cut out many bits to make it suit the reality of the Middle Ages. It was a blessing when some parts could well remain unchanged.

Lily retold *The Blue Carbuncle*, *A Scandal in Bohemia*, and *The Sussex Vampire*. She even managed to adapt *The Hound of the Baskervilles*. Arthur Conan Doyle would have turned in his coffin upon finding out about such a travesty. Lily thought that some film adaptations and fan-fiction she had seen were even worse.

The princesses listened with their mouths open. It was obvious that the only books they were allowed to read were religious texts and a few romance stories, nothing else.

Noble or not, the princesses were children, above all. They craved to hear scary tales and exciting adventure stories. Mirrie became the Tolkien of the Middle Ages, even though she did not know who Tolkien was. The girls had already managed to drink a few glasses of wine; it was made weaker for children. Mirrie emphatically refused a drink and exclaimed that her mother would have taken her head off if she found out.

Angelina and Joliette stared at her in confusion. Yes, explained Mirrie, Lilian banned her from having any spirits until the age of fifteen. After that age, Mirrie was allowed to drink whatever she wanted. It was

Lily's opinion that alcohol was harmful to a growing body. Mirrie could drink water, tea, juice, anything but wine.

The girls had to send the maid for a jug of juice and a tub of rose water. Otherwise Mirrie refused to eat her cake.

The girl had rinsed her fingers and cutlery with rose water before eating her cake. It did not stop her from narrating.

"The scream woke up all the inhabitants, even those who lived on the far edge of the village…"

The knock on the door dispelled the tension. It was Alicia.

"Your Highness Angelina, Your Highness Joliette, forgive me for my impudence. Lady Miranda, your mother came to get you."

"Mother!"

The girl was overly excited; she had had enough of action that day. Lily took her in her arms and patted her head, putting the bow in its place with a swift movement.

"How are you, my little girl?"

"I am safe and sound. Can you join us for one moment?"

"Why?"

"Angelina and Joliette do not believe that you would give me a horse!"

Lily noticed the princess' faces peering out of the doorway; she let go of her daughter and curtsied to the princesses.

"Your Majesties."

"Dear Countess, we hope you can spare us a couple of moments," pleaded Angelina.

Lily sighed. Her headache was killing her. *But how could I refuse?*

***

Two hours later, Lily was sitting in the carriage, heading back to the estate. Beside her was Mirrie snoozing on Leif; Alicia sat opposite them and watched her daughter-in-law with genuine respect. It was true that Lily was good with children, even with teenagers. She only needed to make them interested to make an impression.

For starters, she had had to teach them French braiding; after that, she confirmed that the prince of Khanganat was coming to court; she also showed the girls how to use their fans correctly and told them another one of Sherlock Holmes' stories called *The Copper Beeches*.

The girls were charmed. They sincerely wished for Lily to come again. She had to agree; she would still have to return in a couple of days.

"Dear daughter-in-law, it seems like it all went very well." Alicia was sincerely pleased.

But Lily frowned, "Actually, everything is not so rosy."

"What happened? Was it anything to do with His Majesty?"

"His Majesty was pleased with me. He promised to send me an invitation to a big reception, as well as to the embassy of Khanganat."

"This is wonderful. But what was it that went wrong?"

Lily wrinkled her nose and told Alicia about the meeting in the corridor. Alicia's brows drew together.

"Reynolds? I know who he is. I would let the King know tomorrow! Let them drive him away with sticks! Cattle! He absolutely lost his mind!"

"Maybe we should not? My word is nothing against his, no one would prove a thing..."

"And what about Falion?"

"Do you think he would testify against his friend?"

Alicia reflected. "I know both Reynolds and Falion. It's hard to say whether Falion would speak up or not; knowing him he would not want to stir a scandal."

"I do not want one either. It has not even been a day without–"

"Okay," interrupted Alicia, "I'll take Reynolds on myself. He would regret his impudence...bastard!"

"You said bastard?"

"He is a baron in a sixth generation."

"A *nouveau riche,* I see. What does he have to do with Falion?"

"He simply tags along. He flatters everyone; I suppose he is desperate to get noticed in the company of the more famed and rich. Perhaps he thinks it makes him look more respectable. Falion is not a bad boy, he is smart, he breeds racehorses for sale. His horses are famous across several kingdoms, after the Avars, of course."

"The Avar horses are the best," sighed Lily.

"No doubt, but Khangans do not want to sell their horses, and no one else is capable of producing this breed."

"Not knowing genetics does not free one of problems," silently whispered Lily.

"What did you say?"

"Nothing. I was only thinking aloud. Alicia, would this argument have any consequences for me?"

"There was no one around who might have heard, right?"

"Not a soul. Only a servant."

"He does not count. Servants might gossip and their testimony is never held credible. Falion would keep silent, Reynolds, too. You did everything right. Do not forget, you are the Countess Earton. Jerrison is the King's nephew."

"And the King loves him very much." Lily looked pensively out of the window. Alicia cast a worried look at her.

"His Majesty loved Jessamine very much. He and Jyce were very close. King Edward, formerly the prince, confided in Jyce, who was the only person who knew about the affair with Jessamine."

"It must have been very hard for Jessamine. How long did she and the prince see each other?"

"Ten years. That is eight years as it was, and two years after the death of her Majesty Imogene, during the great Royal Mourning."

"I don't know if I could have lived like that. In hiding... It was not even possible to have children for they would be cast out as illegitimate."

"That is life, and life is often cruel."

Lily nodded. Still, it was terrible. She had her own, darker suspicions, but she did not want to voice them. She would remember them just in case, to argue with her husband. She would think about it later.

"Miranda got tired."

"Would you take her to the reception next time?"

"I don't know. I wouldn't take her, if I am being honest. She is still a child..."

"I can ask the princesses to look after her."

"That is not a bad idea at all."

"Would they agree?"

"Ay, they must. Angelina and Joliette...I have never seen them in such high spirits."

"They are children, after all. Being of royal blood is a secondary part of their identity."

"What a strange thought."

"I can cease to be a countess. But I would remain Lilian, whatever happens."

"Are you sure that such thoughts are not harmful to Miranda?"

"I am more than sure."

Alicia shook her head in doubt. When they got home, they saw a messenger with a scroll. Amalia Ivelen was giving birth. Alicia was invited to come. The woman made a discontented face. And surprisingly asked Lily to come with her.

"Shall we go together?"

Lily sighed.

"I would talk with Tahir and Jamie and tell them to pack."

"Why?"

"I suppose it would be more than useful to have a competent doctor in the room."

"A midwife should manage."

"She should? And does she know about her obligation?"

"What do you mean?"

But at this point Lily ceased to respond.

"Tahir! Jamie! Get ready. We are going to assist a childbirth."

"Take your time. She is in the country estate of Ivelen."

"How far?"

"It is a three hour ride by horse from here. It would take slightly longer with an equipage. If we leave now we will get there just past midnight."

"And what do you suggest?"

"To go in the morning, when the sun rises."

Lily raised her eyebrows.

"My darling Alicia, I have the best doctor of Khanganat with me. Would he not be needed there?"

The woman paused. She did not want to go. *How would a mother act? A mother would come running immediately. Lilian Earton is clever. What would happen if she decides that I behave in the wrong way? I cannot let this happen.*

"Give me two minutes. I would take a couple of sips of wine and we shall depart."

"Two minutes."

Lily rushed up the stairs, simultaneously calling friends on her way and giving out valuable instructions. Martha had to take Mirrie and put her to bed. Leis had to think where to get a pair of puppies for the princesses. Pastor Vopler was asked to pray for the mother and her child. Ingrid was ordered to plan how to rebuild the estate and think about the required materials. Lons had to talk to the Khangans about the approaching reception. He was also asked to get the horses ready for the Countess and her party.

Alicia was petrified at watching Lily create a whirlwind of activity around her.

It is the Broklend blood boiling in her. There is nothing one can do about it. I only hope that she will not be mad at Jess. Otherwise, the poor fellow will simply get blown away.

***

Amalia did not understand a thing. It was very painful. The birth went wrong. If the first two births had been easy and quick, this one was not.

Her contractions were sharp and painful. The child would not get out. The midwife frowned. Peter was pacing up and down the living room. His father, Loran Ivelen, sat in his armchair frowning. He did not like what was happening, but he could do nothing. All that remained for them to do was to pray to Aldonai.

Chapter 4

New Relatives

Lidarh moved ahead with such a speed that it caught Lily unaware. She patted the horse on the neck.

"Steady, boy. We will get to ride. But now we have to wait for the others."

Lidarh looked at Lily from the corner of his big purple eye and Lily heartily patted his mane.

"Everything will come in its own time, my lovely."

She loved her horse. Ali did a good job choosing him and Lily was immensely grateful for that. Lidarh was clever and handsome. He loved his mistress and was ready to go through fire and hell for her. Lily was also prepared to kill anyone who would dare to harm her stallion. She brushed and cleaned him herself and tried to dedicate more time to him. Such an attitude had been rewarding. Little by little, the horse and his rider had become one.

Lidarh slowed his stride and galloped around Alicia's carriage.

"I am going to move on a bit further because Lidarh is becoming stiff."

Leis nodded to a couple of his people and they took off to follow the Countess.

It was fine to go fast outside the city. Lilian understood everything and she wouldn't leave the guards. One never knew what might happen on the road.

The golden horse was almost flying over the road. The rider merged with him into one, she bent low to his steep neck; it was clear that they felt each other. It was not a mistress and her horse; it was two creatures united by the flight.

Alicia admired the sight from a distance. It was unreal, incredibly beautiful.

The strands of Lily's braid disheveled, and her golden tresses fell loose between the horse's mane. The sunset flared in the golden hair and the embroidery on Lily's yellow shirt, matching with the fiery fur of the Avarian stallion. It seemed that the horse was taking the rider right to the sun.

Alicia wished she could stop the moment. She wanted the people of the kingdom to see Lily like that.

How could Jess have failed to see her for what she is? Jess is not a fool. Yes, he is spoilt and picky, but he is not a fool. But to fail to see such qualities in a woman... He is an arrogant brat! Alicia was lost in her guessing. She wrinkled her nose.

I have to be careful and watch my behavior better. After so many years, I have gotten too relaxed, used to things. But the Countess is watching me. She sees my indifference behind my words of love for Amalia.

Even so...Lilian Earton is smart. Even if she draws correct conclusions she will still say nothing.

How is Amalia, I wonder?

Alicia turned her head toward the window. They had taken the carriage just for her. The rest of the party was going by horses. Even the grey-bearded old man whom Lily introduced as the best doctor of the Khanganat preferred a horse.

Should I have ridden with them as well?

***

Loran Ivelen was sipping his wine. There was something wrong with Amalia, something seriously wrong. The midwife frowned more often; she even grumbled a couple of times that she hoped they would not have to choose between the life of the mother and the life of the child. Two doctors who were invited just in case listened to the midwife but kept silent. It was the last resort, to rescue either the mother or the baby. They all hoped it would not come to this. Good thing they had sent the children to ride horses as soon as it all started. If worse comes to worst, they would make them stay in their city home.

Peter's face was pale green. If they let him, he would have slipped into his wife's room.

He loved Amalia with all his heart. It was not enough to say that he loved her selflessly. Peter lived, breathed and loved only because she was near.

Loran was scared for his son. If something went wrong, Peter would not bear it. He also expected the worst, as was his old habit.

One thing he did not expect was to hear the servant's bleating, "My Lady, the Countess of Earton, and the widowing Countess of Earton."

Lily entered the room like a golden whirlwind. She drew a lot of attention to herself against her own will. One of the gifts Ali had given her was a piece of yellow cloth. Its color was bright and full of life. Lily could not resist and had made a shirt from it that drew attention to her even more. She also wore brown combo trousers which looked like a skirt. Her matching sleeveless jacket was embroidered in golden thread; it matched the golden silk of her hair, which fell loosely against her dress. Her hair was almost down, having come undone during the ride.

Everyone else looked pale in comparison to Lily.

Loran did not even notice the moment he went up his feet.

"My Lady…your brilliance." It was only now that Loran noticed Alicia, always strict, always uptight, in a simple green dress, with a gorgeous lace shawl that cost his monthly earnings. He wondered where she got such a luxurious object and resolved to find out later.

"Let me introduce my daughter-in-law, the Countess Lilian Earton."

Lily slightly bowed. It was a family greeting with a touch of friendly disposition. Lons taught her that when there was a meeting between two relatives, it was enough to give a slight nod.

"I am very…" Loran stuttered. He did not expect to see such a beauty with golden tresses show up in his living room. "I am very happy to greet you, My Lady, in the walls of my humble estate."

The lady lightly smiled. Her green eyes flared in mocking sparkles.

Lily realized the powers of her charm and used them without a twinge of conscience.

"I am also happy to be here. Especially for such an important family occasion. May I congratulate you already?"

Loran's expression darkened. Before he could respond, the midwife entered the room without a knock.

"Your Grace, the marchioness is losing her strength. If this continues, we will have to choose between the life of the mother or the life of the child. I pray for a miracle."

Lily did not even move but the room filled up with her energy.

"I have the best doctor of Khanganat with me, Tahir Djiaman din Dashar. Your Grace, I ask for your indulgence to–"

"Yes, Yes!" Peter intervened so abruptly that even Alicia flinched. "I implore you, dear Countess, maybe your doctor is able to help."

"Tahir! Jamie!"

Loran was startled. It turned out that there was a whole crowd of people following the Countess. Two people from the crowd stepped forward.

One of them was a very young man with messy blonde curls. The other one was an old man with a grey beard dressed in a Khangan traditional dress.

"My Lady," the old man bowed. "I am ready to follow you."

"In that case, Your Grace, call the servants forward!"

Confused, Loran produced a clap.

"Jim!"

The servant appeared immediately and was given a job straight away. "Is there any hot water in the kitchen?"

"Yes, Your Grace."

"Lead us toward the kitchen."

"But—"

"We came from the road and need to wash our hands and face." Explained Lily. "Heat up as much water as you can."

Lily did not carry any illusions about the hygiene in that place. The duke's distinct smell spoke for itself.

***

The servants were shocked to see Lily in the kitchen. It was the noble Countess, after all, and she was free to do what she wanted. If someone did not like it, they would be sent off immediately.

"My Lady," Tahir's voice lowered into a whisper. "I have never assisted births,"

"What about the harem?"

"It was punished by death to look at the wives of the Khangan. They used a doll to show me what hurt and where. I was also allowed to speak to the women only through a curtain."

Lily gave off a whistle.

What a joke! How do they even live with such a level of medicine? There are so many women in the Khanganat!

"I am also not very experienced. The only time I assisted births was back in Altver," joined in Jamie.

Lily sighed. She had had a midwife experience, in that other life. She assisted a caesarean section a couple of times. She was very lucky. The gynecology professor did not pass them until they had each assisted at least three births. Three births were a pass. They had to assist even more if they wanted a high grade.

Her previous experience involved careful supervision and sensitive guidance; it highly helped that women in labor reached the point when they did not care. But it was at least something. Lily strongly suspected that, in comparison with local midwives, she was a pinnacle of medicine.

The midwife in place also smelled bad. Her nails were so black with dirt that it was possible to plant potatoes under them, in three perfect rows.

The servants cautiously glanced at each other at seeing the woman and the men thoroughly washing their hands and rubbing their faces. Lily fastened her hair and put it under her vest. They had white medical robes with them, too, but they would put them on once in the room, to not shock any more people.

They opened the door and entered the bedroom.

***

Amalia was lying still. The last contraction had exhausted her to the limit. Her mind was hazy with pain. The baby was still inside. So when a gentle woman's face leaned over her, she thought it was a vision.

The herbal infusion that her midwife gave her to soothe the pain was making her brain burn. The strange woman smiled. Breaking through a small window, the sun flared up her golden hair. Such an image made Amalia believe that she was dying.

"Are you my guardian angel?"

The woman shook her head.

Amalia grabbed her arm. "Do not take me away! I cannot leave now! Not yet!"

"I won't…"

Lily freed her palm from the tenacious fingers.

"Let's see what we have here…" What they had was bad.

The cervix had opened, her water had broken, but the child did not yet wish to appear. Not good. A few more hours like that, and they would have had to get the baby piece by piece to save his mother, if she could still be saved.

Lily wondered if the child inside was alive; she put a hand-made wooden stethoscope to the woman's belly. At least she had one, even though it was not perfect. She could hear the baby's heartbeat. It was uneven, it did not sound right, but it was there. Both the baby and the mother were alive, and her job was to help them. She regretted not having specialized in obstetrics.

Disgusted at the sight of dirt, Lily removed a filthy sheet from the bed. Something heavy fell on the floor. It was a dagger! A dagger encrusted in gold and jewels.

"What is this stuff doing here?"

The midwife straightened her back and pursed her lips.

"It is compulsory to put a dagger in the mother's bed. It will cut through the pain. If it is a boy, he would get out quicker for the weapon would attract him."

Ugh! Thought Lily. *At least they did not put the dagger inside her!*

"Jamie! Tahir!"

The men helped to carefully put a clean cloth under the mother's body. Lily exhaled and gathered her spirits. This was one of the things she hated the most about gynecology. But the hands remained the most important tool of a good doctor. If the baby lay in the wrong position, if the child got caught in the cord...

The woman sighed. She needed a mirror, or a torch... but the only thing she had was a candle, which she was not going to stick inside.

Lily looked at the birth canal.

"Goodness me!" The first good thing was that Lily's new body also had thin bones, another good thing was that Lily had managed to lose weight. Former Lily would not have been able to cope.

Lily's hand slipped inside. To keep Tahir and Jamie aware of the process, she commented on her actions along the way. "So, what we have here is clearly not the head. And if that is so... Aha! I have caught you."

Lily addressed the men.

"The fetus is in the wrong position; he is not able to turn around by himself. Now I will feel him and try to turn..."

"What are you doing?" the midwife was too wound up. "Aldonai commanded women to be in pain when delivering their children!"

"Did he also command them to die?" inquired Lily in a harsh tone.

"All is at the will of Aldonai."

"Jamie!"

Without a word the young man took the midwife by her shoulders and dragged her to the door. The hag tried to escape, but he opened the door and directed her way by giving her a farewell kick in the butt.

"Shoo, you crow!"

The door slammed and was bolted. Jamie could see Leis' guards standing in front of them. He returned to the Countess.

Now, under her sensitive guidance, Tahir studied obstetrics. It had definitely been a new experience for a Khangan.

Amalia groaned from another spasm. And Lily decided to act. It seems that there were no pathologies. An ordinary child, not particularly large, even small...

"Do we have medication for pain relief? Jamie, give her a small dose."

The young man obeyed. He poured a spoonful of bitter potion down her throat, which she mechanically swallowed. He watched as the Countess' hand disappeared inside the woman's body causing her to moan from pain.

"It is nothing. A little bit more, girl, a little bit more..."

Lily carefully began to unfold the fruit. Very slowly, very neatly she stumbled upon one of the main tricks of obstetrics.

The child was not able to free himself. It was a loop from the umbilical cord on the leg which had prevented him from doing so. *It was good that it had not been wrapped around his neck!*

Lily swore.

Slippery, rubbish... and where are you now? Long live my nails! Although short, they are enough to pull.

The umbilical cord gave in neatly and a little baby slipped out into Lilian's fingers.

"And now a little turn..."

Amalia produced a faint moan and the child came out. He was small and covered in slime…and also alive. He opened his mouth and yelled so loud that it made the chandelier swing. Without casting an eye on him, Lily handed the child to Jamie and went back to the woman. But Amalia did not require help any more. She moaned, tightened her muscles again and another time, and a second living lump fell out on the bed. It made Tahir immensely happy. The Countess herself prepared to wait for the placenta to come out. *Ten minutes, maybe twenty?* Amalia was now delivering babies like a cat. The placenta came out in a couple of minutes. Lily stretched it out, looked at it and made sure it came out whole. Everything was in its place.

It was a real blessing that Amalia did not bleed; the prospect of that scared Lily the most.

Now, Lily had to attend to the children. She had to tighten each cord, wait for a few minutes, cut it off… Rub the children clean. But Tahir and Jamie were already at it. The newborns were squeaking. *It is at such moments, that I realize I do not live in vain!*

Amalia moaned again, and Lily went up to her so that the woman could see her face. Her blue eyes were hazed by the painkiller, but there was some reason in them.

"Am I dead?"

"No, everything is good. You have two healthy children."

Lily didn't even think to check their sex; she had been busy saving them.

"Two boys!" exclaimed Tahir.

"You gave birth to two boys. Can you breastfeed them?"

Amalia made a faint movement and Lily nodded to the men. The babies, wrapped in white cloth, were put onto their mother's breast. They yelled with all their heart, feeling the brotherly competition.

"Tahir, have you made a note of who was born first?" Lily doubted her ability to tell between the children. They all looked similar to her, red and wrinkled.

"Yes, my teacher."

Lily's eyes shined, and Tahir bowed in a calm, ceremonial way; his hands were on his chest, his eyes were cast down to the ground.

"Madam, I thank you for the new light of knowledge."

"Thank you for your help, my friend."

Lily thought gloomily that now she could not avoid the task of writing a gynecology textbook.

***

That day Peter survived a couple of near-death moments.

Loran was right, the heir of Ivelen loved his wife more than anything else. If there came up question of whether to sacrifice the mother or the child, he would choose to save Amalia. If his wife died in childbirth, he would end his days shortly after. He died his first death when the childbirth started. His wife was in pain; it was the child who caused it. It was Peter who was the root of all his wife's suffering.

Peter was not scared of pain. He had to accept duels and fights, but it was different for men. They were stronger, smarter, braver; they could, after all, defend themselves.

But Amalia was a woman. *The weak one, the loved one, the only one.*

The only thing she was left to do was to pray to Aldonai. Peter knew that the outcome of childbirth heavily depended on Aldonai. His last resort was a prayer.

Alas. Perhaps I was not been righteous enough, or perhaps the gods did not hear me. Aldonai does not wish to listen. Peter could hear his wife's shrieks more and more frequently, the most inhuman sounds. The midwife's face turned darker and darker.

Lily's arrival did not mean anything for Peter. *What could she do? Hold my wife's hand?*

If they offered him to sacrifice the lives of everyone present in the room to save Amalia's he would have agreed. But the offer was not in place. When the Countess mentioned her doctor a beam of hope sparked in Peter's heart.

A Khangan? Be it even Maldonaya herself! Anything to help Amalia. It must help…

The doctor turned out to be strange. He asked for a lot of hot water to wash himself from the journey instead of going straight to Amalia. But maybe it was their strange custom. It was most surprising to see the young man and the Countess also washing their hands and face. The three went upstairs together, to attend to Amalia. Peter's father wanted to prevent this, but Alicia grabbed his arm and exclaimed, "Duke, do not get in their way!"

"Why do you say so, Countess?" Loran was agitated and Alicia did not fail to give a correct explanation.

"Tahir is the best doctor, even across the far lands of the Khanganat. The prince himself, Amir Gulim, is currently in Ativerna."

"Well, Tahir is a doctor. Who are the other two?"

"Jamie is a botanist. He is good with herbs."

Loran became softer. A botanist was necessary.

"What about your daughter-in-law?"

"Tahir refused to return to the Khanganat because of Lilian. She is his favorite student and he cannot leave her."

"A student?"

"My daughter-in-law had lost her child. And she decided to learn anything she could to prevent it from happening again."

"Everything is in the powers of Aldonai."

"Except the enemies' schemes!"

"What do you mean?"

"My daughter-in-law had lost a child because of somebody evil who wanted to kill her. The King promised to find the villain," explained Alicia.

Peter did not listen to their conversation. His thoughts were busy as it was. He could hear Amalia's moaning from upstairs. Sometimes she was quiet and that gave the man a sense of hope. But the infant cry did not come and the moans of Amalia became even more desperate.

Soon they ceased. *Maybe I just can't hear them?* Peter immediately noticed the midwife who angrily entered the room.

"What happened?"

"I got kicked out!" The woman was outraged. "If no one needs me I am leaving!"

The midwife had a right to be angry. She was called to the wealthiest of households and people regarded her as the best. And look at what they had done! A certain countess (who might also need a midwife one day) ordered to get her out of the room and a certain young man obeyed, closing the doors behind her.

Besides, the midwife had witnessed such cases and knew that this childbirth would surely end with the death of either the mother or the child. It would be better for her reputation to stay away.

"Wait!" Loran stood up, "We have paid you, so would you be so kind to return and help?"

"Your Grace, they kicked me out and closed the door behind," repeated the midwife slowly.

"Who did?"

"The Countess."

"But…"

The moans suddenly ceased, or went quieter. Peter sprinted up the stairs.

Is it so that a man cannot be present at the childbirth? I don't care. That is my wife and my child in there!

But the door was guarded by the two strangers.

"You cannot come in."

"What!"

Such an answer did not make Peter angry but rather put him in shock. He was the Marquess of Ivelen, this was his own house…

"The Countess ordered to not let anyone in."

"Do you understand who you are speaking to! I will order you to be whipped in the stables!" Peter said angrily.

The two men looked absolutely indifferent.

"Your Grace, the Countess ordered to not let anyone in. We are doing our job."

"I am the master here!"

"The Countess is helping your wife. If you get involved, you might make things worse. Your Grace, please understand, we are not acting from our own will. If we let you in the Countess will order us to be beaten," Jean Courier lied shamelessly.

He knew very well that Lilian would never give the order. It was most likely that she would kick them out. But the two did not want that to happen. Working for the Countess was exciting. They were given the uniform, taught new things, fed well, paid generously. In addition, what attracted people to Lilian was that she had never cared for the class system. She never put herself higher just because she was a countess and they were nobody. She always listened and one could always tell her their problems; if the truth were on their side the Countess would help them to settle the matter to their benefit.

Jean did not notice how he started to be truly loyal to Lily—not because he was scared or because he needed money, but simply because she was being herself, the Countess Lilian Earton. If she ordered, even through Jamie, to not let anyone in, they would not, even if they had to fight. However, it was obvious that it would never escalate into a fight, the young man was evidently not a big fighter.

Jean was right. Peter collapsed on the filthy floor and bellowed, "Aldonai! Help!"

The man was desperate. He knew that if Amalia died, he would also end his life; he would stab himself with a dagger. *Away with everything. I will not be able to live without Amalia.* The thought of it made him want to die.

Peter was prepared for the worst. It might have been a year or an instant until he heard an infant cry coming from the room. It was fierce and loud and broke the veil of despair. And that is when Peter died for the third time. *What did he care about that child?* The main thing for him was that

Amalia was alive. But the crying continued. It had become twice as loud and fierce and full of life.

Soon Peter heard the cracking of the door.

The Countess Earton stood in the doorway. She was wrapped in white cloth from head to toe. Her arms were bare to the elbows; both the white cloth and her tender skin were stained with drops of blood and a slimy substance. Her thick braid unwound again, but her green eyes were shining.

"You have twins, Your Grace. Two boys, both in good health and quite handsome."

"Amalia?" uttered Peter, almost going numb from terror.

"She will be all right. I gave her a sleeping drug. You need to find your children a nursemaid."

Lily barely finished her sentence before Peter Ivelen, the duke's heir, an aristocrat from a highly noble family, took her in his arms and hugged her so hard that she could hardly breathe. He had a lot of strength and happiness that he took out on the Countess.

"Let go, Your Grace! You will crush me!"

Peter spun Lily around the room and eventually let her go. He ran to the place where on the blood-stained bed his wife lay in a peaceful sleep. Next to her, squeaking, were two little lumps wrapped in white. He went down on his knees, touched his wife's rosy cheek and felt its warmth. It was only at that moment, that he really believed everything was fine.

"Dear Countess, I owe you my life for this."

Lily smiled modestly. Never before had she seen such happiness as was dazzling in Peter's eyes at that moment.

"It is nothing, Your Grace. Only ask someone to change the sheets. Sir din Dashar and I would like to wash off the blood."

It was only then that the marquess noticed Tahir and Jamie; he swiftly ran to their feet.

"Dear sirs! Dearest din Dashar! Dear sir—."

"Meitle. Jamie Meitl, the botanist," the young man introduced himself. Until his title was confirmed, being the botanist would do.

"Dear sir Meitl. If ever you need any help, I swear on my life, Ivelen is at your service."

"This is our job, Your Grace." Tahir was majestic like never before.

"It was a miracle that drew you to my house."

"My Lady Lilian Earton is a wonderful woman," blissfully agreed Tahir.

Lily did not contradict. She put back her braid and dismissed her people.

"Your Grace, I suppose your servants can attend to us in your place. It is better if you spend time with your wife and children."

Peter happily agreed.

"Yes, dear Countess."

"We will have time to see each other. For now, I will speak to your father. You had a difficult day. Get some rest."

Peter nodded and kneeled at his wife's bedside.

The servants came. They changed the bedding and Amalia's clothes, and washed her with a moist sponge. But Peter cared for nothing; the Countess Earton saved his wife and his children.

***

Jean and Rem led the way, Lily followed them; Tahir and Jamie walked behind. After the adrenaline in her blood went down, Lily found herself shaking. She was not a midwife; this was her first time. She felt the need to take Alicia's carriage on the way back, or at least rest for an hour before the ride.

She decided she had deserved her good grade for gynecology. She had also helped her mother in the old times at the front where they were prepared to treat people in any kind of emergency.

But this was her first time doing it on her own. It was her first time diagnosing the position of the fetus, her first time turning the baby over; she had cut the cord before. She also had practice in cases when the cord had been too long and wrapped around the baby. The midwife she had shadowed showed her this and taught her how to deal with it. As soon as the baby's head was out, the loop was taken off with the speed of lightning. At moments like that, only Batman moved faster than the midwife. But it had been different back then. She had experienced and clever people around who could help at any time. They also had painkillers, antiseptics, drips and were skilled at assisting a caesarean delivery. That was back then.

But now… Not until the very last moment did Lily realize that there were two children inside Amalia. All her actions were correct out of sheer luck. Thinking about it afterwards made her nauseous; her legs were shaky, her head was spinning; all the symptoms of stress were coming together.

"I need a shot right now, like on the front line," said Lily.

"Did you say something, My Lady?"

"I want a drink," confessed Lily to Tahir.

"Why not? You deserve it. My Lady, would the marchioness have managed without our help?"

Lily shook her head.

"The two children got in each other's way. The damned cord entangled them. If the baby had been alone, he would have been able to turn by himself. If the cord had been out of the… No. She would not have managed without help. If we had not helped her, she would have died there."

"Died?"

It was at that precise moment that the doors opened before Lily. Loran Ivelen had caught only the last words.

"She died? What about the baby?"

"Peace, Your Grace," Lily waved her hand. "Despite all the efforts of the midwife, the baby is alive...both of them. Amalia is also alive. She is with Peter now. I gave her a sleeping drug to make her rest."

"What happened to my daughter-in-law?"

"The baby needed help to turn around; he could not do it himself. When there are two babies, they get into each other's way," replied Tahir, and Lily was immensely grateful to him for joining the conversation.

"Were you the one who did this?"

"No, it was the Countess, under my supervision," Tahir was splendid and noble.

"What?"

"Out of us three, the Countess had the thinnest arms. It made a great difference. There are things that men could never succeed at, but women deal with them with ease."

Ivelen could only shake his head. He did not expect such a statement coming from Tahir. Alicia was also surprised to hear such words.

"Is my daughter well, Lily?"

"You are a grandmother once again, Alicia," Lily gave the brightest of her smiles. "In fact, twice. Amalia gave birth to twins. How are you going to tell between them, Your Grace?"

"Hmmm..."

"We tied ribbons to their hands. The elder one is with a white ribbon, the younger has a green one."

"My Lady, I am forever your servant. Aldonai himself sent you and your people to my house. And you!"

Ivelen addressed the old hag, that useless midwife who was trying to escape the room unnoticed. "Where are you heading to? You said that either the mother or the child had to be sacrificed, you said that we had to choose! I will order you to be beaten in the stables, you hag!"

"Your Grace, today is a day of joy. Forgive her," whispered Lily. The last thing she wanted was to have someone argue in her presence. Had it been any other day, she would not have intervened. Lily was tired to the bone. She needed a hot bath.

The midwife gave Lily a grateful look. The duke did not contradict Lily's wishes.

"So be it. Go! If the Countess is asking, someone, show her the exit! Can I be of any help to you, dear Countess?"

"Yes, Your Grace. I need a wash. You can see for yourself that both my teacher and I are covered in blood."

"Dear Countess, I suggest you stay here overnight. I will obviously offer you, and Alicia...and your whole party to stay."

Lily took a moment to think. She could take off into the night. But a lot of weird people walked around the dark, that was a fact. She did not want to risk the lives and health of her people. Amalia needed to be under a close watch, at least until the morning. Furthermore, with Alicia around, her reputation would not suffer if she accepted the invitation.

"Your Grace, thank you for such a generous proposition. We will be happy to accept your invitation." Lily immediately caught the approving eye of Alicia.

∗∗∗

Half an hour later, Lily sat in the guestroom and rubbed the stains of blood from her hands and skin. She was happy with the outcome. If Amalia had bled in the process of delivery, Lily would have failed to help her, but everything ended well. Fortune was on Lily's side.

Another thing to develop here would be a school of obstetrics and gynecology. Would I manage it all? A school... Well, I could open one.

Lily bit her lip and continued her blissful thoughts.

Tahir could teach anatomy. Hmmm...we need to dissect somebody, after all, to make sure there are no physiological differences. This world is different to the one I knew. Maybe the locals have their livers in place of their spleens? Or maybe they don't have an appendix? Who knows! Jamie can teach them botany. I could teach some things. But it would be useful to train people in different kinds of medicine. Pharmaceutics, paramedics, midwives...like in a medical school. Three years, and you're ready to treat all the sinners in the depths of hell...or worse, in a local hospital. Certainly, some district hospitals have not evolved since the Middle Ages!

If you are ill, my dear, go to Lebedan, or Zakopitkino, or Skopino! In short, every state official should go to their local general practitioner instead of going to Switzerland or England! It would make them immediately impose European standards in every hospital in every district. It often happened that a district hospital did not even have a drip! How terrible!

She needed to think it over and talk with the King. Edward would surely be interested in creating a military hospital. One certified doctor per regiment would decrease the number of deaths significantly. Lily contemplated this further. *I could take the orphans from the street, educate them and create boarding schools. Some thousand years will need to pass before the human rights activists will disagree with such a course of action.*

If Lily could, she would make all the state officials in Russia get treatment in district hospitals. And the children, on the other hand, would get a good education and a useful profession.

***

Lily's plan to rest failed. Her bed roamed with fleas; the parasites did not care for titles, they bit everyone. Lily spent half the night dreaming about bug-bombs. Eventually, she gave up on sleep and took the thick cover from her bed, wrapped up inside it, and spent the rest of the night in an armchair. The fleas could also get her there, but there were now considerably less of them.

So, in the morning, the woman woke up kind as a bee. There was a reason for this. As soon as she fell asleep, the fleas started biting. Lily would wake up, scratch herself, try to sleep, suffering all over again. Eventually, she heard someone knocking on the door and when they entered, she was already prepared to conquer the world. At moments like these, she was ready to kill a dragon, for instance, or to finish off the stinking Duke of Ivelen for such a "kind" offer to stay in a bed full of fleas. *Enough of that anger.*

She had to excuse them, feel sorry for the people. They all had to live like that. They were not guilty. Lily asked the servant for a tub with hot water, which left him quite surprised, and began her morning exercise.

A warm-up—aerobics. She had to move quickly. A mixture of military exercise with shaping was doing wonders for her body. The fat disappeared, her muscle grew. The key was not feeling sorry for herself. Lily completed all her exercise with a rare sense of anger. If she swung her arm, it was aimed to hit the enemy's nose or else, his liver. Then she would practice a leg kick. The key was not to give up. Morning exercise was a good way to warm up and release her anger. Lily moved onto stretching. She didn't aim for a split, but she went for a good low stretch. She went down in a plié, a move she learned in her dancing classes, and then jumped up; she finished this exercise in her initial plié position. It was a good way to fight cellulite and her second chin, especially after the warm up. She ended her routine in a martial arts pose, a horse stance and remained standing thus for five minutes. *Why not?* Lily still had to give birth. She wasn't going to spend her life in a nunnery. She would have children, sooner or later. Therefore, it was necessary to prepare for the pregnancy at least three years in advance in order to train the necessary muscles.

It was clear as day. Lily could picture the women moaning in maternity homes and gynecological clinics exclaiming *Painful!*, *My back hurts for no reason*, *My uterus is falling out*, *Oh, something is wrong with me, help me, Doctor*…

A shark was at movement its whole life and did not complain about its uterus falling out. Those women, on the other hand, were the classic office workers. Their muscles were as stiff as bone. They sat in their chairs all day long; the most serious exercise they could expect to get was moving a folder with some papers from one place to another. After work, those women got into their cars and went straight home. To get to their flat, they used elevators; once in the flat, every chore was taken care of by household appliances. Their only exercise was sex, which also didn't happen every day. Their husbands were exhausted, too, and their erotic life was limited to weekends. *What did those women expect then? All the muscle inside them had turned to muck.* It was obviously difficult for them to carry and give birth to a baby. One shouldn't be surprised at that. But many people did not realize it until it was too late, and the problem was already there.

What happened was that a potential mother was at first happy on her visit to a doctor; only after a few months did she realize that she was in trouble. The doctors obviously had a right to be angry with her. It was not because they were mean, but because 70 percent of illnesses happened precisely from a lack of movement. The doctors could not cure it by pills. Sometimes, they got angry seeing a newborn baby and realizing there was nothing they could do because the mother had refused to help herself during her pregnancy. The doctors turned sick, and their hearts ached.

Lily thought that a woman was a beautiful plant. The more it loosened up its petals—so to speak, body parts—to open into a flower, the faster she drooped. One had to always remember that, every day and every hour, and take appropriate measures. Crying over spilled milk was not productive. Pain, tears, and silly illnesses were the price to pay for one's laziness. A neglected body is not capable of producing a healthy offspring. Such truth might sound cruel, but life is never an easy thing.

Lily jumped up from her squat position, kicked her legs a couple of times and smiled to herself. *This is not bad compared to how I was before. I used to look like a cow. Well, I am far from being a top model because I am not a hanger for clothes. I have breasts, I have a butt… forgive me for being straight-forward, but I am not a squished pumpkin anymore, but a normal Russian woman. Wide hips? I will work on having a thinner waist. And it will look great. More training becomes a habit, an iron fist and a beastly attitude. Let that attitude sting my butt and not let me put it down on a soft pillow. I expect to be left surprised at the result.*

Somebody knocked on the door. Lily wrapped herself in her duvet and let the servants come in. They brought a tub and Lily was delighted to splash hot water on her face and limbs. She would take a bath at home. It was at least something. She could rub herself with a flannel, wipe herself dry and put on some clean… Yet, there was one downfall to this morning routine. Lily hadn't bothered to take a change of underwear. She hadn't thought they would stay overnight. What she had with her was slightly smelly. *How else?* She was riding on a horse earlier, then she was helping to deliver a baby…

How is Lidarh, I wonder?

Yesterday she had not been in a state to take care of the horses, so today she had to take a piece of salted bread and a couple of apples to make it up to the boy. He was used to Lily's hand and probably got offended by her neglecting him.

There was nobody downstairs yet. Lily called a servant and explained what she wanted. The servant nodded and let the woman into the kitchen. The same cook she had met yesterday gave Lily what she asked for. Lily only shook her head in surprise.

Poor discipline, she thought. *If it was my kitchen… No, Loria would have also given everything she was asked for. But she would also report back to her mistress, and obviously watch.*

It was different on that estate, and much easier for Lily. The stables turned out to be a massive building, as big as a military barrack. Every horse was kept in a separate stall the size of a one-bedroom flat. Even though Lidarh was put in a huge stable, the Avarian looked… Lily didn't know how to describe what she saw in his eyes.

Once you had tamed an animal, you began thinking and seeing them in a different light; you began to notice a lot of human traits in them, you started understanding their thoughts and respecting them; you gave them room for their own opinion. Take only their face… Someone might have said that Nanook had a snout. Lily, on the other hand, thought that Damis Reis had one. Nanook and Lidarh had *faces*, which looked human and quite sophisticated. They were creatures like us, with their own personality, principles, and logic…

Lidarh spotted his mistress and began neighing. It was as if he was telling her off for leaving him alone, but despite his frustration he was happy to see her.

Lily fed him some salted bread and a couple of apples; she asked a stablehand who was standing nearby for a scraper and started grooming the horse. The Avarian stallion was overcome with pleasure. It was not that he needed special care, for the stablemen took great care of horses. It was that rule of being responsible for the ones we tamed, and it included sacrificing her nice clothes, or at least what was left of them.

Yesterday Lily's dress looked well; she had expected her visit to Ivelen to consist of baby showers and nice family greetings. The decision to bring Tahir and Jamie had been spontaneous, Lily had brought them along 'just in case'. But things turned on their head. At first, she had to ride in these clothes for three hours, then she assisted childbirth wearing them… She managed to avoid getting her clothes dirty with blood, but her sweat made them soaking wet from head to toe. The emergency was a sure way to lose at least five pounds. She had no energy to think to give her clothes a wash, or at least put them to hang outside. Therefore, it was debatable who smelled worse, Lily or her stallion.

The woman spent her time speaking to the horse. She whispered to Lidarh that there was no better horse in the whole world; she brushed his gorgeous mane and enjoyed the process. Everyone had their own methods of relaxation. Lily did not care for her clothing. She was a countess; she could afford to buy new stuff. After all, she could earn her living.

"My Lady..."

So much was she was invested in her conversation with the horse that she jerked in surprise. It was Duke Ivelen.

"Good morning, Your Grace. How is the marchioness feeling?"

"I have not checked on her yet, but Peter spent the whole night by her side. I suppose that if something was wrong, we would have been awake and on our feet a long time ago."

Lily sighed. *Where could I find such a man? Clever, good-looking, from a good family and loving. Only in a fairytale, was the answer, where every second hero was like that. In real life I am more likely to find a tadpole and try to give him a manly upbringing. Alas!*

"I expect Tahir will want to attend to the marchioness one more time before his departure. I hope you will not mind."

"How could I be against it, dear Countess? You may call me Loran; we are relatives, after all. And I owe you. If anything had happened to Amalia last night, Peter would have gone insane."

"If not died," commented Lily with a tinge of gloom in her voice. "He did not look good yesterday. You may call me Lilian, by the way, since we are relatives."

The Duke liked Lily's playful smile. The Countess was smart enough not to refuse the offer of friendship and gratitude. She also realized the existence of certain limits. Putting everything aside, the Duke remembered that she saved the life of his daughter-in-law, as well as his grandchildren.

"Lilian, why do you bother with studying medicine? Do not tell me that you are going to become a medicus."

"Obviously not. My knowledge is ten times… a *hundred times* better than the knowledge of your medicuses. But sometimes it could bring good results. For example, if it were not for us showing up yesterday, Amalia would have died. I would be of no use if sir din Dashar did not agree to be my teacher. The baby needed to be turned around and Tahir's arms were not thin enough. So I had to do it myself."

Lily's words made Loran shudder.

"It is not a fit task for a noble lady."

"Yes, but one does not always get to choose. Your Grace, I want to make a proposition."

"I am Loran for you."

"Of course, Loran. Amalia will need someone to look after her for at least a month. Her childbirth was difficult."

"Yes, and you suggest?"

"Tahir teaches me everything he knows. He also happens to teach Virman women to nurse the patients."

"You said Virman women?"

"Yes, it happens so."

"I thought that the Virmans never left their island."

"Such were the circumstances," shrugged Lily. "I can send you a couple of women who will take good care of the mother. Marchioness Ivelen deserves to get the best care, is it not so?"

"Are you saying that you want me to let the Virmans become part of our household?" As he spoke, Loran's eyes were playful and lenient.

"Yes. These women are specially trained to be able to spot any danger and take care of both the mother and her children."

"Hmm, I suppose they might bring good."

Lily slightly tilted her head to hide her victorious look. One bee was already in her honey pot. Her reputation as a doctor needed a boost. *Why not?* One of her first patients was the marchioness herself, not an ordinary peasant.

The words of Albert Einstein befitted the occasion, "It is necessary to speak everything about one's relatives, for these things would be too rude to be put into print."

Tatiana Victorovna (Aliya's mother) had a brother. This brother had nearly overwhelmed his *own* mother to get a tiny flat in a crippling Soviet building. The situation had been ugly. Although the story had ended relatively well (Lily's grandma even taught her to knit), the woman subconsciously remembered that being relatives did not ensure a good relationship, especially when money was involved.

The Eartons were richer than the Ivelens; their marriage made them rich. *God knew how much money the Ivelens had, but it is my golden rule to not trust too soon.*

The Virmans could become useful for a background check. Servants knew a lot of things. No matter how well one hid them, the gossip would still spread; a word here, a word there… It was useful to gather any possible information about the enemy. And when it came to money, even the closest relative could turn out to be unkind.

Lidarh lightly pushed against the Countess' shoulder to get her attention.

"Forgive me, my sweetheart… I have forgotten about you, handsome. Wait a minute, I will return to you shortly… Loran, do you mind if I—"

"Of course not. This is a wonderful horse and he deserves the best care."

"As does the marchioness."

"Yes, send your Virmans over. I give my permission."

"Perfect, Loran, perfect." She turned back to the horse. "Turn around, my sweetheart. That's it, good boy. I will give you a s—"

"Countess, would you want to sell your horse? I will pay you any money."

Lily shook her head.

"Forgive me, Your Grace, but I received him as a gift."

The duke frowned but nodded in understanding.

"A royal gift, I suppose."

Lily refrained from saying that the horse was supposed to be reserved for the King. It was Ali who managed to get him for Lily instead.

"Oh, yes."

"I will need to ask the Earl where he got such a rare horse."

"It was not the Earl who gave him to me. Ali Ahmet din Tahirjan from the caravan trail guard gave me Lidarh as a gift for saving his life."

"For saving his life?"

"It was in Altver. Sir din Tahirjan happened to walk up on an enraged bull that, did not care for titles. The beast would have killed him if it hadn't been for my guards and me. So he gave me this Avarian stallion as a gift for saving him."

Lily did not disclose all the details. *Why would I?* It was not a confession; Ivelen heard enough.

"I see, Countess. You have a real talent for appearing in the right place in the right time."

Lily shrugged. "I never thought about it in that way. Everything is in the hands of Aldonai."

***

Alicia was expecting them in the living room together with Tahir and Jamie.

"Lilian, darling, did you sleep well?"

Lily smiled at her mother-in-law. "My bed had fleas. Otherwise, it was all fine. How is Amalia?"

"I was waiting for you to join me for a medical examination," intervened Tahir.

Lily smiled. "Do you mind, Loran?"

"Go ahead, Lilian."

Alicia only raised her eyebrows. As soon as Lily and her people left the room, Alicia began questioning the Duke.

"I can see that you got along with my daughter-in-law."

"Lilian Earton is quite an interesting person." Loran smiled delightedly. "She is very...extraordinary."

"Well, she is a Broklend." Alicia had always noticed that Lily was special...on the verge between insane and eccentric. "What can I say, she is August's daughter after all."

"Broklend, oh yes. That shipbuilder who comes from a family of peasants..."

Alicia noticed a tinge of disrespect in the Duke's voice. "Do not put it like that in front of Lily. She would go through fire and hell to protect the honor of her father; indeed, she would fiercely defend any member of her family."

"What a peculiar habit."

"She is August's daughter. Her father brought her up alone, in the wilderness; until she got married, she had no contact with the outside world."

"Why did your son keep such a splendid woman out of sight, in the village? I would understand if she was involved in a scandal or got pregnant before marriage. Perhaps there is something else to it."

"I suppose they just did not get along."

What else can I say? That my son Jess is an idiot?

Loran did not believe a word of this story, but he nodded politely. Alicia realized that she and Lily needed to agree on what to say to different people. Until then, personality clash was the official version.

Alicia only wished everyone would mind their own business.

* * *

Amalia lay in her bed. Peter sat next to her, holding her hand. Lily only sighed.

Where is my husband, who would sit next to me? He is having fun somewhere else, and I am saddened being away from him.

"Good morning, Marquess, Marchioness."

Peter dropped his wife's hand, stood up and bowed.

"Countess, I am delighted to see you."

"It is mutual, dear Marquess. But I am afraid we are here for some business to settle."

"Is anything wrong?" Peter was on guard.

"Before we leave, I wanted to look at the mother and the children once again, to make sure everything is fine," intervened Tahir.

Peter only nodded.

"Yes. Of course. Do you require my presence?"

"If you want. There will be nothing inappropriate," the last phrase was directed at Amalia, who got a little nervous. Meanwhile, Lily was looking at her husband's sister. She was a beautiful woman. The night before, Lily had had other things on her mind. Today, she noticed her gorgeous dark hair, big blue eyes and beautiful smile.

I know Jess looks like her. However, I do not eat candy wrappers. I will judge the book by its content, not its cover.

"Yesterday, it appeared to me that you were an angel from heaven," uttered Amalia.

"I would like you to address me as Lilian," Lily smiled. "We are relatives, after all, especially considering the events of yesterday. I assure you, I am only a real, living woman."

"I am very grateful to you. Peter told me everything."

Amalia glanced at her husband in a way that worried Lily. *Something is wrong, but what is it?*

"We did not do much. It is a common practice in the Khanganat."

"Don't be so modest, Lilian. You saved my life and the lives of my children. I am grateful to you."

Lily shrugged. "The main thing is that everyone is safe and sound. With your permission, dear marchioness, I would like to only..."

"Yes, of course."

Tahir approached the bed and threw away the cover. Amalia whose nightgown was the size and thickness of a sleeping bag turned red.

"I am sorry, Marchioness, but I cannot inspect you with a cover on."

"Y-yes. I understand."

Lily watched carefully. Tahir was working, and it made the woman satisfied with herself. He did his job well and asked the right questions like, *Was anything tense inside*, *Does anything hurt* and so on. Lily knew she would be better at it, but she also had more experience. She was listening carefully, but it seemed like they managed to avoid any postpartum complications. It was especially important that Amalia avoid blood infection. The Virman women would take care of it; it would be good practice for them, too.

Ingrid also said that she would not leave Lily's side before childbirth, because the death rate was too big on Virma, around fifty percent among children. Every fifth childbirth was fatal for the mother. *What would you expect, having to give birth five steps from a sheep stable, or on a dinner table that had not even been wiped?* In terms of hygiene, the most civilized of all medieval people were the Khangans. Even though they lived in a desert, it was their habit to wash every day, or at least wipe the body with a damp cloth.

"As you can see, My Lady," Tahir finished examining his patient and turned to Lily, "the stage of puerperium is going as it should. The temperature is stable; the patient is feeling adequate."

Lily nodded.

"I can see. Marchioness, we have agreed with your father-in-law that I am going to send in a couple of specially trained women this evening."

"What for?" With a brisk movement Amalia pulled her blanket over her body.

"Because you will need to stay in bed for at least ten more days." Lily gave a longer period for reassurance.

"If you think I need it…"

"It is highly compulsory. We will come back in three days to check up on you with sir din Dashar and sir Meitl. We want to make sure that you are completely out of danger."

"Of course. And what about the children?"

Lily, Tahir and Jamie approached the cradle near the bed. Without asking, the two medics took the children out of the cradle and started unwrapping them. Jamie did not miss a second to help; he realized well that his turn to marry and have children would also come in no time. It was best to learn now rather than wait until it was too late.

The children looked healthy, considering that they were twins. Each was around five and a half pounds. The firstborn was slightly smaller than the second child. They were just fine. The most important thing was for their navels to heal; otherwise, it looked like they were going to survive. The people here were tough.

That was what the doctors reported to the parents in the most elaborate form. Both mother and father were relieved and happy, but there was something that bothered Lily. She could sense that something was wrong. At first sight, everything looked perfect. There was a loving grandfather; the spouses admired each other; they had children and prosperity…but something darker hung in the air. *What is it? Only God knows.*

Lily could not figure it out, at least not then. *I will figure it out later. I am homebound now.*

***

The next day had no promise of letting Lily breathe easy. The Royal messenger showed up in the early morning, holding a formal invitation from the King, which was decorated with gold stamps and vignettes.

In short, His Majesty, King Edward the Eighth, expected the Prince of Khanganat and his people for lunch the following day.

The invitation was long and contained a lot of blabber about neighborly relations and mutual understanding. Lily only sighed. She strongly suspected that she and Alicia were going to get the same invitations, and rightly so.

***

It did not take them a long time to pack, at least not Lilian.

She had a trunk of dresses, sewn and knitted by her maids. Her only task was to choose one and put it on. The hair was also not difficult to style; Lily knew dozens of different braiding methods. Although in the other life, Aliya's hair had been short, she used to have flat mates who required braiding day and night.

What about jewelry? Emeralds suited her well. Amber was also an option, either yellow or white. Helke was still doing her magic with it.

Lily was planning to show off a new piece of jewelry at the palace. It was a golden chain with an emerald drop pendant. Too simple, one could say. It was too small for a necklace, but what if she put it on her forehead? A ferronnière was a very elegant thing. The chain was wired in a very complex way. Lily had deliberately asked Helke to choose gold that would match the color of her hair. The chain got lost in her hair but it looked as if Lily had a burning emerald star shining on her forehead. It looked extraordinarily beautiful. No one there had seen such a thing before.

Helke made a bet on the success of this idea. There were a lot of Eveerian goldsmiths in Laveri, and Helke wrote a letter to his relatives describing the new invention. *Why miss such an opportunity? It is a goldmine. Half of the court ladies would immediately want to have the same ferronnières; The second half would order them to be made immediately.*

They could be sold in so many kinds and worn in different ways, with different pendants, without pendants, triple-chained; one chain encircled the wearer's forehead and another one ran in the middle, through the wearer's hair. Lily did not remember its name but she saw pictures of it. It took a moment to make.

And making them for sale… Helke could appreciate the power of advertisement. If the Countess Earton, and maybe also the princesses, wore them…he would make a fortune. Amir could give it to the princesses as a present. *Why not? He had to give them something anyway, and a small symbolic gift would be enough.* Lily remembered the classic "flowers for women, ice-cream for kids" saying and almost chuckled. She found the whole situation quite funny.

Speaking of the present for His Majesty, it was way harder to think of even anything small. They decided to give silk and incenses brought from the embassy and a dagger encrusted with jewels found by Helke. The present was fit for a semi-official visit.

The Khangans spent unthinkably long getting ready.

***

"You there, make way, quick!"

"You there, let the most important man through!"

Lily felt like a protagonist of some animated movie; only a genie, an elephant and a villain named Jaffar were missing. Well, the palace was also different to the one in the movie, but the rest was in place.

There were dancers—six of them—and warriors. *Three dozen persons!* Amir ordered every person from the embassy to join. They took people from the ships, even the Virmans... In short, they added a lot of extras for their theatrical entry to the palace.

There were people who carried palanquins; musicians; ordinary servants with gifts. *How else would they be carried? In a palanquin? Sitting inside of it already required one to curl up into a ball like a newborn baby.*

Lily had stated that she would not go inside the rat-trap. *Alas, it is necessary to follow the rules of etiquette.* In all honesty, she had only agreed because of Amir. *After all, I cannot refuse my patient.*

Not once during the whole time did she put her head out of the carriage. Lily preferred to hide inside, she was terribly sick and a couple of times she almost vomited. Besides, she was sure that she looked stupid. Miniature beauties in oriental dresses were fit to be put inside a palanquin, but she was never miniature and never from the Middle East. And not even... *Well, I am pretty, but I do not consider myself beautiful.*

The people here were not cultured. They came running from all corners to watch, as if it was a circus performance. Lily did not need such fame at all. *What if they throw dirt at me?* Instead, they threw flowers, but to get hit by a rose in the nose was also not very pleasant.

It took them some time to get to the palace. On numerous occasions along the way, Lily made a note to herself that she had to invent mints; they might have helped to fight motion sickness. The palanquin stopped, and the head of the royal guard stuck his head inside it.

"Well, well, well, My Lady!" Her emeralds were shining bright.

"Countess Lilian Elizabeth Mariella Earton," she introduced herself.

"I thank you, Countess."

The curtain dropped again. The procession continued moving along the park with the sound of music, dancing and warriors, who now and then would bang their swords against their shields. The only positive thing about traveling inside the palanquin was that Lily's shoes and dress remained undamaged. She treasured her clothes and did not want to ruin them.

She had decided to dress simple, wearing all white.

Who is the fool who said that big women cannot wear white? She just needed to choose the right combination of style and color. As a result, Lily chose to wear a white silk empire dress that went tight at her ample breasts. She threw a green knitted lace cape over her shoulders. It looked like a gown fastened with a big emerald buckle. The cape added a lot to the look, especially because in those parts, lace was of value. Alicia doubted whether it would be appropriate to wear, but Lily did not care for anyone else's opinion. There were jealous and hating people everywhere at all times. *Let them be angry.* As long as Lily was useful, they would not touch her. She would put up a fight if need be.

Anyway, it was not the time to think unpleasant thoughts. The doors to the royal hall were about to open. Lily could hear the butler's loud voice announcing the arrival of the Prince of Khanganat.

From behind the curtain of the palanquin, Lily watched Amir get out and bow down before the King. She heard him give a long speech. He spoke for about ten minutes, in his own language, of course.

It was Lily's idea. Living a couple of months in Earton considerably improved the prince's knowledge of her language, but one had to be careful.

The speeches of kings were as precious as gold, and the same went for princes. Having a translator allowed the prince to have a tolerable margin for error, he could claim it was not his words and threaten to punish his translator for such unthinkable impudence. The ambassador embraced Lily's idea with vehemence, so Amir had to agree, but only on the condition that Lily would arrive as part of his entourage.

Lily hissed, but did not object. Although she had planned to arrive at the castle earlier, it did not matter after all. *Whoever needs me,* thought Lily, *can find me themselves.* The only thing that vexed her was her status. *Why am I a part of the entourage?* She was not from the Khanganat; she was not even related to the embassy. *What is my role then?*

When Lily asked Amir that question back at the estate, the prince jokingly suggested he introduce her as his future mother-in-law. In response, Lily promised to cut all his useless parts off if he dared to make such jokes again. Lily showed him her fist and turned to Alicia. *To hell with such ideas!* The last thing they needed was to find Miranda in a Khangan harem-where death from poison and childbirth were everyday occurrences and where doctors attended to dolls instead of real patients. *It did not make sense because it was nonsense!*

Therefore, Amir introduced Lily differently. "This is the lady who was so kind as to offer me her home... My Lady, Countess Lilian Elizabeth Mariella Earton,"

The curtain opened, and Lily was given a hand. She got out as elegantly as she could. Back at the estate, she had spent an hour getting in and out of it, until she was convinced that she could avoid face-planting in front of everyone.

The room immediately filled with the jealous ahhing of females voices. Lily looked fairly impressive; no one took notice of such nonsense as a few creases on her elegant dress. The lace looked luxuriant.

Amir Gulim stood beside the palanquin and gave Lily a hand; the woman accepted help and let him escort her to the throne. Alicia made sure that Edward was aware of all the details of the visit, so he looked calm and even approving. After all, he had ordered the boy to the palace at any cost.

Thus, he had to endure everything, including another speech that lasted about five minutes. It followed from Amir's words that the friendship between Tahir Djiaman din Dashar and Lily was a real miracle, for sir din Dashar was the best medicus of all; were it not for Lily, the poor prince would have died a year ago on the dot. The prince said he owed Lily his life. He also added that if it were in the will of His Gracious Majesty King Edward, the Prince would admire to prolong his visit in the Countess' household. *Shame be to anyone who regarded it as improper.*

Edward did give his generous permission. *How could he not?* He almost had a deal with the Khanganat in his pocket. The only thing left to do was to improve his relationship with the prince. It required meetings, presents, time…but it all became a possibility because of Lilian. The King had to give her credit.

The exchange between the King and the prince was a ping-pong game of compliments: *We are glad to see you, No, we are glad to see you even more, We are so glad that you are glad that we are glad* and so on.

Lily got bored pretty fast and began to shoot her glances at the people around her. There were the young princesses. They wore mittens and held the fans she had given them; they were all dressed up and looked greedily at her ferronnière. Lily met the look of the first princess and shortly caught the glances of the second one. She lowered her eyes slowly, as if implying, *You will have whatever you wish, take my word for it.* The girls understood and their faces immediately brightened up.

Lily did not take the dogs with her, but Leif gave an oath to the girls that he would bring them two puppies, a male puppy and a female one. He was ready to scan every inch of Laveri for them, he was going to get them at all costs.

Lily saw Alicia standing aside looking content and happy.

Sure thing, the Eartons are a big name at court now. Lily also spotted Loran. *Did he come from his estate? How curious.*

Hans Tremain was also there.

Oh sure, his status allows him to be present at such receptions. I will need to get hold of him to speak about important business.

Lily spotted a couple of other familiar faces, the Marquess Falion and his friend. The former looked quite friendly; the latter stood squinting his shiny little eyes in a way that made Lily want to gouge them.

You can glisten your eyes as much as you want. If need be, I will squish you with my left foot. How much harm could a dependent baron cause to a countess? Almost none.

Lily felt someone's stare. It was the King's favorite, the mistress of His Majesty. She looked at Lily with the eyes of a hungry cobra. *What if I answer her with an innocent look and a gentle smile?*

A smile had many shades: it could be friendly, cruel, arrogant...or maybe promising; as if inviting a dialogue, as if saying, *I am not dangerous, I don't want a feud. I want to have a conversation.* It seemed the Baroness understood it; her look slightly softened. As if in response, Lily inadvertently shook her little bag containing a box with a ferronnière. *Why not?*

A night cuckoo also had to be pleased, to prevent her "choo-choos" from choking you to death. Lily preferred bird poop to choking and resolved to remain on the friendly side.

The speeches finally ended, and His Majesty announced a break –a lunch of some kind. Huge trays with drinks and appetizers glided around the hall and the whole room transformed into a ballroom. The rules of the court were quite liberal and modern. It was perfectly fine to take a seat even when the King was present, on the condition that one's hands were busy with cards or dice. There were a few playing tables for games in the corner of the hall; Lily never got near them. She was not interested. Besides, her family was never big on card games.

Remaining solo, the Countess got quickly bored with watching the crowd. She was not surprised to find herself alone; being a new face at court, she was a difficult one to figure out for the others. Nevertheless, her peace was soon disturbed.

"My Lady," whispered a voice behind her back, "Baroness Ormt wishes you to join her company." Lily turned around and saw a servant in golden livery.

On the one hand, Ormt was the King's favorite. It was not good to spoil the relationship before it even started; however, it would have been more convenient had the Baroness approached Lily in person; Lily was a countess and a part of the royal family, she was a bird flying high. Therefore, it seemed unfit for Lily to approach Ormt at the first call, for the Baroness was only the King's "night butterfly."

Lily was faced with a dilemma.

"I suppose the Baroness can wait. You can tell her that the Countess is busy talking to His Majesty."

Lily sent a warm smile to Amir. The servant disappeared.

"Thank you for saving me…Your Majesty."

Lily had started addressing her patient by his first name a long time ago. However, in the palace she had to remain formal.

"Countess, it is my pleasure to serve you. Besides, Miranda would never forgive me…"

"Were you not supposed to be accompanying the princesses?"

"They departed for a while…" Amir's face was a strange mixture of mocking and disgust.

"To…"

"Yes…"

Amir pointed at the niche that one could smell from a mile away. Lily wrinkled her nose. Yes, it was common here, to have a pot behind a screen for a toilet; it was lucky that they even had pots instead of the floor. What a combination, the velvet of dresses and filthy straw on the floor; golden embroidery and 'potties' containing human filth, disposed of right at the back entrance or in the park.

Yuck!

Amir was obviously disgusted. As far as Lily understood, such a sight was not common in the Khanganat. Any kind of sewage or slop would reek terribly and spread disease if left under the blazing sun. For this reason, the Khangans dug out pits in the ground and used them for defecation. After a certain point, the pits were filled with sand. It was unthinkable to have pits dug out on the grounds of the palaces or inside of houses.

To make it worse for the prince, there were garbage heaps all around Laveri; the Khangans, on the other hand, transported their garbage outside of settlements and buried it in the ground. Therefore, it was quite understandable that the habits of Laveri made Amir uncomfortable, and he shared his impressions with Lily.

"I thought that here would be the same as in Earton."

"Your Majesty, Earton is an exception, not a rule."

"I understand, but it is still revolting."

The princesses returned, and approached Lilian upon noticing Amir. The elder princess was twittering on about nothing, trying to engage the prince. The younger one copied her and made small talk with Lilian. Lily helped the girl as much as she could. Yes, Joliette still had room for improvement, but so did Lily.

Gradually, Alicia and August Broklend joined the company. Lily curtsied to her father and he kissed her on both cheeks; the shipbuilder declared that his daughter was the prettiest woman alive. Amir noted that beauty had no bounds and used it as an opportunity to present the ferronnièrs to the young princesses.

Baroness Ormt cast an evil look on them from the corner of the room but did not dare to approach. It seemed like the princesses did not like her; consequently, the woman decided that it was best to stay out. Lily resolved to ignore it for now. *One cannot please everyone.*

They had a small conversation and a light dinner, which was munched and slurped with open mouths. As for the quality of the food, the abundance of spice disclosed the fact that some foods were off, at least in Lily's opinion. Soon, Edward announced the lunch over and asked all the courtiers for a walk around the park. The Baroness was invited first. Ormt gave everyone a malicious look, revealing a badly concealed triumph; she followed His Majesty outside. It was a funny sight. Edward was far from being short, and the Baroness hardly reached to his chest. It reminded Lily of a childhood fairy tale about a girl and her monkey called Anfisa—the moment where the monkey meets her father. Amir looked around and offered his right hand to Angelina and left hand to Joliette. August took Alicia by her elbow. Lily was left alone again. Then suddenly, a clear voice addressed her from behind.

"My Lady, would you let me?"

***

The man's grey eyes met Lily's green. She had never been particularly fond of Alexander Falion. He was nothing more than an unsympathetic bore. She had met people like him, terribly annoying and intrusive. *They would not leave you alone until they got right up your nose!* The marquess did not especially fancy Lily either. He preferred dark-haired, miniature women with small breasts and dark eyes. But this woman looked as if she had stepped from the pages of a Virman ballad.

She had something in her, something special which lured one in and did not leave him in peace. At first glance, she looked innocent and quiet, but one had to only look into her eyes to spot something untraceable at the very bottom of her soul. This charm of hers made every man consider himself.

Falion had another reason to speak with Countess Earton. He could not quite approach her when she was surrounded by the two princesses and the prince. They were from high society and could even dismiss him. Falion could not allow this to happen, so he stayed away and waited until the Countess was left alone.

"I thank you, Marquess."

Lily took his hand and the pair headed toward the door. The Countess remained silent, which was unusual for Falion. Usually women sought to get his attention; this woman, on the contrary, was not making the first move.

"My Lady, how did you like the palace?"

"It needs a bit of a polish with soap and water," she said dreamily. "Next time, I shall like it even more."

"Do you find it dirty here?"

"Not at all," she hid her eyes behind her lashes, "it is wonderful."

Falion did not understand whether he was being mocked, but decided to take Lily's words seriously.

"You are very friendly with the Khangans, My Lady."

"Yes, it worked out that way, Marquess."

"I apologize for being too direct, Madam, but the word goes that you happen to own a purebred Avarian stallion, is that so?"

"Yes," Lily confirmed.

"Would you be interested in selling him?"

"Sell Lidarh? Over my dead body!" Lily even forgot about politeness.

Falion smiled upon finding out that he and Lily shared a mutual passion.

"Of course not, dear Countess. That would be a crime against the kingdom. But maybe you would agree to lend me your horse for breeding?"

Lily raised her eyebrows.

"I have heard that you are an avid horse keeper."

"Yes, madam. And I swear that all measures will be taken to make sure that your horse is safe."

***

Lily had no intention of agreeing straight away. Never in her life had she had such a proposition, so she decided to take things slowly.

"I will think about it, Your Grace. You see, it is all very unexpected for me…"

"Yes, dear Countess. I understand."

"Lidarh is like a child to me he has truly become a part of me."

"I understand you very well, dear Countess."

"How long since you began specializing in horses, Marquess?"

It only takes asking a man about his hobby to get his attention. To listen to him is not a must, and one's cues could be reduced to *Really, Incredible* and *You are so clever, I would never think of it myself!* The rest can be left to a man. He will tell you what a clever and attentive companion you are.

Falion said something about purebred Avarians and, complained how the Khangans do not let any mare, or even a stallion, leave the Khangan lands. Lily was kind of half listening and trying to find an excuse to leave, when suddenly they heard a shriek from behind some trees. *Was it a moan? Was someone sick?*

Lily reacted without realizing what was happening. Her reflexes were of a true medic; she would first rush to rescue and think about the consequences later. Lily inherited the reflex from her mother; it was an innate part of her personality.

"My Lady," Tahir appeared out of nowhere.

She saw a woman on the ground, convulsing, with white foam coming out of her mouth and her eyes rolled upwards. A short plump man kneeled next to her, unsuccessfully trying to hold her head.

"She is possessed," whispered someone nearby.

What nonsense, thought Lily. Without the slightest disgust Lily kneeled down and managed to get hold of the woman's head. When she saw her pupils, she realized that she had diagnosed correctly. It was hard to confuse a clinical case of an epileptic seizure with anything else.

Lily could do nothing but wait and make sure that the woman did not hurt herself.

"Tahir, hold her so she does not hit herself against anything."

She turned the woman's head to the side to prevent her from accidentally choking; it was necessary to wait.

"What is happening to her?"

"It is epilepsy."

Lily had completely forgotten about Falion. She had a sick person before her. The patient needed urgent help. Everything else was of secondary importance.

One minute, one and a half, two minutes…it was over. Lily could physically feel the seizure coming to a stop. The body was on the ground motionless, its limbs softened and breathing effaced. There was now even more saliva coming out of the woman's mouth.

"It seems like it ended," said Lily.

"Do you think so?" doubted Tahir.

"Yes. She needs rest now; it is lucky that we came in time."

"In time for what?"

Lily looked up. At least it happened in the park and not during the reception. *But what is His Majesty doing here?* Fair enough if he was with the Baroness, Lily would have managed to put her in her place. *But no.* To the right hand of His Majesty stood an aldon. She could not mistake him for anyone else. He was tall in posture and grey-haired; his old eyes resembled the famous Tomas de Torquemada; the aldon was wearing a long cassock and jewels on his chest and hands. Thoughts about the holy inquisition started invading Lily's mind.

Come on, girl. Either you prove that the lady is not possessed, or you join her in prison.

"Just in time to help this person," Lily calmly continued.

"To help with what?"

Lily sighed and somehow managed to get up from the ground. She ignored how dirty her dress had turned. Saving people's lives, not her dress, was her priority, after all.

"Epilepsy happens to particularly sensitive people. They have a very fragile soul and such seizures can occur to them when they are worried or concerned, or when there are a lot of people and not enough air to breathe. It is her plight, not her fault."

"Is that so?"

"Yes. It happens when a woman does not get enough sleep or if she is nervous...In addition, it is harder for women than it is for men."

"Why so?"

"Men are strong. We women are fragile and weak. Even a withered flower can make us cry. How many men would join us in the sorrow over a withered flower?"

"Does this happen to many, Countess?" Falion decided to join the discussion.

"No. Only those who have a particularly sensitive soul and a delicate heart."

They heard a groan from below; The woman clearly did not realize where she was and what she was doing. Lily rushed to help her.

"Lie still and do not try to rise. Tahir!"

"I will look after her. How long does she need to lie down? Around ten minutes?"

"Yes. And two hours after that, in a more comfortable place. Is this the first time that this has happened to you?"

The lady responded with a muffled sound.

"And it happens when you are worried, unwell, or nervous, right? Okay, this is not the time for asking questions. Let us try to get you to the nearest sofa."

Tahir was ready to help and had already reached out when a tall figure lowered on his knees next to Lily.

"Madam, put your arms around me…can you?"

Lily raised her eyebrows. She did not expect Marquess Falion to be offering help; it surprised her that this insensitive young man was suddenly not afraid of smearing his suit.

With unexpected ease Falion picked up the fleshy woman's body and looked around.

"To the pergola, Marquess," prompted His Majesty softly. "I suppose that sir Din Dashar would like to join your company. And the Countess will explain to us what happened."

Lily lowered in a curtsey. She cursed the place for being so dirty; her dress was ruined. Not that it was very noticeable, but she found it unpleasant.

"Your Majesty, your order is the law for me."

"We, too, in the Khanganat, have people suffering from the disease of the sun," Tahir remarked. "We thought it was from our heat..."

"No, my friend," Lily sighed. "It is not heat, although that can also trigger the disease. It happens. A person is prone to the disease if he or she has a very sensitive soul and cannot bear the cruelty of this world; for our world is imperfect and it makes the person pass out, and induces such convulsions upon their body."

"Do they have a name, Countess?"

"In the old scroll it was called epilepsy."

"Why is it that only some people suffer from it, and mostly women? It is possible that the woman is after all possessed by the evil spirits. She is a shilda!" the aldon's eyes narrowed to slits.

"No, My Lord," Lily shook her head and calmly met the gaze of the aldon's grey eyes.

"This woman is not a 'shilda'. This is a disease and a misfortune because a person having a seizure is completely helpless. One can cause themselves harm, choke on their saliva, or bite off their tongue. The person can die if he or she is not helped in time. This is where the answer lies. What will become of a man suffering from such a disease if he happens to have a seizure on the battlefield? That would be an end of him, that is how he would meet his death. Alas!"

"Is that so! You think that anyone could be prone to this illness, but at the same time you are saying that it is the environment that induces it..."

The aldon was clever. But Lily was also not so simple.

"I would have never allowed myself to be so impudent as to assume things, My Lord. This was written by men who lived a couple of hundred years before my birth. This is their old wisdom. I am only a humble student of sir din Dashar."

"Is that why it was him who followed your instructions, and not the other way around?"

Lily batted her eyelashes.

"In times of danger, even a soldier can give an order to his commander. If the student's instruction is reasonable, why would the teacher refuse to follow? We had no time to contemplate the issue. We had to rescue the woman."

The aldon clearly did not like the answer, but he ran out of arguments.

Lily could not hold back from speaking out.

"The same books regarded a prayer to be the best medicine against such disease. A prayer could soothe the soul and give peace to a troubled mind. I suppose it would be good to call a good pastor... "

The aldon grimaced but retorted with dignity. "Countess, who gave you these books?"

Lily was innocent.

"I think it would be better if you asked my husband about the books in the Earton library. In all honesty, he might not even know himself for the books are old and were bought by his grandmother who is long gone now, Aldonai, save her soul. I was actually looking for a book about Saint Ridaline, but instead came across... Indeed, I must go and pray to the saint, it is her holy presence that saved the unfortunate woman."

Lily put her hands together in a Khangan fashion and rolled her eyes in an elegant manner. The sight was theatrically delightful, and the people appreciated this gesture. The danger had passed. His Majesty lowered his head.

"Countess, we think that you should approach the diseased woman and explain to her in detail—if sir din Dashar has not done so already—the conditions of her illness."

Lily curtsied.

"Do not leave without saying goodbye. We would like to converse with you a bit later."

Lily curtsied once more; she approached the aldon and spoke.

"I am asking you, Father, to give me a blessing for treating epilepsy."

The man frowned; he suspected Lily to be mocking him, but her eyes were innocent and her curtsy was filled with deep reverence. So, the man decided to maintain peaceful appearances. He touched Lilian's head, muttered something indefinite and blessed her with the sign of Aldonai.

"Go, child of light, and remember that only light dispels the darkness within us."

"In the name of Aldonai," echoed Lily and headed toward the pergola.

What did I get myself into?

She produced a long sigh. She understood the danger of getting into this, but she would not leave the sick woman like that. She was a doctor and gave the Hippocratic Oath. She did not care that there was no Hippocrates in this world. *I will invent him, too!*

Falion stood next to the pergola with that sponger who had tried to swear at Lily. She could not quite remember his name... *Tarney, that's it.*

"Marquess, I have to apologize for getting you into this situation."

"Everything is well, Countess. Do you know who she is?"

How would I know? Lily shook her head in denial.

"Countess Marvel is known around the court as a recluse. Her husband does show up at social occasions, but she does not usually appear at either receptions or balls."

"It is understandable, Marquess. She probably knows about her illness and does not want to have a seizure in front of everyone. The question is, why did she show up in public this time?"

"She had no choice in the matter. His Majesty the King sent her an invitation, and his will..."

"...Is law. Would you mind?"

Lily entered the pergola.

If it were not for the stains of human feces on the floor, the pergola would seem cozy; gleaming through the leaves of ivy, the sunlight embraced the shaded walkway.

Countess Marvel was lying down on something that looked like a bench, comforted by Tahir. A short, round man stood by their side and held the Countess' hand. Was it the Count? It seemed like he loved his wife; however, it was very unlikely that he could manage to carry her without Falion's help.

He and his friend had obviously followed Lily inside the pergola. She sat down next to the Countess.

"How are you feeling? Look at me, sweetheart."

Her pupils looked fine; her pulse was weak, as expected…but she was coming back to normal.

The thing that Lily was scared about the most was the possibility of a concussion. It often happened during seizures, when a person fell flat on their head; but it seemed that the ground was not hard enough to hurt Countess Marvel.

"Everything seems fine, but you need to be taken home immediately, dear Countess."

The Countess let out a sob and burst into tears. Lily overcame her squeamishness and stroked the woman on her dirty head. Lady Marvel's hair was ruined and needed a thorough wash. *They forgot to vacuum the garden today*, jokingly thought Lily.

"Do not worry, the illness receded. But if you wish to prevent such attacks in the future, you must take care of yourself. Epilepsy is not the best thing one can get."

"Epi... What?" The Countess was lost.

"I'm talking about your illness, which causes such seizures," explained Lily. "It's called epilepsy. There is nothing wrong with it, but it looks very unpleasant. And so, if you want it to never come back, or at least occur as little as possible, you must take care of yourself."

"So this is an illness?" the Countess suddenly revived. "Does it mean that I am not possessed?"

"Of course not. It's just a sickness, harmful, nasty and annoying, but a mere malady. I can show you the scroll where it is described."

"It is just a malady," the Count repeated slowly. Suddenly he grabbed Lily's hand.

"I owe you, My Lady!" He covered her hand in kisses.

"Countess! You are a miracle! But how were you able to…"

"My Lady, you and your dear husband really need to be taken home," interrupted Falion. "Did you arrive with a carriage?"

"Y-yes..." the Count looked at Falion.

"I'll send the servants down now."

"Make them come to the palace. It is better not to make the patient walk too much," intervened Lily. "And another thing, Countess Marvel, if, within a few days, you find your whole body aching, do not be surprised. Such a disease can cause a sharp muscle contraction which results in a spasm. Once the muscles relax, you might get the aching in your body. I can extrapolate on it later."

"Thank you! Thank you, Countess!"

During official receptions one had to wear official jewelry to mark their title. Lilian's emeralds, therefore, were not merely seen as trinkets. These were the hallmarks of her status; the Count realized this immediately.

"Will you be willing to accept a formal invitation to attend our household once my wife recovers from her…malady?"

"With great pleasure. I hope that you will not mind if my teacher, Tahir Djiaman din Dashar—one of the best doctors in the Khanganat—visits you tomorrow? It will be simply to ensure the quickest recovery."

"My wife and I will be very grateful to you, Countess."

Indeed, Countess Marvel was recovering before their eyes. Lily understood the woman. If Lilian had been far away from her, the harmless woman would have been accused of witchcraft. There was no way anyone could brand her as possessed now. There was a scroll, there were testimonies from the doctors...she was not a shilda, Lily would vouch for it. *And the aldon? He was a problem.*

But if they accepted what Lily was going to offer them, she would never have problems with the Church; she would not even be surprised if they decided to canonize her.

"Countess, was it really not a demon?"

Falion quietly came up behind Lily.

"No, Your Grace," she answered flatly. "I understand that the symptoms might look similar, but all diseases are insidious."

"And what causes this disease?"

"The way in which one's soul is organized; it could be lack of fresh air or unhealthy lifestyle…anything, really."

"How interesting…"

"You can learn more from Sir Din Dashar. I am only his student," said Lily very casually, but something in her words got Falion interested.

"Does Sir Din Dashar stay at your estate?"

"Yes, he and His Highness Amir Gulim."

"I suppose you will not mind me paying you a visit soon ..."

"Is it to speak with Sir Din Dashar?"

"Of course."

A crooked grin twisted Lily's lips. "I'm often busy, but sir Din Dashar..." She glanced at Tahir.

"I will be glad to see Your Grace after our classes with the Countess Earton."

Tahir played his part well.

After Alicia's lectures on the *milieu* of the court, Lily regarded such offers of visits with a certain enmity. Falion's snobbery was no better than the Ivelen's. Such people preferred to invite everyone they wanted to see to their own home. They considered it an honor from their side.

In any other circumstances, Falion would rather offer Tahir pay him a visit. However, he could sense that the doctor would be likely to refuse. He could say that he was busy with a patient, after all. As for Amir

Gulim, he would never do something that his beloved Countess Savior would not approve of. To invite the Countess to his own estate would be unthinkable, too. To accompany her outside during a royal reception was one thing. A completely different thing would be to invite her for a private visit when her husband was not around. So, harboring his own interests, the marquess was politely sent off to Maldonaya.

***

Falion understood it well. However, he needed Lilian—not Lilian herself, but the information about that illness called epilepsy. That is why Falion had to compromise.

The servant reported that the carriage of Count Marvel had arrived. Lily looked at the Count's family.

"My Lady, did you understand? You are not possessed. You are just sick, and you can cure it. We will have a chance to sit together and talk about it very soon; do not worry. It is when you worry that this malady gets right to your bone."

The Countess nodded. The Count also nodded his head a couple of times and once again tried to cover her hand with kisses, but the woman prudently stepped away.

"Tarney," Falion said to the sponger, "show them the way!"

"Sir din Dashar," immediately called out Lily, "would you be so kind as to escort the Countess?" Tahir was kind enough to agree…since he was standing closer, he took the woman by her arm and helped her to stand up from the bench. The other hand of the sick Countess was held by her husband. Tarney was left with nothing, trailing behind the doctor and the Count's family. The worst thing was that there was nothing they could do about it.

It was clearly Lily's statement that she did not trust him. If he had tried to object, he would have surely been laughed at. There was no way of hurting the bloody Khangan, either; the King would wipe him out. *What a shrew!*

Lily stared at the leaving countess and then turned to Falion.

"Marquess, would you mind walking me to my father and my mother-in-law?"

"Surely, My Lady."

***

Lily somehow managed to exit the pergola, and the pair started searching for the rest of the people. It did not take them long, for one could hear August from far away. *Who else would talk so loudly about the differences between a frigate and a Viking ship?*

"Lily," gasped Alicia upon seeing her daughter-in-law. "What happened?"

Lily briefly described what happened and got told off for being reckless. But the woman could not stay angry for too long. She expressed her gratitude at Falion and looked at August.

"I suppose it would be best if Lily and I waited for the end of the reception in the princess' bedroom."

"Very well. I will take a walk. His Majesty mentioned that he wanted to talk with both of us."

Lily nodded. She stood up like a royal, for her plumpness made her movements slower, and said farewell to Falion without offering her hand for a kiss. There had been enough kissing for today.

"Countess," Falion politely bowed, "I hope to be worthy of your future hospitality."

Lily slightly lowered her eyelashes and followed Alicia out of the room. As the old song went, "hope is a compass of the Earth", and Lily was going to put a magnet beside the hope of Falion.

***

The princesses had already returned from their walk and were glad to see Countess Earton. Lily liked to mess around with them, too, but they did not chat for long.

Lily barely had time to tell another scary story about Holmes and promised to get them puppies as soon as they brought them from Virma, before she was called forward to the King.

His Majesty, King Edward the Eighth, was moderately unhappy, and he informed Lily about it. Lily lowered her head and let the King know that she was extremely upset about offending His Majesty and would do anything in her power to make amends.

Edward sighed, looked at how genuinely upset the woman was and eased off the pressure.

"I will talk to the aldon, dear Countess. But you also will have to give him an explanation."

Lily shrugged, "Any time, Your Majesty. It is a real sickness, and I am able to show the scroll and tell him everything I know… Besides, His Majesty Amir also confirmed that they had the same illness in the Khanganat."

"Yes, My Lady. For that I am grateful. Amir is a good young man. If he replaces his father on the throne, we will establish a friendly relationship with the Khanganat."

Lily slightly lowered her eyelashes. "Serving you is an honor, Your Majesty."

Edward smiled.

"Countess, I appreciate your loyalty, and I will think about a way to reward you. Let us talk about business. Do you remember our conversation about lace and glass factories?"

"Yes, Your Majesty."

"Let us get the other interested parties involved in our discussion."

Edward rang the bell, and in a few moments August and a stout short man in his fifties walked in. The eyes of the man were sharp and clear.

"Duke Weinstein, the head of the Treasury."

"I am pleased to meet you," Lily curtsied once again.

"So, the workshops," the King said. "I have a suitable place for them. The Taral Estate."

Lily remained calm. This name did not mean anything to her. August, on the other hand, rubbed his hands.

"It became part of the Crown after the death of its last owner, Baron Taral. It is only a couple of hours' journey from your mother-in-law's home; this estate is essentially a castle on the beach. Taral itself is a strip of rock where nothing could be grown; even fish do not breed there."

"Why not, Your Majesty?"

"The same situation as in Earton. Reefs and shallow water and quicksand. Not even smugglers go there. It is impossible to dock there. In short, no one wanted it. But the castle itself is wonderful. I will give the order to strengthen its foundation and let your people settle there. Your task is to organize a workshop, employ the artisans… I will find glassblowers and seamstresses; I will let your people choose their apprentices and I promise that no one will interfere in their affairs."

People said the same thing about Earton, that it was a hole and no one could pass through its reeds.

"It is so generous of you, Your Majesty."

"Countess, the kingdom will get seventy percent of the profit, which would leave you with thirty; you, however, will be solely responsible for all the production. Is that clear?"

"I will do anything in my power, Your Majesty." Lily's look was calm and confident.

"And even more, Countess. Your know-how is splendid, but I need—"

"To produce in bulk. Is that correct, Your Majesty?"

"Exactly, dear Countess. In bulk. The more, the merrier."

"Your will is law to me, Your Majesty."

"In that case, I suggest we discuss the details, Countess. Duke, please take over."

The next two hours left Lily perplexed. The matter was discussed inside and out. It seemed like the treasurer had been quite happy with himself.

"It is a big castle and we need servants. The question is, what kind of servants? How many of them? The servants need to be paid. How much? We need horses, we need carriages to transport goods and raw materials, we need furniture in the rooms, we need to feed the artisans, we need to equip the workshops…"

We need this, we need that!

If it had not been for August, Lily would have been left utterly destroyed. But the only thing August could do was promise, control, and offer help and unconditional support.

It gave Lily a headache thinking about everything at the same time. Finally, she gave up, took out a small notebook from her elegant handbag and asked the King for permission to write things down.

A notebook? was read on the curious faces. *Well, it is nothing complicated.* Two metal rings made by Helke; the rings held the paper made by the Countess herself. It was far from perfect but it would do the job. One step at a time. The main thing was to record and remember every detail of the affair.

There were two things on Lily's mind. The first was security. She could make her father's people or those of the duke take the organizing side on themselves… Lily would simply be left to keep an eye on them to ensure they did not steal. Another thing was the travel.

The castle was too far away. *Where would I live in order to keep everything under careful control?*

The King reassured Lily that both of these problems were fixable. Security? They would sort it out; the King had enough guards. He also told them it was fine to leave the Virmans as home servants.

"Who shall we put in charge of it all?" inquired His Majesty. "Perhaps Hans Tremain. You know each other, you are close-knit, you have worked together, through thick and thin…Are you satisfied to work as a team with Hans? More than so? Excellent. And now let us go back to organizational issues."

The King could feel that all this was new to Lily and offered to give her one of the officials from the Royal Treasury to help.

She answered, "Not yet." She did not know who she could trust yet.

"Do you not trust the servants of the King?"

"No, Your Majesty. I simply do not know who is able to show sufficient prudence and wisdom to work with a woman."

"It is understandable. Very well. Tell us who you trust, talk to them; we will give you admission to the Treasury. Let it be. As to the question of dwelling, you cannot live in the Taral castle without any of the older relatives with you. It has to be either your father or Alicia. Otherwise, your spouse will be disgraced. You do not want that, do you?"

"That's right, Your Majesty."

"Therefore you must live at home, and yes, you will have to waste your time on the way there and back. It might be comforting for you to know that it only takes a couple of hours in the carriage. Riding by horse is faster. Does that sound better?"

"It sounds perfect."

"Get to work, dear Countess. Here is an order to the Treasury, here is a command to the Royal Guilds. You will get the money once you present us with the costs. Look for provisions and proceed with work. August will help you. You can go now, both of you."

Lily took a bow and departed. August looked at his daughter with pity.

Working for three days as a carpenter would have been easier, these discussions have worn her to the point of utter exhaustion. One thing is of comfort; having seen her inexperience and total ignorance of certain issues, the King is now considerably less worried. There are too many oddities surrounding the person of Countess Earton.

That same Countess Earton was homebound. She needed sleep. The work could wait until tomorrow.

***

The ships cut through the smooth surface of Lima River. The river took them into its bosom and gently swayed them on its small waves, carrying them to the embassy of Ativerna.

Richard and Jess were sitting on the deck of the flagship, preoccupied with something important–backgammon.

Richard, who liked the game very much, asked Gardwig to give it to him and taught his cousin to play, for his own good.

Those who happened to get carried away playing backgammon knew that it could easily turn into an obsession. It sucked one in no worse than quicksand, and escaping out of it required a lot of will.

But the guys did not want to escape. Ivernea was still miles away and backgammon was the only thing that kept them busy.

"Yes! Six, five!"

"Well, what do I have here I wonder... Four fives! Gotcha, Jess!"

"Don't be so sure! You locked me, but now try to keep me from escaping!"

"I will!"

Duke Falion watched them from a distance. He liked the game. He also liked the peace that reigned on the ship. But the thing he liked the most was a reward in case the diplomatic mission succeeded. The only thing that got on his nerves was the third ship.

The duke glanced across the blue waters.

Alas, it would be good to find an excuse to send this boat back home.

But it was out of the question. The embassy had already been formed; its members were selected by all the interested parties; it would have caused a logical confusion had Bernard found out that the appointed members were replaced.

Only Aldonai knew the criteria by which The Earl of Earton picked his crew. If the Earl were his son, he would have been beaten day and night. Jerrison was good at using people for his own ends, there was no doubt about that, but to judge a person's character was beyond his abilities. Anyway, it would be good if he learned from bad experiences, thought Duke Falion, however, if Earton got killed because of his own carelessness, the duke would not shed tears. His main worry was the prince and his marriage, not his idiot cousin. Even though the King was close to this loafer, Duke Falion was not going to tie shoelaces for Earton, and especially would remain on guard lest Earton's crew messed up.

If Earton wanted to frequent brothels, he could do so. If he wanted to bring his girl with him, let him deal with the consequences. The duke was not going to babysit him; he had enough of his own children. The memory of his son made Falion frown for some reason.

There was a secret harbored in the duke's chest, who was once known under the name of Old Pike.

***

Adelaide Wells sat in her cabin and embroidered out of boredom. It turned out badly, but it was merely to waste time. The lady had had a hard time.

Now and again, the court ladies wanted to disgrace her name. She often received indecent proposals from men directly to her face. Duke Falion stared at her like a wolf. Jess did not notice her. As for Richard, he looked right past her from the very beginning. It was bad and sickening. Only Altres Lort's promise warmed Adelaide's heart.

The Count was clever and realized that they would do her no harm unless the embassy was dismantled. In case it happened, if she did everything right, they would help her hide and live a normal life—a good life. She would even be happy to marry an elderly man.

The main thing she was looking for in a husband was wealth. Luckily, there were enough bonny grooms to make up for the rest.

There will be another battle to fight. Lady Wells does not give up so fast.

***

"May I come in, father?"

Bernard the Second of Ivernea lifted his head and sighed.

"Come in, Liddie."

He loved his daughter, so Lidia of Ivernea slipped into his study without fear. He would not throw an inkpot at her like he did when her brothers came in. She would not be kicked out of the room with the promise of being whipped at the stables, like many of the courtiers.

"Father, may I? I wish to talk with you…"

"Take a seat."

Bernard pointed at the chair standing beside his. The furniture in the study had seen its better days; it needed to be replaced, but the avarice of Bernard had long become proverbial. "Aldonai would sooner come down to Earth than Bernard turn generous," said the people. They were somewhat right. Either way, having received the half-ruined kingdom from his spindrift father, Bernard had not only managed to put it back on its feet, but was also able to fill his Treasury with a decent amount of gold.

Bernard was a tall, balding man who in appearance reminded one of a spider-haymaker.

Sadly, the daughter was the spitting image of her father. She looked like a twenty-first century fashion model, in other words, like a stretched out skeleton. She inherited the same pale-blue eyes and the same heavy jawline. Her hair was the color of grey dust and tightened up in a tiny knot on top of her head. She fully repeated her father's looks, not to mention his habits…

For instance, she had worn the same dress for years; she kept re-making and re-decorating this dress forever: a bean here, a patch of lace there… *They were short on money, after all; they always had to save,* she thought.

This resulted in the court of Ivernea looking quite miserable, for it was unthinkable for the courtiers to look better than their King, and the ladies to shine brighter than the princess, herself. Even though everyone had a hard time watching to not overdress, it was better than getting thrown into prison for offending the Crown.

"What is it, daughter?"

"Richard from Ativerna is heading toward Ivernea to ask for my hand."

"Not exactly, daughter. The prince is coming to have a look at you. Once he meets you, he will decide for himself whether to ask for your hand or to make a deal with Gardwig.

"It is going to be his own decision?"

"Yes, I also think that this is stupid. But Edward gave his son too much freedom."

"Father, if he likes me—"

"It is only a marriage and you should understand it perfectly well. It is the basis for a peace treaty between Ativerna and Ivernea. Besides, it is about time you got married."

"I do not want to leave my native home," her pale eyes were filled with tears. "Father, have mercy on me!"

"It is up to Richard, my daughter."

"And if he chooses me, will you give me away?"

"Yes, with a decent dowry, too. A thousand, maybe even two thousand golden ducats…we will see."

Lidia gasped. "Father, but it is such a waste!"

"Yes, but you are my only daughter. Therefore, even despite our poverty, I will show generosity."

Fortunately, Bernard did not know about the existence of province Balia. The promised thousand ducats looked like a pathetic charity. Had Lidia been a daughter of a rich baron or at least a poor count, the dowry he offered would have been quite decent, but not for a princess.

Lidia thanked her father and left the study. She ran to her bedroom and fell on her bed…

She did not want to marry. She did not want to go to Ativerna. She had reasons not to. Nevertheless, the thing she loathed even more was fighting with her father. Lidia decided for herself to push Richard away as much as possible. *Why not? He has a choice, he could make Gardwig his relative! Why do I have to sacrifice my life and wellbeing for the sake of my father's interests? I do not want to marry. No one can make me. This is what I am going to do instead…*

Lidia lay on her bed, her eyes dry and tearless, pondering a plan of action.

***

Lily came to her senses only back at home. August brewed some herbal tea for his daughter and ensured her that nothing had gone wrong. On the contrary, one could only dream of such a fortunate outcome, he said.

Lily became a partner of the state and would receive a lifetime income that amounted to thirty percent. *Maybe my children will become rich from this, who knows?* It depended on the will of the King. In other words, the factories would be working day and night as long as the King wished them to, which meant an endless flow of income.

Lily did not have to worry about spending on raw materials, machinery, or hiring and accommodating workers. She simply had an opportunity to organize everything to her liking. It was true that the whole affair depended on the royal word that was law. However, the conditions of the offer were truly royal.

There is no getting out of committing my time solely to this business. But what else would I have had to do instead? Go to balls and receptions? No way.

Upon hearing his daughter bluntly dismiss all balls and receptions, August snorted. She was just like her father. He also preferred to spend his time on his trade; he was always in the shipyards.

Besides, Lily's tasks had been far from terrible or impossible. She had to speak to the lace-makers and glassblowers about organizing the training for new artisans. Next, was to show up at the Royal Guilds with the order from the King and ask for apprentices. *Yes, the guilds would not like this, but why would I care?* Besides, many artisans made their apprentices work twice as hard for the same miserable price. The young men could get a chance in life when working for Lily.

Lily remembered her own artisans. There was no need for her to do everything alone.

August can take care of them. The first thing on the list is Edward. Second thing, hiring artisans. The *third task is to find a good manager. The fourth thing is to make Hans Tremain do a background check on every person involved in the trade. Number five, is to go the estate itself, in order to complete the sixth task of hiring the servants to work in Taral, previously checked by Tremain.*

This would leave everything ready for the others to do their jobs. The servants would need to wash and clean, the manager, present with the bills.... The artisans would have to get the trade going and start creating, as well as wait for the Countess to tell them her valuable ideas. It turned out that Lily did not have to be obsessing about every little thing. She only had to find the right people. The woman sighed in relief.

"Father, what about you?"

"Here is the thing... I have one man, he is a nice fellow and smart too; I want to switch him with Taris and send him to Earton instead. Do you mind?"

Lily shook her head.

Taris Brock was a perfect candidate. He was a clever, educated, serious man; he and Lily had worked together in the past and it turned out well. She had no objections, but she was worried about running out of time.

"Could I take his place for now, until he arrives?" It was Helke. He appeared out of nowhere.

"Sit down with us if you have something to offer," beckoned August.

August respected Eveers for their exceptional intelligence and their ability to trade; he often did business with them and was immediately able to get along with Helke. The men drank a bottle of homemade whiskey and it got them talking.

"Have you already thought about sales?" asked Helke.

Lily shrugged her shoulders.

"What is there to think about?"

"I would like to talk to you about this. As you might know, I have nephews..."

"Are you referring to the elder...Tores, right?"

"Yes, My Lady. The boy was not born a goldsmith. But he is good at getting along with people, splendid at keeping up with conversations, making deals, managing the whole process... In this, he is second to none.

I even got upset once. I know what you might be thinking, who on earth would put his trust into an Eveer? But I assure you..."

"I will speak to Tores," decided Lily, "If we get along, why not? At first, he can help to sort out the Taral estate; when Toris Brock arrives we will move your nephew to the sales unit, the time will be just right."

"What do you have in mind for the sales?" asked Helke again.

Lily answered honestly that she had not thought about it yet.

"What if I speak to our elders, My Lady?"

Lily raised her eyebrows exhibiting her utter confusion. August and Helke began explaining. The Eveers were not welcomed by anyone. Therefore, they had to hold on to one another and settle into communes. The governing of the commune was shared between three or four elders, who were selected out of the most respectable old men. The elders' role was to act as judges, advisers and settlers of conflicts. Every working Eveer paid tax to the commune, in order to help their less fortunate brothers.

In short, one could spend hours describing the customs of the Eveers. However, the most significant feature of the commune was that the Eveers were tradesmen. They had developed a network of shops and connections across the whole continent. If the Countess agreed to work with them at interest, it would still be a lot better than if she developed the business on her own. Lily contemplated this and agreed.

"I will speak to the King. If he agrees to it, I see no reason why not. We could make a contract, discuss the duties and rights of both parties, and set penalties for their violation, especially since I will only act as an intermediary. The interested party will be His Majesty."

Helke looked sad. It looked like the crafty Eveer was going to make a shady profit from this transaction. But it was not possible to make a shady profit from the transaction with Edward. However, it was not only money at stake. The Eveer could profit from getting protection, he could secure the abolishment of certain tariffs... The jeweler realized this very quickly.

"Do you really think that such an option is possible, My Lady?"

"Of course,"

Lily paused. *Yes, it was possible to do business with the Eveers, but it would be best if I stay out of it and leave it to the state.* She would speak to the King about it. *Besides, it would be a good opportunity to ask about Jamie. Alicia could test the waters first.*

Lily liked her mother-in-law, she could always trust in her willingness to help out. Even the nicest ladies were jealous of their son's wives. But Alicia seemed to be completely undisturbed by that Freudian game.

Lily's thoughts were getting out of hand. *What else could be done to improve the sales?* She had little flair for management. *Where did all the famous fashion-makers start?* They started by creating a Fashion House, as simple as that.

Theirs could be built around the trademark Mariella, in honor of the Countess' mother, with a red cross for its label.

Another thing was to open the first store. She could open it in the capital, designate a separate building for it, build a proper grand entrance. One could get lace in it, admire oneself in a huge mirror, drink something exotic from glass goblets, gossip a little, maybe have something exotic to eat... *Why not dream big?*

Lily needed to think about it further. But first, it was necessary to talk to the artisans.

***

Lily had to postpone the conversation with the girls because Tahir and Jamie demanded an explanation. What was epilepsy, where was its natural habitat, what did one treat her with and how does one fight it? There was no way out of giving them answers.

The Countess spent about ten minutes explaining the difference between an epileptic seizure and a hysterical fit. The two got confused quite often.

"My Lady, is there a cure? Back in the palace your reaction was strange..."

Lily lowered her eyelashes.

"Yes, I know. There is no medication against this disease, no root one can brew to make a potion, no stitches to close it up. I suspect that the cure will not be there for a long time."

"Usually, you suggest the ways to help. Back there…"

"I did everything I could there. First, I did not let the woman cause herself any harm. Second, I convinced her that her condition was simply an illness, and not the work of evil spirits. Living in fear of the next seizure or in fear of being persecuted would, itself, cause an illness."

"Why did you not tell us before?" Jamie could not resist asking.

"I feel like I never leave you in peace with my explanations!" Lily smiled. "It is impossible to wrestle with an immensity of knowledge, Jamie. People study medical science for decades before becoming professionals, and you want to master it in a year. Not even! It has not even been half a year, sir!"

Jamie looked down. There was truth in her words. If they had raised the boy like a baron, he would have become one. But he was raised as a medicus and it grew on him. Well, at least it meant that the Barony of Donter would always be healthy.

"You would not tell the patient that the illness is incurable, right?"

"No. I already said too much back there, but I had no choice."

Lily covered her eyes. She was exhausted. *What was she left to do? Yes, I did a foolish thing. Yes, in front of an aldon. Yes, I put myself at terrible risk. I wish I could think before I act. Is there anyone who can solidly pursue their ideal strategy in a critical situation?*

"Well," muttered Tahir, "If you said before that there was no cure…"

"There is no cure only if it is sent from above," intervened Jamie, "as a punishment."

"And then the Church intervenes," Lily sighed. "Of course the Church says that…"

She left the second half of the sentence hanging in the air. The Church and the doctors never got along very well. The former considered sickness to be a punishment for human sins. The latter cared nothing for retribution, but tried to help people. Hence, there was a conflict. Everyone who was present in the room was on the same page; but there were things that had to be left unsaid even around friends. It was safer that way.

"Therefore back there I had to exaggerate some things a little and tone down some others. But I would say that my words were a good treatment for her. First, the placebo effect…"

Having been familiar with the concept already the men nodded amicably.

"Second, my words removed the constant fear, which hung over the patient like an axe. Since all diseases start in the head…well, not all, but a high percentage of them—"

"It will make her life easier—"

"And the life of her husband, too. Every day, she lived in fear of a seizure, of being denounced to the Church or sent to the monastery. There is not much joy in such a life. This disease is neurological. One could expect anything, even insanity. Considering that she did not go insane, we can assume that the lady is strong, and her disease is mild."

"What could be done to help it?"

"Fresh air. A brew of soothing herbs…that is about it. Well, another thing that could be done is relaxing the muscles after a seizure…a hot bath with salt or oil…perhaps a massage…"

"And what can cause this disease?"

"Anything. A reaction to color, smell, sound, or all the three combined."

"I wonder…but can I really find out?" Tahir became interested.

Lily shrugged.

"Maybe. But this requires examining more than one case."

"What if I try to at least question her?"

"You are a famous healer from Khanganat, Tahir-jan. You hold all the cards."

Tahir grinned. He might have been famous, but it was the Countess who did all the healing and teaching. But one must hold a good face during a bad game. Tahir did exactly that.

"As you wish, My Lady."

Lily smiled gratefully. "Well, if there are no more questions, I'll go. I want to have a rest..."

***

Upon hearing the latest news, Marcia and the girls showed an unexpected reaction. They started crying their eyes out. Lily had to spend about two hours calming them down before they could explain what was wrong. The collective fit of female hysterics was famously a self-sustained condition.

It turned out that the women were immensely happy. It was a grand prestige. But they suggested it might be a good idea to talk to His Majesty. Before Lily's revolutionary idea, the lace had been woven in single narrow strips by ordinary dressmakers. But now, the work was going to have no end; they suggested it might be worth creating a royal Guild of Lace-makers. The Crown could provide support and protection.

Lily wrote the idea down in her notebook and decided to ask Edward about the guilds when she went to the palace with Jamie.

As it turned out, the girls were over the moon. They would become the most desired brides, they would be able to marry merchants. On the other hand, they were reluctant to part with the Countess. *But how could they combine their work with the new responsibilities?* Lily suggested a simple way out. To waste their talent remaining simple housemaids would have been a crime. It was not hard to help someone put on a dress, but to make such precious lace required great skill.

Hence Lily's order was for the girls to find students and move to the Taral estate. They would see enough of Lily there. Of course, if she needed to have a dress made or get something knitted for herself, they would be the first ones to know. That was the general consensus.

The boys, on the other hand, reacted differently. Both glassblower and blacksmith chuckled in delight. They were already thinking of working together, since they worked so well as a team. Before Lily's arrival, they could not even have dreamed of getting their own workshops and their own apprentices. Some artisans had to work for sixty years to get to that stage, but the age of the two combined barely reached forty.

Lily was pleased that for all of her artisans, dreams were coming true.

Chapter 5

The contacts in high and low societies

Amalia Ivelen looked at the twins in the crib. They were her children, hers and Peter's. Two boys, Roman and Jacob. *Peter is filled with so much joy!*

Amalia, on the other hand remembered only pain, a red sheet of pain that had covered the light and twisted her intestines in mortal spasms. There was a moment when she thought she would have died and was surprisingly not scared.

Death was only scary if there was no one waiting on the other side. She had someone who would be waiting. She knew it. Suddenly, she thought about Sessie and Jess. *I cannot leave them alone, can I?* Once again she tried to come back, but the pain was pushing her out, not letting her take a breath…she was losing the will to resist; and then it was better. A female face bent down over her, and Amalia thought she saw a saint. The saint was saying soothing speeches, and the pain receded, gradually…until she heard the cry of her newborn babies and realized she was alive.

Only after, did she realize that the saint had been Lilian Earton; only later, did she understand that the bright halo around the saint's head had been the sunset…only later…and it surprised her.

She had heard her dear brother call his wife a cow. Lilian was anything but a cow. Her eyes shined with extraordinary wisdom, her pink lips smiled, and her stature was prominent but not at all gross. She carried herself and her body with such dignity that it filled the room with awe.

The woman knew her own price, and the price was high. Before Amalia knew it, Lily was gone, replaced by three Virman women. The doctors recommended her to stay in bed for at least ten days, and she followed their instructions. The Virmans washed, scrubbed, polished and made the servants run around to and fro; if anyone complained they would reply by saying that illnesses begin when hygiene ends and that the Countess ordered them to take care of the marchioness.

Soon, Amalia noticed that she could breathe with more ease, that her children cried less, and that being rubbed with perfumed water thrice a day made her feel better. She was astonished even more when she received Lilian Earton's presents to mark the birthday of her children.

Amalia appreciated the ferronnière as well as the long shirt; the part designed to cover the breasts was made of lace and the rest was pure silk. Lily also sent other little things made of lace.

All this was made in Earton! In the middle of nowhere! At Jess's estate! Incredible.

Amalia could not wait to get out of bed. She really wanted to speak to her new relative, to understand where she got such things from, to figure out how her brother could overlook Lilian.

***

Lilian herself did not even have a spare second to write to Amalia. She was totally busy with other things. For days, Lily was trapped in her own house. She could not accept an invitation from anyone because her husband was away, and although she had been invited to attend court, she remained formally unintroduced to anyone but the aldon. It was highly unlikely that the latter would want her company.

All those curious women were trying to find a way to meet Lilian again. They could invite Alicia, but then there was a danger of her coming alone and informing that her daughter-in-law was busy and had no time for parties. To invite Alicia over alone and ask her about Lilian was another option. However, no one fancied to gossip with a viperess, lest she turn the gossip against them. The only thing left to do was to make the first step and visit Lilian; or pay Alicia a visit, to be more precise. *How else*? No one had been introduced to Lilian yet, they had only seen her at the palace.

Such twists of the local etiquette put a genuine smile on Lily's face. She said she could go somewhere with Alicia if she wanted to. But the old viperess retorted sharply.

"My darling Lily, you are a new celebrity of the court. They will show up at your door without an invitation, out of sheer curiosity. But you should keep the appearances."

" How can I do?"

"You can host them, or you can refuse."

It was Lily's time to disagree now. She could refuse them, but she must not. Her products were a novelty and had to be advertised. What were the ads like in the Middle Ages? They were simple demonstrations and verbal promotion. She needed to spread as much information about the product as she could. For this reason, it was unwise to drive the visitors away, even Maldonaya herself.

"But how do I need to hold myself in front of the visitors?"

"In any way that suits you," replied Alicia. "You are the Countess of Earton. Your husband is the King's nephew."

"But I am also a shipbuilder's daughter."

"Yes. But are you ashamed of it?"

"Not at all, but the courtiers might look down on me because of it."

"And will you let them do so?"

Lily replied with a smile. *No way.* On the one hand, the art of gossip and wit was more developed in the Middle Ages, not counting mass media. On the other hand, a person from the twenty-first century was quicker to process information. Being an undergraduate in medicine also sharpened Lily's tongue, for one could become a victim of poisonous bullying unless he could stand up for himself. As the famous university joke went, the viper on the medical emblem was a physician extracting his poison; there was a truth to this joke.

Therefore, Lily was not afraid, but the future prospects caused her to yawn. She had no choice, it was necessary to meet all these people.

So, Lily ordered her servants to clean the house once more. The first thing the servants were ordered to do upon meeting the guests was to show them the way to the bathroom, which was a wooden shed in the garden. *If I see anyone shitting under my bushes, I will bury them alive right there, to improve the compost. They can turn their own palaces and houses to shitholes, but it will never happen in the house of Countess Earton.*

***

Lily was right in her guessing. The house had seen no rest from visitors for days. Ladies came flowing in great numbers, alone and with relatives, in groups from three to five people. One thing they all shared was immense curiosity.

Lilian Earton turned into a celebrity. Her clothes, her lace, and her glass were famous, especially since her products suited men and women alike. Her clients were of all ages and all types, and they all had money.

Lilian knew that success could be achieved by knowing her client: *Tina had this but Mina did not! Mina would torture her husband until she got it, and it had to be no worse, or ideally, even better than Tina's.*

Lily smiled. She spent around six or seven hours in the living room, smiling. She spoke about her products, demonstrated them. She demonstrated lace on herself and sometimes on Miranda. But most times the little miss was not allowed in the living room, and neither were the dogs or the Khangans. They were forbidden from entering for one simple reason, because those greatest courtiers of the kingdom carried fleas with them wherever they went.

Yes, lice and fleas were always on offer, in great quantities. Therefore, Lily tried to sit as far away from the guests as she could. She tied her hair in a tight knot and had put leaves of wormwood around the room. She even put a couple underneath her skirts, for having fleas was definitely more uncomfortable.

Everyone who came around to see Lily was left surprised to find Alicia's house so clean. They were surprised at the carpets in front of every doorway, to wipe one's feet and not bring shoe dirt into the rooms.

They were equally surprised at the absence of toilet pots and the little house with *W/C* written on its doors. The first thing Lily did was order the servants to dig out ten holes in order to ensure no one had to wait and prevent the courtiers from pooping outside.

The courtiers raised their eyebrows, as if asking why she bothered with it.

"So that the others do not have to bother later when they have to scrape off the poop from the soles of their expensive shoes!" *It is highly unbecoming for gentlemen, and especially, for ladies, to happen to smell like shit.* The comment was met with silence. Perfume and incense were highly popular in this world, and used in great quantities.

Lily enjoyed explaining how the toilet was built. It was not a difficult construction. It was built like a little deconstructable house. You used it, you covered the holes with sand, and you moved to a new place. *Is it not convenient?* One could even plant things on places where there were holes, they would grow well.

The courtiers were surprised, but considered it to be one of the many weird things about Countess Earton. She liked when the house was clean; she also liked when the house smelled of flowers; she would put huge heaps of them in colorful glass vases around the house, which were seen as an incredible luxury. The women wondered if they had to do the same for fear of getting behind on fashion, the thing they feared the most.

Lily did not try to convince anyone, she did not advertise anything, only referred to the old scrolls, to the Khangans and the artisans who invented everything. She only happened to be in the right place at the right time; she only tried to do as best she could.

She also produced ethanol and the many pleasantries made with it. Oils were not in fashion in that world, but it was always possible to make something fragrant—mint, lilac, rose, lily, wormwood. Lily was not going to bother with making essential oils—it was not worth the effort—but she could make certain fragrances. They were more alcohol based, but still quite good. Lily turned it into a habit to offer towels soaked in fragrance, for one's face and hands. Thank God, makeup was not in fashion either; they had not yet invented white lead face pigment. Some fashion-followers used chalk for face foundation, which easily crumbled and vanished; beetroot would smear, soot was not the most resistant colorant for eyebrows and eyelashes. Therefore, it was not common to paint one's face and go to sleep with the same makeup to renew it in the morning. The women had to either scrape off their makeup or wipe it with a towel soaked in aromatic water infused with herbs or flowers to then put on new makeup.

The ladies were quick to appreciate Lily's eau de cologne. It took off all makeup almost without a trace; when Lily told them that the product could also improve skin quality, the women bought it immediately.

The homemade distillery worked non-stop, and Lily was going to make another six, or better ten, flasks of cologne. The Countess warned that ingesting the mixture was forbidden because it could cause poisoning. But rubbing it on skin was allowed in all quantities.

"Where did you get it from?" the women asked.

From the Khanganat. It was a blessing that the Khanganat was far, so they could not check it even if they wanted to.

"Where could we get it from?" asked the women.

"Impossible," replied Lily, "impossible yet. It will be available very soon. My father August Broklend and I are going to open something like a Fashion House in the capital."

"What is a Fashion House?"

"It is a place where great ladies can come for a cup of herbal brew with honey or a glass of wine, eat a piece of cake, and get themselves some things made of glass or lace. They will be shown all the newest items. In a word, it is the most prestigious little place."

"Where will it be?"

"We are currently looking for a building in the capital."

August was truly obsessed with the idea. He himself spoke to the heads of the guilds and handed the job over to Helke's nephew. His name was Tores Gerein, whom Lily called by his surname. Gerein quickly managed to buy a couple of buildings in the center of the city and began the construction process. They planned to join the buildings together and create a big salon with a couple of fitting rooms, storage, and the second floor for servants and artisans who would live there. This task was given to Gerein as a test of whether he was suitable for serious work or not. But the young Eveer, inspired by iridescent prospects, worked not out of fear but conscientiously.

Lily clenched her teeth, bowed, demonstrated and explained over and over again, at the same time dreaming of shooting everyone down with an AK-47. The formalities and small talk drove her up the wall.

***

The visit of Baroness Ormt made things more entertaining. Lily spoke to Alicia about her and they concluded that she was not worth the hassle. After the death of Jessamine, Edward had had two dozen women like her, each fling did not last for more than three months, to stop these favorites from getting too proud. After that term expired, each mistress was usually dismissed with a small gift in her teeth. If any of them dared to kick up a fuss, Edward kicked them out of court. It followed that, no matter what the Baroness assumed herself to be, she was a dime a dozen. Judging from Alicia's speech, the Baroness was particularly shallow, shortsighted, scandalous and stupid enough to be yapping at elephants.

The Baroness did not resist coming, after all. Her curiosity surpassed her pride, and she showed up at Lily's accompanied by her two girlfriends. They were both ugly like the atomic war and could not hold a candle to Ormt. The favorite herself, in her turn, looked pathetic next to Lilian; the Baroness realized it, and it drove her mad. She hissed and turned red. Lily was genuinely entertained watching how the Baroness was torn between the wish to bite and to learn more.

"It is such a shame, Countess, that you have to wear this mourning green color." The Baroness sighed hypocritically.

"Do not worry about me, sweetheart," laughed Lily. "I wear this green to mourn for my enemies."

"Do you have so many enemies, My Lady?"

"Of course not, Baroness. I do not mourn for living people."

A good enemy is a enemy dead. If you are not going to be good, I will murder you.

The conversation would move onto discussing novelties, ferronnières, but the Baroness always returned to the same old song.

"You have such a sweet country blush, Countess. The life in the blackwoods must be most exciting!"

"If a woman is intelligent, she will find something interesting anywhere, and will always be interesting herself. If not, it means that she is not that intelligent."

"Either way, I would not have been able to live in such a wilderness. My husband would never send me there, though. He values me highly."

"Of course, such a wife like you has to be valued highly," retorted Lily. "I have no doubt that your...talents are highly valued across the kingdom."

Ormt's eyes turned wild. She was still trying to bite.

"And why did your husband not take you with him to the embassy, Countess?"

Lily raised her eyebrows. She was tempted to mention the pregnancy. *But why?* This rumor had to be trickled into the world by Alicia, not through three old hags who advanced themselves using their intimate parts.

"The embassy commission was made up and confirmed by His Majesty. And the will of the King is law for his subjects, which is made to execute, not to discuss. Perhaps you can ask His Majesty this question?"

The hint was quite thick. But the Baroness took it indifferently.

"Oh, yes, His Majesty trusts me..."

"Of course, he trusts you to handle his most valuable things," Lily said sarcastically.

The Baroness flared up. Her friends giggled but broke off immediately.

"What are you implying, Countess?"

"Of course I mean handling state affairs. What did you think?"

But the smile on Lily's lips clearly hinted at something else.

Like any woman who achieves everything with intelligence and effort, Lily did not like ladies who tried to achieve the same in bed. She worked like a mule, studied hard, passed exams, and her classmates got the same diploma with distinction for blowing on the professor's...flute.

Back at university, a friend of Lily's had wanted to get a place in the graduate school, but the parish was the same as its priest. They chose another student, the one who was proud of her ability to perform almost all the poses from the *Kama Sutra*.

The Baroness left after a couple of hours, as malicious as Maldonaya herself. Lily fell on her bed in her room, exhausted. Hard labor was easier than maintaining social appearances.

Strange as it seemed, the visit of Marquess Falion was the only good news.

***

Alexander arrived alone on a horse. He greeted Alicia, who happened to be at home, and wiped his face and hands with a fragrant towel.

The tidiness of the household left him amazed. He brought Lily a big bunch of flowers, and a toy horse for Miranda. Falion started a lively conversation and almost immediately brought up Lidarh, after which they slowly moved to the stables. As soon as Lily saw Falion in his favorite place she had forgiven him for being boring and stiff earlier.

The marquess' heart melted upon seeing Lidarh. He walked around the Avarian like a cat around a pot of cream, not knowing how to approach him. His eyes were shining and his lips were curled in an enthusiastic smile which did not leave his face for hours after. He accepted a couple of apples, which Lily gave him to feed the horse, like royal regalia and fed the horse with them reverently.

Lidarh also liked the man, his plush nose tucked under the arm of Falion. Lily patted the horse on his gorgeous mane.

"You are a flatterer, boy! A pampered, indulged, charming rascal."

Falion smiled. "He is magnificent, Countess."

Lily nodded.

"He is wonderful. You must understand that it is impossible to part with this handsome beast."

It was written all over Falion's face that he would have never given up such a horse, even if they threatened to shoot him.

"You would not mind if I…I have a couple of very nice mares."

Lily sighed and nodded.

"I will let you have him for that only if you promise to keep him in a clean stable and be careful with him."

"How can you doubt this, My Lady!"

The marquess was genuinely offended. Lily smiled.

"I know, but you also have to understand me. My horse is very precious to me."

"That's right."

The marquess stroked the horse dreamily, and the flatterer loved it. Lily smiled.

"If you really want to you can ride him. I will not mind."

Judging from the marquess' eyes he appreciated her offer, but did not hurry to accept it.

"My Lady, I value your generosity and I have one more question to ask you."

Lily challenged Falion with her eyes.

"Tahir Djiaman din Dashar."

Lily could not resist making a joke.

"The option of riding him is not on offer at the moment."

For a few seconds the marquess looked at her in a mad, confused way, but the joke was eventually heard. Lily did not expect that the marquess capable of laughing in such a loud and joyful way. And so contagiously, too! This annoyed Lidarh and he snorted, deafened by the explosion of laughter. It took Falion about five minutes to compose himself.

"My Lady," said the marquess at last, "do you think sir din Dashar can ride with me to my estate?"

Lily sighed.

"He is a free man, not my servant or my slave. What exactly do you need? Is anybody sick?"

Falion made a meaningful gesture by lowering his eyes in anguish.

Fine. She would not lose anything by going. She could check out how they treated horses there; besides, it would be useful for Tahir's medical practice. She would not mind getting out of the house. She was a countess, after all, not a production man and not a manager. She was first and foremost a doctor. Her job was to treat people, not to 'combine an urchin and a snake to get ten meters of barbed wire', as the old Russian joke went.

"Your Grace, you can speak to him. If he agrees to go, I will not mind."

"You are very kind, My Lady."

Tahir would only agree if the Countess went with him, along with another one of his students. The marquess' honor should not be damaged, for Lily was a countess, and Jamie was almost a baron. It somehow bothered the marquess that Jamie's title was uncertain, but Tahir was adamant about it, and Falion gave in.

The next day, three doctors with the Virmans as guards went to visit the marquess. But Lily was not going to put herself in danger; she explained everything to Tahir. She would help him to examine the patient, if needed, but it was better not to get her involved.

***

The marquess greeted them at the entrance to the house. He bowed, managed to kiss Lily's hand without her getting off her saddle, received a cheerful smile in return, and went suddenly gloomy. He brought up the issue only after they had entered the house.

"Gentlemen...My Lady... I must ask you to keep everything you see and hear in secret. I understand that you might doubt the reasons why–"

With a gesture of his hand Tahir brushed off Falion's apology.

"I am a healer, Your Grace, and everything that happens between me and the patient will remain between us and the Heavenly Mare. No one else will ever find out."

Falion nodded, but it seemed that he still had doubts.

The doors to one room were different than to the others. They were made of dark oak and strips of iron and had a lock and a guard.

"How is she today?" asked Falion.

"Today was quiet."

"Look through here first, sir din Dashar." The marquess opened a little window on the door. Tahir glanced through and nodded to Lily.

"My Lady…"

It took Lily no time to set a diagnosis. She saw a half-naked woman, her shirt all holes, her body covered in dirt, her hair hanging in lumps. The woman was about thirty, and she had saliva coming out of her mouth; and such empty eyes. To diagnose her was not hard. There were options…schizophrenia, psychosis, other manic states… Lily was not strong in psychiatry. *But is it important to give it a label?* The other, more important thing, was to help, and that was not possible, not possible at all.

Lily could not even give the woman tranquilizers or haloperidol.

"How long has she been like that?"

"It started after she had a miscarriage. It worsened gradually, she started attacking people trying to kill them."

Lily nodded. They were the signs of bipolar depression.

"Was there anyone in her family who had previously suffered from anything similar?"

Falion nodded.

"Her mother killed herself. I found out after the wedding…" Judging from the faces of Lily and Tahir, Falion realized that his wife would not get help.

"Is it—"

"It is incurable," Tahir was sad but calm. "The medicine is powerless against it. We know enough to treat the ailments of the body, but not the soul."

"The soul?"

"Yes."

"What about a prayer?"

Lily did not dare to voice her thoughts. Even if Falion prayed day and night, it would change nothing.

"Do you have children?"

"A daughter."

Tahir nodded. Everything looked way worse than he had thought at first. First, the daughter was in danger of inheriting her mother's illness. Second, Falion could not get rid of his wife. If he had not had children, at least he could have changed something, provided he paid long visits to the aldon and offered him big sums. Otherwise, he was powerless. He had children, his wife was faithful. Concerning her sanity, the aldon would surely advise him to pray to Aldonai and ask for his mercy. Tahir thought that the people in the Khanganat were more intelligent.

Falion sighed and asked Lily and Tahir to keep what they saw in the highest secret. The party was invited for tea and cake, or wine and some appetizers.

The marquess promised to think about breeding Lidarh, either by bringing the mare over to Earton or by taking the stallion to his estate, whatever would suit them best. Lily had officially agreed. At last, Falion asked Tahir to have a look at his daughter when she returned from the village.

The girl was already fifteen and fit for marriage and lived in Falion, on the border with Wellster. That was where the marquess would send his wife, a thing he should have done a long time ago, since every doctor confirmed that there was no treatment.

All three medics headed home in the evening. Lily was sad. Tahir kept asking her about neurological disorders; and Jamie contemplated the issue of choosing the right woman to marry.

***

Hans Tremain was waiting for Lily at home.

"My Lady, we need to talk."

Hans looked so serious that Lily swallowed all her excuses.

"Did anything happen?"

"Yes, My Lady."

"What is it?"

They walked to the study and sat in the chairs. Hans gave Lily a meaningful look.

"My Lady, you asked me to find out who was standing behind the activities of Karl Treloney."

"And have you managed it?"

"I asked the Darcy family. Then I found the ships that Karl spoke about."

"The 'Scarlett Seagull' and 'Golden Lady'."

"They belong to the trading company Rockrest and Sons. I started slowly digging around about them and I cannot say that the news is good."

"Long story short." Lily's eyes sparked.

"Rockrest Anvar, forty-five years old. He set up his company not so long ago, around ten years."

"With what money?"

"And here is where it gets interesting. He is married, My Lady, married happily, with the daughter of a nice man called Giulio Femo."

"Who is this Femo guy?"

"It gets more exciting here. Femo works as a butler at Ivelen."

"Where?"

"Yes, for Loran Ivelen, the duke."

"And you think that he financed the whole mess?"

"I do not have any documented proof of this."

Lily plunged deep into her thoughts and mechanically nodded.

"So, this means that he can easily get away with it. The King will not give permission to interrogate him."

"That's right."

The Countess was once again looking right at the core of the problem. Even Hans struggled to find out the truth. The King would not care about who Femo was married to. It was not proof of the crime. The

Ivelens, on the other hand, were one of the oldest and most respectable families in the kingdom. Peter Ivelen was married to the sister of the Earl of Earton. This was another reason why the King would not believe. Although there were a lot of people who would sell their own mother for a couple of copper ducats.

Hans was afraid of Lilian's reaction. He had brought her the news about her relatives, after all, after that childbirth story. But the Countess surprised him with her calm response; she smiled and spoke about it in a matter-of-fact tone of voice.

"Hans. I am not going to teach you how to do things. I need to know everything about the Ivelens and their butler, to the nearest detail, up to how many times they visit the bathroom. Fair enough, it would be difficult to spy on them in the estate, but in the city…"

"I will do my best, My Lady."

"I also wanted to suggest another idea that you will definitely like. Hans, have you already thought about who you are going to recruit for my service?"

The man sighed. "As usual. There are a lot of people on the streets who would work for a penny, or do you have another idea?"

The last sentence was said with hope. He was aware of the kind of ideas the Countess usually had. They were often insanely ambitious, but if one modified them a little, they turned out great.

"The Squad of Hans Tremain."

"My Lady?"

At first, Hans thought Lily was going to bribe the Civil Guard officers. Then he questioned her sanity. In the end, it seemed like a good idea to him.

It has the potential to work out. It will be cheap and it will bring good results…

***

Misty hid behind a pile of garbage; it was a good heap of trash, nice and big. He was going to sit there for at least an hour. First, he had to chew up the crust of bread recently stolen from the bakery. The rest of the bread he put underneath his shirt, planning to take it back home. He had to eat some, too, because being starved to death, he struggled to even walk. Second, Fat Ronnie happened to stop his cart right in the middle of that very street; he furiously haggled with big Maggie over the price of bread. If that parasite spotted Misty, he would definitely demand payment.

There was no way Misty, also known as Maris Ramsay, was going to pay Fat Ronnie, especially a whole copper ducat a day, as he asked for. *Shameless greedy bastard!* Where could a boy expect to earn a copper a day? It was lucky when he managed to scrape up some food or other findings. If Misty had had a copper ducat, he would never have given it to Fat Ronnie. He would rather get something for the little ones back home, for they were always hungry. He was the oldest, he already had ten years of age. He was the breadwinner of the family. He helped his momma, brought some crumbs and bits home, but at least it was something. *Where am I supposed to earn a living? As an assistant?* That required paying a fee. It could also be that the master would choose to feed him instead of paying him money, which meant that Misty would not have been able to help his momma out.

By the time he learned…if, of course, the master did not happen to be a goon and refuse to advance him; such apprentices were called tyros, for they were permanently students. Misty knew two such cases. One of those men already had a white beard and was still a tyro. *To Maldonaya with that!* Speaking about other jobs, it was hard to earn a living in Laveri, extremely hard.

Fat Ronnie suddenly fell silent. His yelling and the yelling of Maggie unexpectedly ceased.

It was the appearance of a dandy that caused all the hassle. Misty saw a wealthy, well-dressed man with a sword at the waist, gold embroidery on his tunic, and a feather on his head, and even gloves.

Upon seeing him, Ronnie stopped haggling, threw a piece of bread at Maggie and went down the street. Misty knew the reason perfectly well. He would whistle to Crooked Louis to meet the dandy in some dark alleyway. The aftermath would be one more naked mutilated corpse, not big news for the city guards.

It got Misty thinking. *What if he tried to speak to the dandy?* Misty could try to get him out and get a ducat for it. *Why not?*

Fat Ronnie was angry at Misty as it was; it could not get worse. Misty could run away, if anything. He was light and climbed roofs like a cat.

The man had just passed by Misty's rubbish pile and the boy decided to act. "Hey, uncle!"

Hans Tremain turned around and smiled at the sooty little face that stared at him apprehensively.

"What do you want, nephew?"

"Do you care about dying?"

Hans snorted. "I have other plans. Why?"

"Fat Ronnie will soon call his gang forward and meet you in the alleyway. They will not care to even leave you a rag to cover up your shame," hissed the lad.

"Could happen," Hans shrugged. "What is your interest in warning me? Have you decided to pursue aldonship? You are too young; they won't take you."

The boy giggled, revealing a hole in place of a baby tooth.

"It is too early for me to go there. Fancy me to lead you down a secret path?"

"Fancy."

"What will you give me?"

"One ducat. Enough?"

"Three ducats" haggled the boy, excited with his own audacity.

"Two, and that's my last word."

Misty slipped out of the pile but was careful to come near.

"Show me the dough!"

Hans waved a coin in the air. Then he spat on the ground and rubbed it with his heel.

"I'd die sooner than cheat you!" The royal trustee knew the street oaths; it was his job.

Misty nodded. "Follow me, uncle."

He ran in the opposite direction of Fat Ronnie, keeping distance between him and the client, just in case. Hans followed him. He looked around quickly. It was not nighttime yet. There were still people on the streets. He himself was a mighty beast.

It was impossible for them to escape trouble.

The fatty turned out to be quite agile. When the way was blocked by three men, Misty suddenly went pale.

"Fat Ronnie!"

"I will get you, little rat!" The bloke had also recognized the boy. "As soon as we finish this courtier... Hey, you, moneybag, if you do not strike about, we promise to not mutilate your corpse. The fee for walking down our street must be paid, I'm afraid."

Hans turned around. Two more blokes were approaching them from behind. Five on one was quite a number, but not if you had a couple of aces in your sleeve. Literally.

"Is the tax high?"

"It is worth everything you have on you right now... YOUR MAJESTY." replied another one, threateningly swinging a club in his hand. It was short with a leaden end, a scary weapon in a skilled hand.

Hans looked at the trembling boy.

"Can you manage to not get in the way?"

Misty nodded briskly. He would climb any hose on any wall, his employer, on the other hand... Hans did not need to run.

He pushed the boy on the shoulder. "Go on!"

Misty ran to the nearest house, and in a blink of an eye, was up on its roof. The trio took a step forward.

But despite all expectations, Hans did not step back to fall into the hands of the blokes behind him. He ran forward so quickly that no one had time to react. A red cloud was thrown in the faces of the men. It was pepper powder. Although it was expensive, one was prepared to pay for such a great find.

The Countess recommended it and had given some to Hans. A long time ago in the other world, when nineties Russia was full of thugs stalking their victims in alleyways and the ends of dark streets, Aliya's parents did not have to worry. Their child was able to defend herself against a couple of pickpockets. They always made sure she had a couple of bags of pepper powder in her pocket. Lean and mean, she only had to throw an open pack into the face of her attacker, and it would keep him busy for a long time. Besides, it was not a self-defense spray, nothing like that. She could say she had a packet in her hands and dropped it out of fright. It only happened that it flew into his eye; it probably ripped in flight. Things like that happened. Aliya had had to use it a couple of times. Once against a dog that someone ordered to attack her, another against a man.

It was only in silly films that the hero kicked and hit a bunch of men and never managed to kill them. In real life, there was only one way for a single man to fight against three: to beat them to death.

Hans distracted his attackers and managed to slash one with a knife, hurt the other one with his own dagger, and kick the third one so hard that he dropped onto the ground. Upon turning around toward the other two, Hans realized they were gone. *Those slumdogs did not want to fight; it was not their job.*

Hans turned around for fear of having lost the boy. The lad sat on the roof and watched. "Wow, are you from the royal guards?"

"No. So are you going to show me the way or not?"

Misty climbed off the roof. The fat one was unlucky; Hans had slashed him with a knife. It was not surprising for he was the one who spoke the most. Hans understood perfectly well that to hurt the leader would make the others back off.

"Dead?"

Hans shrugged indifferently.

"He deserved it."

The boy scrupulously searched the pockets of the wounded men, took away a couple of ducats and glanced at Hans.

"Will you finish him?"

Hans paused. He stuck his sword twice. *Remorse?* He only knew what they wanted to do to him. He also knew that the only things that dirty scum were capable of were stealing, murdering and playing dirty tricks on others. *Would the world not be a better place without them?*

Well, let Aldonai punish me, if I did wrong. Aldonai remained silent, so Hans decided to consider his deed benevolent.

He followed the boy out of the slums to reward him with three ducats. Misty was knocked off his feet. He had many copper ducats now, more than the fingers on his hand, maybe more than the fingers on both hands. The dandy did not cheat him, he even gave him more and finished Fat Ronnie.

The boy wiped his nose. "Here, if you need me, ask for Misty."

"And will you come to help?"

"Why not help, if you pay, sir?" Misty tried to sound professional.

Hans pretended to think about it, although he had already decided everything for himself.

"You know, I happen to need a dozen boys for a good job."

"What job?" The lad tried to come across as an adult.

"Is there anywhere to eat? Let's head there, and I will tell you. You will get paid a good price."

"I do not agree to every job," Misty warned him.

"I do not offer you every job." Hans smiled. "Where is some food?"

The boy paused a little and pointed at the tavern nearby. "Smokey Tentacles,"

The place sounded grim, but Hans nodded. "Lead the way." It smelled so bad in the tavern that it was clear its tentacles were long rotten and decomposed. But Misty did not notice, and Hans did not care.

He was going to recruit his first boy for a detective job—the first for his Tremain Squad.

Within a week, Hans would have around thirty such boys who were ready to work for a couple of coppers a month and a bit of food. They were fearless and would work conscientiously. The network began to form.

***

Lily did not lose time, either. She was now being attacked by Pastor Vopler, the idea of book printing fondly harbored in the mind of the man. He began going around his pastoral organizations, but, because he was walking with a few printed pieces of text and told everyone that this was to benefit the Church, he was soon called forward to the aldon. Although he had to wait for hours in the waiting room, the result was worth the effort.

The rumors about Lilian Earton were spreading fast, and the aldon, himself, had witnessed the results of her deeds. The idea of printing seemed to fit her image. However, the aldon treated Vopler unfavorably to keep up the discipline. Aldon Roman was the son of a landless nobleman. It had cost the aldon a lot of blood, money, and resourcefulness to get to the top.

He carefully examined the printed text. "What is this?"

"It is paper, Reverend Father."

"Pa-per?"

"Yes. The Countess found a method for getting it out of the simplest weeds."

"What is it used for?"

"The Countess said it was made for the Church, Your Reverence."

Having put a few more pages on the table, Vopler started explaining. There were very few handwritten books, he said, and they were very expensive. The Countess' invention would help to spread religious texts all around the kingdom; even the most faraway chapels would have the ability to read sacred texts. Besides, one could even make illustrations with teachings. The Church could take it on themselves. The Countess did not insist on having a monopoly. On the contrary, she wished to leave the rights to either Edward or the aldon.

Aldon Roman listened carefully.

It could really become useful; but he could not agree to something so alien so fast.

No, I have to think thoroughly.

***

It was true that Lily did not want to have the laurels of book printing. Upon careful consideration, she realized that it was a waste of effort, and she had to preoccupy herself with her own specialty. She was a doctor, so she was going to pursue it.

But the problem was, in order to practice medicine, she had to have money and a roof. The Guild of Medicine did not get paid for nothing, they would crush anyone who tried to get into their profession.

The money was not a problem. If the Taral project succeeded, she would not have to worry about money. Even her grandchildren would gamble with peers with precious stones in place of rocks.

Edward worshipped Lily even just for her invention of the telescope. Moreover, she would surely introduce another useful thing to this world. A person who did not spend his days playing video games knew a lot of things.

Her second protection would be the Church. Lily seriously thought about book printing and realized that there were only two scenarios: either the Crown and the Church tear one another to death over it or they could peacefully share its benefits, with Lily as a mediator.

The Countess, in her turn, would have the approval from both sides, as well as her modest share. Twenty percent would satisfy her. The technology of book printing was, after all, primitive. Everyone would be left satisfied. Both the state and the Church would be able to print their own texts. In the midst of all this chaos, Lily would quietly print and promote medicine books and books for children. They used to say that, in a battle between the lion and the tiger, the winner was the monkey, who watched from a distance. Therefore, she would sit on her butt and begin monkeying around.

She took it calmly when Pastor Vopler brought news from the aldon. She was ready to talk, but first, she had to refresh the rules of etiquette in her memory.

***

It was time for Lily to step inside the holy place.

All aldons lived in temples. Her particular aldon dwelled in the main temple of Laveri. The Royal Sunday Service took place in that temple; the Church Treasury was located there; and the word went that the bowels of the temple had a prison with interrogation cells.

Lily contemplated a little and decided to take precautions. She told Alicia where and why she was going. In addition to writing a letter, she asked Hans Tremain to report everything to the King in case she got into an unfortunate accident and disappeared.

Lily was scared. To begin with, the average twenty-first-century Russian was religiously illiterate. The previous generation had either been wildly atheist, vehemently agnostic, or religiously obsessed. Either way, none of these people could sit down and explain what they stood for.

In the other world, Aliya had not been involved in matters of religion. She had quickly realized that believing in God was different from following a religion. She did believe in God, like the majority of doctors. Religion, on the other hand, with its customs and rituals, reminded her of shamans with tambourines. She was not very interested in it. *Why would I be?* God, himself, wrote only ten commandments, the rest of Christian wisdom was written and created by people, at least that was how the old joke went.

Following from that, Lily knew little about the Church and its history. The only thing Aliya could remember was the inquisition that occupied itself with torturing every woman in Europe who happened to be prettier than a scarecrow. Maybe not all women, but the history books made it seem so.

Lily did not expect anything good from the Church in her new world. *What good could it bring?* Back in Soviet times, they used to say that the Church did not need thinkers, it needed followers. Religion made people angry, believers and non-believers alike.

In short, Lily was nervous and grumpy. Pastor Vopler tried to console her, but all was in vain. He nearly got shouted at.

So, the Countess arrived at the main temple. It was beautiful, no doubt. The walls were painted blue and gold; the temple had big windows and a lot of light. One downfall was the incredible amount of filth. Lily wished to clean the temple with soap and water.

Aldon Roman was waiting for the Countess in his study. As a sign of respect to a woman, Lily was not made to boil in a hot waiting room. Lily appreciated that and politely smiled to the secretary. The boy nearly jerked from the sight of Lily's grimace, for she was nervous. The Countess entered. Vopler held the door for her and wanted to follow her inside, but the aldon refused him, and Vopler was left outside to worry about his mistress.

Lily took three steps forward, as was the custom, and dropped in a low curtsey. She looked strict and simple. She was not wearing anything expensive or exquisite. It was a white silk dress, with autumn green and yellow leaves embroidered along its hem and collar. No cleavage, no side cuts, no lace. The only thing that Lily allowed herself was lace gloves. Otherwise, she would have started biting her nails, a habit she could not get rid of even if they threatened to shoot her. A ring, a bracelet, earrings with emeralds, and her hair was braided in a French braid with white, green, and yellow strings entwined into it. It was simple and tidy.

"Rise from the low, child of light." The aldon finally acknowledged her.

Lily obeyed but did not yet lift her eyes.

"My Lady," the voice of the aldon was soft. "I am glad to receive you as my guest."

Lily looked up. "Your Reverence, your invitation is a great honor for me."

"You deserved it, dear Countess. Please, be seated."

Lily appreciated the softness of the chair and its cunning purpose, too.

On the one hand, it was a simple chair, soft and comfortable as a tribute of respect to the guest. On the other hand, it positioned the guest twenty inches below the aldon. Moreover, the chair was difficult to rise from.

Lily obediently sat on the very edge of the chair. "I thank you, Your Grace."

"Would you like some wine, Countess?"

"With your permission, just water."

"But…"

"I do not drink wine. It makes a man weak and a woman promiscuous."

The aldon nodded in appreciation of Lily's wisdom.

"You are smart, Countess. I could spend a lot of time speaking about trivialities, but let us move on to the matter. Pastor Vopler came to me with this."

He put a couple of sheets of paper on the table.

Lily glanced over.

It was a fairy tale—the life of a saint taken from the Earton library and copied and printed by Lily.

"Is that your work?"

"That is my idea. It is the work of my people."

"What is this material?"

"It is paper, cheaper than parchment. One only needs plants to make it, although not every plant would be suitable."

"How did you find out about it?"

"From the old scrolls."

"Where did you get these scrolls from?"

Lily innocently shrugged. She said she did not know, because the Earton library had existed for generations. It must have been one of them who bought the scrolls.

"Fine. Tell me, Countess, you lived in Earton for three years, in peace and quiet. Why have you become so pro-active now?"

Lily looked down. She hesitated. *To say that before she had lived in a different world? That back then they had not tried to kill her? Or that she lost her child?*

The aldon unknowingly helped her out. "Do not be shy, My Lady. Do not be afraid. You can tell me everything. Nothing will leave the walls of my study."

Will I be able to leave these walls and how far will I be allowed to go? The Countess lifted her eyes. "Your Righteousness, you know me well. I am both ashamed and scared. I have my own reasons for it."

"Is that so, Countess? What are your reasons?"

Lily was not going to make the priest happy and tell him about her dark sins.

"Your Grace, I am ashamed to talk with you about the most intimate things. You are a man, and I am a woman. Yes, I am scared, scared of being wrongly understood. I am scared that out of my own stupidity, I will fail to explain myself."

"You and stupidity are incompatible. One can call you anything but silly. Another thing you should know is that I am not a man. I am a servant of Aldonai. It is my calling to listen to people's worries and sorrows. Put trust in me."

Lily hesitated like a schoolgirl on her first date. "Your Grace, I ask you to not impose judgment on me if my words might sound harsh."

"I will not, Countess. Try to tell me everything and I am sure that we will find a common language."

Lily sighed. "I do not know where to start."

"Start from the beginning. A few years ago, you married Earl Jerrison Earton and moved to his estate. You lived there happily until last summer. But then something changed. What was it?"

"I lost my child, Your Grace," Lily looked down to conceal the malice in her eyes. "I do not know how to explain. When a new life grows inside of you, when you dream about this child, imagine him or her, dream of breastfeeding and carrying the child in your hands, singing him songs… You dream of your husband looking at you approvingly… Only to have these dreams be taken away from you. They took away everything from me." Lily paused.

"I woke up on the ashes of my broken hopes," she continued. "You know, I did not expect from life anything more than what every ordinary woman is entitled to… marriage, love, childbirth, bringing up her husband's children, seeing their happiness, and looking after her own children. Not a lot to ask for, is it?"

Lily looked up, straight into the aldon's eyes. She no longer had to lie. Aliya Skorelenok wanted this, too. This and her favorite job of a medic, but this was secondary.

"That is what every woman desires, Countess. Not everyone receives it."

"All in the will of Aldonai."

"That is correct. So, you lived peacefully…"

"Until I lost my baby. Only then, did I realize that it was out of my own stupidity. If only I had noticed that they had been poisoning me… If I had paid closer attention to that maid ... My lack of will cost my son's life."

"Your lack of will? Countess, I was told something about your husband. He had sent you to the wilderness where the manager was stealing, ten days of travel from the nearest town only to pay visits a couple of times a year. This is not proper behavior."

Lily lowered her eyelashes.

Oh, I could have said a lot about my husband, but I wont. "I cannot judge my husband. He probably had his own reasons for it."

"Oh really? Countess, did you not think that your spouse was also responsible for your misfortunes?"

Lily sighed. She realized that if she started complaining about her husband, the aldon would use it against her later. *I will not let this happen! Why don't you look for blackmail elsewhere? I will not be the one to tell you about my husband's sins.*

"Dear Father, we are so used to blaming someone else for our own troubles. We blame neighbors, relatives, friends, fate... Is it not time to find fault in ourselves and our actions?"

"This is an unusual approach, Countess."

"Understand me, Father. We are the ones to blame for what is happening to us. Yes, Aldonai's will is above us, but a lot depends on our own will."

The aldon bit his lip. He had expected anything but this. Women usually complained to him about their fate, their husbands, about everything that the Countess listed, but she was different from the rest. She blamed herself, and she tried to fix things. It was not common for a woman to think that way.

"My Lady, you lost a child. What happened next?"

"Next, I realized that I can fix things myself. There were children dying on the lands of my county, dying from starvation. Even though they are not my children, but the children of the peasants, they are still children. They are innocent. I failed to save my own child, but I can at least help these other children."

"These intentions are noble, Countess. I do not understand why you were ashamed to tell me."

"Your Grace, I believe that one should do good things without talking about it. I do not think that Aldonai is in favor of empty boasting."

The aldon rolled his eyes. "Countess, I understand why you prefer not to talk about your opinions. They are so different from most women's."

"Yes, Your Grace. I hope you understand me."

Aldon Roman shook his head. "Fine, Countess, let us move onto the subject of scrolls. How did you happen to come across them?"

"After my illness, after I lost my child, I was very weak and could do nothing apart from reading. My servant Martha brought me this scroll from the library." Lily did not lie much, Martha had brought her scrolls about the lives of saints. "It had something strange. It spoke about healing people. I did not quite understand everything it said."

"Is that when you decided to treat people?"

"If only I knew how to help myself, I would have been able to hold my own child in my hands right now… I beg you, Your Righteousness, do not make me talk about it!"

For a brief moment, the aldon felt a stab of consciousness.

"Countess, can you bring these scrolls here for me to study them?"

"I can order them brought. I have some with me."

Lily decided to give away the scroll about pharmacology. *There is no way a person could figure out what it said sober, unless they had studied it before.* Another one she could spare was a scroll on histology. *Or would it be better to give him the one about hygiene and epidemiology? Probably yes, as a PR campaign for keeping things clean.*

"All right, I will send my servant along."

"As you wish, Your Grace. I am happy to help."

"Let us move on to your invention…your pa-per."

"Dear Father, I think that it would be best if you spoke about it to His Majesty, not to me."

"Is that so?"

"There are things that people must know. One of those things is a book of Aldonai. It can be produced on paper. It will be cheap, and book printing will help to spread it around the whole kingdom. Even the poorest family will be able to have it."

Roman nodded.

"You are possibly right. But it can also bring a lot of harm. The people will be able to interpret the text as they want."

"You can print both the book and the explanation of it. Or preach and explain in the sermon itself."

Aldon Roman nodded.

"That is true. But His Majesty would—"

"Why not? Religious literature is one thing. The state could also use printing for their own good. Laws, orders, chronicles…they have to be copied by hand. If we introduce printing, we could write it only once and make hundreds of copies to spread around. It would save a lot of time."

"This is also true."

"My humble opinion is that such important things as printing should be controlled by the Church and the Crown."

"Do you not want anything for yourself, Countess?"

"I do, Father."

Aldon Roman nodded. The conversation began to make more sense. Selfless acts were conspicuously suspicious.

"First, I want to have a share of the profit."

"Right, and what is the second thing?"

"I want to print my scrolls. Even if not everything is crystal-clear now, it can become of use for our children and grandchildren. They will be able to figure it out."

"That's how it is."

"Your Grace, I am not selfless. I am ashamed to admit to it, but I have a dream. I need a lot of money to make it come true."

"Well, what is your dream?"

"You Righteousness, do you know what the doctors said to me after I revived from the illness?"

"Do not speak in puzzles, Countess…"

"They said that they treated me with enemas, bloodletting, and vomiting."

"From your miscarriage?"

"From maternity fever."

"And what helped you?"

"Only the will of Aldonai. Otherwise, I would not have survived. Your Grace, I do not want children to die because of such doctors. Tahir Djiaman din Dashar teaches me. I want to create a school…you know we have many orphans. Where are they going to end up?"

The aldon frowned. The question was not a pleasant one.

"At the very bottom of society, where else? The boys would become thieves; the girls would turn into whores. There is little joy in such prospects, but there is no other alternative for them either."

"I think that our Church can help. We can take the orphan girls and give them an education—at least basic medical practices, to help those like Duchess Marvel. They can nurse the wounded and the ill, obviously, under the patronage of the Church and with the will of Aldonai. He sends us illness but, being wise, he also delivers us from suffering so that we can contemplate what we do wrong and repent. To teach these girls would be…"

"Who would pay for educating them? The Treasury?"

"I do not ask for a share of profit for myself. I am asking to invest it in a good cause."

"Is that so, Countess? What does your husband think about it?"

"I suppose you can convince him about the benefits of my decision, either Your Grace or His Majesty the King. I wish I had had someone well-educated to help me back then, my baby could have survived."

"What will we do with your girls after?"

"Make them use their knowledge of medicine. We can send them to outposts, assign them to detachments… We can teach boys and girls at the same time. There are many people dying on the battlefields and many of them from non life-threatening wounds simply because they did not receive proper medical care."

"Hmm."

It got Aldon Roman thinking. Everything the Countess said had been quite rational, but he could not give a hasty answer.

"I will think about your proposal, Countess."

"This is more than I could expect from you, Your Grace."

"Is it not my responsibility to listen to people?"

The Countess' green eyes glimmered mischievously. "Listening is different to hearing, is it not?"

"It is very interesting how you put it."

"Correct me if I am wrong, but you, dear Father, could have simply listened to me. You could have ordered me thrown into prison. You could even have kicked me out. You could have done many things. You could have, and you still can."

"Are you not afraid?"

"I am," Lily said, "but I am not afraid of you as a person. I am afraid of your power and the things it obliges you to do."

"It is not often that I hear such words, Countess."

"In that case I will keep silent."

Did I cross the line? Did I dispel the image of a suffering woman? Lily lifted her eyelashes and met a joyful spark in the aldon's eye.

"Oh no, I will think about your proposal, but I will ask you to pay a special price for it."

There was a question in Lily's eyes.

"I would like to see you sometimes and talk with you."

"The will of Aldonai is law. Your will is law to me as well."

Aldon Roman smiled. Lily was truly an interesting woman. She was strange and different, but it seemed that she was not mean. *Why did Jerrison Earton hide her away in the wilderness this whole time?* Anyone would be proud of having such a wife. Aldon Roman had no doubt about Lily soon becoming a court celebrity. *Why would he hide such a gem?*

The aldon was utterly confused.

***

Lily arrived home late. She gave the aldon's messenger a few scrolls and plunged down in her chair. The conversation had seemed to go well. At least the aldon did not think her a witch. She avoided an anathema and was not cast away as a servant of Maldonaya. *At least not yet.* Today she walked on thin ice. *Considering my weight—* Despite everything, Lily tried not to be too hard on herself. She was quite a good-looking woman now. But one wrong move could cost her a lot. Nothing would save her from death. They would not necessarily hang her, but her murder could be made to seem like an unfortunate accident.

She had to talk to Tahir. She had to let her father know. She also had to introduce Jamie to the King as soon as possible. If something happened to her, her people would at least have a chance in life. Besides, her knowledge would not be wasted, or at least a tiny part of it.

***

Lily introduced Jamie to the King two days later.

In addition, she brought up the Taral estate. Lily's visit to the castle had left her unsatisfied. On the one hand, it was a perfect place. It was easy to guard and difficult to spy in. On the other hand, there were many things that needed to be transported there, including the food. It was not very convenient. It was one thing if it was a small-scale production, but what would they do when the scale increased? However, Lily realized that it was unrealistic to find a big spot next to the capital that would be cheap, functional, and did not cross anyone's interests. The suburbs were in high demand.

For that visit, thank God, there were no formalities or posh receptions. With Alicia's help, they had managed to enter the palace without making a fuss. They were allowed to use the back entrance and would leave the palace in the same quiet way.

Edward looked at the botanist without affection.

"So, Jamie Meitl, also known as Baron Donter, is that so?"

Jamie bowed and was glad for having picked up proper manners from Chevalier Avels.

"Your Majesty, will you allow me to relate my story to you?"

"You may."

Jamie did not fail. He honestly told the King everything he heard from his mother and his stepfather—how his father died and how Jamie lived with his grandmother; how he moved to Earton, where he came across Clive Donter.

He showed evidence; he took out miniature copies of portraits from Donter. It was evident that he was related to them. Jamie was the spitting image of some of the Donters. Edward carefully looked over everything and nodded gloomily.

"Yes, I suppose I will have to believe your story. So, you want a barony and a title."

"I am asking you to return what is mine by birthright. I promise to serve you faithfully, Your Majesty, the same as my ancestors served you.

"I will think about it. What will you do after I return your title, Baron?"

"Your Majesty, I would have liked to finish my studies. Tahir Djiaman din Dashar is my teacher."

"Is that so?"

"When we went to assist the Marchioness Ivelen's childbirth—"

"How is she doing, by the way?"

"Amalia sent a letter. She says she is in good health and she invites Alicia and the rest of us to visit them," reported Lily.

Edward's gaze softened. He loved his daughter. *After all, these two helped her.* Well, it was Tahir Djiaman din Dashar who did all the work, but he would not have been there if it was not for Lilian.

"This is good. So, Baron?"

"Yes, I thought, what if it had been my wife struggling? I would not have been able to help her."

"Hmm," Edward sighed. He realized how distressing it felt to be bent down by the weight of helplessness. When Jessamine was giving birth, he was so restless he almost wore a hole in the floor from walking up and down. This happened all four times. He would have felt much better knowing that he could help her.

"It makes sense, Baron. I agree; you need to finish your study. What will you do once you are done?"

"I will do anything that pleases Your Majesty. If you tell me to leave, I will leave. If you tell me to stay I will obey, too."

"What would you personally wish for yourself?"

"Methinks it would be incredible to join the Guild of Medicine, Your Majesty."

"A baron and a medicus?"

"It is better to be a good doctor than a bad baron. You can take my title away at any time. But my skill will remain with me forever."

Edward smiled. "I can kick you out or I can execute you."

"Everything is in your hands, Your Majesty."

"Fine, you may go, dear Baron. My people will inform you of my decision. Countess, you stay."

Lily, who had just swiftly got up from her chair, dropped in a curtsy and returned to her seat. Yes, it was the sign of royal mercy to be seated in the presence of the King. Jamie had to stand, but Lily was asked to sit down on a chair. They had brought her a truly royal one.

"I spoke with the aldon about your idea. You are right, it is not wise to leave everything in the hands of the Church, but it would also be wrong to leave the Church out of book printing. We agreed that fifty percent of the main profit would belong to the state. The aldons will get thirty, you will be entitled to what you asked for, twenty percent."

"You are so generous, Your Majesty."

"The money would return to the Royal Treasury anyway. Aldon Roman also told me about your idea with schools."

"Yes, Your Majesty?"

"I find it reasonable. My troops need doctors, literate and educated. But will you be able to"

Lily already had an answer to his question.

"Your Majesty, Tahir taught around twenty Virman women to treat and tend the wounded soldiers. I suppose they could teach the basics of medicine. The rest can be taught by one of us three. Besides, the Virman women are eager to learn more."

"I have informed you before, Countess, that I do not approve of your brotherhood with these sea pirates."

"I know that they are pirates, Your Majesty, but that is because of the treatment they get. They cannot survive otherwise. If we show them that there can be other means of making a profit, maybe they will change their trade."

"You are a true dreamer, Countess."

"I suppose so, Your Majesty. But my Virmans are proof that I am not a hopeless one, after all."

Edward smiled. "Fine. How many people are you going to educate?"

Lily took a deep breath and began explaining.

At first, she would hire around ten to fifteen people. She would employ those orphan boys Hans recruited to his Tremain Squad, or anyone else who might be useful. They would easily manage such a classroom, they already had enough practice; the ones they educated could teach the next generations. Well, it was impossible to train a surgeon in this manner, but their school would graduate many skillful nurses. *Why not? Does one have to have a medical diploma to be able to nurse someone at home?* The lives of these children and women had already taught them many skills. Lily wished to teach them nursing and the basics of surgery. That would be enough. The subjects like therapy, pediatrics and pharmacology would be reserved for those who pursued further study.

If Lily had not managed to get the approval of the Church and the Crown, she would have gotten a lot of hissing. But now she was free to do whatever she wished.

I want everyone to know that the aldon, himself, has blessed my activities!

He looked at me as if I was an idiot, but still approved. Although he did say that charity was only good in small doses. So now, Lily was not a heretic. Everything she did was blessed by Aldonai. *There are so many things one could hide behind that claim!*

Lily was going to work, teach and learn. That could only be done if she ensured she was safe from persecution. It was not that she was completely exempt from all responsibility, but it was progress.

Let's get to work!

***

Jess and Richard looked at the capital of Ivernea.

Faldero did not strike one as a gorgeous city. Laveri was at least a sea town and half of the dirt was washed off into the sea by rains and thunderstorms. Laveri was beautiful because of the sea and sand, white sails of ships and wings of seagulls. Faldero, on the other hand, was grey and miserable.

"This view makes me sick somehow," Jess broke the silence.

"It smells like mold," Richard almost regretted coming.

"Let us hope that the princess smells better." Jess winked.

Richard grimaced at him. Jess laughed and hit his cousin on the shoulder.

"Do not worry; Gardwig will always be waiting for you. And so will big-breasted Anna.

Richard sighed in sorrow. *Where art thou, my queen?*

***

The embassy of Ativerna was no better. If they could at least expect to get all facilities at Gardwig's, in Ivernea nobody even invited them to stay at the palace. Bernard was saving money on every little thing.

A few hours after their arrival, an old ambassador told them that Bernard's children resembled their father very much, including the daughter.

"I am not sure that you will like her, Prince. Lidia has a very peculiar personality. She does not part with her books; she is very economical and does not like to dress up; and when they tell her she is a young, beautiful girl, she replies that the Treasury has no spare money to spend on silly things like tinsel."

"Hmm." Richard did not know whether that was a good thing or not. It was true that such a wife was priceless in some respects, but only if the two got along together. *But what if they did not? Would I have to receive constant reprimands for every button? Would I have to sew them on myself?*

"Who else is in the family?"

"Six brothers. The eldest one, Rafael, is the heir; the others are called Adrian, Gabriel, Miguel, Julio and Esteban. The eldest brother is your age; the youngest is eight. All of them adore their sister, or at least seem to."

"Well, well!"

"In public, the royal family comes across all peace and calm. I tried to find out what passions boiled inside the family and discovered from the servants and scraps of information that His Majesty often beats the sons. It seems like he loves his daughter, though. She is a copy of her father."

"I had not realized that Bernard liked books."

"He does, but tries not to show it."

"Fine. What else can you tell me about the court?"

The story lasted until early morning. Jess yawned, but endured. Richard listened with interest. Duke Falion was even asking questions. Dried Old Pike was toothy because he was always on guard.

The first reception was going to take place in ten days. Richard relaxed after the journey, walked, played backgammon... Nothing seemed to portend trouble until Jess was suddenly overwhelmed with a heap of letters.

***

Richard, who also received a letter from his father, was sitting in the study.

My dear son,

I hope that you and your retinue are well. I also hope that you will be more careful in Ivernea than in Wellster. Duke Falion will advise you well.

We are well. Your sisters send you greetings. Now, about unpleasant things. If Jess starts to go around whorehouses, you should stop him. His wife arrived at court, and I think that she can bring a lot of use. It would be best if she remained Countess Earton and not an angry, divorced woman. If I hear any gossip, both of you will meet my wrath.

Write to me if you need anything. I hope that you will manage to choose yourself a wife.

Your loving father,

Edward the Eighth of Ativerna

Richard only blinked.

What happened that father found it necessary to write about Lilian Earton? About what she was doing, how she was feeling... Richard shook his head and plunged into deep thoughts. He only noticed that Jess had entered the room when he dropped a big pile of letters on the table.

"Read!"

Richard glanced at his cousin. The latter was evidently on edge. His eyes were lit up, his hair was messy, his fists clenched. Had he a tail, he would snap.

"What is the meaning of this?"

"Letters from Ativerna and Earton."

"Earton?"

"My *wife*," pronounced Jess in an unspeakable way, "writes to me. Have a read!"

Richard shrugged and opened the letter. The first one was from Lilian Earton.

My beloved husband,

I consider it my duty to inform you that His Majesty is asking me to come to the capital, whereabouts I am heading with all my people who happened by the will of chance to spend winter in Earton. I assure you that the estate will be left in good hands. I have found a person who will not steal (or at least who would steal in moderation).

Miranda is coming with me. I promise to look after the girl well.

Otherwise, all is well.

I pray for your health and for your fast return home.

Lilian Elizabeth Mariella Earton

"How interesting," said Richard.

"Interesting? She did not mention a word about the Khangans! Not a word! Is she taking me for a fool?"

"Well, you often took her for a fool, what goes around comes around…"

Jess was inventive with his choice of adjectives in addressing Richard's remark. Richard only snorted and took another letter from the pile.

"Miranda?"

"Yes. Just read this!"

Dear Papa,

It is great in Earton, but we are going to the capital. Lily says that they need us there! I am curious. Amir, the Prince of Khanganat, is also coming with us. He also knows a lot of fairy tales, and not like the ones Lily tells about Baron Holmes, but the Khangan ones. Also, Tahir tells me many things about medicine. I, too, will be a medicus when I grow up. If I do not become a countess like Lily, of course.

We are probably going to live in the capital, and I will write to you very often. I hope that you are well, and I will pray to Aldonai for your fast return.

Papa, can you please bring me some books as a present? Better in the Elvanian language because we learn both

Khanganian and Virmanian, but not Elvanian yet. Bring something for Lou-Lou as well. She is saying hello. She will soon grow up and have puppies.

I love you.

Miranda Catherine, Viscountess of Earton

"What is this letter?" Richard was completely confused, "I do not understand anything!"

"Me neither. It is Miranda's hand, only she writes better now. But still, Elvanian?"

"So what? It seems like she is learning it. What is wrong?"

"She never liked studying, and now this!"

"I suppose you need to talk about this with your wife."

Jess held Lily's letter by its edge like it was a dead mouse.

"I do need to talk with her, but I cannot! And what about the rest? My baby doll wants to treat people! I thought she was scared of everything!"

Richard could not find words.

"And how can the Prince of the Khanganat tell my daughter fairy tales?"

Richard was also curious about this. He had never heard any Khangan tales and never told any tales to his sisters. Maybe he should have.

"I do not know. I suppose he is recovered now?"

"At least some good news. I would not want to see the Khangan's wrath."

"The wrath of my father is already enough."

"How do you know?"

"Did he write to you, too?" questioned Richard.

Jess fell into a chair.

"He did. Have a read. All the letters are there."

The Earl of Earton,

I order you to behave according to your title. I do not want to hear about any scandal linked with your estate. Otherwise, I will send you to the border, a place without women. Be kind to your wife. I will check myself. Do not worry about your daughter, she is under my protection and care, the same as the Countess.

Edward the Eighth of Ativerna

"That's it. No greeting, no farewell."

"Yes, father got angry. Let's hope he forgets it upon our return."

"Tell me about it."

"Do not get annoyed, but for now, you will have to behave yourself like an angel."

"I am aware, thank you very much."

"And keep your trousers tight."

Jess grimaced but did not object. Richard began going through other letters and grabbed his head in distress.

Alicia Earton had written to her son that he was an idiot. She praised her daughter-in-law in most elegant expressions and chided her son for not having noticed such a diamond. She also praised Miranda and underlined the role of her mother in her upbringing. He could read her anger between the lines, as if implying that Jess had contributed nothing.

She wrote about how everyone adored Miranda for being so charming and how Prince Amir had become very friendly with her.

Richard was speechless. He began reading the last letter, which was the most shocking. It was from Count Leonard Toulon, one of the main gossipers of Ativerna. He addressed Jess. The beginning of the letter contained the news of the court, after which the Count related the news about the arrival of Countess Earton. He complimented her in abundance: *Your wife is charming, The Countess is sweet and witty, The way she dealt with Baroness Ormt deserves admiration, Your cunningness in hiding such a precious woman in the wilderness is understandable, any husband would be jealous of such a wife.*

Richard finished reading, carefully put the letter in the pile and looked at Jess.

"Is he in his right mind?"

"Can you believe that all of it is about my cow of a wife?"

Although it was unfit for a prince, Richard could not refrain from swearing. "I do not understand! How did it all come to this?"

"No idea. What is going on with this world, Richard? It seems like I am going mad."

***

Lily had no time to think about her husband. As opposed to Alicia, she had written him a long time ago, when she was still in Earton. She sent her and Miranda's letters to the embassy of Ativerna in Ivernea, supposing that her husband would be there, and had removed him from her thoughts.

Sod-off husband. I am busy as it is. The first thing that had to be done was the Taral estate. It had to be cleaned from basement to roof. In general, Lily liked Taral. It had a nice tower, and its four wings made its shape resemble a cross.

Lily decided to reserve the tower for herself and her people.

One wing was dedicated to lace-making, another; to glassblowing; the third wing was for medicine; and the fourth went to blacksmiths and book printing. The rest was up to convenience. Things were well under way. Hans reported back about creating a street boy squad that would spy on the Ivelens. As payment, Lily suggested taking some of their brothers and sisters as students of lace-makers and glassblowers.

Helke, too, could use some help if he found someone with a good eye and a steady hand, although the invention of the magnifying glass made his job a lot easier. Now, it could be fastened over the desk for examining stones. It was much more convenient.

His Majesty was skeptical about the agreement with the Eveers, but suggested the Countess try it out on the batch that she brought, if it was possible.

Lily spoke to Helke and agreed on a meeting with the Eveer Elders the next day. They were considered stupid medieval people. It was not at all like that.

It was Lily who felt stupid when they started talking about finances. If it had not been for August and his treasurer, she would have failed on all accounts. Lily regretted not having studied economics and finance.

They had finally agreed, and the Eveers heartedly accepted the gifts of lace, colored amber, and other rarities.

Lily immediately invested all the profit back and agreed on getting half of the profit in raw materials for a wholesale price. *Why not?*

They needed thread, sand for glass, and a lot of other things; best if delivered home.

Lily also had to think what to do with the road. For example, she could put rubble on it, even though this world had never seen such methods. However, Lily had to transport the products, and glass was fragile.

Another thing she needed was to hire servants, ask Hans to do background checks, reserve places for artisans to conduct interviews… After long negotiations with August, the guilds had agreed to provide them with second-rate specialists, but Lily did not care.

First, people worked well when they were paid well. Second, the employees needed to have a genuine interest in their trade. The first one was up to her, the second one was up to her people.

Lily visited the palace a couple of times more, but the meetings went rather sluggishly. They were quite informal. His Majesty simply invited the treasurer, listened to reports, and nodded. Everything had satisfied him so far.

Lily did not overspend the money allocated from the treasury; she also provided a written record of all expenses; every penny was used wisely. *What else did one need? Results? They will come in their own time.*

It was impossible to subvert the natural flow of things, in the same way that one could not make a woman give birth to a baby in a month, even by hiring nine mothers to do the job. Everyone realized it and did not hurry. Besides, the results were in place already. Lily left her house at dawn and came back no earlier than evening. This was her normal working day. She spent time with Miranda, spoke to Alicia, conversed with the Virmans...

Hans was working like a bee and had already found four spies that were paid by the guilds. Lily did not fire them. She decided to give them cleaning jobs in Taral, with either Lons or herself reporting back to the guilds in their place.

Chevalier Avels tagged along with Lily. He had long become a skillful secretary to her, and the woman was rather happy with his work.

It was the others who were unsatisfied. Alicia argued for no apparent reason, and August would tell her off for her lack of tact. His Majesty, on the other hand, kept silent, he listened and absorbed.

The aldon's messengers also came along. Lily gave them two scrolls and let them know that they were copies. She left the old ones in Earton because she was scared of losing them. They told her to bring them anyway and so she sent the ships and asked them to wait two weeks there and back by ship. The journey by land was way longer and way more tedious. Going by ship, on the other hand, was much faster, if one took the right course.

As strange as it may have seemed, Marquess Alexander Falion became a common guest at Earton. He usually arrived in the evening and as a rule spent around thirty minutes or more with Lidarh, but Lily also received his attention.

He gave her flowers, sweets, and even presented her with singing birds in a cage; Mirrie also received sweets, but that meant nothing to Lily. She did not think that Falion was even infatuated by her, and women have an instinct for such things. Alexander treated her in a very particular way. She was presented with gifts, but they were given as if in passing, they were of secondary importance. Being able to breed Lidarh was of first importance. There was also another thing...

Falion had had to conceal his wife for so long, that now he was happy to talk about her at least to someone, especially knowing that the truth about his wife would never pass Lily's lips.

As the Countess figured out, there had never been any love between Alexander and his wife. It had simply been an arranged marriage, a financial contract. Things went fine at the beginning. They had one child, and then another, but when Falion's wife got pregnant with a third child… Renée always used to be too scandalous and too ill-tempered, but Falion did not pay much attention to it at the beginning.

Her temperament got worse after each pregnancy, but Falion did not find it surprising. Childbirth was not an easy task. The first two childbirths were successful. The third one, however… Renée lost the child and became seriously ill. She spent almost ten days in severe fever, and when she seemed to have recovered, everything went downhill—from hysterias to scandals; from scandals to psychotic fits; from fits to oblivion during which her person was replaced by a humanoid animal in her body.

They noticed it too late. Apart from mixed responses, the doctors gave her healing mixtures, from expensive wines to frog juice. Nothing seemed to help. Falion started losing hope, and when his son died in an accident, his spirits almost collapsed. In addition, everything had to be kept in secret.

Who would choose to have mad relatives? In the name of Aldonai, do not let me go insane.

Lily was like a scalpel opening a painful wound. Falion poured his tortured soul out to her. Lily did not mind. She pursued her own goals.

When Falion was not prattling on about his wife, he was an interesting interlocutor. Lily liked talking to him. In addition, he took a bath about once every ten days. One could call him a metrosexual. Being his friend was quite acceptable, in all respects. In addition, Falion knew a lot about the court and told Lily about the most outstanding of its representatives. Lily listened and learned.

Another interesting fact was that Alexander had been a close friend of Jerrison Earton. Lily spoke about him quite often, making Falion tell her about his friend. For Lily, the Earl of Earton remained an unsolved mathematical equation. Besides, Lily always went to the fields with Falion without taking too many guards along…until the attempt on her life.

***

The danger came out of the blue. When they had had enough of horse riding along the fields, Lily and Falion rode alongside one another, engaged in a peaceful conversation. The marquess was quite well-versed in classical poetry, and Lily also showed herself to be educated. She told him about Pushkin, Lermontov, Blok, Ahmatova...she taught him about all the Russian poets of the Romantic era.

Falion was enjoying listening, when the wind blew a handful of dust into Lily's face. She started coughing, slowed down her horse and reached for a handkerchief. The rest was blurred into a colorless film.

It was either a bee or a horsefly which bit the horse of one of the guardsmen. The horse jerked forward, and a mute whistle was heard.

The guard grabbed his shoulder. His name was Tristan, and he found an arrow with dark feathers sticking out of his flesh. The arrow was not short; it went right through the man's shoulder. The next instant, somebody's hands took Lily off her horse.

"Stay on the ground!"

The Countess obeyed and remained on the ground splayed like a starfish. Silly thoughts occupied her head, *The dress will be fine; we have soap, It is good that I lost weight otherwise my stomach would get in the way and Lidarh...*

Lidarh was held by the reins by the wounded Tristan. His face twisted from the pain but he still held the horse with his wounded hand. The horse went slightly anxious upon sensing the blood. The Avarians were clever creatures, so Lidarh stood still like a statue. This is what helped Tristan to hold his reins, because his other hand was holding onto the handle of his dagger. The wound made him vulnerable, but not less dangerous. Leis made sure the Countess' guards were the best men, and Tristan could trap a fly with a throw of a dagger.

"Can I stand up?"

"Not yet, mistress."

"How long do I have to lie down?"

Tristan squinted and peered into the distance; Lily could not see a thing.

"It seems like not long."

She heard the galloping of Falion's horse and the man jumped off his horse beside Lily.

"Are you hurt, Lilian?"

He did not notice how he had started calling Lily by her first name.

"Not at all," Lily wiped the road dust from her forehead. At least it was not damp. "What about…"

"He has escaped, bastard! Excuse my language, Countess."

Lily was also tempted to swear, but the sight of Tristan made her forget about everything. The man grew weak and had to sit down on the ground.

There was only one thing before Lily, a man who needed first aid, or better, to stabilize the arrow to prevent more blood loss, put a bandage on and head home.

Lily had to be the one to do all the work, the man only looked around. The marquess took off the feathered end of the arrow to facilitate getting it out later.

The murderer disappeared.

***

To put it mildly, the house had turned into havoc.

Alicia was agitated, Miranda held on to her stepmother's neck, Leif and Leis were telling Lily off for being careless.

She did not care for their chiding remarks; her main mission was to help Tristan.

The man was feeling worse. He had an end-to-end wound, a torn vessel, blood loss, and a threat of infection. The infirmary filled up with people. Ingrid came running with Tahir, who was already dressed in a white robe and had put his beard away in order to assist Lily.

"Scalpel."

With a sure move, Lily took the dirty stick out of the man's shoulder, washed the wound, stitched it up, and put in a drain. Tahir admired her economical, precise moves. This was practice to him; he could not have learned it from books.

Finally, Lily straightened up and tightened the last stitch.

"Now you will have to stay in bed. If everything goes fine you will not get a blood infection.

"I will appoint people to attend to him. Lily, maybe you need to rest?" Ingrid also addressed the Countess by her first name, although not usually in public.

"I will sit in the study for now. Ingrid, I leave you in charge. Call me if you need me."

Hans Tremain was swift to arrive. Upon finding out about the attack, he took his dogs and people and went off to where it had happened, but was unable to find the villain. The dogs took the trail but could not follow it far. The murderer turned out to be clever and had walked through the stream.

Despite Tahir's and Jamie's efforts to put her to bed, Lily sat in the study, carefully analyzing everything that had happened.

Who would do such a thing and why? Maybe it was the Ivelens? But Hans watched their every move. Who else might have anything against her? The King's favorite? That fool cannot take revenge on everyone who puts her down, that would be unlikely. Who else?

Lily had no other ideas as to who might have committed the crime. It made her angry. Now, she had to leave the house under guard.

"My Lady?"

It was Marquess Falion. Lily greeted him with a weak smile. "I am glad to see you, Marquess."

"Are you all right?"

"No."

The marquess stood in the doorway hesitating and eventually walked in.

"Do you have wine?"

"No."

"You need to have a drink."

"I don't."

The woman rose from her seat abruptly and started pacing the room.

"Lilian…"

"Don't!" snapped Lily. "Has anyone ever told you that women get used to wine very quickly, and later it disastrously affects their children, their mind, and their lives! Did you know that? So, do not offer me that stuff! Leave me alone!"

At that point, anyone would turn around and leave to never come back, but instead, he took a step forward. He took her in his confident arms and pulled her close to his chest.

"Everything is fine, girl. All is well. You are alive, and so is everybody else."

"But what if it was not fine?"

"The circle of life ends with death. It is natural. Sooner or later, we will all be gone."

"But I don't want someone else's death to be my fault!"

"Of course it would not be your fault. You had nothing to do with it. Relax, girl. You need to cry. Tears will help."

Lily let out a sob. She grabbed Falion, holding on to him like a rope over an abyss, and hot tears streamed down her face.

***

The marquess stroked her hair and thought that torturing the attackers would not be a severe enough punishment. *Bastards… I need to talk to the captain of her guard, to somehow improve her protection. I will not let anyone hurt her!*

It took Lily a long time before she could stop sniveling. Finally, she stopped weeping and started thinking straight. She pulled away from Falion and wiped her face.

"Thank you, Marquess."

"Alexander."

"Thank you, Alexander."

"You are always welcome. I will still bring you some mulled wine, otherwise you will not be able to fall asleep tonight."

"A little bit of wine, mulling spices, and fruit, if possible…"

***

Falion kissed the Countess' hand and left Lily thinking about the attempted murder.

It happened, but no one died. Fine. I will need to do something to make sure it never happens again; for example, improve the patrolling. I will manage. We must get these bastards! What kind of fashion is it, to try to kill a small, fragile and vulnerable woman! They could at least have chosen to target my husband! She would even thank them for it.

***

Meanwhile, her husband was approaching the palace in Ivernea. Richard sat in the carriage, angered and frustrated. It had been quite a while since they arrived in Ivernea, but they heard nothing from Bernard. Gardwig was far more welcoming.

If the daughter was like her father he needed to run away as fast as he could, but first it was necessary at least to meet her.

The palace was a miserable sight. The garden was overgrown with weeds, perhaps for the lack of money to pay someone to take care of it. The walls were grey. Every second window was covered with parchment; heavy wooden blinds on all windows… and the dirt. Every corner was evidently a place to relieve oneself. Jess would not mind the dirt, but he noticed the rusty weapons on the walls, crippling tapestries with threads coming out of all sides; the courtiers were dressed so poorly that in Ativerna they would have been taken for some unfortunate merchants.

The most unpleasant thing was the lean expressions on people's faces. It made Jess slightly shiver.

Richard also felt uneasy. The court of Gardwig stood out as exceptionally over-extravagant, whereas in Ativerna they preferred being modest... but Ivernea was a whole new level.

Yuck! Narrow corridors, torches, dusty heavy curtains of uncertain faded color...and the throne room.

It was brighter in there. Big windows were open. The breeze was playfully messing with the ladies' hair, going under their petticoats, fiddling with men's vests...Richard, on the other hand, was not feeling it and made frequent glances at the exit. His face went darker every minute.

Bernard should have been born a hoarder, not a king. He was a grey man; he had a grey tunic, grey trousers, grey face, dusty grey hair... Only the crown animated his whole image, but even its gold failed to shine, as if touched by that profound all-embracing sadness of the palace. The King's face was also dull. His eyes were somehow lost in it, somewhere between the long cartilaginous nose and the massive chin. His lips were thin and narrow, almost invisible, as if to balance out his bulky features, to match with his unremarkable eyes.

His eyes were small, grey, frankly judgmental. Under his blank stare, Richard suddenly felt himself looking out of place, whereas Jess simply got mad. He was annoyed at everything: at this greyness, the misery that was felt in every corner of the palace, the glances of courtiers who stood as a wall as if they concealed someone behind. The Earl suddenly felt an urgent need to get drunk and kick someone's ass.

They were not welcome here.

"Your Majesty." Richard was first to greet the King. "I am filled with joy to be accepted at your court. It is a great honor for me."

Bernard slightly tilted his head. "We are also happy to see you here. We hope that your stay will be fruitful for both parties." His voice creaked like a rusty door.

"Let me introduce you to my wife. Her Majesty Dalia."

The queen looked somehow…plain. Richard remembered Jessie being a bright sparkling flame, Milia was a caring mother, Anna would have looked like a courtesan queen, but Dalia…she was a blank space. She was a shadow of her husband. One could even call her pretty, with blue eyes and light brown hair, were it not for the expression of stupid obedience and dull indifference on her face.

"And here are my sons. My eldest son and heir, Rafael. Adrian is my second son, followed by Gabriel and Miguel."

Richard noticed that the sons looked just like their father; the same brown-grey hair, the same unremarkable lips and eyes, identical long chins and noses. Julio and Esteban must have been too young to be present.

"My daughter, Lidia."

The brothers moved aside to reveal Lidia. She was not ugly. If one considered the features of her face separately, they would find her to be good-looking. She was tall and bony, like a stick, without breasts and butt. Her hair was the same mousy color, and she had her father's eyes, only slightly more blue.

It was the expression on her face that made all the difference to Richard. Men do not perceive a woman in fragments but look at her as a whole. In general, Richard did not like the girl.

There was something else in her, perhaps dislike of the proposed groom.

"Your Majesty," Richard bowed. Lidia responded with a curtsey and a hostile look.

"I suppose you can go for a walk around the park, obviously accompanied by the young man."

Richard assured the King that it was a dream of his life and gallantly offered his hand to Lidia. The princess accepted it, and the whole party plodded toward the garden.

When they left, Bernard smirked. "Do you think it is going to happen?"

Dalia shrugged. She had learned a long time ago to say what her husband wanted to hear.

"If it pleases you, Your Majesty."

Bernard was satisfied. Of course, everything was in his will. He was a king after all.

***

Richard led the princess along the garden. She was slightly shorter than him which made it comfortable to walk beside her. Two princes, her brothers, followed at a very close distance. It was the elder one and possibly the one after him… Maybe Richard would learn to distinguish between them, but for now they looked to him too much like their father.

Richard suddenly remembered that he ought to make conversation. He started with standardized, all too familiar phrases. "Your Majesty, your eyes…they are the color of the sea..."

"My teeth are pearls, and my lips are corals…" continued Lidia. "Thank you, I've heard it many times."

"Who dared to do so!" Richard protested theatrically, "Just say a word, Your Majesty!"

"Everyone who had little imagination to come up with something new."

Lidia was not going to build bridges, but Richard could not retreat, he had no other option.

"Your Majesty, I promise not to make any more cliché compliments. But maybe you will tell me something about yourself? What are your hobbies? What do you like?"

"Loneliness."

It was clear as day: an explicit rejection. If it were a beautiful woman, he would have thought about whether to bother.

She must think she is so swell! Boy, her looks alone make me want to cry! And what airs she puts on! It is as if I was not a prince who came asking her for her hand, but a stable boy who pinched her on the buttocks!

"I really feel you, Princess." Richard unburdened his soul. "It is true, sometimes it is better to be alone—"

"Instead of spending it in a terrible company."

They reached a mutual understanding, which was far from a peace treaty. Richard remembered Anna tiptoeing around him and frowned.

***

Lidia thought of saying more nasty things. She did not need that handsome man who looked at her with such superiority. *Does he expect me to throw myself at him and cry from happiness? He showed up to choose whether he liked me for a bride or not, what a great deed! Not a chance, boy.*

The princess remained stubbornly silent. Richard, too, was silent for a while, but after all brought himself to ask, "Princess, how do you feel about poetry?"

"I have nothing to do with it, Your Highness."

"Perhaps you would like me to read you something? I know a lot of poetry; you will like it."

"If I want to read something, I can read it myself."

***

It was impossible to express oneself more clearly. Richard looked around. Lidia's brothers fell behind. *Should I be direct?*

"Your Highness, why do you dislike me so much?"

Such a direct question made Lidia freeze for a moment. She then gave him a clear reply. "You are not a gold coin to me that I have to like. It is the first time in my life that I have seen you, Your Highness."

"Yes, with such a significant purpose as well."

"And that, too, contributes to my feeling toward you."

"Do you not want to get married, Lidia?"

"Not to you," the girl answered shortly.

Richard was surprised. *Have there really been any hunters for such prey?* "You can refuse me and I will leave right away."

"I cannot," Lidia knitted her transparent brows, "My Father will be upset with me if I do."

"And how much time do we need to spend together to not get him upset?"

"I believe that one month will be enough to convince him of the lack of mutual sympathy," Lidia abandoned all manners and appearances and spoke directly. "You do not like me; I do not like you. A month should be an optimal period. My father will understand that we do not fit each other, and you will leave."

"And what if you change your mind?"

Lidia snorted.

"I have heard you," nodded Richard. The situation entertained him. *All the beauties of Ativerna queue up to marry me, in Wellster and Ivernea as well...except for this scarecrow in ancient rags! She is a princess only in name.*

"I suggest we make a pact," continued Richard.

"What pact?"

"A peace pact. You do not hiss at me this month, and I court you to convince your father that we have tried."

Lidia nodded.

"Yes, it will be better. Do you mind if I call you Richard?"

"No. I am too allowed to call you Lidia then, I guess?"

"Let us go somewhere where we will not be heard."

"Deal."

***

Richard did not feel offended. Lidia, though ugly, was a princess, equal to him by status. She could say what she wanted. *She does not want me? Great! Good riddance to bad rubbish.*

He would still need to pass the time here. And after, he could go to Anna. She was a better candidate. At least, she felt good to the touch. *Who would want to bruise himself lying on top of Lidia's bony breasts?*

Yuck.

However, this situation was more insulting to Jess. "Are you serious?"

"Quite. She clearly does not want me for a husband."

"If every woman started figuring out what she wanted…"

"Are not you talking about your wife?" teased Richard.

"Yes, about her as well. It is unbelievable, everywhere I turn there is Lily. Lily, Lily, everywhere is Lily! Miranda cannot imagine her life without Lily!"

"She can, but she does not want to."

"I will sort this out," said Jess. "By the way, can you be my censor?"

"What do you mean?"

"I wrote letters to my wife and Miranda."

"Come closer, let me see." Richard was too lazy too stand up.

He quickly ran his eyes over Jess's letter to Miranda. It was nothing special. *I love you, sending you kisses, will bring you presents, promise to write more often. Love and kisses, Study well and I will be sure to bring you…*

The letter to his wife was more of a big deal.

My beloved wife,

I will be glad to see you when you return home. How did you receive my mother? And what about my sister? I hope you are doing well. As for Earton, I fully approve of your decision.

I shall be back in Ativerna by autumn, we can talk in detail then.

Richard only shook his head.

"You would even write more to a mistress…"

"Yes, she is not my mistress! She is my wife."

"Exactly."

"Richard, I have no idea what to write about!" exploded Jess. "Kill me now. I do not know. My uncle is enraged; Miranda is delighted; this gossiper praises my *cow*, Maldonaya take him! My mind is going around. If I write something the uncle does not like, he might send me to the border forever."

"You would not want that?"

"Would you?"

"Fine, do not get angry. The letter will do. You can sort things out once you are back."

"Yes, true. Besides you do not want to marry this horse."

"Lidia?"

"Who else!"

Indeed, Jess spotted correctly; there was something horse-like about Lidia.

"She does not want me either."

"What a fool. She does not even understand what she is losing."

"It is even better for me like that. Let us wait for a month and go home."

"Well, yes." Jess sighed. "You know, sometimes I get scared. I am afraid that I will come home and everything will be changed—Ativerna, Laveri, everything!"

Richard only shook his head. It was time to rescue his cousin from such depression. "Jess, can you pour me some wine?"

The cousin complied with the request, but his blue eyes remained sad and tired.

***

Altres Lort read the report of his agent.

Very good. Lidia and Richard did not like each other. Lidia swiftly gave him the brush-off. Altres expected this. *But is it necessary to take protective measures? Of course.* The man began to think about his future plan of action. He needed to give instructions to that slut from the embassy. He also needed to give orders to his agent. There was no need for a public scandal. As for a small one, a family drama kind of conflict... *Why not? It could open the prince's eyes to certain flaws of his potential bride.*

***

Time flew ahead like an arrow shot from a crossbow.

Lily worked like a convict. Her only comfort was that her work was repetitive. Everything was clear and straight-forward. She already had experience with equipping the artisans' workshops, instructing people, and cleaning the castle. The only difference was in scale and also at Taral she was under total guard.

Leif appointed the Virmans, Leis arranged for guarding the nearby surroundings. Although, they did not catch the killer, at least there were no new attempts. Upon finding out about the incident, His Majesty was quite angry and put his wrath on Hans. The latter managed to excuse himself, but his feelings toward the Crown were noticeably weaker. At least, Lily could trust his loyalty, which was very well paid for.

Approximately ten percent of the products went on presents. The rest was given to Helke—to be precise, to his brothers in trade. The received sum surpassed all expectations. Marcia and the girls worked day and night. Ladies queued up for their products. These women haggled for the right to be ahead of their rival, they fought, bribed the clerks, made schemes. When Lily heard about the bribing for the first time, she was furious. She wanted to put the scoundrel clerk to beating and kick him out, but Helke talked her out of it. *Were the Eveers famous for being corrupt scoundrels? Very well, they would sell that reputation and invest the bribes in building the Fashion House.*

Once they began to recruit staff, they would change everything around. As for now, the Countess was a weak, fragile woman. She might not realize that the Eveer was conning her. *Would he agree to become the scapegoat?*

"Countess, we will choose someone who deserves it. There are a lot of lousy goats in any family and any nation."

Lily gave it thought and agreed, but only for the time being. She would change this later.

Lily could have asked her own father for a loan. August had offered it on numerous occasions. She could try to borrow from Alicia, or the King…

No way! I can share my production, but not my Fashion House. I can already see a fashion salon with a little café. It could bring a lot of money. It would take a long time for something like this to appear in this world, but the women's wishes remain the same in every century.

As for the hospital, Lily had no idea how she would organize it, but she was sure to have one. It would also host paramedic, nursing, and surgical schools. Every bit of knowledge she had, she would pass on to the people.

Lily also wished to print children's books—a project she would not trust to anyone but herself—fairy tales, stories, legends and alphabet books. At first, they would be expensive, but later, she would make sure to sell them at an affordable price.

Lily was not the kind of person to sit still. She was not going to do everything at once, because she realized that she would not be able to manage to do it all well. There were some things that she did not have a talent for.

Therefore, she resolved to find a competent manager and an accountant who would control the expenses. Her trade was medicine, and she would spend her time healing people. The rest was just a cover-up.

As for now, she needed to get a lot of work done. She needed to dedicate her time to her daughter and to her people and spend her nights quietly crying from melancholy. She wanted to love, to be loved, to have a family, children, a home, her favorite job…and her Alex.

What did she get instead? Middle ages, a ton of things to do that she did not give a damn about. She was with strange people in a strange land, with her husband God–knows-where, and even his arrival was not a promising event. Lily still harbored some hopes for having a family, at the same time realizing her utter loneliness. It was her total constant loneliness that she felt deeply in her chest. Even if she got married, even if she had children, she would still feel alone. She would never risk revealing her secret.

Always lonely, doomed for loneliness… Why? What have I done? It hurts so much…

***

Alicia looked calmly at His Majesty King Edward. It pleased His Majesty to be displeased.

"Countess, is your daughter-in-law really so busy that she cannot find time to attend my receptions?"

Lily was guilty of skipping all her courtly duties. She did not want to go to court. *Why the heck would I? It is stuffy, dirty and the odor is terrible.* It was better to let Mirrie go and communicate with her cousins and show them some novelties at the same time. The girls quickly found a common language. After Leif found two puppies for the princesses, Mirrie became like a sister to them. Although the girl was younger in age, she knew a lot of incredible things and her cousins found her interesting to be around. In addition, Mirrie could give advice on how to train the puppies. Edward liked that Mirrie and his daughters were friends, but he wanted to see the Countess, too.

***

She seemed to avoid coming to the palace. Of course she showed up on official occasions, even twice this month, just to disappear from them like a ghost. Edward suspected Alicia had something to do with that, but since he had not managed to catch them in the act of conspiracy, he could say nothing.

She had become hard to talk to, as if she closed a door to her heart.

The treasurer received another business report from Lily, and it made him incredibly happy. The digit in the income column exceeded the digit in the spending column. Everything was clearly written out—how much, what for, to whom and when. It was nice to read. Every word in the document had a purpose. Lily was ready to talk about business, but she missed the spark that the King spotted in her upon their first meeting. She seemed to have hidden it somewhere deep inside. The flame in her somehow faded.

His Majesty did not know how to get the once sarcastic woman back. *Why do I even need to get her back? Because I find her interesting.* There was something in her that made the King feel good. She made him curious.

"Your Majesty," the sole thing that differentiated Alicia from other court ladies was the lack of fluttering eyelashes. "Lilian does work day and night. Even her daughter gets to see her no more than one hour a day."

"Do the tasks I give her take up so much time?"

"Lily is trying to do everything well. She is a gem, Your Majesty, and a very responsible person."

"But still."

"Your Majesty, you put a load on her that not every man would have been able to bear."

"I did not think that she would do everything on her own," Edward frowned. "Women are not made to do business."

"Well, it seems like Lily is an exception to the rule."

"That's true. Countess, what else can you tell me about her? What is she like now, once you became friends and got to know her well?"

Alicia bit her lower lip, but did not lie.

"What can I say? She is very clever. At the same time, her wit is different."

"What do you mean?"

Alicia fell silent. *How can I explain something I do not understand?* She noticed Lily's original solutions, words, actions…even her gestures were something else. Everything was clear and straight-forward, but Alicia could not piece it together. She shook her head. "I do not know. She is clever, but in a different way. For instance, her tales about Baron Holmes."

"Did she tell them to Miranda?"

"Yes. I told her the girl should not be exposed to tales of murder, but Lily replied that the girl must learn to think sharply so she would never find herself in Lily's position."

"And the Countess teaches the little one to think by using the method of storytelling?"

Alicia nodded. "Yes."

"It is most curious. Alicia, I would like you to pass on my words to her. It is not an order, but rather my wishful thinking. I would like to see her at court more often."

"I will pass on your wish to her; but do not forget that she is a Broklend."

Edward sighed. It was very difficult to lure August Broklend to court. *Is it a coincidence or is personality hereditary?"*

The King suddenly considered the possibility of visiting Taral. He could check what was going on there. Lily was a woman, after all. Yes, he put everything into August's hands and appointed his own people there, but the Countess also had a say in the matter.

What is a woman capable of? We shall see…

***

Lily had a lot of things to do. Ingrid could not help as much as before, Chevalier Avels was also extremely busy, and Lily drowned in a heap of documents. She could not even spend as much time with her daughter as she used to. She would let Miranda go to court to play. At least, it would keep her busy. Lily asked Leif to appoint guards to accompany her, but that did not stop her from being constantly worried. If anyone wanted to get at Lily, Mirrie was the first person to target. The

Virmans realized it well. Each Virman guarded the girl like she was the apple of his eye.

Lily's life was monotonously routine. Morning, work, day, work, evening, work... Only the return of Erik brightened it up, but he did not come for leisure.

Six ships of white sails entered the harbor. Erik headed to Lily, and the Virman embassy, to Edward.

***

Mirrie was the first one to spot Erik. She shrieked in excitement and embraced his neck with both hands, her feet dancing in the air.

"Uncle Erik! Hurray!"

Her happiness was quite natural. Despite his scary looks, Erik loved children and very often played with them.

"Are you staying for good?"

"We shall see. I will need to talk with your mother about that."

"Mother is at her end! She is head over heels in work!"

"Are you running away from her work then?"

"Leis will be teaching us to throw knives. Tristan got wounded, so Leis plays with us now."

Erik smirked. "It is well that I arrived now!"

He enclosed a little knife into the girl's hand. Miranda removed it from the sheath and whistled. "Wow!"

The girl could tell a good weapon. Erik was the one who taught her. She tested the knife's outstanding balance, the sharpness of its edge, the blueish shine of steel, and the handle made of shark skin.

"Is it for me?"

"For you."

"Thank you!"

Miranda embraced Erik, kissed him on both cheeks and hurried away.

Erik shook his head and proceeded toward Lily's study.

Countess Lilian Earton... The Virman could not himself determine what feelings she invoked in him. *Admiration? Certainly. Respect? Of course. Love? No, I feel no love toward her yet, but the Virmans can appreciate strong and clever women. The foolish ones cannot survive there, due to the climate, perhaps...*

"My Lady?"

When Lily saw Erik standing in the doorway of the study her eyes flared up so much that Lons unwillingly bit his lip. The woman's smile was exceptional. It was bright, open; it came from her very heart.

"Erik! Come in! Lons, could you order something to eat? Would you like some wine?"

"I keep my usual ways."

The Virmans did not favor alcohol. They thought wine made a woman compliant and a man weak. They would surely not survive if they loved wine. So, the Virmans got to appreciate other drinks, such as weak brews and blackcurrant juice—especially brews. Erik loved brews.

Lons left the room. Erik got comfortable in the chair and looked at the Countess with his happy, blue eyes. *She is beautiful, indeed.* Lily bent over, not noticing that the cut of her dress revealed her cleavage.

"Erik, what did they say on Virma?"

"My Lady, I come to you with great news."

"Come on, tell me!" Lily hit the table with her fist and immediately caught a non-spill inkpot.

"As you may be aware, we do not have one ruler on Virma."

"But you have a Clan Government Council, I know."

"I demonstrated everything that you gave me,"

Lily had given him crocheted shawls, socks, gloves... The knitted stuff was a novelty for the Virman women, the best of its kind. She also presented them with a telescope and a magnifying glass, invaluable finds for shipbuilders with experience; medical alcohol for disinfection, one could even take a little inside; and the technology of obtaining salt from seawater, the benefits were apparent.

Lily could think of a lot of things to show them, just off the top of her head. However, Virma was a cruel and a cold island. Therefore, they needed to be shown how they could use it for their own advantage and how much she could give them.

"So, what decision did the Elders reach?"

"They decided to start negotiations with Edward."

"About what?"

"There is war between us, but there are things which can benefit both sides. We have a lot to offer. Your husband trades. We can guard his ships."

Lily winced. She would rather have someone drown her husband's ship.

"Guards, help, defense, and in case you decide one day to move to Virma…"

Lily nodded.

"That is from your side. What do you want from Ativerna in return?"

"Salt is important for us. It will be easier for us now. But it is not everything you can offer, am I wrong?"

"Not at all. You should speak to the King about that, and he, in turn, will negotiate with the Elders. As for me, your artisans, your technology… I like Virma, and I hope for a good neighborly relationship."

Erik's lips stretched into a gleeful grin revealing a hole in his teeth.

"My Lady, good people can always find a compromise."

***

Lily responded with the same smile and thought about scurvy. The simplest task was to explain where it comes from and how to deal with it.

She would give him a recipe for pickled cabbage and seaweed as well. She knew a dozen such recipes, if not more.

Indeed, knowing medicine helps you survive anywhere.

Chapter 6

Top-level negotiations

To say that Edward did not expect to host the Virman Embassy was an understatement. He would not dare drive them away, after all. He was thinking about his ships. *Indeed, one side of the scales is Virma and the other one is Loris. These jackals bite one another.*

But if Virma was a clan island, Loris was…an 'Isla Tortuga'. In this world, however, Tortuga was owned by Elvana. Because the Elvanians did not have a good navy, they killed two birds with one stone. They exiled every scum there, far away from normal people. They took prey from them for cheap, lower than the market price. If anyone asked them about Loris, their eyes grew wide. *We know nothing; we have not heard; it was not us.*

They refused to clean up the mess because Loris was convenient. It was also too difficult a job, for if the Loris people united, it would raise a lot of issues. As a result, it became a breeding ground for pirates. The only ones who killed all their fun were the Virmans. The grey wolves did not like competition, so they pinched the pirates with all their might. Edward also did not like Loris, but it was too far. *To send ships across the continent? It is easier to let the merchants suffer.*

It suddenly occurred to the King that he could collaborate with the Virmans to protect his trade. *What brought them hither?*

"I will host them tomorrow morning," ordered the King. "As for now, assign them a place in the bay and arrange for lodging and watchmen."

The Virmans obviously did not need any watchmen, but it was done so that the local jackals did not bother them. His Majesty had no idea to what he owed the pleasure of hosting such people.

"Your Majesty, Alicia, the widowed Countess of Earton."

"Ask her in."

Her sudden appearance in the palace was bizarre.

Everything became clear in a few moments, when Alicia put an envelope before the King.

"Your Majesty, Lilian Earton is asking you to receive her immediately."

"What happened?"

"The Virman delegation."

"Is she responsible for this?"

To say that the King was astonished would not do it justice.

"Where is she?"

"With the princesses now."

"Just like that?"

"She came to me, but the girls just grabbed her and pulled away. They demand new stories about Baron Holmes."

"What kind of stories does she tell them to stir up so much interest?"

"If it pleases you, Your Majesty, we can go and listen."

Edward smiled playfully.

As strange as it seemed, the old viperess was one of those people around whom Edward felt at peace. She was a part of his youth, a part of his happiness with Jessie, his love... It meant quite a lot.

"Let's go, Alicia..."

Judging from the golden sparks dancing in Alicia's eyes, the viperess understood this well.

$$***$$

"And then they found the dog of the killed man on the shore..."

"Did he die from grief?"

"No, everything was not so simple. When Baron Holmes inspected the hound, he noticed the same marks on the body of the animal as the ones on the body of his master. It was harder to see it through the fur, but they were there, as if someone had dropped a red-hot grid fence…"

Lily told them *The adventures of the Lion's Mane*. There were some tales about Holmes that could be told without mentioning the inventions of technological progress, but there were also others…

Edward and Alicia stood behind a curtain, enchanted by the story. When the story ended, they did not hurry to reveal themselves. Alicia was the first one to speak up.

"Lily, have you ever seen such jellyfish yourself?"

"I have not seen them with my own eyes, but I have heard about them."

"Who told you?"

"The Virmans. They sail everywhere. Besides, nature is full of secrets. For instance, a horse has eighteen bones more than a human. And have you ever seen an octopus' eye?"

"Is it round?"

"Not at all. You live by the sea and have not seen an octopus? His eyes are squares."

"No!" joined in Joliette.

"Go and see for yourself," Lily teased them. "It might be that a couple of octopuses live right in the kitchen."

"We will surely go," nodded Angelina. "Tell us more, Lily!"

"For example, a great tit feeds her birdies one thousand times a day. In a night, a mole could dig a tunnel two hundred and twenty feet in length, maybe a tiny bit less. A snail has twenty-five-thousand teeth."

"No!"

"Check it. I never say what I don't know." Lily was evidently having fun.

"But how?"

"Well," teased the Countess, "one could catch a snail and count her teeth!"

The girls burst into loud laughter.

"Lily, will you tell us more about Baron Holmes?"

As much as Edward would have liked to listen to another story, his time was precious. He made a coughing sound and came out of hiding.

"Your Majesty." Lily immediately stood up and dropped into a deep curtsey.

"Stand up, My Lady. Did you wish to see me?"

"Yes, Your Majesty."

"In that case, let us proceed to my study. Girls, Countess Earton will tell you stories another time."

Lily obeyed but winked at the princesses behind the King's back, as if saying, *Miranda will tell you. She knows…*

Angelina and Joliette simultaneously sighed. They were distressed. Every time they found an interesting person, their father had to spoil all the fun.

***

Once in the study, His Majesty ordered the women to sit down and nodded to the secretary. "Wine, spring water, sweets and fruit. Now, tell me, Lilian, what connection do you have with the Virman Embassy?"

"Your Majesty, I am afraid that I have the most direct relationship with it."

"What is the meaning of it?"

"I am guilty. I hired the Virmans and failed to keep track of what they did there. They failed me…"

From Lily's words of repentance, once the Virmans realized that they could get Lily's trust, they decided to try their luck with the King.

"Why do they want peace talks? The Virmans are no fools."

Lily told the King the Virman she had hired had returned to offer peace negotiations to achieve dual benefits.

"I see." His Majesty raised his hand. "Now, let me think."

Lily fell silent. Edward was not angry.

Well, the Virman freemen were a constant issue, but there were positive sides to the situation as well. Maybe I could find a way to appoint these sea wolves for my own service, teach them the customs of Ativerna... Is it too difficult a task?

If I started this enterprise now, Richard could continue it in the future. At least Loris would keep away from the ships that were guarded by the Virmans. At present, every fifth ship suffers.

The Countess, of course, assumed the guilt by blaming it on her naivety, but her direct involvement was evident. She put it across as if this whole affair happened without her knowledge. But he was not going to stir a fuss. *This idea could become beneficial for the state, and the benefit would be big.*

"Countess, you have truly been careless." But the expressions of all three revealed mutual disbelief and a trace of a smile appeared on each. "I hope that this will never happen again."

Lily passionately reassured the King that there was no way on earth, and the King dismissed her. She hurried out to withdraw home. Alicia remained sitting in Edward's study.

"Were you aware of this idea of hers, Countess?"

"No, Your Majesty."

"You tell me that she did it by herself... Is it not too much credit for one woman? One day, she quietly sits in her nook, the next day, she invents a lot of novelties, becomes a student of a famous medicus, and now, she also influences state policy. Are you saying there was no one standing behind her?"

Alicia shook her head. "Your Majesty, you have to remember that she is a daughter of her father and a granddaughter of her grandfather."

Edward let out a strange grunt. *Fine, of course, August is an extremely talented man.* He is a shipbuilder who was gifted by Aldonai. From that, it followed that his daughter must also be talented in her own trade, of course. There was no fault in it. But the stately wisdom was a completely different thing, one could not acquire it at birth.

Lilian was a risk-taker and could take responsibility for her actions. *Wherefore did she acquire such qualities?* August is not a remarkable statesman, as for his father… Lilian's grandfather did not get his Barony for nothing. Back in the day he used to be a mongrel boy. He became one of the first royal representatives purely by chance. He resolved a handful of the most dangerous conspiracies against the state. One could say that it was his efforts and work that ensured Edward's peaceful reign. The Crown owed plenty to Lily's grandfather.

"Is it due to her ancestral blood? Perhaps you are right…"

"Your Majesty, she is not a shilda, she is not in contact with evil spirits. She converses with the aldon, goes to church, the pastor is always by her side."

"I can see it myself. But as for her other possible liaisons…"

"She does not see anyone. I am keeping watch, as do my maids."

"And you claim that she does not see anyone on the side?"

"She treats everyone as equals. She is strictly faithful to her husband. Although the Marquess Falion has begun to frequent the estate, but I personally see no harm in that."

"So, she does see men, after all."

"There is no romance in that relationship, but pure friendship. Besides, he is married."

"Does that ever stop anyone?"

Alicia glanced sharply. "Your Majesty, there are no men in Lilian Earton's life. If you are implying adultery, there will be no such thing in Lily's life. She knows her worth and defends her honor."

"Are you sure about that?"

Alicia returned the monarch's look once more. "If I were in her place, I would not have been able to resist temptation. Since we are alone, I will be honest with Your Majesty. For all of his great finesse, my son deserves not only horns, but also hooves." A tinge of irony, sharp as a knife, struck the King's ear.

"But Lily will not allow this to happen. She loves Miranda like her own daughter. I strongly suspect that if Lily tries to make peace with her husband, it will be for Miranda's sake and hers alone."

"Jess might screw up again,"

"Now, it is our job to not let that happen,"

"Fine. The Virmans first, My Lady. Let us return to the subject."

* * *

Lily pleased Erik with the news. The King was open to negotiations, so Virma had the chance of becoming rich and prosperous.

Erik asked the Countess about his next mission. Lily had no task to give him; his question was fair enough, she hired them for service until spring.

"Do you not need people anymore?" asked Erik. "Because we would be happy to work for you."

At that moment Lily caught the eye of Hans Tremain, who entered the room with a grimace on his face and a fat folder in his hands. The folder was surely another report.... Poor rulers, thought Lily. *How do they even manage to read all the documents that come through?*

Lily glanced at Hans and Erik.

"Leir Hans, could you spare me a few minutes?"

Upon noticing the playful sparks in Lily's eyes, Hans faltered, only to find himself quite content a few moments after.

"Here is a Virman for you. He has his own crew, and you may teach him. You told me you needed reliable and serious people for your job, is that not so? You already have your schoolboys running around and gathering information. They know many things. Now, you will also have someone to teach. Take the Virmans and turn them into soldiers."

Erik scowled but did not object. The Countess was pleased with him. She made him one of her own people, she praised him relentlessly, he was given a good salary. Being in Hans's service would only mean that he was not Lily's personal guard any more. It was even better that way.

Hans inspected the Virman and remembered him from the last time they worked together.

"I agree, My Lady. I have another thing to tell you."

"Anything important?"

"Yes. It would also be good to invite artisan Helke to join."

Lily sighed and nodded to the maid to bring Helke.

"Shall we proceed over to my study?"

***

Half an hour later, Lily was angry. She expected it to happen, but not at this early stage. One of the Eveers named Varil Shalim turned out to be either a rat, a thief, or maybe both. Either way, his actions spoke louder than words. That snake managed to cook the books and steal almost half of the profit-; the documents in Han's file confirmed it.

Lily did expect theft to happen, but not that soon. The first merchants were selected by Helke, and it was him they called forward to question.

He sat on a chair, glanced through the papers and looked up with cunning mockery.

"So, he does steal, after all! The bastard!"

"Were you aware of it?"

"I suspected that he was prone to theft."

"And why did you pick him then?"

"My Lady, I am an Eveer."

"Yes I am aware of it," mumbled Lily. It made Hans smile.

"Yes! I am an Eveer, and you still hired me, gave me shelter and care. Only once I started serving you, I found out what it was to have peace and quiet. You spoil me with the pay, too. Not to mention your ideas! Any goldsmith and jeweler would give an arm and a leg for such a life. Loria is not worried about the children. You give them an education fit for the nobles. You placed my elder son in a good trade. It is not in my interest to con you, My Lady. My whole family is bound to you."

"So what?"

"There will always be the ones who fool you. Varil is scum, no one likes him. He manages to betray even his own people. No one has ever caught him red-handed, but everyone is aware of his nature and they try not to do business with him."

"Well, what about me?"

"Sooner or later, someone would try to steal from you anyway. You will teach that thief a lesson, and they will hold a grudge, and so on."

Lily nodded. She knew that she should not leave the crime unpunished, even once. But the Eveers stood up for each other.

"So, you selected him to teach me an exemplary lesson?"

There was a twinkle in his eye. "How else, My Lady. My trusted people will not mind if you kick him out."

"They should also get it in their head to not meddle with the Countess…" Hans articulated slowly.

Helke responded to him with a naïve smile. "You are such a—! That is solid." The jeweler took no offense. It was a daily matter. If someone else had found out about it, they would have made a lot of noise. But the Countess did not do that. She was wise, and it was a pleasure to work with her. The trinkets she invented were truly precious. The ferronnière took only half an hour to make, but turned a profit.

Lily looked at Hans. "Leir Hans, here is a job for you. Erik came on time; he can help you."

"My Lady."

"It will not be necessary to kill him, but I suppose the Virmans know how to punish thieves."

Hans nodded. They did know. The Virmans never killed their thieves but made sure that they remembered the punishment for a long time.

"Do I have a right to deal with thieves by myself?"

"You do, My Lady. If you have proof, the King will not object."

"Do I need to notify him about it?"

"Leave it to me, My Lady."

Lily nodded.

"Go then, get everything ready. If you need me to be present, let me know."

"Will you manage to witness such a sight, my Lady?"

Lily shrugged.

Dear Hans, I wish you had seen me as a freshman dissecting dead corpses in the morgue. The others around me passed out, but I stood strong and did my job. So the sight of punishing a villain should not scare me in the least.

Hans headed off to do his job. Lily looked at Helke.

"Sir artisan, I have another idea for you."

The idea was simple. Ferronnières were a great success, but they could also make some variations. Indian headpieces like *maang tika* and *lalatika* were slightly more difficult to make. Parts of them could be made by apprentices.

Maybe later, Lily would tell Helke about *haathphool*, but it was not productive to bring up every idea at once.

✳✳✳

Helke listened, made notes and drew pictures. He also thought that he had chosen himself a good mistress. Although he was already old, he was employed by a truly wonderful woman and friend whom he could always trust with the wellbeing of his family. He wondered what other ideas Lily wanted to share with him in the future.

The ideas she already offered him were enough to immortalize his name for centuries, but Helke was dying of curiosity.

✳✳✳

Varil Shalim was satisfied with himself, and also with his profit. He counted the coins paid to him for selling lace, put some aside, thought about it and put away a little more. He weighed a heavy sack of gold on his hand.

Splendid!

Like every other scoundrel, Varil considered himself an honest man, and now he was only splitting the profit in a fairer way: a little bit more for himself, a little bit less for Countess Earton...and a tiny little bit more for himself.

He was not even surprised when they chose him to be a trading intermediary. He always did the right thing. Well, to trick and make losses for his employer was a way to split fair and square...no man was without sin. This time was no exception. *First, every woman is as silly as a goose, so the Countess would not even suspect she might have received less than there was. Second, I am a man, so I will spend the money more wisely. Third, this feather-head of a countess did not need so much money! She would be just fine. On the other hand—me! A smart serious man!* If he handled the trade of her products for another year, he would be able to think about marriage. Nobody wanted to give their daughters in marriage to Varil. *But what if I were rich? Who would refuse me then? I will show them all!*

There was no knock or creak of the door, for Erik had taken great pleasure in taking it off its hinges. Hans forbid him to make noise ahead of time, and Varil was caught red-handed, as he was stacking the gold into many little sacks and contemplating whether to take a little more, or wait for later. Suddenly, the Virman shadows towered over him.

The Virmans looked very scary. Wearing leather jackets, they were armed with axes, swords and malicious smirks on their faces. The man jumped out of his seat, but a hard blow on the jaw knocked him against the wall and out, into the grey oblivion.

***

Varil was brought to his senses with hard slaps to his face. The tradesman did not find the situation agreeable. No one would like sitting in a chair, hands and feet tied down, with a couple of Virmans standing around, staring with bad intentions, and the woman sitting opposite.

It was Countess Lilian Earton. Behind her, with a hand resting on the back of her chair, stood Hans Tremain. Their last encounter had been friendly, but that did not make Varil any happier.

Everyone stared at him with a detached, cold interest. *Do they want to hang me, or maybe to take mercy? Definitely hang.*

"Good evening, sir."

Varil tried to say something but a gag in his mouth stopped him from doing so.

"Can you guess what might have brought us here?"

Varil moaned. But Hans did not even think of removing the gag.

"Over there, on the table, golden coins. Something tells me that they are earned from selling the goods of Mariella. The money for them, on the other hand, was not received by the owner. Does it not seem slightly wrong to you?"

Varil shook his head.

"It does to me. A little birdie told me that this is not the first time. That is why we are here. Why are you moaning? Do you have something to tell us? Well, tell us! But if you raise your voice even once, my friend Erik will cut off your ear and put it inside your mouth instead of a gag. Do you understand?"

Varil repeatedly nodded his head.

He wished he could somehow get away with it, at least this time. Although, the woman is silly, he thought, he could make her believe his lies. Moreover, she is the one in charge. She would let him go. Besides, women are scared of blood...most definitely...

He did not scream when they removed the gag.

"My Lady, it is all slander!"

"Is that really so?" The Countess squinted, "I know what you sold, how much for, and to whom. Here is written proof. Did you really think that I would trust you with my products and not check on you? How absurd."

"I am… I only…"

"For example, you sold a lace collar to Marchioness Layster for twenty golden ducats. But the price here says ten, plus I pay you a share. How greedy. There is also Countess Merel, Duchess Tarves and a couple of wives and daughters of merchants. Did you think I would not find out?"

Varil only blinked. *What is the point in shouting and justifying myself?*

"My Lady, Maldonaya tempted me!"

"Yes, all evil comes from women," Lily agreed in melancholy. "What else can you say?"

"Do not ruin me…do not orphan my children…my poor wife will be left a widow…It was a devil who tempted me, and I will never do it again…have mercy!"

He invented the wife and children, but if he could, he would have thrown himself at her feet, he would have crawled like a reptile, he would have licked the soles of her shoes and so on.

Lily bit her lip. She was disgusted to death, but she had no choice.

"Erik?"

Upon understanding that something bad was going to happen to him, Varil tried to scream, "The King will not forgive you, and neither will the guild or the Eveers! They will not forgive!"

But all was in vain.

Erik swiftly put a gag over Varil's mouth. The Eveer got silent, realizing his destiny was being decided now.

"So, the most *un-noble* sir Varil," Lily said quietly. "I could forgive you, but you would not learn from it, and new thieves would be quick to follow your example. His Majesty knows everything. Leir Hans?"

The man took a scroll from his pocket. "Issued to Countess Earton. She has a full right to administer justice over Varil Shalim, for the above mentioned stole with stupidity and impudence not suitable to his rank. Moreover, you, Countess, pay interest to the Treasury, meaning that the times he robbed you, he was robbing the King."

Varil whined. A yellow puddle started forming on the floor.

"So, my *un-dear* sir, I will be just fine. The thieves will get what they deserve. They long ago learned how to deal with the likes of you. Erik?"

"We will deal with him, My Lady," smirked the Virman.

"Hans?"

"Will you stay present?"

"Not for long. I still have things to do today."

Erik took out a short sharp, knife from his boot. Varil grunted and cringed, but all in vain. The punishment for theft on Virma was threefold. Chopping off both thumbs to prevent them from holding vessels, cutting out the tongue so they could not tell lies, and finally cutting off the tip of the nose, so one could spot a thief from a mile. It was cruel, but it worked. There were very few thieves on Virma.

***

The moon peered through the window, pale and cold—the same moon in a different world. Her slippers were completely noiseless. Lily walked around the room while Mirrie peacefully slept in her bed under a warm cover.

The bedroom was big, almost fifteen steps from wall to wall, so Lily had a lot of room for pacing. Miranda was fast asleep, but Lily had insomnia. Before her eyes, was the senseless stupid face of a man she ordered disfigured. It was ugly, scary and covered in blood. She overestimated herself. A morgue was one thing; an operation was to save people. It was another thing to use a knife for punishment. *What have you become, Aliya Skorolenok? Who did you turn into? Before you could not kill Etor, although that villain deserved death way more. Do you remember how you used to be? When you came to your senses you only chased the scoundrel out, nothing more. Have you not paid a big price for your kindness? Had you killed him straight away, you would not have had to suffer later... But is it humane? He is a human being, after all. It does not matter if he is good or bad, he is a man, after all. After prison, he would have a chance to reform himself, change his ways. But now he is simply doomed to live in misery.*

It is okay, Lily! He has stolen enough. Let him go and dig potatoes...

What you have done is inhumane...

What I have done was approved by the King...

But it is cruel; it is unreasonably cruel. What next, Aliya? Chopping off hands on a public square?

Why not hands? They practice it here. The only difference is that I did it in silence and privacy.

What have you done to yourself? Lily grabbed her head with her hands, moaned and fell silent. The last thing she wanted was to wake up Mirrie.

Two dogs looked at their mistress in surprise.

Am I cruel?

But he robbed me.

The discordant voices came out of her head and joined together in one passionate speech: *I could have given him a different punishment. A tortureless one. I did not have to mutilate him. I could have, but also not. I am a woman. From the start, they treat me way worse than men. They think I can be deceived, conned and betrayed only because I am a woman. They picked Varil to teach me a lesson precisely because I was not the first one. The others will be scared now. And what about the shrieks? Were they the voice of justice, or the burps of The Geneva and Hague conventions? Not really. Is it better to close the dam now when one drop trickled through, or to later deal with the current? A small cruelty now or a big one later? What is worse? The principle of the lesser of two evils.*

Lily was not justifying herself. She did not deserve to be excused. She was guilty and was going to take full responsibility for her actions. Her parents would not understand her, or maybe they would.

A long time ago, back in that other life, she and her father had been watching the news. Upon hearing about the execution of some drug dealer in the Middle East (she could not remember all the details), Vladimir Vasilievich approvingly said "Yes!"

It was cruel and ugly, but drugs in Iraq, Iran, Indonesia and some other places were punished by death, and rightly so. Those scumbags murdered many people. God save the relatives of people who abused drugs.

Lily's was a completely different matter. The dry residue of it was unjustifiable cruelty. *Although no, the cruelty was justified, by the King, by the Eveers, by other people as well. It is a common practice here. They could beat a child to death for stealing a loaf of bread.*

That was ugly. *As for Varil, did he have starving children? Was he starving himself? Did he have sick parents or a wife? No. He just thought that he could eat everything at once, even the things which did not fit into his stomach. And that was why he choked. Was it not just?*

But how much money would I get from it?

The amount is miserable.

Lily was perfectly aware that she spent almost nothing on herself.

She paid a salary to her people, improved Earton, developed trade, built a Fashion House. The profit she got from sales, she would spend on building a hospital and teaching medicine.

Am I similar to Dzerzhinsky, The Soviet statesman? How many people did he destroy, and how many did he give a chance in life? How many orphans and abandoned children did he save?

Lily savagely bit her nails.

Ugly. Money, blood, and filth always come together. In this mercantile world, one learns to step over dead bodies.

Back during her university years, a very rich classmate of Aliya was trying to show herself superior. Aliya would not have even paid attention; she had other things on her mind. But the young lady began to get in her way. She began getting on her nerves during breaks, she was snobby almost to her face. Aliya avoided the conflict as long as she could, but when the snob called her a pauper, she lost her temper.

"How many people has your father convicted to death in order to buy you these haute couture knickers? How many people lost everything because of him, became drunks and druggies? What happened to their families? Your wealth is built on blood and bones. Do you understand? There is nothing to be proud of."

Lily was now no better than that snobby girl from class. Her wealth would be built on blood and bones; there were no excuses for it, at least not yet. Tomorrow was a new day.

The sunshine will fill the room, and Mirrie will be laughing, oblivious that she could have even been dead by now. All of my people will welcome the sun, as well as the people I have saved and the ones I will save later.

Lily was not defending herself, but she hoped she could make up for her sin. Yes, it was cruel, but medicine was also a cruel trade. Sometimes, the healing process could be painful for the patient. Varil was a contagion for her trade. He was amputated, like gangrene. If need be, Lily was ready to organize a public hearing. Her witness was God, himself. She did not do it for money. She cared nothing for money, it was not her aim. What she would be able to achieve was more important. No one could stop her plans.

Lily put her hair away. There was enough pacing for one night, she would drink mint tea and go to sleep. If it failed to put her to sleep, it would at least warm her up a little. She had a hard day ahead and getting a cold was not in her plans.

She finally managed to stop dwelling on the subject, for it became incredibly painful to think.

***

Richard parted his blonde hair to the side and turned to his friend.

"Jess, where are you heading to this evening?"

"I wanted to visit one salon."

"You will have to skip it."

"Is that so?"

"You are going with me, because I could die of boredom if I go alone to Bernard's."

"Do you want me to lie with you?"

"No, I want at least one person in that place to be adequate."

"You want me to be your court jester?"

"You can call it whatever you wish, but you must come along!"

Jess grimaced but did not protest. He could understand Richard. The evenings at Bernard's were boring.

They offered no drinks, apart from wine, which was such bad quality that one would refuse to wash the hooves of his horse with it. There were no women, because in the court of Bernard, chastity was very strictly observed. The King himself, on the other hand, used such vulgar expressions that he should have been sentenced to public beating for debauchery. There was no need to mention entertainment. Gaming, races, fighting and tournaments were all forbidden, for they pleased Maldonaya alone.

They did have dancing, but it was boring to death. Everything was ceremonious, sublime…there was no way to even just mingle with somebody in the corner. The guards and courtiers would detect it and break it off.

"You understand why I need you there, right?"

Jess sighed. The only entertainment Richard had was Lidia. Every other woman avoided coming close.

Lidia, in her turn, preferred books to everything else. A certain princess in an enchanted tower; the princess from the fairy tale was at least beautiful, but Lidia looked horrible. Like a rat who snapped at his every phrase.

* * *

Richard was not entirely objective about the girl, but Lidia knew the thought of seeing everything with her eyes did not appear to him once. Lidia was also unhappy with what was going on. She was the one treated as an object for sale. She was the one regarded as a piece of meat sold to an arrogant, boyish-looking prince.

He could not even imagine asking her what she was thinking about, dreaming of, what her feelings were… Instead, he simply showed up expecting her to be in seventh heaven, as if he had descended from the heavens. *Who would have liked that? His good looks were a double-edged sword.*

Lidia was clever enough to see herself in the mirror as a woman, not a princess. She realized her flaws. She was too thin, too tall, too pale, and unremarkable. She also knew that she could marry a prince, but she would still go to bed with a man. As for a man like Richard, he was all too attractive to not see other women on the side. *Call me a witch if I am wrong! A king who is cheating and a queen for appearances? No, thank you.*

Lidia could have explained this to young men, but she did not want to. She assumed that she made her position clear. But some things that appeared obvious to women needed to be forced down upon men with a heavy bat. The same went the other way around. Women might have not noticed something that seemed obvious to men, until it hit them on the head- three times.

In other words, there was no mutual understanding between the prince and the princess. As for solidarity, one could suppose that there was none either. However, they were required to speak to each other and keep up appearances.

***

"Could I invite you for a dance, Your Majesty?"

Lidia gave such a condescending look that Jess felt himself a miserable cockroach.

"No."

"Your Majesty, you will break my heart."

Lidia's stare made Jess fall silent. "My Lord, relieve me of the burden of your company."

Jess's eyes flared with anger, but he backed off regardless of his hurt pride.

Richard squinted. "Your Majesty, Jess did not mean any harm."

"It is unwise and unthinkable to think otherwise." Lidia wrinkled her nose in a demonstration of her regard for Jess.

"Your Majesty…" Richard's voice was full of reproach, but Lidia only shrugged.

"How soon will you depart, Your Royal Highness?"

"In approximately twenty days."

"Good."

"Why are you so happy about it?"

"Should I be crying instead?"

Richard was discouraged. No one had ever spoken to him like this stick-tall awkward girl did, and he did not like the feeling.

"Well, kind of…"

"I should be sad as per the etiquette, no more, no less. I will be struck with grief in front of my father." Lidia was on a horse, slaying enemies one by one. "But I do not see it necessary to play a part in front of you. Neither you, nor your people, excite kind feelings in me."

"I also do not like your court!" retorted Richard, perfectly aware of the fact that Lidia would not report his words to the King for fear of him finding out the full message of the conversation. "I have never seen such a lack of generosity."

"Let me tell you," Lidia flared up like a matchstick. "You call it lack of generosity, but both my grandfather and great-grandfather did nothing but throw money around. When my father came to the throne, the treasury was completely empty. Even the treasurer did not steal, because there was *nothing* to steal!"

"Maybe he had stolen it earlier,"

"Very funny. The neighbors were pressing on, and what was my father left to do? Yes, he is very economical, sometimes too economical, but what would you have done in his place? Would you have drunk poor peasants' blood or milked the courtiers?"

Richard was ashamed. *What would I have done?*

"I would try to develop trade, industries, and would never allow the churchmen to be so liberal," Richard replied honestly.

Lidia sighed. "I also wish we did not give them so much freedom, but we had no choice."

"Is that really true?"

"Do you have any idea how much it cost to save the kingdom? The money was given to us by the aldons."

Richard scratched his nose. He did know that the aldons accumulated a lot of wealth, but not to that extent.

"Yes, it is true." It was as if Lidia had read his thoughts.

"I do not have a habit of underestimating either the power or the wealth of the Church. If we need to bend down and comply for the sake of keeping our land safe, to keep Ivernea away from the greedy neighbors, we will do it."

"The result might turn out even worse,"

Lidia shook her head. "With the right government, my nephews will manage to return Ivernea's lost wealth. We will survive the dark times."

"We as in yourself and your family?"

"It might surprise you, but a woman does not necessarily need to follow the path from the kitchen to bed and to the nursery," snapped Lidia. "I am good at finances and I am helping my father. My brothers are also smart, but not as gifted as I am."

There was so much pride in Lidia's voice that the prince brought himself to bow.

I see nothing to be proud of! She is such a fool.

"Do you not want a little bit more fun, joy, colorful dresses—"

Lidia's ice-cold look cut off Richard's speech.

"Do you know how much it all costs? Ivernea cannot afford it!"

"Being economical is surely important, but you will sooner or later want to have a home, a family, children…"

Lidia shook her head.

"I do not see a reason for it. My experience tells me that every husband will turn into a tyrant."

"Every husband? For sure?"

"Not for sure, however you will."

"You think very badly of me, Your Majesty…"

"You have not done anything for me to change my opinion," retorted Lidia. "I wish you left sooner, all these balls are a waste of my time. I despise all this small talk and mannerisms. Do you have any idea how busy I am? Get married to someone else and leave Ivernea alone!"

"I will follow your orders with great pleasure." Richard, who was already raging inside, grit his teeth.

Lidia proudly nodded. "Make sure you do. You may be dismissed."

Richard bid farewell and left the hall. Upon noticing that something was wrong, Jess caught up with him hastily.

"Richard!"

His Majesty kicked a statue with all his might, hurt his foot, swore, and flopped into a chair.

***

Jess found out a lot of new things about Lidia in the next ten minutes. One must say that her parents did not suspect her of belonging to the class of pervert animals. Had Bernard heard about it, Richard would have been kicked out of the palace immediately for his cursing, but the garden was dark and quiet.

"What came over you?" Jess was genuinely surprised.

Richard swore again. "Bloody hell! God forbid to marry such a hag. Bitch, shrew, ogress! Jess, do you remember your mother?"

"Of course," Jess did not have any idea why he brought up Alicia, but nodded. "This one is ten times worse!"

"And she is younger, too."

"Precisely! When she is your mother's age, I promise you, not even a fly will buzz her way, because it would die on the way from the poison she exhales into thin air!"

"So, I conclude that Anna is a better option?"

"By all means! I will write to father and Gardwig."

***

Lidia stared at Richard as he was leaving. She snorted.

Arrogant, self-admiring prick! Those like him genuinely think the whole world is at their feet and get surprised upon finding out that it is not so.

Poor women. Such handsome men marry only after having slept around for years, and they successfully continue doing so after marriage. It is enough to remember unhappy Imogene, poor woman. Her husband openly lived with another woman, and the queen had to endure. Disgusting! If Jessamine were here, they would have quickly classified her as one of the servants of Maldonaya and exiled her to the convent to pray for her sins. What a whore! To live with someone else's husband, without being married... Disgusting!

Lidia grimaced. She may have had different views had she not been brought up in her family. The aldons were strict governesses and nannies. Bernard never spared a wet rod for beating his children, even for the smallest faults. As a result, Lidia had soon learned to behave in a way to avoid punishment. The first thing, was to obey her father and to follow the teachings of the Church. Unfortunately, quantity turned into quality. If you always call a man a goat he will soon start to bleat.

Another thing was that she knew her father's interests, particularly in terms of finance. Lidia was a successful financer. She was not interested in her looks, but more in her soul, and had no way to appreciate another person, except by judging him for his sins that displeased Aldonai. In addition, Lidia understood perfectly well that she was not a beauty, and was not afraid of openly manipulating it.

Yes, I am not that pretty, but I have a beautiful soul. What is your worth?

She grew ignorant and failed to realize that everything in a person should be harmonious, and it turned her into a religious feminist, as sad as it was. No one could stop her. Her father was pleased with his daughter being a business-oriented accountant. Somehow, Lidia always managed to find the way of making money.

Her mother was indifferent to everything that was going on around her. The queen had long ago become a shadow of her husband and it became her habit.

As for her brothers, they all suffered from a flaw typical to all brothers. All of them loved their sister enormously and were ready to behead anyone who would not appreciate her for her worth; as well as those who would. Her title made her superior to any member of the court. As a consequence, Prince Richard was the only bachelor around who could be fit to marry her. Even so, he made them very jealous.

The princes despised the potential husband of their sister, and Richard considered them genuinely boring.

＊＊＊

The prince thought Lidia was genuinely dull; all her achievements were nothing to him. *How could he value her if she was ugly and did not listen to him with respect?* Moreover, she thought herself to be smarter than Richard, an unforgivable flaw. Richard was clearly astonished at finding someone encroaching on his sacred dignity. *Was she foolish enough to do so?*

Thus, Richard counted the minutes until his departure, and so did Jess. The news from Ativerna burned Jess like acid; the letters would not stop arriving.

He had received a letter from his sister who expressed her admiration toward Lilian Earton. If it were not for Lily, Amalia said, she would not be alive. The strangest thing was that she scolded him for being a foolish husband to have locked such a beautiful and intelligent wife in the wilderness; Jess's sister was speechless. She could not imagine how Jess could have said such bad things about his wife.

Jess rolled his eyes and showed Richard the letter. The prince had been of no help to his friend; all he could do was scratch his head. Where such speeches came from and on what grounds was a mystery to both. After that, Jess received a letter from his mother, with an enclosed note from Miranda.

Miranda was happy. She was all wonderful. She referred to the two princesses as being swell and called His Majesty a great old man. Lily was a bright ray of sunshine, whereas Alicia was a great example of how to "hush everyone down". Amir allegedly ordered a couple of Avarian stallions to be sent to Earton, and Mirrie could choose herself a horse.

Alicia also wrote, but her words were less joyful. She told him that even though Countess Earton used to live as a recluse, she managed to become one of the most fashionable ladies in the kingdom. Her outfits were copied by others to the best of their ability. King Edward was very pleased with the Countess and treated her with favor. Any attempts to send his wife off to Earton and forget about her should be abandoned because it could lead to very painful and unpleasant consequences. She wondered what her beloved son thought with when talking to his wife—his head or a piece of wood? If so, she said it was important to invite woodpeckers so they could make a hole for inserting the brains. Otherwise, it might leave His Majesty unhappy with the situation.

It was the last letter which struck the final blow. The letter was from one of the gossipers of the court.

***

Dear friend,

Now, I understand why you used to hide your wife in the wilderness. I would hide her too if I happened to possess such a precious woman. The Countess' appearance left an unforgettable impression. Her manners and her dresses have become proverbial in all tongues and a subject of envy for the ladies. They have truly valued her for her worth. However, if I was in your place, I would pay attention to her overly-liberal behavior. Her Virman guards have crossed all boundaries in their impudence.

He did not tell Jess that the line crossed alluded to the guards punishing the gossiper for making improper and insolent comments about her friendship with Falion. His face was rolled in the mud and dipped in a puddle of manure. He held a grudge against the Countess and decided to turn the tables by writing to Jess. *To tell on Falion? Aldonai forbid*. He wanted to live. So, he resolved to complain about the Countess and her guards, her "pagan," "unpredictable" Virmans. He made his hints very clear.

They do not respect anyone and say that they are around your wife day and night. They even accompany her to the palace, against the will of the King. As your most sincere friend, I must let you know that it stirs a certain confusion.

***

Jess showed this letter to his cousin, but Richard only shrugged, as if saying, *you are a fool, my friend.*

"How could they be guarding her 'around the clock', and what 'violations of the rules of propriety'? In the house of your mother? With her stepdaughter being always there? Think with your head!"

Jess did try to think rationally, but he had so many thoughts that his head reminded him of a boiling tea-pot. The percentage of clever thoughts was very little. The Earl's blood boiled with anger at his wife. *How else? All my relatives thought me a fool at best.* He also was angry at himself. It was true that he had failed to follow the news about his wife and what she was up to.

Miranda's letters added some dissonance to the picture. It was clear that the girl adored her stepmother, and the love was big. Jess loved his daughter and understood perfectly well that he could not separate her from her beloved Lily. She would not forgive that. In addition, the Earl was tormented by his own feelings.

His wife was an iceberg made of fat, and genuinely stupid, too. He could remember her mumbling something, her big cowish eyes. *What was the use of those eyes?* He could not even remember their color. Her hair was probably of light color, but the rest was a blur of pink cloud; he could picture her fat pink face—all was pink.

Ugh!

Jess and Richard occasionally relieved the stress with wine, since they could not see any women. Of course, Bernard had everything under control. Richard also realized that as soon as he married Lidia he would also be grabbed by his member. *No!* Anna is a better choice; the decision was final.

* * *

It could be said that Adelaide Wells was enjoying her life, periodically reporting back to the court jester about Richard's moves. The prince was evidently not going to marry, so Anna had no rivals. A different thing bothered her. *What will happen when I return home?*

But Altres Lort relieved her worries. "Do not worry, My Lady," he said. "You will go to Wellster. There is nothing to worry about. We will take care of you."

In reality, Altres did not need this whore anywhere, neither in Ativerna nor in Wellster. On the other hand, there were no outsiders in life, everyone could have their place in the sun. He could make her marry some chevalier or old man and put her to her intended use. Altres had long ago spotted a fit candidate, and he was going to dwell on it upon his arrival.

As for now, Adelaide was trying to remain in Lidia's society, together with other ladies-in-waiting. What she saw put her in silent shock. Lidia was not a woman; she was a digit in a skirt. The skirt was tattered and the digit was fanatic and dumb. Counting gold could not substitute for human understanding or warmth and care. Richard could also see it. Despite her being a whore, Adelaide was not dumb; her wit was practical. She was not bestowed with wings, but the heavens gave her swift legs and suckers. She was like a spider or remora fish. To slip through doors and tag along with someone was her everyday business. Adelaide's practical wit made her see that if Lidia were to shake off the shell of her religious fanaticism, stinginess, and other flaws, she would make a good wife. *But alas!*

It is impossible to change a man. He can only change himself, but only on the outside. The stem will remain and come out in the most extreme situations, and it will strike very hard, so hold on tight. Adelaide did not believe that Lidia could change. She also suspected that Gardwig would only be glad to find out about such a course of events, which meant that her jester would also be happy. But she had to still ensure it, just in case.

A princess is a creature much desired. Is there not a single hunter for her heart? If only she could find out something that could be used for blackmail. Altres would appreciate it; besides, it was best to be armed.

Adelaide thought a lover was not a ghostly substance but a real man who left traces, who required time. She started watching.

The first days left her genuinely upset. Lidia's footsteps could be traced to her chamber, to the library, to the King and the treasurer, and to the church to pray and confess. As for her chamber, according to the old custom, the bedrooms of the royal family members were a suite of rooms joined together. It was useful in cases of emergency, for the royal family could quickly get hold of the heir and run away via the back exit together. That was a plus. A minus was that it was unfit for hosting lovers. The chamber could be entered at any moment. It could be her brothers, mother, father or servants. Having someone stay there would have been too risky.

During one of her visits, Adelaide was smart enough to inspect the princess' chamber, which made her conclude that it was unfit for a romantic *rendezvous*. The locks were too unreliable; a sneeze was enough to break them. There was no place for a lover to hide in case someone walked in. It was as if the chamber belonged to a poor nun, not a young princess. It possessed an evident air of asceticism; there was not even a canopy over the bed. Even a moth would be disgusted to eat such curtains. If a thief broke into her chamber, he would cry and offer charity.

Adelaide exaggerated, but it did not change the main thing: the room was invaded by servants in the morning and the royal family in the evening. *No, Lidia would not risk so much.*

Adelaide inspected the library, which she also dismissed as unfit for the purpose. First, the librarian was around fifty years old and looked like a dry pear. Second, the library was adjacent to Bernard's study, and the King often visited it to take some manuscripts or consult the librarian. The princes also spent their time there often. From Adelaide's point of view, the library was also unfit for visits. The King's study and the treasury were out of the question. The only thing left was the church.

Adelaide began to follow Lidia to the church, mumbling about her sins and forgiveness, as well as glancing from side to side. Her efforts were rewarded, although not straight away. Adelaide was clever and noticed things that others tried to hide. For instance, she noticed that the church priest was quite young and good-looking. He had brown hair, deep blue eyes, and a well-kept beard. Even the green cassock suited him.

Adelaide also noticed that Lidia's voice trembled every time she looked at the handsome priest. Another suspicious thing was that she went to confessions way too often—every two days. Every time, Lidia chose the same confession room, in the corner of the church. Adelaide visited it as well and found out that the metal lattice between them was purely symbolic. One could even move it aside, given possession of the key, and Adelaide was sure the priest had the key.

Adelaide concluded that once in two days the princess used an opportunity to pay private visits to Pastor Reymer. She rubbed her hands and started thinking. *What do I want to achieve, to catch the princess in the act? If so, what will I do next?* She would more likely be punished than rewarded for her finding. Bernard would not be happy to find out. It would make Richard leave immediately, but that was not likely to soften Adelaide's punishment.

The woman resolved to meet with the agent of Altres Lort and give him the information. It was not her responsibility to think of how to use it. She did her job, and now it was up to the others to bear the consequences. The agent was satisfied with the news. He immediately wrote to his master and waited for instructions.

***

In the aftermath of the Virman delegation, Lily was rewarded. The King was happy because he made a lucrative deal with Virma. They agreed to develop the production of salt in both Virma and Ativerna. Glass would remain in Ativerna, but the agreement of cooperation would be in place. The Virmans started feeling at ease in Ativerna. They were assigned to accompany trade ships and drown the pirates of Loris.

In return, Edward would deliver goods and buy wool and whatever else the Virmans decided to sell. They could sell many things. They received a large discount at the shipyards, and many other things, as well. The Virmans separately discussed the possibility for the Virman children to study medicine from Tahir Djiaman din Dashar at Lily's school. They hinted that if it was not for Lily, it was unlikely that anyone would even accept them outside of Virma. Those speeches got into Edward, and as a result of the talks, Lily was given permission to open her clinic. The King even promised to finance it. He resolved to invest part of the shares received by the treasury from Mariella trading house into building the hospital.

***

Lily was also immensely grateful to the Crown because a delegacy of mediuses showed up to see her. They abhorred Lily's initiative, as well as the news about Medicus Craybey. The word went that Craybey was a trickster, and that the guilds taught only tricksters and poisoners. That was the first thing. The second thing was that Lilian invited the main doctor of the Khanganat to teach new doctors and herself, and they wondered what would happen to the mediuses after new doctors finished their studies.

Sir din Dashar was already helping more people than the guild itself. He and his people saved Marchioness Ivelen and helped her give birth to the twins. The doctors who were present there did not help at all… *What were they doing? Sitting and waiting. What for? Aldonai?* Countess Marvel began to appear in public much more often. Neither Lily nor Tahir minded having people coming for consultations. The guild obviously did not like it, and soon Lily was visited by a procession of seven long-bearded doctors in blue tunics.

She had no choice but to accept them. The visit followed all formalities. It began with greetings, then proceeded on to a slight indignation. They said that Tahir was not a member of the guild and his practice was not entirely legal. If they complained to the Crown, His Majesty would not trample on his own laws. The guild of the doctors was honorable, and such rumors harmed its reputation.

It all boiled down to an extremely polite ultimatum. Either Tahir entered the guild and accepted the consequences, or the guild would create as many problems for him as they could. They had a lot of power to do so. Everyone got ill, from goldsmiths to aldons, and during illness, people tended to listen to the medicus' advice over anyone else's.

***

Lily went to the King, and in a week's time, she held a royal charter in her hand to create another guild for her own medics. Tahir Djiaman din Dashar was appointed as the head of the guild. Exactly five minutes later, Lilian Earton and Jamie Meitl, now titled Baron Donter, were accepted as the guild's full members. Jamie was now earning money to reconstruct his estate. He did not want to trade slaves, so he saved gold, which was not difficult when working with Lilian. As a disciple of Tahir, Jamie was always in demand. He did not accept all the calls, usually consulting with Alicia or Lilian, and soon found himself a desirable doctor upon discovering that he knew a lot. He could identify many maladies, and cure them, too.

This was the difference between the guild of medicuses and the guild of doctors. The former was there to treat for money. The latter sought to cure the patient, the sooner the better. They did not work for free, but as a rule, if they cured a person once, the same illness would never bother them again. At present, Lily's task was to recruit students.

The Virman women could teach them the basics, following the scrolls that Lily wrote herself. There were a lot of university professors who taught the subject by the book. If a person wished to learn, he would learn. The results would show. It would take at least a year and a half to learn the basics, and after, that she could send her people to work in the clinic. It was better to learn in practice. At first, they could be qualified as paramedics, not therapists or pediatricians, but that could be changed.

To do everything at once would mean sacrificing quality. A good paramedic, on the other hand, was very valuable. There were times when paramedics were the only doctors in villages. They saved people, assisted childbirth, cut people open and sewed them back up. Even a good nurse was better than a *specialist* who would use their dirty hands to heal the wound or smear the birth canal with honey to lure the baby out. There was no doubt about that.

The medicuses were extremely dissatisfied with the new guild. Their wailing ceased after the aldon approved of the newly formed doctor's guild. The medicuses could not go against the will of the Church. They could try, but the Church was famous for its hard-line approach.

***

Lily worked day and night, as did everyone around her. Her conscience was slightly hurt by the conversation with Pastor Vopler.

"Child, was it necessary to be that cruel?"

"What are you on about, Pastor?"

"About how you dealt with that poor Eveer. Although they are pagan, is such cruelty really necessary?"

Lily shook her head. "Pastor, do not blame me. He was stealing, not from me, from the Crown. What is the punishment for it?"

"The death penalty and seizure of private property."

"Exactly. The reason why he was stealing was because I am a woman. I am a fool in his eyes that can be easily conned by a clever Eveer. Did he do it out of poverty? Out of grief? Did his crying children make him do it? Were his parents struggling to get by?"

"Nothing of the kind?"

"No, Pastor. He simply wanted to make a little business out of fooling me. That is why I had to…play by the rules, there is no other word for it."

"That game is dangerous."

"Who has doubts about that? I had to speak to the King, I had to deal with the Eveers, I also had to be present when they chopped off his thumbs and put a stamp on him. I nearly fainted there. I could not eat for three days, as far as I can remember. Do you think it was because of my love of money?"

The pastor shrugged.

"You are mistaken, Pastor. If it was in my power, I would have never done that. But he was hired as a test. If I let him get away with it this time, the whole affair would be shredded to bits. Think about it, Pastor. Ativerna is becoming richer thanks to glass and lace. It will attract more sailors, tradesmen …not to speak of the benefits for the Church and treating the sick…I do not want to get distracted from it every time I need to kick some thief's ass! It makes sense to nip it in the bud."

"It is pride, Countess."

"I know, and I will answer for my sins. But I had no other choice."

"You had none, or you did not see one?"

"True, I failed to see another option."

"Perhaps you did not want to see it?"

"This is also possible."

"Maybe there was another way out, without such cruelty?"

Lily shook her head. "Pastor, I did not take pleasure in it. If need be, I will chop off any thief's legs until they realize that they cannot steal from me, no option given. You may call it cruel, ugly, proud, and you will be right a hundred times! But sadly I do not get to choose."

***

The pastor only shook his head. He was no fool. He saw that Lily was tired, that she was relying on her last strength; she was afraid for Miranda and herself... He saw a lot of things.

"Aldonai will forgive you. He will forgive us all. He loves us, no matter what we do. Will you forgive yourself for this sin?"

Lily shook her head. "My sin cannot be forgiven. I know."

"Nonetheless..."

"I was merciful to him. He is alive, and I only took away what he had stolen. As for my own peace of mind... It will not kill me. I shall recover, as I always do."

The pastor sighed. "Let Aldonai follow you on your path."

Lily also made the sign of Aldonai. "Let the sun of truth always shine over us."

***

The truth was painful. Just take the conversation with the Eveers. Lily explained quite harshly that she wanted it to be the first and the last time they decided to test her. If someone dared to steal once more, she would punish the whole Eveerian commune; not only punish, she would leave them making pasta on Virma instead of serving at her estate.

Lily completely forgot about pasta, and about a lot of other culinary recipes. She needed to tell Helke's nephew to look for a place to open a restaurant; she rejoiced that sanitary inspectors, firefighters, and other bloodsuckers remained in the twenty-first century. Their jobs were surely useful, but the amount of bribery in those institutions almost canceled out their benefits.

The speech got under the skin of each Eveer. Helke was especially alarmed after Lily notified him in popular language that the second such test without her knowledge would portend a much more serious conversation, not with Erik, but with the angry King. Edward held a high authority and from that time on, no one dared to set up any tests for Lily.

* * *

She did not think once about her husband, and would not have remembered him at all, if it were not for Alexander.

Falion became a true friend to Lily. He visited her, gave her presents, held long conversations; Lily's breakdown made Falion see her anew.

Yes, Lilian was strong, intelligent and beautiful, but she still remained a woman. No one seemed to acknowledge the feminine side of her. They viewed her like they regarded a battleship and noticed the number of its guns. They paid no attention to the color of its sails. They failed to see its beauty and fragility.

He himself had not seen it before. He saw a woman of knowledge, strength, intelligence and a habit to subject others. Women like her left a mark in history. At the same time, they were unhappy, because they were Iron Ladies, cold, determined, desperate to burn out for their chosen career. Among them were warriors and court ladies. They did exist, and their memory was forever engraved in history. At first, Falion thought that Lilian was the same, but soon he started recognizing other things.

She adored her horse and tenderly loved her stepdaughter. Although Miranda was not her own, Lilian loved her immensely. Some women, like his mother, did not even love their own children. Lily was ready to give her stepdaughter anything, whether possible or impossible. Falion noticed it.

Lilian Earton was good at switching her masks, but they came off every time she opened her arms to greet Miranda. Every time, without fail, her eyes would shine with incredible love and warmth. It was coming right from her soul; there was no doubt about it.

Lily was kind and loving to all her people alike, such an attitude was impossible to fake. As a result, everyone loved her in return. The only person who Falion never heard Lily mention was Jerrison, Earl of Earton.

Alexander was friendly with him, they even liked each other. He had now realized that it was best to talk about her husband. Lilian did not mean him ill, he saw it quite clearly, but their friendship would bring nothing good either. Alexander even clenched his teeth upon facing the facts; he knew Jerrison. His primary confusion upon finding out about their friendship would quickly change to aggression. The consequences might be unpredictable.

That day Alexander planned to take the first little step to prevent it. He resolved to talk with Lilian. Although it seemed like none of his business, maybe he could bring it up because Lilian knew about his family problems. She never betrayed his secret, not with word or gesture, but she pitied him, and it was clear. She understood him and helped to take the heavy load from his shoulders. He wanted to return her kindness.

He found the Countess with Hans. They were evidently busy, drawing some circles and arrows on a sheet of paper.

"Lilian."

The woman turned around. Her green eyes sparked, her smile brightened up her face. *A beauty! There was no other way to describe her.* When the inner light of the soul shone through like that, the shape of nose or ears became unimportant. She was shining, and it looked almost like a miracle.

"Good day, Alexander. I am happy to see you."

Her speech was never trivial. She was genuinely glad to be seeing Falion.

"I wanted to ask you if you wished to ride in the fields with me. Have you been out today?"

"I need to go to Taral. Will you join me?"

Falion nodded. They could talk on the way there.

***

Lily was not naïve. She noticed Falion's glances, and they made her nervous.

I pray that Falion is not in love with me! It would be utterly out of place to lose a friend for the questionable pleasure of sex.

Why questionable? Because she was utterly exhausted. She wanted to get some sleep, have rest, relax... *No one let me enjoy those pleasures!* There was no pleasure in her life at the moment, only stress.

But what can I do if that is the case? Change the subject? Or maybe...?

She chose the second option.

"Alexander, did you want to speak with me about something?"

"Yes, Lilian. I want you to understand me correctly...I am going to touch on some personal subjects..."

"I promise to listen carefully." Lily's face radiated calmness.

Falion sighed and dove headfirst into cold waters. "Lilian. You became extremely popular at court. You are beautiful, intelligent, every woman tries to resemble you, you have the King's favor, you are now ahead of everyone...And what follows such success?"

Lily shrugged. "I do not know. I have no choice in the matter. I just live my life."

"You wish to spend your whole life living like that? Without a husband, and without children, always busy..."

The woman cast down her eyes. Falion hit Lily's most painful spot.

"No, I do want to love and be loved, I want a family, I want children... But it does not depend solely on me."

"Yes, it depends on you and Jerrison. Lilian, I beg you to understand me right. You have become precious to me; Jerrison is my friend. If I saw that you needed nothing more than power, I would have not said a word to you, but you are not like that. You are warm, you need a home, you had no other choice than to become like this. But if it was possible, you would have chosen to—"

Lily shook her head. "I would have happily lived a peaceful life, if I was not under the constant threat of getting killed. If I did not have to…well, you know everything yourself. Should I tell you again?"

"No. I remember. But do you remember that you are the Countess of Earton?"

"I would be glad to forget it."

"And what about your husband, Jess?"

"What about him?"

"He is far away now. And what do you do?"

"I am saving my life and the life of his daughter!" snapped Lily.

* * *

Falion's grey eyes were filled with so much care that Lily unwillingly softened. Falion possessed a certain quality that repressed the most savage fits of rage. It was not akin to religious humility. It was his inner strength, a solid determination that made one take a step back. Lily retreated. She was the first to cast her eyes to the ground.

"That is true. No one would dare to judge you for it. You are saving yourself. But at the same time, do you realize that men are selfish creatures?"

"Yes, so I have heard."

"You are leaving him without a stone to build his sense of pride. Tell me, for instance, he is coming back soon. How do you imagine your meeting with him?"

Lily was glad to be sitting down. If she were standing up, she would have fallen to the ground. *I don't know!*

"Perhaps, we would have a conversation…"

"Will you have things to talk about?"

Lily glanced at Falion.

"If I did not consider you a friend I would never have started this conversation."

Lily sighed and put her hand in a thin lace glove on top of Alexander's. "Forgive me. I know you are a friend."

"And I want to remain your friend."

Deep down, at the bottom of his soul he harbored the hope of being able to see her and remain her friend if she would remain in the capital. She needed to talk to her husband about that. They would soon lead separate lives, but when he first saw her...

Alexander knew her husband. He would ignore all chiding and hatred. *They could not exile him further than Virma!* He would do such things out of anger, misunderstanding and hatred.

He had to let Lilian know before it was too late.

***

Lily knew it was true that she treated her husband as something abstract and distant. *What will I do with him once he is back?* If he turned out to be an enemy, it was best to poison him straight away. Mirrie also could not stand her before, and now she was like a bird who was not afraid to take food from Lily's hand. *Besides, I want to...yes, it is a very girlish thing to do and it might be silly, but I want revenge for the poor fatty, who was not loved but only used.* The best revenge was to turn the tables. Her husband would be the one who got all the hatred.

"Alexander, I genuinely do not know."

"I know. Lily, you told me about yourself."

Yes, I did, although it was an altered version of my story. Not about her travel to the past, but about her waking up from the drug coma and realizing that she could not go on living like that. The foundations of her personality were laid by her father; it did not matter that she only saw him a couple of hours a month, it was genetics, no doubt.

"So what?"

"The times when your husband spoke to you, were you...normal? I am sorry for my choice of words..."

"No, it's fine."

"Not drugged, not under the influence of …"

"No. Not once."

"Why did you not write to him and tell him everything as it was?"

"Why do you think that I did not write?"

Lily was curious, but Falion only shook his head. "I am sure that you never did. It is most likely that he wrote to you still thinking that you were intoxicated, and you took his manner of speaking to you badly and got offended. If you wrote, it was not out of love."

Well, except that it was not the drug but my old personality, Falion's guessing was pretty accurate.

"You think?"

"I am sure."

"You are right. I will send him a letter right away. I will do it today. I promise."

"Do it, Lilian. Do you really need a family drama? You want home, children, and a loving husband, is it not so?"

"How do you know that I …"

"Well, I have never happened to be wanting a husband…" Falion smiled mockingly. "As for everything else…"

Lily burst out laughing. The conversation turned into something light-hearted and playful, but Falion's words got stuck in Lily's head like a nail hammered into a piece of wood. On the one hand, she was right. But on the other, she would have to live with Jerrison. The King was in favor of her marriage with the Earl of Earton, and divorcing would mean taking losses.

She herself was not sure she wanted a divorce. *How many people,* she wondered, *see me as Lily, and how many look at me as Countess Earton?* She would find herself in a worse position if she did not start improving the relationship with her husband. She had a total right to be offended, for both Poor Fatty Lilian and for herself. Her husband should receive all the kicks and whacks he deserved.

She could picture one possible course of events. Jess would arrive, ignite a scandal with the breaking of plates and all the attributes of it… No man would stand to be running errands for his wife. It is very likely that he would be tempted to rip Lily's head off. *What next?*

They would defend her; her husband would be exiled to some wild parts; and she would never see a normal life. She could find herself a lover, but she would still have no family, and she did not like the idea of meeting her significant other in secret. She would have no children, nothing.

There was a second option. Even if she wanted to live separately from her husband, she had to try to come to a peaceful agreement. In other words, she would have to start stirring the cauldron now.

She was not defenseless anymore so she could let herself set up an illusion. She would show herself slightly weaker than she was, and then strike first if she needed to. If Jess was not a fool, he would agree to a peace treaty, but only if he was going to think with his brains, not another part of his anatomy.

If he was a fool, after all, she would strike from her highest caliber weapon, because there would not be much to lose.

Lily wondered why Falion brought this conversation up.

I will think about it later. Jerrison Earton is my main focus now. I have dealt with murderers and slave-traders. Will I fail to deal with a medieval earl? You, Jess, will soon be trained to take food from my hand. I will tame you.

***

That night, when Mirrie was already sniffling in sleep, Lily sat down to write a letter.

My beloved lord and husband,

No way I am writing that! She crossed the words with a thick line and took a new sheet of paper.

"Your Lordship?" *It reads like I am his humble slave. Yuck!*

"Jerrison?" *That's better.*

Jerrison, the Earl of Earton, I send you my greetings.

I hope that you are doing well, as much as it is a fit description.

I also hope that you will not throw away this letter as soon as you read it, but at least will try to think about what I am trying to convey.

I suppose the last few months have been most difficult for you. I also went through a lot of hardship. They tried to rob me, kill me, and seduce me. I cannot say that any attempt by the above mentioned succeeded, or that it brought me pleasure, but you should know about what happened. Miranda was also in danger of being kidnapped and murdered. Yes, the villainous attempts were not successful, but they did take place. Why am I writing all this to you? To explain why I left Earton and why I behave in the way I do.

I really wanted to live. I suppose anyone in my shoes would have done the same. Or would you have obediently waited for your death? I doubt it.

Do not be surprised by the rumors that reach you. Just remember who my father is and think what I could inherit from him. My mother, too, was not particularly gentle and obedient, but this subject is better to speak about in person.

I never think about you, I must admit. You can take it as an offense and throw the letter away now, but I will continue nevertheless.

I have spent all our married life intoxicated. Before the wedding, I was intoxicated by love. If you ask any married woman (and I think you are acquainted with such), she would tell you that young girls go completely mad before the marriage. After that, I was being drugged, pushed off the stairs, put on the edge of the grave. I have told you this before already.

I am sure that it was difficult for you, too. However, I am asking myself, how could one not notice that his wife was being poisoned? How could you give so much freedom to your overseer? Is that because you did not want to see it?

It can be comprehensible, but not justifiable. In fact, it is clear as day. An ugly and unloved wife was just an addition to the dowry, the shipyards of her father. You probably wanted to get her out of sight and out of your mind. If she survived, oh well, if she did not , very well. Your only wish was for her—for me—to give birth to a boy. Am I wrong?

I was very hurt when I realized it. I do not know how you feel about it.

What next?

Once you land in Ativerna, a strange woman will meet you there, the woman you are married to. A man who is a stranger to me will come to my door. And we will have to try to somehow live together. I am telling you honestly, I would not try to bring the dead horse that is our marriage to life. The reason for my efforts is Miranda. I started loving this girl with all my heart, and I am ready to do much for the sake of her happiness, including seeking to find a common language with a man who wishes me dead.

I still struggle to imagine how we could find that common language. You are probably angry at me. I also have many reasons to be angry. Nevertheless...

How do you picture the future of our family? Let us try to speak a common language at least now, after being struck by the grief of a lost child. I will try my best, but marriage is a two-way road.

Lilian, as of yet, Countess of Earton

Just like that. Not Broklend, not Earton, not counts and barons. The conversation was between a man and a woman. A signature, a fold, a drop of wax, a titular seal. If Lily's dear husband was not a fool, he would quickly understand that her letter was the holding out of a peace pipe. If he was a fool, after all, he would not even be worthy of her pity. There were a lot of counts, but she did not have a second self, and so she had to protect her well-being.

She thought about issuing an order to express her gratitude to Falion, or give him something. He was a good man, a sound person.

Lily fell asleep as soon as her head touched the pillow. In her sleep, she saw the grey eyes of Alexander, grey and grieving. He did what he should have done, but it made him extremely sad.

***

Gardwig's spy at the court of Ivernea appreciated the news from Adelaide, provided the knowledge that Lidia and Richard did not like each other anyway.

Either way, blackmail would always come in useful. That is why it was of extreme importance to listen to the conversation between the pastor and Lidia, or better to peek on top of that. *But how will we pull it off?* Although confession rooms stood practically next to each other, someone could still notice a stranger listening to conversations. *But if a spy managed to walk into one of the rooms…*

Green cassocks were not in deficit. As soon as Lidia slipped into her confession room, a spy in a cassock with a bucket and a rag would enter the neighboring confession cell—a cleaner, the most inconspicuous character of all. The most important thing was for him to have his eyes and ears open. No one would object to him doing the sacred act of cleaning.

His efforts were not in vain. Although the gain was not as big as he had hoped. There was no kissing, no love confessions, although sometimes he could recognize them in Lidia's trembling voice, in the way she touched the boy's hand… The young woman was surely in love. Her love was platonic. The boy, on the other hand, was too handsome and too prudent to fall in love, especially with such an ugly duckling. One thing he wanted was to become an aldon.

What was the best way to achieve it? If one had money he could be anything he wanted, even a king—there have been precedents of the kind. Therefore, the platonic friends were eagerly discussing trade, investment, and other things.

Everything on Lidia's side was innocent. However, the spy was not naïve enough to believe in the innocence of the priest. The next day, the priest was put under a very close watch. They grazed him like a sheep, day and night. They snuck into his chamber, the church, searched everything. In a week or so, the spy was grinning and rubbing his hands. Adelaide turned out to be quite useful. *Maybe it is not worth killing her after all?* She misunderstood the content of this couple's "prayers," but the rest was accurate.

The priest turned out to be quite ambitious, and he was plotting against the Crown.

What would be the easiest way to get rid of the royal family? It was very primitive. They could gather all of them in the church for the ceremony, with a couple of courtiers. He had found several options of how he could pull it off, to burn the building down, to poison the holy water... The one who sought always found. The pastor resolved to combine the two options together. He would poison as many people as he could and then burn the church down.

The Khangans had a nice substance that, once on fire, could not be put out. It would leave no evidence. He would bring himself from rags to riches in a split second. As for the poison, the boy was going to add something to the censers. It would put everybody to sleep. That sleep would be lethal if it lasted for longer than three hours.

He planned to do it soon, in approximately ten to twenty days, whenever Richard left. Everything would be like in a fairy tale—the savage murder of the royal family in a church.

Who would be found guilty? It would be the aldon's fault, for sure!

Who, on the other hand, would save the only surviving person? Pastor Reymer. He obviously would be made an aldon, and would reign together with Lidia. As for the princess and the fact she had no knowledge of the plan, the pastor did not think she was required to know. She would protest, get scared, look to save her relatives...

The experienced spy had already searched over the pastor's dwelling, without stirring a flea in his bed. He concluded a sad fact. Everything was ready for the deed. The boy had the poison ready, and his mercenaries were waiting for his command.

What would be the most beneficial to Altres Lort, the attempt, or its absence? It was clear as day that the attempts on the royal lives were best to be prevented; such thinking was not out of being humane, but rather because a successful experience in one country could well be repeated in another.

Lidia, as well, upon staying alone, could start to find protection and a strong man's shoulder. One thing that no one could take away from Richard was his charm.

The agent needed to deal with this matter quickly. However, the spy understood perfectly well, that all papers, even the ones indirectly related to Lidia, must disappear. But if he stole everything, the boy could get nervous and run away before the time. *How can I get around this?*

*＊＊

The perfect moment arrived in four days. The royal court decided to go on a pilgrimage to one of the most beautiful temples in the country. Naturally, every member of the family attended. Our young priest went with them, too.

The secret agent rubbed his hands. The next night, as if by Aldonai's providence, all letters and notes from Lidia to the priest disappeared from his chamber, as well as all the evidence that could indicate her involvement in the plot. The priest had made sure to have materials for blackmailing Lidia, in case her love for him suddenly ended.

By the same Aldonai's providence, some such exemplary letters appeared in every state institution of Ivernea. It appeared in the King's study, in the study of the first minister, in the hands of the head of the Royal Guard and so on. Someone should be taking action. The leader of the race after the conspirator appeared to be Chancellor Gaius, who got sick and could not go on the pilgrimage. Yes, rheumatism was hell; the moment it attacked left the chancellor bedridden for days. He was the one who supervised the guards; under his command they found the poison and prepared a report for His Majesty, as well as sent off letters to notify the King and his guards and order the villainous pastor to be placed under arrest and interrogated.

The letter was met with His Majesty's full approval. He did not mind the suggested punishment at all and expressed it with the dirtiest colloquialisms. Lidia fainted and could not recover for hours. The aldon grabbed his head in regret at having trusted the snake.

Richard and Jess did not react. It was unpleasant, but they were out of danger, for the plan was going to unfold after they departed from Ivernea. Richard was still not going to marry Lidia, their mutual border with Ivernea was after all not so big. In a word, the guests from Ativerna were not particularly worried.

As for the people of Ivernea, had Bernard been a little bit smarter, he would have used this attempt as an excuse to tighten the belt around the power of the Church. Lidia would possibly protest, but that was not a fact. Her love was after all directed at one particular priest, not at the whole Church at once. Her heart was now broken and swelling heavy in her bosom.

Lidia walked around gloomily, did not speak with anyone, and would constantly break into tears. Even Bernard got worried. The princess managed to explain her behavior by saying that her spirit was too fragile. She was a believer, and her faith in Aldonai had been so cruelly deceived.

***

Maybe her fault was in that first letter...

"Your Highness."

Lidia lifted her tired eyes at the courtier. She did not know who he was but there were a lot of them at court, youngest sons, chevaliers and so on...

"What do you want, sir?"

"I suppose that my name will tell you nothing..."

Lidia raised her eyebrows.

"However this letter might well do."

Lidia held out her hand, and the next moment she was petrified. It was one of the letters which she had written to Pastor Reymer a long time ago, in the very beginning of their relationship.

I hope for your understanding and prudence... I have no doubt that our interests are mutual...

She wanted to scream, call the guards, ask for help... But Lidia was absolutely helpless. She was trapped by the existence of this parchment. The letter was composed in such a way that it was unclear what it had been about. Lidia, of course, knew that it was about the friendship between her and Pastor Reymer. Everything worked out as she wanted. Although their sympathy was completely innocent, as the only thing the boy allowed himself was to hold her hand or kiss her on the cheek. However, the subject of the letter was unclear; it could have well been about the plot.

She was not the first or the last princess seeking to take over the royal throne. *What will my father do if the letter is presented to him in a wrong light?* He would execute her. He would make it quick, if she was lucky. Lidia raised her eyes and glanced at the stranger.

"What do you want from me?"

"Nothing that you don't want," the man was calm. "Am I right in thinking that you do not want to marry Richard from Ativerna?"

Lidia raised her eyebrows.

"No, I do not. But—"

"Good. I urge you to leave it like that. I promise you that, when you and Richard are nothing, the letters will also be nothing. They will disappear."

"It is blackmail," hissed Lidia. "You are a bastard!"

"You can call me whatever you want as long as you have understood what is required of you."

All his softness suddenly disappeared. Lidia was facing a real werewolf, except the saliva dripping from his fangs was missing.

Lidia flashed her eyes, but she was left with no choice.

"I understand. Give me the letter." The man enclosed the parchment into her outstretched palm.

"Enjoy, Your Highness. I have another dozen of them."

The stranger disappeared into the crowd. Lidia had an urge to moan. She was caught on the blackmailer's hook.

***

Jess was deeply astonished by Lily's letter. He expected nothing of the like. In fact, he did not expect anything that had befallen him, neither the governor who was a thief, nor the murderers, and especially such statements from his wife.

The first of his impulses was to rip the letter into pieces and let it be consumed by fire. *As if she is some sort of a hero! First, she humiliated me in front of the whole kingdom and then she made me look guilty!*

The second urge was to read through the letter again. The third was to get advice from Richard.

Jess was not stupid. He could resolve a standard situation. However, everything in this one had been out of bounds. The saddest thing was that he could not protest against his wife's testimony, for every word of it was true.

Am I guilty? In a way he was. He did send her away out of sight; he did neglect his family; and he did dream for her to die. Lily had a genuine right to put forward such accusations. It was also clear as to why she did not do it earlier. Datura was a strong drug. Jerrison had never tried it himself, but he knew people who lost their minds from being under its effect. It was a true miracle that Lily survived and remained in her right mind. *Although it is sharp, maybe it is not so right? Is she a bit insane?*

It is clear as day. An ugly and unloved wife was just an addition to the dowry, the shipyards of her father. You probably wanted to get her out of sight and out of your mind. If she survived, oh well, if she did not, very well. Your only wish was for her—for me—to give birth to a boy. Am I wrong? I was very hurt when I realized it.

Jess responded to this bit of his wife's letter aloud like a madman. "What on earth are you capable of understanding, you pink cow? You used to only sit on your ass and eat sweets all day. It was disgusting to even be in the same room with you, let alone touch you!" he bellowed.

"I have done my job. I took you, a merchant's daughter, as my wife. I have given you my name. You lived in my house, and I was really trying hard to give you a child. What else would you need?"

Jess looked at the scroll and angrily threw it against the wall. He contemplated a little, lifted it up from the floor and headed to see Richard. After all, he needed to send a reply. The only thoughts which came to his head were the sacramental "screw you." Maybe his cousin could help him think of something, or at least help him unwind.

***

Richard did help. He looked at his friend, evaluated his mental state by judging the state of his heart and asked a brief question: "A drink?"

As a result, they only turned to the letter in the morning, after the wonderful medicine against heartache called booze. Both of their heads exploded.

Richard read carefully and looked at his friend.

"How much truth is in it?"

"There is no truth in it whatsoever," retorted Jess, "I gave her everything, a title, a place in the sun, and she could not even manage to bear a child!"

Richard shook his head. "Are you being just? Is that why you are so wrathful?"

"What do you mean by that?"

"A title? She is not a peasant."

"Her title is not hereditary."

"Nevertheless, she is the daughter of a baron. A rich baron, not to mention the shipyards. You know very well that August is the best shipbuilder in the whole vast region!"

"I know."

"So, she does not need a title so much, after all. A place in the sun? What 'high society' are you referring to there?"

"Uh…"

"Or do you have a court in Earton?"

"It has certainly turned into a criminal court, for I have got a thief!"

"Right, that sounds more like the truth. How could you have overlooked the mess that was going on in Earton this whole time?"

Jess shrugged. *Did I have anything to notice? Yes, I handed out orders about the stables and the kennels when I was around, but the rest…*

"I was hunting all day and went to sleep with my wife at night."

"Right, so you did not see because you did not look."

Jess sighed. "Well, not to spare that."

"You just did not want to meddle in the affairs, you refused to find the guilty, to rebuild Earton castle. Why would you? You chose to neglect and forget about it, a very prominent quality of yours. Do you really think that ignoring the irritant would make it go away?"

"You are being a smart-ass."

"You did come for advice."

Jess was angry, but still listening to him. "Of course, go. Finish me off."

"What is there to finish off? The only times I heard you speak about your wife was when you called her a cow, a fat cow, a fatty… moooo!"

Jess burst out laughing, but it was a sad kind of laugh. Richard also smirked gloomily.

"That's right. She also failed to bear the child because she was poisoned. They drugged her, they pushed her down the staircase, it is lucky that she survived herself!"

Jess' face was so full of emotion that Richard only tapped him on the head with a finger. "Think about it! If it were to come out after her death, it would have taken you a century to clear your name."

Jess squinted.

"No, my friend, you are the lucky one and you do not even realize it. Is she telling the truth about her death? Yes, she is. And what do you choose to do?"

"For now, nothing."

"Exactly. What you should have done is be grateful for her giving you a chance. Your wife is a gem, she is trying to fix your relationship, although its downfall is mainly your fault."

"Yes, it is! So what!?" groaned Jess. "I did not notice her, did not try to understand, insulted, humiliated, scoffed at her! Now, she will take revenge! Even the horses will be laughing at me in the capital!"

"All is in your hands."

"Oh really?"

"If you come and start a scandal, certainly not. But if you reconcile with your wife and together develop a mutually beneficial strategy, maybe show up together a couple of times, you declare in front of everyone that you would do anything to make sure nobody takes away your treasure of a wife from you and so on..."

"If there was such a hero I would have even paid him to take her away."

"Moreover, you would have to pay on top, with the shipyards."

"Ugh!"

Jess needed the shipyards, whether he liked it or not. He was trading in luxury goods, which he bought in the Khanganat, in Elvan, Avester... August had ships that proved very handy. Together they would be better off.

"Lilian is clearly not foolish. Have you read this letter carefully?"

Jess shook his head. "What do you mean?"

"Listen, you need to start thinking with your head! You are sitting here like a statue of Aldonai! Have you tried to analyze it at all? The woman clearly knows about your faults. Tell me, what would...Adele, for instance... What would she do?"

"She would blackmail me with it until I was a dead man."

"You see. There is nothing of the like in this letter. She only says that she is hurt, that is all. The rest indicates that she is ready for a dialogue."

Jess only sighed. "The question is whether I will be ready for it."

"Do you have any doubts about that?"

"You see, I am physically ill affected by her mere appearance. Before, I could at least forget about that nightmare. But now, when she is always by my side, when every single person around me is ranting about her and praising her in their letters... It makes me scared to even write home."

"Why?"

"Because, think about it. I have a feeling that the world had a fit of collective madness. Well, all right, I can write home. But what reply would I get? The reply will be no different than the letters now."

Richard sniffed. "You suppose you will not hear anything new?"

"On the contrary, I have received so much news that I don't know how to digest it!"

"Have you tried to write to anyone yourself?"

Jess sighed. "Who would I write to? My wife drove the governor away. Shirvey as well, although I trusted him. Bastards. I will bother about them later. Miranda, my mother, sister, even His Majesty, my uncle, have written to me. I am scared. Who else can I write to? Someone from my friends? Only imagine—dear friend, can you please check whether my wife has suddenly become pretty and clever? If that is so, please describe to me what exactly has happened, because I struggle to believe in miracles."

"What about your trusted people?"

"Servants, Richard, servants. They like to gossip. In addition, someone undesirable might read the letter. I am going to just... I am going crazy!"

"Is there really no one to write to?"

Jess shook his head. "Richard, when the first letter came, I puzzled over it for so long, even back in Wellster. I went through every single person I know, and every one had either seen me drinking or been with me to brothels... It doesn't matter. I realized that I have a sea of acquaintances, but as for friends, I only have you. Tell me, Richard, how many friends do you really have?"

Richard paused to think.

"Exactly. And how many of your convenience friends see the real you in you? As in, how many of them see Richard?"

"Explain?"

"Not Richard of Ativerna, not the heir to the throne, but just a guy called Richard. And how many people really see my real self behind my title?"

Richard's face changed into a painful grimace.

"You know yourself."

"I know. And it does not make me happy. You, too, are struggling methinks..."

"There is nothing to rejoice about. So what have you decided?"

"For now, I will live and enjoy my life. I will still have to decide what to do on the spot, so why sit and wonder now? In all honesty, I still suspect that someone might be standing behind Lilian."

"Yeah. In your mother's house, under her vigilant eye, and under the supervision of the King—of course not!"

"So you think..."

"Everything is just like she said. Before the wedding, your wife was in shock, a mad woman, all right? You are not a freak, not a fool...she was madly in love with you."

"I am starting to doubt whether I am not a fool and not the mad one."

"It means that you are getting smarter. In short—judging by the court ladies—anyone can fall in love with you, which she did. And you? What did you do?"

Jess sighed, remembering his wedding night. To be more precise, all he could remember was its shreds floating in the alcohol fog. If it were not for his stubble, his face would have surely turned red. Luckily, he managed to hide his embarrassment.

"Well yeah...I remember."

"You took all your disappointment out on the girl and exiled her to Earton, where they started poisoning her, after which point she turned completely mad."

"You are really making me a beast..."

"I think this is precisely what your wife thinks of you. After everything you have done to her. Think about it from her point of view."

Jess dropped his hungover head. He did not want to repent. He did not feel particularly guilty, but something needed to be done about the situation.

"So what should I do now?"

"To begin with, you should write to her- and tell her you are ready for a dialogue."

"I can write. But what is the use in it? They will attack me all the same! My uncle will surely burn me alive."

"We will talk to the messenger right before he sets off, and we will send the letter in secret. Remember not to write anything nasty to her."

"I will try, although I am very tempted to. Maybe we can pick some gift for her, Miranda, Amalia, mother..."

"That's it, walk around the jewelry stalls. These Eveerian tricksters have some interesting things in stock."

"True. And once we are back in the capital, we can figure out what to do with my wife."

"Are there any options? You have to build bridges, whether you like it or not."

"Well yes. It is not you who lives with this cow!"

"And now imagine that I had to marry Lidia..."

"Ugh. It would be scary to lie on top of her bones, lest they stab you to death."

"Her bones are only half of the problem..."

"Yes, her personality, I know."

"What if Lilian was really a changed woman? What would you have said to yourself if you received such a letter, putting all the emotions aside?"

Jess thought about it. "I would think that she is not foolish. I would say that it was written by a man. Listen, maybe someone is standing behind her after all?"

***

The men decided to walk around the jewelry stalls. They looked through different fabric and fur, and walked into one of the Eveerian shops.

An ancient Eveer first started saying a lot of compliments, and after, took many objects from behind the counter.

"Gentlemen, I can see that you are looking for presents for beautiful ladies. I can offer you earrings."

"Earrings?"

The Eveer nodded his head with a smirk on his face.

"Your ladies surely do not have anything of the like. Some of them are made to never fall off their beautiful little ears."

The several types of locks were a novelty to Jess and Richard. The guys looked, tried to open and close them.

"It is quite practical," decided the prince. "I also need to buy a couple for gifts."

"I can offer you tears of the sea Golden, white, red..."

"White? Red?"

The men exchanged glances. Amber of this color was a great rarity. And the earrings were made so exquisitely that the hand was drawn to it by itself.

"Whose work is this?"

"Artisans of Helke Leitz. Here is the brand.

"And this?"

Next to the artisan's stamp there was another mark of a red cross. The jeweler shrugged.

"Artisan Helke did not write me of it. All his crafts are of highest quality."

The men glanced at one another and took a couple of earrings each.

"And this, this is also sent to me by Helke. But the work is mine own. Would you like to have a look?"

The jeweler opened the box. The young men were astonished.

"What is it?"

"A set of cutlery. I hope you understand, gentlemen, that there are all kinds of dishes and it is simply indecent to eat, let's say, soup and dessert with the same spoon. Here you see six large spoons, six small dessert spoons, forks and knives for meat, fish forks, spatulas to lay out everything on plates, ladles—"

Jess only whistled.

"Whoa, what are they for?"

"For small family dinners."

"Are there sets for big dinners?"

"Yes, my lord, thirty items."

Jess began to think. His mischievous eyes beamed brightly.

"I will take a big one."

"What for?" Richard was surprised.

"For Lilian. She loves to eat."

"And you will use it together."

"Of course." Jess's eyes were completely innocent.

"Okay, and I will take a small one for now. How much?"

The price was so big that even the prince whistled, not to mention the paupers of Ivernea.

"Are they made of gold or what?"

"We can offer them in gold, too, my lord. But these are silver. Sir artisan Helke insisted on it. He said that silver was better for the body. We can also engrave a coat of arms on them, just tell me which one."

The price suddenly made sense. The men sighed and laid out the gold.

The earrings did not occupy much space. The cutlery was left in the shop to be engraved and the young men continued their search.

They got stuck in a weapon shop from which they bought a pair of throwing knives; they ate a pair of pies from street vendors; and Richard dragged his friend to the bookshop.

Edmond was the heir, whereas Richard tried to spend as much time in the library as he could. He also liked to hunt and spend time with friends and women, however the library was his most favourite place of all.

Once upon a time, an ancient teacher revealed to Richard the beauty of language, and Richard was forever enchanted by the mystery of symbols written on parchment. They had a power to travel to the depths of the oceans or up to the mountain heights. So now, Jess was bored waiting for Richard to look through the old scrolls, to ask about the authors, to feel the thickness of the parchment.

He discovered the shopkeeper to be a true lover of books and the ordeal lasted for around an hour. They would have spoken for much longer, but a green cassock showed up on the doorstep. The pastor was a tall, dry man. The expression on his face reminded one of a viper after being dragged along the ground by its tail.

"Good day, children of Aldonai."

The sound of his voice resembled the hissing of snakes. A couple of front teeth were missing.

Jess carelessly made the sign of Aldonai, and after a few minutes, Richard followed his example. The shopkeeper overtook them both and was the first one to honor the visitor. He bowed to the priest.

"Pastor Meyvern, I am glad to see you."

"Do you have the teachings of Saint Silion, my son?"

The shopkeeper thought a little and disappeared under the counter.

"Anything for you, Pastor. Although I often get asked for it and sometimes the copyists do not have enough time."

"What else do you order for them to copy?"

"Pastor, sir…"

Even Jess noticed that the shopkeeper was afraid. The pastor glared at the man with his serpent eyes.

"Recently the churchmen found a copyist who wrote forbidden text from the book of Maldonaya. He swore he did it for you."

"Pastor!"

The cry sounded so outraged that it was clear the shopkeeper might have been guilty of a lot of things, but not this one.

"I also did not believe it. But I decided to let you know. You have the best theological copies in the capital; that is why I am telling you that you should be able to—"

"Pastor, never in my life have I held such abominable texts in my hands. I am slandered."

"I believe you. And now, how much do I have to pay for the teaching?"

"It is a gift, as a gesture of my love to our Church, the one and only true church."

"Fine, child of light. But do still take those coins in return for the book."

The Pastor laid several silver coins on the counter and retired with the purchase.

The guys exchanged glances. It was time to get out of there, but the salesman looked around and suddenly seized Richard's sleeve.

"Sir! I implore you…"

"What exactly do you want, sir…"

Richard was unhappy. Jess took a step forward, ready to take off the shopkeeper's head. But the prince stopped him with a raise of the hand. "Wait for now."

"Sir, you also like books, I can see it. Whoever you are, help me!"

"How do you want me to help you?"

"I did not order the book of Maldonaya to be copied, but they named me for a reason."

"What was that reason?"

"Knowledge, My Lord, is the most valuable thing in the world. Any knowledge is precious. To destroy it is a great sin. You're not from Ivernea, are you?"

"How could you tell?"

"Your clothes, your look, and you do not pronounce the words in exactly the same way as we do here."

"I'm from Ativerna."

"It is easier there. You do not persecute people for banned books. And here, the Church does it. They can come and search me, they might find something that in their opinion contradicts the teachings and the interests of the Church, and they will destroy it."

"Well, let it be," said Jess lazily.

"My Lord! Knowledge cannot be destroyed, whatever kind of knowledge it might be, whether it is bad or good. It is a great sin before Aldonai. He gave us these texts, and we throw his gift in his face." The man started to shake, and Richard raised his arm to calm him.

"I understand. Do you have anything that could be taken as an offense to the Church?"

"Yes. Could you take it to Ativerna, My Lord?"

Richard paused to think and finally agreed.

"All right, I will buy all these scrolls and books from you. What do you have?"

"Scrolls, My Lord."

"How much do you want for them?"

The shopkeeper named a modest price. Richard counted the remaining coins and had to even borrow some from Jess.

"Here."

There were a lot of scrolls, and the young men had to carry them together.

"We should have taken the guards with us," said Jess. Richard brushed his comment off.

"I suspect that they might be watching us even now, but at least they do it in secret."

"We would at least have someone to help us carry this!"

"Stop grumbling. We can manage, it won't kill us. I wonder what these scrolls he managed to smuggle are."

"Probably some heresy."

It was no heresy. Among the scrolls there were treatises on the movement of celestial spheres, studies of the human body, and critical reviews of theological books.

***

Three days later, Richard was passing by that same shop and found it closed. He only hoped that they would let the man go. After all, he had nothing left to hide.

Richard would take the scrolls from Ivernea to make the trip at least slightly more useful.

The time went by...

***

Lilian, Countess of Earton, my greetings.

I hope that you are all right, as far as it is fitting to describe so. All is well with us.

Although you are absolutely right. I cannot imagine how hard the last months have been for you, although I suppose that murderers, robbers and seducers are not a fit company for the Countess.

But since you are writing to me, I assume that those threats have now been eliminated. The news makes me rejoice.

If only I had known that Earton was so dangerous, I would have never sent Miranda there. Only one thing makes me happy—that both of you survived.

I hope that you understand that I would never intend to poison or kill you. It was my negligence, and not intent that allowed for such horrible events to unfold.

I suppose I have already been severely punished for my negligence. I have had a hard time this winter. I was attacked by all the people whom I love and respect. Your father, my uncle...

I wish my message to reach you secretly. And I would like to ask you not to disclose its contents to anyone, even Miranda. I shall write to her separately.

And you are absolutely right. Judging by this letter, I did not know you before.

So what do you want, Lilian Earton?

Do you want to remain Countess of Earton, or are you willing to pursue a divorce? Judging by what I have learned from the recent letters, you have the opportunity to do both, and even more. It makes me very angry. Am I angry at you or at myself? I do not know. I do not want to be a public ridicule.

You asked me how I imagine our family. I suppose you do not want to sit in the wilderness. Therefore, I propose a truce. I do not demand that you retire to the family castle, and in return you try to maintain the honor of my name. It is your name, too, after all.

Well, so far, we have only one common love—Miranda. I, too, am ready to sacrifice a lot for my daughter. But I think you understand that one daughter is not enough.

Marriage is a two-way road. I believe that we will discuss it further during our meeting. In the meantime, all words are only air. All words are wind...

Jerrison, Earl of Earton.

***

Lily was torn between the store, Taral, His Majesty who called her to the court a couple of times a week, and his treasurer who suddenly became interested in the Countess. Lily remembered very little about binary accounting, but it was enough to make the treasurer fond of her. He began to give her valuable advice on how to conduct her trade. Lily listened, and learned, even though she was very rarely involved in the actual process of deal-making.

Taral remained under the supervision of Ingrid and Lily. Moreover, Ingrid conducted a lot of changes around the castle and was a decent substitute for Emma. Marcia was responsible for lace-makers, the glass-blower also found a dozen boys and girls, Helke was involved, as well. All these children were carefully inspected by Hans who sent four of them home and advised they find them substitutes. August's treasurer was the one doing all the finances.

Ali's arrival in the middle of the summer brought Lily great joy. He did not arrive alone. Three more Khangan ships anchored in Tivaras Bay with Ali and Omar as captains. Ali decided to stop at Earton on the way in order to bring Taris Brock and a load of processed amber, as a pleasing gesture of appreciation. The amber was not yet calibrated, but already suitable to work with. Lily ordered the tax sent to the treasury and the rest to the laboratory. Part of that amber would be turned into white, the other half into red. Chemistry was their friend.

Ali verbally and physically expressed his gratitude to Lilian, fell to his knees before Amir, praised the Heavenly Mare, and gave Mirrie a foal.

He was little and ginger. One could spot an Avarian stallion from first sight. The foal would grow into a beautiful horse. Shallah was his name, translated as "the breath of a storm." The foal was taken from the royal stables of the Great Khangan.

It was love at first sight. If Lily had let her, the girl would have slept in the stables, or else would take the foal to her chamber, since the size permitted.

Lily had to intervene and remind Mirrie about the lessons and other joys of life. Mirrie pouted, but not for long. Lily had promised her an Avarian, and Lily kept her promise.

Well, how could I not love her?

***

My dear husband,

I bring to your notice that I found a worthy manager for Earton. I received a load of amber from there, paid royal tax and sold the rest to the jewelers. I will try to invest the profit, and we can discuss the benefits of it in person. I want to emphasize that I would never wish to offend your business interests.

All of us are alive and well, which is what we wish for you. I must say that it took me a lot of trouble to eliminate the threats, and there remain many of them even today. Alas...

If I was plotting against you, I would not have written to you. I am happy to realize that you are an intelligent man, and I suggest we do not blame each other. We are both more or less guilty, especially because we did not find time to listen and converse with each other. Imagine, let's say, that I am your partner in trade. Our marriage has been a business deal from the very beginning, so let us treat it like that. You assume that we would be able to discuss our wishes upon our meeting? That sounds perfect to me. I also think that it is impossible to communicate everything through letters. I hope we will be able to talk about the recent attempts on my life and the life of Miranda. This issue cannot wait and must be resolved.

I suppose that you understand that the attempts are directed not at me. Why would anyone take so much interest in me? These attempts are targeted at you. I have inquired about certain things and found out that I am your third wife. If you did not have any heirs from me, you would be left with only one option. To marry for the fourth time would be difficult. Would you be able to protect your fourth wife? Do not take it as an offense, but this requires a lot of experience.

I do not know what is waiting for me ahead, or if there will be such a thing as "us" in the future, or if our roads will split. But my love for Miranda grows stronger and stronger, and I do not want any bastards to try to take her life.

That is why I resolved to follow the plan of Leir Hans Tremain—I suppose you have heard of his person—which will make these villains come into sight as quickly as mushrooms after the rain.

This letter will remain our secret. Send your reply with the same messenger. In the official correspondence, however, make sure you express your deepest sympathy and admiration; state that you are ready to start working on making a new heir, or maybe more than one; say that you will take me to Earton as soon as you arrive...

If you are lucky... I suppose widowhood would not make you sad? Either way, I do not want to live my life under the executioner's axe, let alone be threatened by the people around me, lest they turn to plotting my murder. Therefore, I shall consider your agreement to my plan as a step toward mutual understanding.

Lilian, Countess of Earton.

* * *

Altres Lort was pensive. So far, everything turned out to be not so bad. Anna was ready for the wedding. Gardwig felt more or less well. Lilian Earton's advice proved very useful when His Majesty followed it. As for Gardwig's health, doctors expected him to live for another year or two.

If Richard married Anna, he would get a strong alliance and a queen he could control. Anna was a fool, but one did not need wits to change the husband's mind. Having big boobs would suffice. Maybe in ten years or so, Richard would turn more intelligent and see through her tricks, but for now, they would work. It was in the manly character to seek to defend the interests of the weak and poor, especially if they have big breasts. Anna was exactly the type, at least she seemed to be.

There was a lot of material for blackmailing Lidia. So she would sit still without yapping. The mistress of the Earl of Earton turned out to be worthy, after all. *Perhaps it is better not to get rid of her so soon. She could bring a lot of good. She might not be very intelligent, but she is very good at spying.*

Waste not, want not. What if I can get Lilian Earton on my side? Why not? The Countess can always come in for a visit. She can also stay over. Let us assume that the Countess' husband died an accidental death, tripped on a stone and hit his head. The Countess could fall in love with some nice nobleman, preferably with land and title.

The news that reached Altres made him think about what benefit the Countess had from the state. Salt, lace… They tried to extract salt from seawater before, but there was no use in it. It caused terrible indigestion. The Countess, on the other hand, managed to produce very good salt. It was a bit more bitter, but that did not make much difference. Lace was also on the go. The main thing, however, was not her inventions, it was the Prince of the Khanganat. He was alive and feeling quite healthy now. In addition to this, it was priceless to have a crowd of Khangans following the Countess' every step. It would have been quite good for Altres to make friends with them. Besides, if the Countess managed to cure the young prince, then she could maybe help Gardwig—if not save him, at least prolong his life a little.

Altres was ready to do much for his brother, let alone setting up an unfortunate incident for the Earl of Earton. *No one cares about Earton anyway, only wenches would shed a couple tears. Otherwise, one courtier more, one less…it did not matter at all.*

Altres also wondered about Lilian Earton, herself. He realized that she was not a fool. He read her letters and contemplated. Every time he returned to the conclusion that he should only proceed with murdering Earton after he let the Countess know.

Why not?

Suppose the Earl arrives home, and his arrival ignites a domestic fight. The couple quarrel, the Earl starts to exert more pressure. What will the Countess do? She will not seek help from the King, she would never complain to him about his beloved nephew. I will have to plan the liquidation very carefully. I shall think on it later.

As for the Countess's protection, the King will never help her, and the woman will start seeking help elsewhere. Why not in Wellster? Maybe I could write to her, in a polite, subtle way. I could say, "We are always glad to see you in Wellster. We always appreciate your worth and contribution. You may always rely on our unconditional support."

Why not?

Altres took a golden pen from the table and touched a tiny ball with his finger. He held the non-spill ink pot and twisted it in his hands. *If the woman was able to come up with those it was better to get her into my household.*

Dear Countess Earton…

***

Only one thought pleased Lily in the wild turmoil of affairs: that no one stole from her because there was no one who would.

The incident with Varil showed the Eveers their place. As for the other tradesmen, there was only Torius Avermal. The Baron was smart and did not wish to climb above his head. He understood well that it would be better to earn a ducat once every day and live in calm than receive ten ducats at once and be kicked out of the Countess' circle of trust. He did not need any problems.

The Virman women also required Lily's attention. Now and then, she taught them a lot of useful facts about medicine.

His Majesty organized a reception to honor the Khangans and invited the Countess as well. Lily obeyed. She showed up dressed in all the glory and brightness of her novel fashion inventions, shined her bracelets, and was already leaving when the princesses crossed her path and demanded attention. As a result, the world was enriched with the spell of new stories about Baron Holmes–and not only about him. Sir Arthur

Conan Doyle wrote a lot of other books, and she knew them all. For instance, *The Secret of Cousin Geoffrey's Chamber*, and *The Brazilian Cat*...these stories were also fitting for the epoch. She only had to change a few details.

The princesses listened with quiet admiration. The other courtiers were green with envy. There were some who tried to join their circle, but the princesses only dismissed the rude fellows with a wave of their royal hand. The whole evening was spent telling stories, the exception being when Marquess Falion invited Lily for a dance. They danced twice, no more, for more would be improper. The rest of the evening, the marquess gave advice about bringing up puppies. He knew a lot about dogs and horses alike.

The princesses envied Miranda and wanted a foal, too. Lily only shrugged and apologized, saying that she did not have power over the Khangans, but one thing she could do was to give them one of Lidarh's children, with the marquess' help, of course.

Edward overheard this and said that such gifts were out of the question. Instead, he invited the marquess to his study after the reception to talk about the breeding of horses. The outcome left Falion immensely happy, and he thanked Lily with the gift of flowers and an exquisite golden chain. Lilian accepted it and wore it with pleasure.

They agreed about the breeding of Lidarh and were getting stables ready. They drowned in the amount of work, let alone the Khangans who tagged along with Lily and noted down her every word. At first Lily, was enraged, but she finally gave up. Tahir would soon leave, his medics would leave, too, and with them the knowledge she gave them.

How could I hold back knowledge that could save people's lives? She wanted her knowledge to spread across the world, but on one condition. Every medic must teach his trade to at least three children, thoroughly and for free. Everyone agreed. Later, Lily found out that Amir promised to sponsor this enterprise. Let them study, thought Lily. Someone would become a good surgeon; someone else would turn into a therapist.

Lily liked the Khangan doctors because of their attitude. They did what they were told and never questioned her knowledge. They would not be like the local mediduses, who first convinced you that the dye is red and then painted the wall green. Such things were common.

Jamie and Lily would always argue over the use of different herbs; it was only after those arguments that he accepted the Countess knew what she was talking about.

What would happen to the local students? The Virman women obeyed without question, but they had no other choice. *The locals, on the other hand....*

Hans Tremain selected a dozen boys and girls for Lily from his Tremain Squad. He chose the ones who were too weak to survive on the streets. At first, they required a thorough wash accompanied by shrieks of terror and a good dinner accompanied by shrieks of excitement. Only then, could they move on to schooling. And the children honestly made an effort. They absorbed information like sponges absorbed water. They copied out scrolls, learned the basics of hygiene and epidemiology...the paper factory was working full force to keep up.

His Majesty was very interested in this project, not to mention Aldon Roman. Both men understood perfectly that something like this would appear sooner or later. *If the time and opportunity are in place, why not?* It was better to have it supervised by the state and the Church. The aldon assigned two dozen monks for Lily to employ and sent a few pastors who were deeply engaged in the study of science. At first, Lily nearly quarreled with them, but then she calmed down, and they gradually found a common language. If they wanted to accompany their every action with a prayer, Lily would let them do so. *The science of medicine is new and alien to them, after all; let it be under the patronage of Aldonai. Besides, the pastors have turned out to be of great help, improving the paper production by making the sheets whiter and stronger.*

It was not surprising that the priests knew what they were doing. The Church in this world was an institution engaged with science. Although much of it was pure alchemy, the reagents were of good quality. *No matter if they pray over cinnabar or not, it contains mercury anyway.* Discovering that the pastors had barium oxide made her even happier. Qualitative reactions to barium were simple – one only needed to check it with acids. She could even get peroxide from it, and even better, hydrogen peroxide. Lily knew that hydrogen peroxide was a key chemical, it was used in bleach, antiseptic. *It is utterly necessary!*

That was the reason she put four priests to work on that reaction alone. After having trained for a week, they began producing peroxide in large quantities. Lily only prayed that they would not run out of barium. The only thing she regretted was the absence of electrolysis. But her knowledge of physics did not suffice. The girl only remembered about rubbing the ebonite wand, or amber. That was the end to her knowledge. She was sure that rubbing thirty wands at once and putting them into a solution was not the recipe for creating discharge.

In a word, the only thing Lily could re-invent was paper. The King also assigned thirty people to work for her, until they moved to Taral. The whole party accommodated themselves in the castle, which was under reconstruction, and had to almost camp in tents. They got to work. Someone was working on making bleach, while the others were making forms.

Three weeks later, Lily presented two dozen sheets of paper to His Majesty. They were all fairly white, thin and durable. Some of the sheets possessed a greenish tinge, others were more yellow. It was of no particular importance. At last, they resolved to release three different kinds of paper—yellowish for books, greenish for Church literature, and white for state documents.

His Majesty rubbed his hands and ordered an increase to production. Fortunately, the costs were minor. The King could substitute the share of the tax with correct plants, which would ensure the factory's operation even through the winter. It was already clear that Taral would fail to accommodate everyone. It was necessary to find another place for paper-makers.

Lily did not mind. It was hard for her to go from one project to the other. Therefore, she already assigned a notebook where she wrote the most important things. She resolved to talk with Helke in order to begin producing notebooks. She also thought about making pencils. Graphite was the same as coal. Alternatively, she could mix burned bone with vegetable glue or burn over the mix of graphite, clay, and water. One could also use sulfur, but the other methods were simpler. She needed to make a slate-pencil and then use the simplest method. She could also picture pen nibs made of gold, silver, simple metals... She thought of even producing colored pens and pencils. Lily was frustrated because she realized her life would be too short for that. Other people would come after her. For now, she needed to give the world as much knowledge as she could.

So, Lily worked hard. Miranda followed her every step. Marquess Falion paid frequent visits to spend time with Lidarh and the foal. He adored both of them. Miranda spent a lot of time with her animal, too. She was strongly convinced that she had to raise her horse by herself. Lily worked a lot, and in her spare time, she practiced throwing knives with Erik. It was a certain happiness, peace, and balance for her tired soul.

***

My Lady,

I wish to notify you about the death of Karl Treloney. He died last night from food poisoning. According to our knowledge, his fatal dinner choice was fish. It seems particularly strange considering that he was allergic to it. It caused his skin to swell.

Yours sincerely,

Baron Avermal

This short note sent by pigeon started Lily thinking. His client got to him only now. *Why now?*

Knowing the answer to this question would lead her to the client. She could not get a clear vision of it. *What is the reason for all of this? Was it a wound? Business? Ah, where are you, dear Sir Sherlock Holmes? Telling Mirrie detective stories did not make me into one!*

There was only one option left. Fishing with bait. Lily was well aware that it was dangerous, that she might die, that it might be an unacceptable risk. But she also knew that they would continue to try to murder her anyway. She would simply anticipate the event and direct it in the right direction.

What if that bastard dares to touch Miranda? I will bury him alive!

Lily sent a letter to Jerrison Earton. She received two answers, a secret one delivered by her private messenger, and another one for the public. Lily had a lot of fun comparing them to each other. The first one was the official version. It was like sugar candy coated in chocolate and filled with syrup. Nevertheless, it managed to communicate the main points.

My beloved wife!

I flatter myself with the hope of our swift reunion. As soon as the embassy delegation returns to its homeland, we will finally be able to resolve our family affairs.

I admit that I have neglected them and hope for your forgiveness.

I also sincerely hope to efface from your memory the terrible episode when you lost our child. Miranda will be delighted if we give her a brother...or a little sister. Personally, I will be happy with either.

As far as I understand, you also do not mind. And if it pleases you, I will take you to give birth at my estate near the sea. It is the place where I spent my childhood. It is very quiet, peaceful, safe and comforting, and has trusted servants.

I look forward to seeing you.

Yours,

Jerrison, Earl of Earton

If, after such a letter, the killer did not take action, he was a cretin. Lily smiled with malice. The second letter was sharply different from the first one. It was uncensored.

My dear wife,

I do not doubt your business acumen, and I am sure that you are doing the business honestly.

Let us reduce our relationship to a business transaction and have a business agreement. As for the rest, let us discuss it in person.

I must admit that I am offended by your hints of luck.

Be it in my will, I would make your life peaceful and happy.

Are you sure that you can prevent the attempted murder by yourself?

Otherwise, luck would abandon you and yourself alone.

I agree with your plan, since I cannot assure you of the purity of my intentions otherwise. And I wish luck to Lier Tremain in catching the villains. If you want to use my people or money to catch the villains, you may.

Give my love and greetings to Miranda.

Jerrison, Earl of Earton

Lily did not know that all the letters from her dearest spouse were a product of collective creativity, with Richard as their co-author. It did not matter. His words were of little consequence to her; she was waiting to see his actions.

After looking through the official letter, Hans advised Lily to publicize it as much as she could. Fortunately, all members of the Ivelen family soon paid them a visit—the old duke, the marquess, the marchioness, and their four children.

The two elder ones were a boy and a girl. Sessie was short for Cecilia, and Jess stood for Jerrison, after his uncle. The younger ones were named Roman and Jacob.

Miranda was entrusted with entertaining Sessie and Jess; Lily was busy with the adults.

The Countess spent ten minutes 'oohing' and 'aahing' over the babies. To be honest she never found newborns pretty, but she got used to watching her parents look at them as if they were angels. So she made a lot of effort to show her admiration: charming eyes from their mother, wonderful little nose from their father, stunning ears from their grandfather, and so on...

Yes, they are charming. I hope to have the same wonderful children. By the way, have you seen what our dear and beloved Jess wrote me? Here is a letter. Of course we would love to gather all together as soon as he arrives.

Amalia was delighted, the men also nodded...everything was wonderful until they heard yelling outside. Lily listened closely. To hear children yelling with zeal was very common. The Virmans were short-tempered people, and during the training, the little ones got a lot of scolding. They never spared the rod for bad education.

But the yelling now sounded alarming. While Lily was trying to figure out what was wrong, Amalia was already outside, with Peter following. Lily ran after them. *What if it is something important?* The old earl would have, run, too if it had not been for his age, so he gave the children to the nanny and left the room with dignity.

* * *

Upon finding out about the cousins' visit, Miranda winced. She could not stand either Sessie or Jess. They were pretentious and nasty. She often suffered from the Ivelens, from their teasing and pushing. The guilty one was always Mirrie whereas the nasty relatives would always get away with it. It was not a coincidence that the girl would go anywhere, except to the Ivelens. Fortunately, she found herself with Lily.

Now, this hostility seemed ridiculous to her. Lily quickly gave an educational talk explaining all about it, kissed her on the nose, and asked her not to kick anyone with her feet. Mirrie promised her not to. *Why would I use my feet if I have Lou-Lou, a little doggie who could easily bite off an arm?* Mirrie almost snorted upon seeing the cousins. They were all dressed up, done up, their clothes uncomfortable, their necks dirty, their eyes stupid. *Eww!*

She never realized that she looked so different. She was wearing a blouse, a vest and an English skirt. Her face had a bronze tan, her hair was braided like Lily's, she had a huge dog by her side and her shoulders back. She was wearing no gold, only a signet ring and tiny sapphire earrings in her ears to match the color of her eyes. Otherwise, jewelry got in the way during her training. The only thing the girl never parted with were the throwing knives given to her by Erik. She even wished she could put them underneath her pillow at night. Lily finally agreed and ordered scabbards, including the hidden ones.

So, the cute little child was as dangerous as a middle-sized snake. The Ivelens, on the other hand, noticed something else.

"Good Aldonai! Mirrie, you got so thin!" gasped Amalia trying to kiss the girl. Mirrie swiftly dodged.

"It is because of training, Auntie. I am glad to see you."

"I would say that Miranda's visit to Earton did her good," remarked Peter. Mirrie remembered him saying a lot of nonsense after her fights with her cousins and was tempted to kick her uncle in the foot. The elder Ivelen inspected Mirrie from head to toe and reminded her of a pigeon sitting on a rail.

Will he poop? Very soon for sure.

"It is about time to think about a husband for the girl. She has grown up."

A husband? To marry? No way on earth.

"I suppose Jerrison will take care of this question when he comes back," Lily innocently remarked. "I am glad to see you. I hope that the road was not too tiring."

The guests began to ensure Lily that they were happy and well and it lasted for about ten minutes.

"Mirrie, take care of Cecilia and Jerrison Junior, please." asked Lily after the hassle and small-talk were over.

"I have homeworks to do. I am going to visit Shallah now."

"Wonderful. Take your cousins with you."

Mirrie winced but Lily's look was strict, and the girl cast her eyes down.

This was one of her "countess responsibilities." Even if she found it unpleasant, she still had to be polite and smiley. Lily taught her those manners.

"My dear cousins, please bring me the joy of your company."

Sessie and Jess glanced at each other and followed Miranda. In the stables, the girl looked over her foal, brushed his mane—not because he needed it, but he liked it a lot—and treated the horse to a bit of salty bread and a promise to come back in the evening. She also patted Lidarh on his back and snuck him an apple. The Avarian smothered it from the girl's palm and pushed against it with plush neighing. A spoiled beggar—so Mirrie had to promise to bring him more in the evening. The Ivelens stood dumbfounded. The first one to break the silence was Jess. He burst into questioning.

"Is he your own?"

"Yes, mine. Shallah. It means 'breath of the storm'.'"

"What language is it in?"

"It is the language of the Khanganat."

"And where did you get an Avarian from?"

"Mother asked the Khangans to give him to me as a gift. Amir agreed. She would be given anything if she asked."

"Who is Amir?"

"Amir Gulim? He is the Prince of the Khanganat."

"And the prince gives you presents?"

"Mother's doctor has cured him. That is why he does. He is generally a grateful young man," Miri repeated Lily's words almost verbatim.

"And they gave you the Avarian? They are insanely expensive!"

"So what? The Great Khangan can afford it." Mirrie shrugged her shoulders. "The big Avarian is my mother's. His name is Lidarh."

"Why do you call her your mother?" intervened Sessie. "She is nobody to you."

Mirrie stroked Shallah one more time and headed to the stable exit.

"Kinship is not determined by blood."

"What?" The cousin did not understand.

"My mother and I may not be blood relatives, but I am still her daughter."

"How is that possible?"

"Your relatives are those people who love you."

"Does she love you?"

Mirrie remembered the look on Lily's face after the kidnapping, when she chided the girl, and nodded emphatically.

"She loves me."

"She's lying to you so that her father does not drive her out of the house," Jess said. "Everyone knows that she did not give birth to a child, she showed up at the capital, and began sticking her nose into other people's business. She is asking for a beating. Her husband must teach her a lesson!"

The boy was repeating someone else's words, but angry Miranda did not understand it. The girl turned around and answered, "Dear cousin. Take your words back immediately."

"What?" Jess was confused. When it finally struck him he roared with laughter. "Never in my life! You understand yourself that your 'mother' is—"

"Who?" Mirrie narrowed her eyes. "Tell me, who?"

"A shilda! There!"

"Apologize immediately," demanded Mirrie.

"And what if I don't? Will you challenge me to a duel?"

"No, I will crush your nose," Mirrie said quietly. The girl's blood boiled, but she remembered that to start a fight hot-headed meant to lose it. Erik told her this many times, and so did Leis.

"I wish I could see you do it!"

Jess stood boldly, with his arms and legs akimbo. He was almost fourteen, and thought himself a grown man; he had his own sword. He did not have an Avarian though, and a Virman dog. He would ask his father for them.

Mirrie did not care that her opponent was taller and twice her weight. The girl started attacking. Since she understood that she could not reach for his nose, she decided to kick him in the feet. She did not throw herself at him or jump out, she only took a tiny step forward, almost unnoticeable. Luckily, the cousin was already standing near. When an opponent was relaxed he could be easily tripped. Jerrison Ivelen dropped to the ground and got winded. It was, after all, very difficult to land on the whole body. Miranda did not lose time and jumped on top to strike him hard in the nose with the back of her knife. His blood was everywhere. Jess started screaming, but Mirrie did not want to wait for his reaction. She stood up from the ground.

The girl suddenly recalled an old conversation with Lilian.

"If you will be a good girl I will teach you to fight."

"But it is not fit for a noble lady…"

"Was the noble lady ever bullied?" squinted Lily.

"You can fight?"

"A countess has to know how to do a lot of things, including self-defense."

Now Mirrie felt that she had gotten her revenge for all her cousins' bullying. A loud yelling pierced the air.

This time it was Sessie, who Lou-Lou was not letting approach either her brother or Miranda; the dog was snarling with her rather big teeth. Mirrie winced upon realizing that in a minute, her cousin's yell would attract a crowd of people. She looked at Jess Junior. He sat on the ground and held onto his nose.

Did I break it? I don't think I did. Even so, who cares? What kind of man is he if a little girl twice as small could smear his face with dirt?

Now, she had to put her knife away and get herself in order. The results of her training were showing. She could not remember how she took out the weapon and turned it hilt first. This meant that it was hammered into her head and turned into a reflex, as Lily would say. That was good.

The first one to come out into the yard was her aunt. Mirrie winced once more and continued cleaning her clothes and hands. Although her clothes were of simple material and made especially for playing outside and falling on the ground, they still managed to get slightly ruined, at least in the eyes of Mirrie… by a single blade of grass for instance.

Lou-Lou hid behind the girl's back and grit her teeth from there. She did not growl anymore. *Why growl if she could simply attack?*

"What is going on here?" yelled Amalia, rushing to her son.

"Sessie?" inquired Peter.

"She attacked him," Sessie pointed at Miranda. The girl pulled a face.

"My dearest cousin, have you not been taught that it is improper to poke your finger. Only common and ignorant people do that. Eww!"

A mad Jess junior sat in the center holding onto his broken nose. He would have to hold on to it for a long time. It looked like a fracture. His sister was standing nearby and poked her finger at Miranda. Mirrie cleaned herself with an independent look, with the dog gritting its teeth behind her. The people in the yard were watching a free circus performance. *Let the magic unfold.*

"Miranda Catherine Earton!" sharply called out Lily. "Please explain why you broke your cousin's nose."

"Yes," grunted Amalia. "I also would like to know."

Mirrie did not even think to back off.

"At first, my cousin said that you should be taught to obey your husband, and after, he called you a shilda. I suggested he take his words back. Otherwise, I promised to break his nose."

"So what?"

"So, I had to break it."

"You want to say that you were defending me?" Lily's harshness melted away.

Mirrie replied with a cunning look, and Lily realized that it had also been an old grudge. *What difference does it make?*

"She's lying!" Sessie stamped her foot in a gesture of indignation. "She's lying!"

The girl's thin finger pointed at Miranda.

"Cecilia Ivelen, please do not poke your finger. It is not nice.

"Huh?"

"I can remind you, dear niece, that you were not alone in the courtyard. I can ask the servants."

"The servants would lie!" yelled Amalia.

"You can ask me, My Lady." Pastor Vopler was splendid. His green mantle was made of expensive linen; his hands were well-groomed, holding amber rosaries... Nothing was left from the village priest that Lily saw at their first meeting. "I became a witness of how this young man started insulting the Countess. I swear before the image of Aldonai."

Amalia flared with anger. She could not accuse the pastor.

"The young gentleman allowed himself to utter highly inappropriate sentences. Furthermore, to insult her mother to the child's face... It was not surprising that the young Viscountess was forced to defend her honor. I suppose that the young man's education and training are far from perfection, if a little girl could knock him down."

Jess's face went pale. Peter and the Duke finally realized the consequences of the incident. The important thing was not how, but rather why the boy's nose had gotten smashed and by whom. If the rumor went around the capital it would ruin them.

Lily smiled.

"Mirrie, honey, was it not the first time that Jess said nasty things to you?"

"I suppose that he will not do it again. Otherwise I promise to break his arm." Miranda's eyes were naïve and innocent. The dog behind her started wagging its tail.

Lily turned to the crimson-red Amalia and pale Peter.

"I suppose that the incident is over?"

"I think so, too," old Ivelen responded instead of Peter. "My Lady, who taught the young lady self-defense?"

"The Virmans."

"Perhaps they would agree to teach this dunce, too?"

Lily squinted not worse than Miranda.

"Only when the young man realizes that insulting young girls is unworthy. Now, get up Jerrison Ivelen and go to the nurses. Mirrie, where are you going?"

"I have horse riding."

"No."

"Mama!"

"I will now look after your cousin's nose. Come and watch how to heal such wounds. Any fool can use their fist."

Mirrie obediently nodded. At least, she did not have to turn her nose to the corner, she could stand and watch something interesting.

***

The nose turned out to be broken, as was the prospect of a good relationship with the Ivelens. Lily could put a bandage on his nose and even promise that it would heal without any consequences, but Amalia looked at her like a witch. Peter was most likely supporting the position of his wife. The Duke simply did not care. *Why does he not?* He asked to teach his grandson and got a negative answer, that was the end to it.

How strange. There is only one good thing. If it is one of the Ivelens who stands behind the attempts of murder, the incident will make him take action.

***

There was little happiness in receiving a letter from the relatives of the second wife of the Earl of Earton. It was from Baron Yerby.

The man wrote that he was going to Laveri and asked for an audience to make sure that his beloved granddaughter was safe and sound.

"Well, let him come. We will hold a visit. We will pull by his ears." Lily grinned upon remembering a childhood rhyme about pulling ears. She also remembered Damis Reis dying in her hands.

Let us talk about why you gave me a gigolo, dear Yerby. I am a kind woman; I will ask without the use of improvised means. The example of Damis will suffice, and you will tell me everything yourself.

So, Lily wrote back that she was happy to host him and got back to work.

* * *

The business gradually grew. They were building the trading house Mariella, as well as repairing Taral and educating children.

Suddenly, she heard a knock.

"My Lady, merchant Limaro Vatar asks for an audience."

Lily looked up at Lons Avels. The chevalier was rather calm and even smiled with the corner of his mouth. He turned out to be a perfect secretary.

"Who is it, Lons?"

"He is the head of the Merchant Guild in Laveri."

"Is he?" Lily nodded in understanding. She should have expected such visitors.

Although Lily was under the King's patronage as well as the protection of the aldons, it was unthinkable for the local Merchant Guild not to try and make some money on the side. Her actions affected too many interests. If she was a woman without a title, they would have already taken her head off. But she was Countess Earton. She had a kinship to the King, although not direct.

The Eveers, too, were very particular people. Lily strongly suspected that their cunningness would crowd out the merchants, but she was not going to act on it in any way. Natural competition was a basis for developments in trade.

"What else can you tell me about him?"

Lons told her that the man was sly, clever and a "...rare bastard. Pardon me for my language, My Lady."

"It would surprise me if he was otherwise. Ask him in."

Lons bowed and disappeared behind the door. In a moment, a man entered the room with the sound of heavy footsteps on the creaking wood.

What a bear, thought Lily, astonished.

The merchant was the height of Erik, only twice as wide. The floorboards beneath him sagged quite palpably.

His expensive cloak added to his volume. The man's beard was combed and braided in several braids, according to Elvanian fashion. His hair was dark and slightly grey; his eyes were also dark and intelligent; his face was deliberately simple. Lily became alert but did not show it. On the outside she remained calm and polite.

"Please, dear Vatar."

The merchant bowed low.

"My Lady, I thank you for your courtesy. I am very glad that you have found time for such an insignificant person as me."

Lily smiled.

"Dear sir, leave your modesty. If you were an insignificant person, they would never place you at the head of a guild, especially the Guild of Merchants."

Vatar carefully looked at the woman but did not say anything. Lily pointed to the chair.

"Please sit down."

"Thank you, My Lady."

Lily smiled innocently.

"Would you like some wine? Cider? Ale? Compote?"

"Compote, My Lady."

"Please pour some for yourself and me." Lily nodded at the glass jug on the table and a few glasses beside her.

The berry brew was delicious, the glasses were beautiful, the Countess was clearly in a good mood, and Vatar relaxed a little. He was preparing for a lot. The rumors about Countess Earton were too contradictory and not at all predicting a kind reception.

Although the woman definitely guessed why he came, she waited.

"My Lady," the merchant finally decided. "I came to talk to you about matters, perhaps they are low—"

"But necessary to discuss. Can I help you a little?" Lily smiled affably. Now, it was possible to meet halfway. "You would like to say that my intrusion in the trade and my contract with the Eveers violates the existing balance. The Merchant Guild has lost a lot of money. So what?"

Limaro Vatar inspected her carefully. The woman was not angry. She did not swear but simply stated the fact.

"You are right, My Lady," he uttered. "And forgive me for getting involved with these offspring of Maldonaya..."

Lily flashed her eyes. Their swords came together. It was a first trial lunge.

"Aldon Roman does not mind," she said simply.

"Everything is in the hands of Aldonai," played along the merchant. "Maldonaya has many disguises. Either way, dear Countess, I understand how low it is for a nobleman to earn money by trade."

"My father is August Broklend," Lily put simply. "If it is not a disgrace for my father to build ships, I find no shame in selling lace."

"However by selling it through our guild, you would have made a lot more profit." Vatar looked serious.

"Perhaps you are right. But I have an agreement for all jewelry with artisan Leitz."

"And what about lace?" Vatar seized the idea.

"Lace, too. The only thing that the Eveers have not gotten into is… Do you like this glass?"

Vatar looked at the goblet in his hands. It was made of beautiful glass.

"Yes. Is this Elvanian glass?"

"No. It is Mariella Glass," she corrected calmly.

"Mariella, My Lady?"

"In honor of my mother."

Vatar began twisting the glass even more—good that he had finished his compote. The glass was beautiful, in the shape of a flower.

"I suppose if His Majesty does not mind, the guild could get the right to trade Mariella Glass around the country and outside of it." Lily smiled. "Do you mind if I invite you to the workshops?"

"It is an honor, My Lady."

***

Wrapped inside his cloak, Vatar almost forgot to offer his hand to the Countess.

Lily smiled. She dealt well with the merchant. They had already discussed such visits with the Royal Treasurer, who warned her that sooner or later the pilgrimage of the guilds would begin. He suggested to turn away glass blowers from the very beginning because they were useless artisans and would more likely cause a lot of harm. In their minds, Lily's glass could not surpass their...shards and fragments.

There were also merchants who made money on sales. It was necessary to roll the dice. Since it was not beneficial to give everything to the Eveers, she could give glass to the merchants. Let them fight with the guild of glassblowers. She would maybe be able to give them a share of lace, when the demand fell and she had to reduce the price. She would leave it up to them to trade her glass, mirrors and goblets as soon as the production was firmly established. She would discuss her benefits once in the capital.

"You are not going to trade by yourself, My Lady, am I correct? Very well. Everyone should do what they are made to do. If you want to create a Fashion House, you may. The produce will not have to be too big. You are happy and your merchants, too."

She got it sorted with the doctors. Book printing was a new trade anyway, as well as the production of paper. It would have to be a new guild. The book scribers were the only ones who could object, but those were few and mainly scattered around the monasteries. She already had an agreement with the aldon. More problems would arise nevertheless, but those would have to be solved as and when they arrived.

For now, Lily's task was to make an agreement with the merchants. If they realized their benefits, they would cooperate well.

Lily was aware that her many successes were due to her title. They were not the achievements of her person. If she had no title, they would have killed her in some accident or set fire to her home a long time ago. But the production of Countess Earton and the patronage of the Crown spoke for themselves and made everyone else shut their mouths.

Vatar was shown the glassmaking workshop; he glanced over the amount of work he had to do and nodded. Only after, did he start asking questions that put Lily in a stupor.

The volume of production, the terms of delivery, the number of workers and amount of produce... She could only give him approximate numbers, and Vatar was not satisfied by them. Lily suggested he discuss it with the Royal Treasurer, to which the merchant replied that he did not believe in the opportunity to ever speak to a man who was so high up in rank. Lily assured him that the treasurer would descend from his high rank to speak to an ordinary merchant; besides, he would happily do so.

Coming from there, they would also be able to sort out their issues of production.

"You should understand that we are not yet putting full force into production because we still have spies and saboteurs crawling about..."

Vatar got the hint, lowered his glance—maybe he was also one of the spying lot—and offered the Countess his help in checking the artisans and their students. The merchants like him knew much.

Lily thought about it and decided she did not mind help. They parted as friends and agreed that Lily would send a messenger as soon as she arranged for the meeting with the Royal Treasurer, and they would go from there.

✳✳✳

Mirrie turned her head drowsily to settle comfily against Lily's shoulder. The woman stroked her dark hair.

"Baby bun."

"Mother, are you mad at me?"

"Why would I be?" asked Lily.

"That I broke Jess's nose."

"Do you want me to be mad?" Lily touched the top of the girl's head with her lips. "I am not angry. But you must understand that a knife is not a toy."

"I know. I hit with the hilt."

"What if it had been the blade?"

"The cousin would have died. Mother, I'm not that stupid. I did not want to kill him..."

"And he did not expect a dirty trick from you. And he was badly prepared. I wonder why? I thought all the boys were being trained to fight?"

Miranda pondered, apparently remembering something.

"Mother, Jess is a whimper. My auntie adores him. She constantly jumps around him..."

"True."

This explained a lot. Mirrie, of course, could not have knocked over a boy almost twice her age. She caught him by surprise, and given that Jess was not used to others fighting back, plus the lack of his military training, Mirrie turned out to be stronger. After her kidnapping, she trained and learned self-defense all the time. The girl's training bore fruit.

"I'm not angry. But you have to be more careful. You are not the best fighter in this world."

"I know, Mother..."

"And so that you do not think that you can get away so easily, you will write to your father tomorrow."

"About what?"

"About the incident with Jess. Grandma will write to your father as well."

"And you?"

"Maybe I will. We will see."

"Are you sure you are not angry? I just could not help it when Jess started saying nasty things about you."

"I would not have been able to stand it either if he were saying nasty things about you."

Mirrie buried her nose in Lily's arm.

"Mother, you are so nice."

Lily stroked her dark hair.

"Sleep tight, baby bun."

***

Mirrie was long asleep, but Lily was still thinking. Being kind, trusting, and calm was good... In this world, on the other hand, her life had been under constant stress. *How much longer will I be able to bear it?* It was good that she had close people, but if it were to continue like that, she would not last long.

I hope that everything resolves. As soon as Jess Earton arrives, everything should fall into place. Either we will come to a mutual agreement and I will finally have someone to trust, or I will have to find somebody else. I am not a business lady; it is a mere coincidence. I want to feel human warmth, to have children, a husband... I am strong. I will manage for sure. If I repeated it six times in a row, maybe my words will have power. Almighty Gods of this world, I am so tired... To think about all those murderers...

Lily thought about sending Miranda to August or to the King. However, she felt more reassured having Mirrie by her side. She was confident in the competence of her own guards, but to send Mirrie to a strange house with strange people... They would manage. They should be fine.

***

The dance finished, and Richard gracefully walked Lidia to the big window.

"Shall we take some rest, Your Majesty?"

"Why not?"

"Do you want wine?"

Lidia shook her head. She had been shaking with a fever for the past week or so. She was silent for a while but resolved to say what she meant. "Are you leaving soon?"

"Yes."

"You will obviously choose to be relatives with Wellster."

"You are correct."

Lidia sighed in relief. "The better. If only the time went faster…"

"Your Highness, I hope you understand that you will nevertheless have to arrive in Ativerna? For I cannot give my answer now, it would be disrespectful."

"Yes, I understand everything," she dismissed him. "I will go and return, only to not marry you."

Richard was a bit offended, but not too much. He was not affected by such statements any more. If Lidia had been beautiful, maybe he would still get offended, but to hear it from an ugly hag… She had no taste and no imagination. If he had married her, he would have run away from home.

"Very well."

He had to swallow his words about Lidia being a fool and an old maid. *Who knows how she would react?* She might burst into tears, and Richard did not need problems from Bernard.

Richard could feel that Bernard was testing him. He made hints, expressed his admiration. It seemed that he loved his daughter sincerely and could not even think that anyone might refuse to take such a "treasure". Richard, on the other hand, thought that living with Lidia would have been a nightmare. So, the task was quite simple. He had to bid farewell and depart as soon as possible. It sounded like an easy thing to do, if only Bernard did not cling to him. It seemed he was determined for Richard to choose Lidia.

It would be impossible to explain to the King that if Lidia happened to find herself in the ocean with sharks, the poor sharks would get poisoned. The only way was to avoid the subject.

***

Richard had long made an agreement with Edward to return home, so today he was calm and happy.

"Your Majesty, I have received a letter. It is calling me home, and I must obey."

"When?"

"As soon as we are ready. I suppose in ten days."

"Perfect!" There was so much enthusiasm in her eyes that Richard even got offended. He could not know that the young woman had already spoken to the saboteur twice and was ready to do anything to make him go away.

"I am glad that my departure brings so much joy to you."

Lidia noticed the irony and could not hold back her emotions. She had to take it out on someone.

"It would bring me more joy if your visit had never happened."

The prince and the princess bid farewell and walked in opposite directions. Richard walked to his friend, and Lidia, to her father, whom she had to persuade not to blast thunder and lightning. She did not like Richard; it was not a big deal. Looking at her father made her think that handsome men never make good husbands. Looking at Richard and Jess strengthened those convictions even further. She would hound her father about it, so he did not get offended.

***

"Home soon…"

"Yes. You know, I even miss it."

"Are you tired of resting?"

"You know, yes, I am sick of it," Jess did not take the joke. "At first, when they send you by force, you begin having fun. You sail, and you do everything else. And then, at one point, it somehow gets annoying. I start wanting to see home, see Miranda, see how my baby girl is doing."

"Yes, you have never left her alone for so long."

"I could not take the girl to the embassy. By the way, what are we going to do about this whore Adelaide once we return home?"

"Already a whore? There had been so much moaning about her…Adelaide, so gentle, so understanding…"

Jess made a face. He could forgive a woman a lot, but certainly not murder, and certainly not making him a fool. It was good that no one found out. Otherwise the whole courtyard would be laughing at him. A mistress tried to kill a lawful wife, in the hope of becoming a new lawful wife… *What would they say about such a husband?*

"You are asking what to do with her? They would send her to some wilderness and marry her to some freak so ugly that even a goat would refuse such a candidate."

"This goat would marry anyone for money."

"I do not promise her a rich husband," Richard said sharply. "She must be grateful for not finding herself in prison."

"Yes, prison would have been a fitting place for her. I want to go home so bad. I am tired of wandering around and doing nothing. How is the regiment doing without me?"

Richard shrugged.

The responsibilities of the commander of the Royal Guard Regiment were not particularly difficult. The guardsmen themselves had only two things to do, guard the royal premises or participate in parades. They did not go to war. This very regiment was for the children of the nobles who wanted them to learn to hold a sword and be out of danger at the same time.

So, the guardsmen spent their time around the court and had affairs with ladies-in-waiting. In other words, their job was to maintain a good image, not chase bandits across the forest. The job of the commander did not require Jess's full dedication. A couple of austere foremen who now and then boxed the young men's ears would have been enough.

The regiment had such captains—four of them. Jess only commanded during the parades; the four captains took the rest on themselves. Richard had long been dying to dismantle this almshouse, but his father explained that it was not so straightforward. If there was a revolt, these were the children and grandchildren of the nobles kept hostage. And even if revolt never happened, it was better to have them all at court and look after them. On the one hand, they could find out certain private details about the royal family, which was not beneficial. However, it went both ways. It was also useful for forming parties and coalitions…the reasons were numerous.

"I suppose they have drunk a dozen more barrels of wine and slept with a dozen more women. As for the rest, do you think anything could change?"

Jess shook his head. "I am sure not, but home is calling."

"It will be soon now, very soon…"

***

Anna was peacefully preparing to go to sleep in her chamber. She sent off the servants as soon as they helped her to unlace her dress. She was now combing her hair by herself, in the way she knew. She found it irritating to have servants in her chamber.

"Are you still awake?"

She stood up from her chair so quickly that it toppled.

Altres Lort languidly raised his hand.

"Do not rise; sit, and throw something on yourself."

Anna squeaked, climbed into bed and sneaked under her covers; she watched the jester from her bed with her eyes wide open, struck by horror.

"I have good news for you. It seems like Richard will choose you after all."

Anna sighed. The icy claws inside her chest weakened their grip on her soul.

"M-me?"

"Yes. So get ready. We will soon leave for Ativerna."

"W-we?"

"I will not go. I am talking about your father."

Anna closed her mouth with her hand. That meant that…

"Exactly so. You should think carefully about your behavior, manners, and conduct. You will need to shine in comparison to Lidia, so when they look at her, they see a scarecrow. You understand?"

Anna nodded.

"You will manage that. The next thing is my people. I will send a couple to go with you. You will find out who they are later. If you need anything, they will be the ones to ask. Do you take what the witch recommended?"

Anna nodded again.

"Fine. Be a good girl. I need this marriage to happen. Therefore, I need you. Do you understand?"

"Y-yes."

"Get ready for the trip."

Altres disappeared from the room.

Anna pulled a fur blanket on top of her cover. The woman was shaking. It was the last stage, the last push… If she was lucky, she would become the queen of Ativerna.

If not…

Upon remembering the snake-green eyes of the jester, Anna started looking for another cover. Despite these covers, fur, and the fire, she was still cold. She was freezing…

✳✳✳

"How are you doing, Gard?"

"Your prayers keep me well," Gardwig responded sarcastically.

Altres made himself comfortable in his brother's room.

"Who else would pray for you if not me? Have you decided for sure that you are going?"

"I have no choice. The matter is most urgent."

"I agree. Gard, can you do me a favor?"

"To bring you a magical sword?" Gardwig smiled upon remembering the children's tale.

"No. There is a certain Countess Earton in Ativerna."

"The wife of that cad?"

"Correct. A famous Khangan doctor lives at her estate. Tahir Djiaman din Dashar."

"And?"

"He saved the Prince of Khanganat. Maybe…"

Gardwig sighed and put a hand on his brother's shoulder.

"Alt, you are doing it as a last resort. What can a woman know about healing?"

"Not the woman, but Tahir."

"Fine. I promise to speak to him. Is that what you want?"

Altres brightened up the room with his brazen smile.

"What else if not this?"

"Do you think he will give me more than a couple of years?"

"Why not?" Altres seriously retorted.

Gardwig shrugged.

"Alt, I am traveling to another county, so here is my last will. I command you to be the protector of the princes. I will not take Milia and the children with me, but if something happens to me…"

Altres quickly made a sign to ward off evil.

"So, if something goes wrong, will you take the regency until my son is of age?"

"I promise."

"Educate him, teach him everything you know, take care of Milia...she is not bad. She gave me so many laddies."

Gardwig smiled in delight. Milia had given birth to another boy that she offered to name Altres. The King and the fool liked it. The child was named after his uncle.

"If something happens, you can count on me," Altres calmly said.

"Good. The order and the rest are in the cache where we used to play as children. You know where it is."

"I do."

The men exchanged meaningful glances. Gardwig was dying, they both knew it, so they tried to arrange for the future of the country.

"The Kings might change, but Wellster must live! This is important!"

The price for it was stealing, betrayal, murder. It didn't really matter. The Kings had their own morals, which were quite cruel. They often did something that made normal people sick. They have done it and will do it again. Such had been their fate.

Altres was now giving an oath to do everything and even more for the sake of Wellster. Gardwig was accepting his oath at that very instant. There were no superfluous words, no pomp, no pathetic tragedy. Instead, there was the crackling of the fire and the two glances coming into one; the hand of the younger brother on the shoulder of the elder.

A brief moment of unity without titles; an eternity in an instant.

***

"Your Majesty,"

Lily joyfully looked at Lons.

"It came? How much?"

"Five ducats for showing him the way to you. He did not know that you were waiting for someone from the merchants," Lons smirked. He was happy and not at all afraid. The coins glistened on his palm. The mistress would not get offended by such trivial little things.

"I hope that you managed to haggle?"

"What kind of question is that! Of course, the secretary of the Countess is not cheaply sold."

"Quite the opposite, an extra prize of five golden ducats." Lily was also smiling. People did not value a thing that they get too easily. Therefore, the merchant left strongly convinced that it took a lot of effort for him to reach her, through fire and water; those "obstacles" were organized by Lons and Hans.

The gold disappeared in the chevalier's pocket.

"My Lady, would you be kind enough to let me—"

"I let you. What is it?"

"The Embassy visited Wellster. According to my information, they will soon leave Ivernea. I also know that there was no mutual understanding between the Princess of Ivernea and Richard. Therefore, Anna remains the only suitable bride—Anna, my wife."

Lily bit on her nail.

"And what exactly do you want?"

"She will come here, there is no doubt about it. I only wanted to—

"

"See her? Talk to her? Pass her a letter? To murder her?"

Lons started thinking.

"For starters, I want to give her a letter, and only then—"

"Do you love her?"

"I do."

Lily carefully looked at Lons.

"Think now. What would a sweet girl rather choose? To be a wife of the secretary of Countess Earton, in the wilderness of Earton, or a queen of Ativerna? You know her best. Do not take it personally, but…"

Lons deeply sighed, "I do not know, My Lady."

"Did you know it before?"

"Before I believed that she loved me, that she would wait for me. And now, she thinks that I am dead. In that case, she becomes a widow and has a legal right to marry anyone she wants."

"You are alive only by chance."

"Yes. Everything would depend on her feelings. If she loves me, I need nothing more. You will not drive me away from Earton, will you?"

"As a last resort, I would ask the Khanganat to give you refuge. Amir will not be against it, he found you a worthy man a long time ago."

Lons nodded.

"Thank you."

"What if her choice does not fall on you? You can resurrect as many times as you want but…"

Lons was looking in one spot. "I do not know, My Lady. I do not know…"

"Will you kill her? Will you leave? Will you scream at the top of your lungs, so the whole of Ativerna hears?"

"I do not know…"

Well, at least an honest answer.

"Think about it then."

"I do!" exploded Lons. "Every night! I love her, is that not clear? You are a woman after all!" The unsaid "although you are like a man" was left hanging in the air. Lily sighed.

Oh Lons, you cannot imagine how much I want to find that strong shoulder and care about nothing. If only all my problems could be resolved by someone strong and clever. He would manage my life, he would protect me. Is that how people think? And what if not?

What if, from the very moment of your birth, you are always under the threat of being destroyed? You live on the edge, and you realize that if something happened, it would blow you to pieces. You always make mistakes and recognize some strange glimmer in the eyes of the people around you… but you also have no choice.

You either go ahead and make mistakes, or you stay where you are and die.

It is impossible for me to find a lover. Although, I am not a robot. Sometimes I think about it, but there is no way I would go through with it.

A faithful wife follows her destined road, an unfaithful one has a road, too, but it leads to the monastery. Therefore, I do not need any source of blackmail. The craving disappears in the same way as it starts, very swiftly.

"I do understand everything. And remember that I am a woman, but Anna is young. How old is she? Even Miranda is more clever. Can you imagine her reaction?"

Lons shook his head. Lily nodded at the table in the corner.

"Take wine, a few sips won't do you any harm."

Lons obediently poured himself some wine, drank it and looked at Lily.

"And?"

"So, imagine this. You do not have any documents; the proof is quite contradictory."

"But at least I can list all her features, all her beauty marks…"

"This, my friend, would be a reason to accuse you of depravity. Do you realize that if you kick up a fuss, no one will give you your princess? They are more likely to take away your life."

"I realize it."

"And my life as well,"

"But…"

"Who would believe that I did not know anything?"

Lons would also not believe.

"So, what now, My Lady?"

"There is only one way out now. Think. I am in no right to trust Hans. If there are more than two people who know about this secret, it will sooner or later come to light. Therefore, we need to think how we can reveal you to your heroine. We need to think of how to organize your meeting in secret and how to take both of you away if need be, or at least how to arrange for you to remain alive. Is that clear?"

"Very."

"So, think."

"I already have an idea."

"What idea?"

She listened to the idea, criticised it, and sent Lons off to think on it more. Lilian approached the window.

Yes, My Lady, you are being pulled into court intrigues against your will… I am completely ignorant of what is going on. Well, I must admit that I do possess some information, but very little of it, very little…

She did not want to lose Lons. She did not like him as a man, handsome boyish-looking lads were not her type. However, as a secretary he was perfect. She needed to talk to Hans and ask him to find a substitute for Lons—at least two people. It would take them time to learn, to understand who is who, etc.

Even if Lons managed to run away to the Khanganat with his "much missed" darling, Lily would still need to find a substitute. Therefore, it was better to do it in advance.

Lily looked at the jar with wine. A moment later, she took it in her hands and threw it against the door. She was overpowered by emotion.

Everyone thought that she was made of iron and concrete, a horse with balls that walked around burning houses.

Lily had once read about a man who was the director of a factory. During the war, the man lived at his factory morning, day, and evening. When the war finished, he went into his room, lay down on his bed, and died. Upon inspecting his body, the doctors found that, although he was forty years old in his passport, in reality, his biological age had been seventy and a bit. Those four years of war had burned the man from the inside. Lily was in a similar state right now. She threw herself into a furnace, she burned, and realized that she had very little time and there was no one near. Maybe only Mirrie could understand her, but it would have to be no sooner than in ten years' time.

Loneliness.

A maid peered inside the room. "My Lady..."

"Get the room clean," Lily made a dry order. "Be careful, do not cut yourself."

She left the room. She wanted some fresh air.

"Marquess?"

Alexander Falion was standing in the reception area and smiled with the corner of his mouth.

"My Lady, may I ask you to go for a walk?"

Lily sighed. She looked at her fingers. Even through gloves, one could notice them shaking.

It is not good to go to the horse in this state of mind. The horse is a creature with a fragile, elegant soul.

"Marquess, it is unlikely for me to be able to ride now."

"I only want to ask you for a walk, nothing more, along the garden, My Lady."

"Let's go."

Alicia had not taken care of the garden before Lily's arrival. Lily had ordered the servants to get it into order, and now there were rose bushes in full bloom. Lily touched one of them.

Like home—the same as home...

"Lilian..."

"Yes, Alexander?"

"I received a letter from my man. The embassy will soon get moving, maybe they are already on the go."

Lily nodded. She touched a rosebud.

"Thank you, Alexander."

"Lilian, I wanted to ask you for one favor, and I hope you will not refuse."

Lily shrugged.

"Ask me if it is in my power."

"I would like to keep seeing you and being your friend even after your husband's arrival."

"If it depends on my will, then I promise you. Alexander, why do you suddenly ask me this?"

"Because I know Jerrison, Lilian, and I know some of his sides that might be concealed from you."

Lily wanted to be sarcastic and say the same about herself. It was unlikely that Alexander would get to spend at least one night with the Earl. But she refrained from making that remark. There was some hidden meaning in the man's serious eyes...

"And?"

"I also know you. If you find a common language, it will make me most happy. It is more likely, though, that your house will turn into a battlefield."

"They came together, wood and wire, poem and novel, ice and fire," murmured Lily—her translation of Pushkin.

"Will you get offended if I ask you a straight-forward question?"

Lily shook her head. It took all her courage to touch Falion's hand with hers. The marquess flinched like from a burn, but did not take his hand away.

"Alexander, you have long become my friend, from the moment when I cried and you gave me comfort. You can tell me whatever you want, and it will not affect our friendship."

The marquess smiled somehow crookedly. "Even if I tell you that I love you?"

Seeing Lilian's face numb with shock made Falion suddenly laugh.

"Close your mouth, Countess, lest a crow makes a nest there."

"You have no shame! You got my hopes up!" Lilian realized that the marquess was joking and lightly hit him on the shoulder. "How dare you give a woman such explicit hopes!"

Grey eyes shined with glee.

"Let me at least offer you my hand, and we can continue."

Lily smiled. "Alexander, have you ever gotten beaten up for your little jokes?"

"Sometimes, they wanted to. But I always turned out to be the first one," admitted Falion. "I still made jokes after."

"Hmm! I would not want to be on your bad side."

"You are already my friend. And Jerrison is my friend too. Therefore, let me speak the honest truth."

Lily nodded. Falion swiftly took a rose from the bush and gave it to Lily.

"You are proud. I can see it. But Jess is the same. And when two proud people meet..."

"Mine will bend over. Is that what you wanted to say?"

"Most often, women are the ones to compromise. But you would not compromise your beliefs, right?"

"I have no room to take a step back, at least not now. I would have gladly returned to Earton, but where is the guarantee that there will be no attempt on my life that might become fatal?"

"I understand, but Jess might not. In order to reach the agreement, you will need to at least make it look like you have complied with his wishes."

"What if I do not want to create anything? I want *him* to compromise at least once! Alexander, I am alive and normal. I was nearly killed when complying with his wishes; Miranda was in danger of death, and do I need to bend over after this? Would it not be too much?"

"That is exactly what I am saying."

"What would you advise me to do?"

"It depends on what you want to get."

"Peace."

"You also need your status as a countess. Otherwise, it will be bad for your business, as well as many other things."

"What do you suggest?"

"I suggest you offer your husband a civil marriage. You have your life; he has his."

"We meet a couple of times to make an heir and then go our separate ways?"

Lily pursed her lips.

"It is not in me, Alexander. I look at such marriage arrangements with abhorrence. Yes, they exist; yes, sometimes they are necessary; but maybe not in my case."

"I have thought about your situation for a long time, and I cannot see any different option for you. You are a proud and a possessive woman. Jess is the same. However, there are two types of men. The first type would be proud of having a wife like you. The second type would get angry and suffer from having a wife who makes them look smaller in the eyes of others."

"Does Jess belong to the second type?"

"Quite possibly. I cannot exclude the possibility of him choosing to be proud of you. But as for now…"

Lily pensively bit on the stem of the rose.

"Yes, it is a problem."

"Think, Lilian. You are beautiful, smart, you are a rival in the eyes of many, but how are you going to deal with your own husband? Either you will break him, or you will break yourself."

"To be flexible…"

"Is that not how all women act? Leave his silly games to himself. If the feelings do not ignite now, they will never ignite. If you manage to balance everything today, what else do you need?"

"Family, children, simple happiness."

"With Jess you can have the first and the second. As for the third, he will not be able to respect you as you are. In his understanding, a woman is a fragile, weak, and vulnerable creature, tender and sentimental, something everyone should protect."

"What the—"

Lily passionately flashed her eyes. She threw her rose and it landed on the pathway.

"Alexander, am I not a woman? Who said that only the bleating goats should win in the survival of the fittest? Beware that goat's children are bucklings and doelings. Besides, if a woman becomes the man's support, the man will be able to achieve much, is that not so?"

"Of course it is so. I am not talking about my own opinion now. I grew up at court."

"And?"

Lily gradually grew calmer. She lifted the rose from the pathway with a sigh. She needed to keep her hands busy. Otherwise, the gloves would not help."

"Do you know about His Majesty's second wife?"

"Jessamine. I know. So?"

"But you have never seen her. Nevertheless, she was exactly the type. A tender rose, head over heels in love with her King."

"What does that have to do with my husband?"

"I thought you realized. The Countess Earton never looked after children. It was always the Earl and his sister, until she became a queen."

Lily moved another bean on her imaginary abacus in favor of her theory.

"Hmm, and you suggest that Jess subconsciously looks for the same in women?"

"I would not put it like that."

"But this is the truth. I see. He will not appreciate me for my worth simply because strong women are nonsense."

"Correct. History knows many examples of it. But an example is one thing, and it is quite another thing to find in your family."

"You are implying that there is no way out. It is either they will start breaking me by force, and considering my assumptions, with the King's help, too, or I pretend that—"

"You will be able to test it yourself. I just wanted to help you."

"Why me? Jess is your friend. I am only his wife, a cow—"

"Lilian!"

"As if I don't know what my precious husband used to call me. They told me all the details! Do you have any idea how many of these 'tender, meek' women come to me? His Majesty temporarily let Alicia go to make them go away. Why are you helping me?"

"Because I see you. I also hope that I understand you a little, too."

"And?"

"You are... If all of this were never to have happened, would you have become like this?"

Lily shrugged.

Lilian would not have. As for Aliya Skorolenok, she only needed medicine and Alex, in any sequence, but surely not producing lace and kaleidoscopes in a strange new world.

"You see. You are only tough temporarily. If Jess is able to give you protection, you will sooner or later become yourself."

"What if he will not?"

"Your mask will merge with your skin. Such things also happen."

Lily was silently looking into Falion's grey eyes. *Why could this man see and understand?*

It was true that war made people mobilize and remain strong until the very last moment. But as soon as peace and victory came, the heroes put their banners aside. They returned home to bake cakes and raise children. These occurrences were part of history.

If a woman chose to fight instead of crying in the corner, it did not mean that she was an Iron Lady. It only indicated the type of her defense mechanism. Some people always faced the fight, others assumed the role of the poor and hurt. Both types of people put themselves through a lot of risk.

If one fought till the end, he or she could get a violent response; if one played the victim, the enemy would start using their weakness, knowing that the weak and the poor never raised their voice.

Lily did not have the "weak and poor" option. Whose shoulder was she to cry on in Earton? On Etor's, may he rest in peace? Her only option was to fight. That was why she became tough. Alexander realized this, but Jess did not…

"He will not see it."

✳✳✳

Alexander was looking at her. *She is so incredible.* Lily somehow reminded him of a diamond—she was as hard and as delicate as that stone.

"I am afraid that it will be like that. I wanted to let you know."

Lily stood on her toes and caressed Falion's cheek with her lips.

"Thank you, Alexander. I will think about your words."

"Have you written to him after all?"

"It is not a correspondence," she smiled bitterly.

"What is it then?"

"A battle."

"Pretend you take a step back."

"I will think about it. Can we talk about something different for now?"

"Of course." The conversation changed to the subject of dogs and horses. Lily had learned to converse about these animals, their croups, necks, hooves... In her new world, a horse was not a miracle from the zoo, but a domestic pet, much like a hamster. Knowing about them was useful.

The woman and the man walked along the garden. The flowers bloomed, the birds sang. Everything was almost pastorally beautiful. They maintained a pleasant conversation.

If Falion was right, Lilian owed him a lot, both for his support and his advice.

Alexander thought that if his assumptions were correct, he would have a chance.

Is it love? No, I do not hope for love. He hoped to at least stay close to Lilian, to be able to see her and talk with her. His damned tongue became completely awkward in her presence.

He would touch her hand and give her roses. *And maybe even...*

His cheek was ablaze, as if from a burn. She kissed him a thank-you from her heart, without a second thought.

His wife was insane. He was burdened for the rest of his life. He would not be able to offer her anything neither his hand, nor his heart or protection. But sometimes, the offer was a mere triviality.

She did not yet need a hand. She stood tall without scaffolding. *A title?* She had her own. *Protection?* she had already taught some foolish people a good lesson and it made the rest hold their poisonous tongues.

What about her heart? His heart was hers anyway. *Forever, no matter what.*

A man and a woman walked along the garden.

Medieval Tale:

First Lessons

The Clearing

Palace Intrigue

The Royal Court

The Price of Happiness

Book Recommendations:

Thank you for reading this book. Please remember to leave a review.

The final part of Medieval Tale, '***The Price of Happiness***', is available for order.

You can find the full series on Amazon: https://amzn.to/2WqhY10

Lina J. Potter's pen now takes us to the mystical lands of the Kingdom of Radenor suffering under the reign of the unjust King. His sister, the Princess of Radenor is determined to have him dethroned. Her half-demon son, Alex conceived by a demon father, becomes the ultimate weapon of her bloody revenge. A magnificent tale of blood magic, necromancy, court intrigue and family revenge.

Order the opening book '***Half-Demon's Revenge***' now.

LitHunters

LitHunters is an innovative global digital publishing house. Born in the minds of literature enthusiasts, LitHunters main focus is the new generation of literature.

Our mission at LitHunters is to find the gems of the modern entertaining literature and bring them to English-language readers. We believe that good books should not exist in isolation, so we want to make the best fantasy novels available to all in the easiest, most accessible way, while providing our readers with the highest quality stories.

Our vision is to create a new, comprehensive publishing ecosystem where the borders of literature and culture are easier to overcome. We are happy to be part of this cause by matching the most talented and creative local authors with the latest technology and top professionals from all areas of publishing. In this way, we connect writers with their global audience.

However, let our books speak for themselves! Check out our selection, which offers series selections for all tastes—from epic or romantic fantasy to LitRPG. You decide which world to discover next!

I would like to draw your attention to some other great works from LitHunters.

NOW available for order, the uplifting Sci-fi Space Opera *Kiran: The Warrior's Daughter* (The Rights Of The Strong) by Ellen Stellar

Meet Kiran; the young, reckless, and wild cadet of the most prestigious university. Beautiful, free-spirited, jolly, clever and fun-loving. Her life is one of organizing underground races, gambling, skipping classes, issuing fake IDs and having passionate love affairs... Until one day she is abducted to her native planet as a captive, forced to marry the strongest warrior by the law of the strong. Her restless soul won't abide, to her cruel father nor to her supposed husband. She is a cadet after all.

Made in the USA
Las Vegas, NV
29 November 2020

11689814R00217